PHONY TINSEL

OTHER FIVE STAR TITLES BY ROBERT S. LEVINSON:

PHONY TINSEL

ROBERT S. LEVINSON

FIVE STAR
A part of Gale, Cengage Learning

GALE
CENGAGE Learning®

Detroit • New York • San Francisco • New Haven, Conn • Waterville, Maine • London

GALE
CENGAGE Learning®

LIBRARY OF CONGRESS CATALOGING-IN-PUBLICATION DATA

Levinson, Robert S.
    Phony tinsel / Robert S. Levinson. — 1st ed.
       p. cm.
    ISBN 978-1-4328-2679-6 (hardcover) — ISBN 1-4328-2679-4 (hardcover)
    1. Motion picture industry—Fiction. 2. Murder—Investigation—Fiction. 3. California, Southern—Fiction. 4. Mystery fiction. 5. Romantic suspense fiction. I. Title.
PS3562.E9218P48 2013
                                    813'.54—dc23   2012032740

First Edition. First Printing: January 2013
Find us on Facebook– https://www.facebook.com/FiveStarCengage
Visit our website– http://www.gale.cengage.com/fivestar/
Contact Five Star™ Publishing at FiveStar@cengage.com

Printed in Mexico
1 2 3 4 5 6 7 17 16 15 14 13

One more for Sandra
LVY

"Strip away the phony tinsel of Hollywood and you'll find the real tinsel underneath."

—Oscar Levant

CHAPTER 1

It was an accident—

Meeting Sarah.

Charlie Dickens thought he was invading the realm of Cecil
B. DeMille when he hopped over the modest brick wall protecting the perfectly manicured forest green lawn and trudged up
the inlaid marble path to the picture-perfect hilltop residence
on DeMille Drive, south across Los Feliz Boulevard from the
winding, tree-lined trails of Ferndell, near the western canyon
entrance to Griffith Park.

Movie people had been nesting in the fashionable Laughlin
Park area since the earliest days of the silents, because of its
proximity to studios like Paramount, Warner Bros., RKO,
Columbia, and the Fox location lot. And, of course, DeMille
was now and had been for years the biggest of the big among
producers and directors.

He was Charlie's first choice to produce and direct *Showdown
at Shadow Creek,* but getting to DeMille was like trying to get
through the gates of Heaven without first dying, nothing that
could happen short of a miracle, especially by an untested commodity in the movie Hell of unemployed screenwriters.

More than his first choice, DeMille—peerless at bringing
miracles to the screen, witness *The Ten Commandments*—was
now his last hope.

The screenplay had been rejected by every studio in town,
his agent Roy Balloon said, just before he fired Charlie as a cli-

ent, claiming, "Nothing personal, Charles, my good man, just that you're awful lousy for my batting average."

"I'm glad it's nothing personal," Charlie said. "How about you taking another run at DeMille before you officially shoot me down?"

"Officially? What was that blowing a hole in your heart just now, gas pains?"

They were in Balloon's office, the postage-stamp size reserved for Elegant Artists junior agents recently upgraded from the mailroom, too tiny to accommodate a visitor's chair, obliging Charlie to press against the wall facing Roy's miniscule desk, arms folded defensively across his chest.

Roy seemed to regret his words immediately. He'd never been good at sustaining the tough-as-nails demeanor that seemed to be part of the black suit–black tie–black heart uniform expected of all Elegant's agents. His basso became less profundo as he told Charlie, "Here's what's what, Charles. The great man did a western two years ago, *The Plainsman,* with Coop and Jean Arthur, remember? He's got another one on tap for thirty-nine, *Union Pacific,* headlining Stanwyck and Joe Mc-Crea, and gets underway soon as he wraps *The Buccaneer* with Freddie March. If you really think he'd ditch the railroad yarn for one by an unknown writer with zilch credits, a reputation to match, it marks you as a candidate for the booby hatch."

"You told me more than once, no uncertain terms, how *Showdown at Shadow Creek* is a great screenplay."

"What else would you expect to hear from your agent? You want to get your screenplay to DeMille, scram over to his house and plant it in his mailbox."

"What's his address?" Charlie said.

Roy gave him a disbelieving stare. "That was a joke, Charles."

"DeMille has a mailbox. I have a screenplay. Funnier things have happened. What's the worst-case scenario—I get arrested for trespassing?"

Roy threw up his hands. "Giving the lie to everyone who ever read *Showdown at Shadow Creek* and told me, *With that screenplay Charlie Dickens will never get arrested in this town.*"

"Like who?"

"Like everyone who's ever read the screenplay?"

Charlie could have made a clean getaway if he'd simply stuck to the plan and left the envelope containing the screenplay and a note urging DeMille to consider *Showdown at Shadow Creek* in the mailbox at the foot of the gated driveway, but the residence was too accessible, too tempting to resist.

He hopped over the wall and headed up the path, inspired by a new and improved idea—

Leave the envelope propped against the front door.

That way it couldn't be missed or ignored in a shuffle of the letters and packages that filled the mailbox.

Advancing, Charlie's head rang with the sound of the voice he knew so well from all the years of hearing DeMille host the weekly Monday evening airings of the Lux Radio Theater, telling him, *Greetings from Hollywood, young man. I read your screenplay and it's positively brilliant. You absolutely must let me have it, please. Won't you do that for a humble filmmaker who bows in the presence of your genius?*

Only it wasn't DeMille's voice he heard when he stooped to position the envelope and the door opened suddenly, throwing him off balance into a fall that landed him on his hands and knees, staring at ten perfectly manicured pink toenails.

The voice demanding to know "Who the hell are you?" introduced him to Sarah Moonglow, not that he didn't know her before this, but only as Sarah Darling the movie star and ever a fashion queen dressed to the nines, unlike right now, only a skimpy bath towel protecting her from total nudity.

She looked older than she did on the silver screen, in her mid- to late forties, her face well into the wear and tear of middle age, a random collection of wrinkles and laugh lines that probably took hours of Max Factor's makeup magic, resourceful lighting and a pound of Vaseline on the camera's lens to hide.

"I asked you a question," she said, sizing him up as he struggled back onto his feet. "Put your eyes back in their sockets and answer me."

"You're Sarah Darling."

"And you're not Earl Stanley."

"Who?"

"Earl Stanley, my gardener." She made a sly face and let the towel slip an inch, as if by accident, exposing a bit of cocoa-colored nipple long enough for Charlie to drink it in like Ovaltine. "He comes every Thursday around this time."

"Today is Wednesday."

"That explains that," she said, repositioning the towel. "Staff's day off. No wonder I've had to do everything for myself. You still haven't answered my question."

"A delivery boy," he said, too embarrassed to admit the truth.

"You look more man than boy to me," she said. "Either case, do you know how to deliver?" He pointed to the envelope. "Hand it over." She took it from him, managing to let the towel slip again, in a way that revealed most of one petite tanned breast; no tan lines.

"It's for Mr. DeMille, Miss Darling."

"Explaining why someone wrote his name on the envelope better than it explains why you want to leave it here, delivery boy, seeing as C.B.'s *casa de la moola* is across the road," she said, using the envelope as a pointer. "The highest elevation in Laughlin Park, a mixture of Victorian and neoclassical styles, on two-plus acres. He bought it in sixteen, two years after it was built." She was sounding like a tour guide. "Later, C.B. bought the house next door from Charlie Chaplin, connected them with an arboretum. This place, Moonglow Manor, is a high-class dump by comparison."

"*Moonglow* Manor?"

"My husband puts his personal stamp on everybody and everything. Formerly Mendelssohn. The name got changed by some immigration clerk at Ellis Island when he got here from Berlin by way of Switzerland four years ago, in thirty-four. The way he tells it, at the time the clerk was listening to the song 'Moonglow' on the radio. You know—Benny Goodman and them others."

"Maxwell Moonglow?"

"You heard of him?"

"The movie producer who escaped Germany one goosestep ahead of Hitler's Nazis. A great filmmaker, who produced some of Germany's finest movies." Charlie snapped his fingers. "You married him three years ago, eloped to Reno after you starred in *Daydreams* for him, the picture that earned you a Best Actress nomination from the Academy."

"And a loss to that Boop-eyed upstart Bette Davis—"

"Who got the Oscar for *Dangerous,* like it was her consolation prize for being shut out the year before for *Of Human Bondage,* where she didn't get a nomination, but all those write-in votes."

"You definitely know your *Photoplay,* delivery man, I'll say that much for you."

"And *Modern Screen,* and for sure I read Louella O. Parsons's column every day in the *Examiner,* and Hedda Hopper since she started writing for the *Times* in February. And something else—I was voting, I would have voted for you over Davis, Hopkins, Hepburn, and the others."

Actually, he'd have voted for Davis, but telling her that would have been rude.

13

"I admire your excellent judgment, delivery man," she said, and lowered the towel to provide him a brief, tantalizing peek-a-boo of both breasts, at the same time undressing him with a seductive stare.

"Something else, Mrs. Moonglow—"

"Miss Darling."

"Something else, Miss Darling, I'm a screenwriter and—"

"That explains why you're working as a delivery man."

"It's my screenplay you're holding. *Showdown at Shadow Creek*. Mr. DeMille is my last hope at getting it produced, why I—"

"Couldn't Max be your last hope?"

"Mr. Moonglow already rejected it. Twice."

"That was before he heard C.B. is anxious to get his hands on *Shadow Creek at Sundown*."

Charlie's pulse skyrocketed. "When did he hear that?" he said, not bothering to correct her about the title.

"Possibly tonight. Third time can be the charm, especially if Max has a chance to achieve the impossible and outdo DeMille. Let's talk about it some more, delivery man. I want to know everything."

She motioned him inside and, in closing the door behind them, lost hold of the towel. Charlie froze, his eyes welded to her perfectly proportioned body. She fed on his admiration and wondered, "Are you sure today is Wednesday, not Thursday, because my garden needs watering real bad."

Twenty minutes later they were in bed.

Charlie was late meeting Polly Wilde at the Nickodell Restaurant's seductively under-lit bar between Paramount and RKO on Melrose, nicknamed "Stage 35" by studio hands who regularly sneaked over during working hours to indulge their need for a quickie pick-me-up or two or three.

It wasn't quite seven o'clock, but the brown leather booths lining the back wall were already full, boisterous conversations and mumbled exchanges overlapping, drowning out songs booming from some invisible jukebox. A number by Bing Crosby, "Dinah," ended and was followed by another of the crooner's big hits, "Out of Nowhere."

Polly was at the counter sharing a loud laugh with an executive type, hers the squeal Charlie could identify in total darkness, like she was summoning hogs to a feeding trough. It was her only feature he found annoying, but he had learned to live with it since they fell in together a year ago, the rest of her too irresistible to, well, to resist.

She was a robust farm girl, like him in her mid-twenties, hair the color of hayride straw and a strawberries-and-cream complexion dotted with freckles and stamped finished by the dimple in her chin. Not beautiful. Pretty in a grown-up Shirley Temple way, sexy like an overripe, athletic Lana Turner whenever she stepped out wearing a sweater and a skirt, her preferred mode of dress most of the time, including the day they met.

She'd struck up a soda fountain conversation with him over morning coffee and sinkers at Schwab's Pharmacy on Sunset, a favorite haunt of the industry's unemployed, Polly wondering if Charlie knew it was here that Turner, a Hollywood High schoolgirl, was discovered by Billy Wilkerson, publisher of the *Hollywood Reporter.*

"Sitting on this very stool," she said, with the exuberance of someone waiting for lightning to strike again.

"Gee whiz, no kidding?" Charlie said, too taken in by her innocent ocean-blue eyes to dash her dream by explaining that Wilkerson first spotted Turner at the Top Hat Café, a student-rendezvous point a mile or so east of Schwab's, at Sunset and McCadden Place.

Robert S. Levinson

"No kidding," Polly said.

"Hollywood High, that where you go?"

"Silly man," she said, slapping his shoulder and initiating him to her laugh, which drew the curious attention of everyone in the pharmacy, including the out-of-work actors who routinely used the magazine rack like a library, scanning *Variety* and *Reporter* for job leads. "I'm an actress is all."

"Have I seen you in anything?"

"Not so far. I'm working at the Farmers Market down on Fairfax while I'm waiting out my big break. Behind the counter at Contento's Guaranteed Garden Fresh Fruits and Vegetables, selling fruits and vegetables. Our tomatoes are especially something special to try you're ever in the mood for tomatoes. They're a fruit, you know, tomatoes?"

"You're some tomato yourself," Charlie said, too smitten by her to engage in any subtlety.

Polly poked his arm and aired her laugh. "I bet you say that to all the girls."

"Not even if I knew all the girls, but you are definitely one girl I'd like to know better."

"Are you a producer? I hear that a lot from producers. Also, there was once a guy who said he was a director, but he really wasn't I found out after."

"I'm a writer. I write movies."

"Like what, for instance?" Challenging him.

He thought about it. "Like *Lost Horizon*."

She squealed. "You wrote that? I loved that picture."

"No, not that, exactly. *Like* that. Mine's *Forbidden City*, where a detective chases a gangster into a desert ghost town inhabited by people who'll never die as long as they stay put, and both fall in love with the same woman."

Polly's jaw fell open and she pressed a palm to her heaving bosom. "I so love it, it's divine. Who's in it, Mr. Clark Gable and Mr. Spencer Tracy, maybe? And Miss Myrna Loy as the girl, or maybe Miss Irene Dunne?"

"My agent couldn't sell it," he confessed, "so it's sitting on my One of These Days When I'm a Hot Property shelf, but the girl I created for *Forbidden City*'s definitely more like you than either Myrna Loy or Irene Dunne."

She measured him with silent uncertainty before stretching out a grim smile. "You are playing with me, right? You sure you're a writer, not a producer or"—rolling her eyes heavenward—"a director?"

"Reading it, would that convince you?"

Polly lit up at the prospect. "I'll let you know after I read it," she said.

Charlie was confident Polly would find herself in the character of Cassandra. He'd written her so any actress could be cast, even a Marie Dressler type, especially if Charles Laughton and Wallace Beery played the detective and the gangster. Vague descriptions, a screenwriter's trick—the way the Hollywood game was played.

Later in the day, Charlie delivered a copy to Polly at Contento's Guaranteed Garden Fresh Fruits and Vegetables, leaving with a complimentary bag of oversized, vine-ripened tomatoes and a date to meet again tomorrow morning at Schwab's.

Instead, she surprised him by showing up shortly before midnight at his miniscule one-room apartment, half a converted garage on a shabby low-rent street in the Westlake Park district, her pounding on the door drawing him out of a dream about her and his first restful sleep in weeks. He thought he might still be dreaming when he opened the door and saw her feasting on him, clutching the screenplay, verging on tears. Her voice broke telling him, "Once I started, I couldn't put it down, not for one second. Your address was on the title page. I had to come and tell you how beautiful and moving the story was, your writing a miracle. And yes, Mr. Charlie Dickens, I am Cassandra."

They made love that night.

Two weeks later he moved in with her.

They'd been together ever since.

Now, her interplay at the Nickodell bar with that guy, whoever he was, raised the usual hackles of jealousy on the back of his neck.

Not that he was possessive, he was—

Possessive.

Yes, he was.

And jealous.

Resentful of anybody who invaded his territory, stole a minute of his girl's time, even now, this minute.

Crosby had been replaced on the overhead by his late rival, Russ Columbo, who'd been accidentally shot and killed four years ago, Columbo's silky voice gliding through his biggest hit, "Prisoner of Love."

That was Charlie, a prisoner of love, even though he was wearing the stain of Sarah Darling on his conscience and his cock-a-doodle-do.

On the drive over he had convinced himself it was a business decision to reward Sarah's lust for the good deed she would be doing him by bringing *Showdown at Shadow Creek* to her husband's attention, selling him on the idea of making it a Max Moonglow production.

Charlie crossed to Polly, rested a hand on her back and said, "Guess who."

Without turning, she said, "Mr. Salmon, say hello to the late Mr. Dickens."

"Hello, late Mr. Dickens," Salmon said, turning to expose a mouthful of teeth the size of mah-jongg tiles. "Your lady friend has been bending my ear about your wonderful screenplays." He sounded in his cups. He toasted Charlie with his highball while his free hand wandered onto Polly's knee.

Charlie's jealousy got the best of him.

He brought one up from the floor.

It landed with a crack on Salmon's aquiline nose. Blood spurted like water from an open fire hydrant on a hot summer afternoon. Salmon toppled backward off the bar stool, landed on his back on the concrete floor, out for the count.

The room, momentarily gone silent, exploded noisily. A dress extra in white tie and tails checked Salmon for a pulse and shouted for someone to phone for an ambulance. One of the three men who had locked onto Charlie and wrestled him into submission added the need for someone to call the police.

Polly gave him a pitiful look, stepped over, and said, "You ought to be ashamed of yourself for what you did to poor Mr. Salmon," and fled, ignoring his pleas for forgiveness.

CHAPTER 2

Shortly before six o'clock, Max's secretary phoned to say Mr. Moonglow would be tied up in a meeting for the balance of the evening. Sarah hung up, wondering who it was tying him up this time, and how Max did enjoy his sex games. If he were playing with her now, she'd be tying his hands behind his back and a noose around his neck on the scaffold built for *Mrs. Quasimodo,* the sequel to *The Hunchback of Notre Dame* that brought them together after she was cast as Esmeralda.

Actually, it was Jack Warner who brought them together.

Not intentionally.

Jack wanted to cast her in some god-awful melodrama, in a role that eventually went to Joan Blondell. When she refused, he loaned her out to RKO as punishment, the way Louis B. Mayer had punished Gable, when he shipped him to Columbia Pictures in Poverty Row for *It Happened One Night.*

Surprise, surprise, Mr. Mayer—

Gable won an Oscar.

So did his costar, Claudette Colbert.

Only lightning didn't strike for Sarah with *Mrs. Quasimodo.*

Instead of an Oscar, she got a Max.

"I begged the studio to capture you away from Warners for my first picture here in America," he told her at their first meeting. "You have been my inspiration, my idol, since I sat spellbound through your first movie back in my native Germany. I told myself, Max, you must have Sarah Darling if you're to achieve greatness as a producer and director, and so we are here now, together, yes?"

His English, mastered as a schoolboy in Berlin, was accent-free, almost as flawless as his powers of persuasion. He had the commanding presence of Reinhardt and Lubitsch and the Continental charm of a Boyer and a Chevalier that more than not offset an average face branded by a dueling scar and a short, stocky body ripe with evidence of the Good Life. He explained how the Nazis offered to forgive his Jewishness if he agreed to run their movie industry. It was the same offer made earlier to Fritz Lang, and his answer was the same as Lang's. He fled the country overnight and quickly landed a lucrative producing contract at RKO.

Mrs. Quasimodo did surprising business at the box office, good enough for Max to sell RKO on the concept of buying up her contract from Warner Bros. Their second movie together, *Daydreams,* got her the Academy nomination she so desperately wanted, but not the Oscar itself.

By then they were husband and wife, living in style in the shadow of C.B. DeMille on DeMille Drive, outwardly happy, although even before their first anniversary theirs had become a marriage of superficial convenience. Max engaged in more affairs than Casanova and she retaliated by matching him hurt for harm.

She wondered sometimes if she still loved him.

As often, she wondered if he still loved her.

The guessing game never lasted for long, never as long as her flings, like the one in progress with Earl Stanley.

And Charlie Dickens?

Only a means to an end—

The end of Maxwell Moonglow.

Sarah had a lonely dinner of fresh lettuce leaves drenched in vinaigrette with garden-fresh carrot and celery sticks on the side and demolished a bottle of Bordeaux before settling down to read Charlie Dickens's screenplay.

It was far better than she had anticipated, not that that really mattered, only that the screenplay was perfect for the plan taking shape in her mind.

She hid *Showdown at Shadow Creek* in her Schiaparelli lamb chop hatbox in the walk-in closet, poured herself a bath and lingered an eternity among the fragrant bubbles, wondering what it would feel like to play the grieving widow again.

Afterward, she phoned Earl Stanley.

"The answer to our prayers just fell into my lap," she said, a smile in every word.

"All's I like falling into your lap is me, so what's that mean exactly?"

"What we've been talking about almost since the day we met."

"This I gotta hear. Spill the beans."

"Face to face is better. You never really can tell if someone's eavesdropping on the party line, so tomorrow, when you're here to prune the roses."

"Along with anything else needs pruning."

"You're the gardener," Sarah said, and giggled like a schoolgirl.

Hanging up, she thought she heard a faint click that suggested someone may have been listening in on the call.

The next morning, they were playing Lady Chatterley and her lover at their favorite spot inside the hedge maze that extended the width of the backyard behind the pool house, under a sun burning a hole in the gray sky, Earl Stanley sweating like a priest in a brothel, when she told him he was fired.

"Fired up, you mean, and you better believe it," Earl Stanley said, sucking in the air. "I'm hotter'n a firecracker on the Fourth of July and getting ready to explode again."

"I mean I want you to make like Judge Crater and disappear is what I'm saying, big boy."

"What's that supposed to be all about? Doesn't sound like no answer to our prayers, the way you were saying on the telephone." He studied her for the joke and, finding none, lifted her off him and set her aside on the grass carpet. Rolled into a sitting position, arms laced across his hairy chest.

"The less you know, the better. Thirty days, maybe a little longer. You'll thank me when Max is dead and buried and you're not the one on trial for his murder."

"Dead? His . . . ?" Earl's face bunched into a question mark. "All the times you talked to me about getting rid of him, I thought you meant about getting a divorce."

"Too messy and expensive, a divorce, and it could put a big blemish on my career. This way, I get a lot of sympathy as the grieving widow, and there won't be any haggling over alimony."

"How you going to do it without getting caught? I don't wanna be worried sick over you."

"You're such a lambie-pie, sweet and considerate . . . Not me, a writer named Charlie Dickens."

"Charlie Dickens." Earl thought about it. "I heard of him. Ain't he over in London or England or somewhere?"

"Somewhere," Sarah said, fighting off a grimace, reminding herself it wasn't Earl's mind that had first attracted her to him.

"And I'm fired because—?"

"Charlie said that's how it should be. He said the less I know, the better, same as I just said to you."

"Not because you got some humpty-hump going with this guy?"

Sarah leaped to her feet and feigned anger. "How could you even think that, you big lug? You're my guy, my one and only, and don't you dare ever again think otherwise." She raised her hand like she was taking an oath. The lying, nowadays it came so easy to her.

"Prove it," Earl said, making come hither with his fingers.

"Consider it a going-away present, something to remember me by," Sarah said, and had him screaming her praises a minute or two later. She joined in the chorus, doing some of her best acting.

Sarah reeled in her tongue from deep inside Earl's cavernous mouth, promised she would let him know the second it was safe for them to be together again, and sent him on his way.

Charlie Dickens called shortly after that.

Sarah wasn't happy to hear his voice and let him know it. "You were supposed to wait until you heard from me, once I spoke to Max about *Shadow Over Sundown Creek*," she said.

"*Showdown at Shadow Creek*, but it was an emergency. The police officer was kind enough to get your number and dial it for me after Information said it was unlisted. I could only make one call by myself, that's the rule. I tipped him my last twenty, and that helped. Wanted to make it a tenner, but he didn't have change."

"The police—Charlie, where are you? What's this all about?"

"I went to meet a friend, have a drink at the Nickodell. One thing led to another and I wound up slugging some guy."

"Why?"

"It was the right thing to do."

"Why the right thing?"

"So, I spent the night here at Ramparts Station, sharing the holding cell with a raggedy bum who smells like a garbage dump and two bruised and battered queers the cops caught playing Hide the Salami behind the bushes at Echo Park," he said, dodging Sarah's question. "They're charging me with assault and battery and taking me downtown to court later today. County Jail after that, I suppose."

She couldn't let that happen.

Charlie behind bars would screw up her plan.

Getting the whole story about Nickodell's out of him would have to wait.

"You get to court, plead not guilty," she said.

"But I am. There were witnesses. They way I'm looking at it, doing time in County Jail will be like researching my next screenplay after *Showdown at Shadow Creek;* a crime story, George Raft or James Cagney gets into a fight in a bar, maybe both, with each other, and—"

"Charlie, listen to me. *Shadow Showdown* will never get made by Max Moonglow once he learns it was written by a jailbird. Scandal is scandal, and nobody wants to tangle with the Breen Office, especially not Max."

"There'll be a trial soon enough, though. Testimony will be stacked against me, the same way it'll be stacked against George Raft and James Cagney. I'm thinking Edward G. Robinson or Paul Muni as the DA."

"Charlie, you're not listening. Max battled the Breen Office over the kiss between me and Cary Grant in *Daydreams.* The close-up ran twenty seconds. Too long, indecent, shocking, Breen said, and wanted it cut from the picture. Max wrestled him to the mat and they finally agreed on a compromise. The kiss would be jake if it lasted five seconds. Max has gone around ever since telling people life's too short for him to ever again do anything that puts Breen on his case. Anything, Charlie, like a screenwriter found guilty of criminal assault."

"I remember that was some hot kiss, even for five seconds."

Sarah banged the air with the phone, trying to get past her frustration with Charlie, whose choo-choo had obviously been derailed by his arrest. This conversation was going nowhere fast, like her grandpap used to say, faster than green grass through a goose.

She hung up on him with one final command to plead not guilty and dialed from memory the private number of an assistant district attorney she once knew in the biblical sense, a cocktail party hors d'oeuvre—George Simon, or was it Simon George?

Tried a different combination when she reached a Chinese hand laundry.

Recognized his bulldog voice on her fourth attempt.

It reminded her of his walrus mustache and how he used it on her like Van Gogh attacking the canvas.

"Simon, it's Sarah. . . . I said, George, it's Sarah, Sarah Darling, darling. . . . Forget you? Who could ever forget you, you silly boy? . . . True, they don't make backseats like they used to. . . . We'll have to do that, test the theory one day soon, but right now I need a favor, George, and I know how discreet you can be."

CHAPTER 3

Polly was stewing in her car in the Nickodell parking lot across Melrose, trembling with indignation, her emotions in shreds, when the patrol car pulled up to the restaurant, all blaring siren and screeching brakes, red lights flashing, and two cops jumped out with their weapons drawn.

A police Receiving Hospital ambulance made its own noisy arrival a minute or two later from the opposite direction, did an impromptu U-turn and pulled up alongside the cop car. An attendant wearing a white shirt and rumpled blue trousers leaped from the rear of the vehicle carrying a doctor's satchel. He dashed into the restaurant while the driver came around, unloaded a stretcher and trailed after him.

Polly cut the motor, suffering second thoughts about abandoning Charlie although there was no excuse for what he had done to poor Leo Salmon. Leo had done nothing to deserve Charlie turning Leo's nose into a blood gusher.

Besides, Leo was a good person.

Honest, sincere and, so far, true to his word.

A casting director without a casting couch—at least, not one she knew about—who was responsible for the modest role she was playing across the street, at Raleigh Studios, in *Bar 20 Justice,* one of Mr. William Boyd's Hopalong Cassidy westerns.

If Charlie had waited to hear that, he would have been hugging Leo, not slugging him, thanking him for getting her those four lines and two close-ups, her first opportunity to sparkle on

27

the silver screen, displaying the talent she had honed in her junior and senior years at Rutherford B. Hayes High School.

After that, she would have sprung the bigger news on Charlie, how Leo had been hearing nice things about her from Mr. William Boyd himself and even Mr. George Gabby Hayes, so maybe there'd be more Hopalong pictures in her future. How Leo had heard Mr. Roy Rogers might be looking for a leading lady for his cowboy movies, so that could also be in her future.

Why Leo was with her at the Nickodell in the first place.

She'd invited him to join them so Charlie could learn the wonderful news straight from the horse's mouth, but that wasn't her true motive. In fact, she had been bragging on Charlie's writing to Leo and wanted them to meet. Leo was only a casting director, but he knew a lot of important picture people, was always rattling off their names. She was sure as the day is long that they'd hit it off like long-lost twin brothers, and Leo would want to help do for Charlie's career what he was doing for hers.

Reality interrupted her rambling thoughts—

Charlie in handcuffs being led from the restaurant, shoved kicking and complaining into the back of the patrol car by the two cops.

Polly jumped out of her car and aimed for them, slowed by traffic challenging the speed limit. Narrowly avoided getting hit by a driver faster on his horn than on the brakes.

The patrol car pulled away from the curb and sped off before she got there, its siren blaring, red lights ablaze as it zigzagged toward Vine Street.

She bent forward, hands on her knees, struggling to catch her breath, and watched the car disappear into the distance.

Turning, she saw Leo on the stretcher being loaded into the ambulance and hurried over calling his name.

Got no response.

Appealed with anxious eyes to the attendant.

"He'll live, best I can do you," the attendant said. "It'll take a doc to tell you better'n me after we get him to Emergency. Room for one more, you want to tag along. Hop in."

She hopped in, held Leo's hand on the ten-minute ride through traffic to Hollywood Receiving Hospital on Wilcox, wondering why she was here and not tracking after Charlie, denying the answer she couldn't scrub from her mind:

Charlie was the present.

Leo Salmon was her future.

"No, no, no, no," she said, unaware she'd made more than a silent denial until Leo's eyes popped open. He seemed to struggle through some fog before he blinked recognition and strained to draw one of his big-toothed smiles, drifted back to sleep, breathing noisily through his mouth, a back of the throat rumble, his nose apparently useless inside a heavy bandage.

She spent the rest of the night in the waiting room, refusing to leave until the doctor assured her Leo was fine beyond a mild concussion and a severely broken nose that would require reconstruction surgery, still out, but resting comfortably. She left a note for him with a nurse, taxied back to the Nickodell parking lot for her car, and headed over the two blocks to Raleigh for her early-morning costume, hair and makeup calls.

Forecasts of rain had forced a change in today's shooting schedule.

Mr. Lesley Selander, the director, was anxious to get a corral scene on film before Hopalong Cassidy's horse, Topper, and the other horses rebelled at the change in weather and refused to cooperate, as had already happened on two other days, when black clouds had hovered ominously overhead before sailing past.

Polly spent all of the morning and well into the afternoon waiting patiently for her scene inside the cantina, where Hopalong and his sidekicks, Windy and Lucky, would call her over and order sarsaparillas all around, and she'd toss her head back, laugh at them and say her big line: *You gents sure you can handle something strong as sarsaparilla?*

She was rehearsing the line, changing attitude and emphasis, determined to make it as perfect as perfection itself when Mr. William Boyd wandered in, gave her a grin as warm as a summer sun, and settled over a cigarette at the next table. Mr. George Gabby Hayes entered a few minutes later and joined him.

This was an opportunity to tell them how grateful she was for—how much she appreciated—their nice words about her and her future to Leo.

Polly sucked in a gallon of air, blew it out the side of her mouth, and called over, "I learned what you said from Mr. Leo Salmon, so thank you very, very, very much, Mr. Boyd, and you too, Mr. Hayes."

They answered her smile in kind, but otherwise looked at her and then each other like they had no idea what she was talking about before falling into a quiet conversation, taking occasional sips from a modest metal hip flask Mr. George Gabby Hayes had been packing in a gun holster.

She decided they didn't want to say anything new to her, get her hopes up higher than they already were, just in case those other Hopalong Cassidy pictures did not come her way for some unpredictable reason. She appreciated their consideration. She couldn't wait to tell Leo.

Polly headed home by way of Hollywood Receiving.

Learned Leo had been released an hour ago from an admissions clerk cultivating black fatty pouches under his tired eyes. "Some babe come and picked him up," he said, patting a yawn. "A looker like you." He shook his head in wonderment. "Some guys got the magic touch."

She spent the rest of the drive thinking about the woman, who she was, why she knew where to find Leo, if Leo had them call the woman to come fetch him.

If so, why?

Why not her?

It was something she'd offered to do in the note she left for Leo, telling him to call her on the set.

She was anxious to repay a debt of gratitude, that's all, so why was she so bothered now?

She was thinking maybe the woman could have been Leo's sister as she pulled into her garage slot behind her apartment building over by La Brea and Sixth and headed up the back entrance to her one-bedroom on the second floor, hoping Charlie was there.

Through the day, she had dropped lots of nickels in a set-side phone booth trying to connect with him. It took numerous callbacks before police headquarters was able to direct her to the Ramparts Station, where she learned he had been taken downtown to court. That started a cycle of calls to the courthouse, finally to the courtroom where he'd be pleading to charges that included disorderly conduct, assault and battery and resisting arrest, except—

Dickens, Charles's case was removed from the docket, a disinterested clerk told her.

"What's that mean?" Polly asked.

"It means it's no longer on the docket."

"Where is he, then?"

"Somewhere, but not here," the clerk said, and hung up on her.

She phoned the Ramparts Station again, was put on hold for five minutes before the disembodied voice returned to tell her, "No Dickens here, now or ever."

"That can't be. I spoke to someone earlier and they said—"

"No Dickens here, now or ever, is the best I can do for you, lady. Maybe you need to try the DA's office?" A sugarcoated spin to the way he made the suggestion.

She made the call.

The DA's office was no help.

There was a case number for a Charlene Dixon, charged with streetwalking, but none for any Charlie Dickens.

Polly entered her apartment calling his name, excited by the fresh smell of his cologne scenting the room.

No response.

She hurried to the bedroom, pushed open the door.

The hopeful look drained from her face when she discovered he had emptied his dresser drawers.

Emptied the closet of his shirts, slacks, sports jacket, shoes, and the one dress suit he owned and only wore for meetings and the rare special occasion, like her last birthday, when he splurged on dinner at the Florentine Gardens.

Left behind a scribbled note taped to her vanity mirror:

I can't see you anymore.

Polly studied the five words in disbelief that he could sum up their relationship in five words and disappear like this.

I can't see you anymore.

It wasn't an explanation.

It wasn't even an excuse.

I can't see you anymore.

Why?

Because he saw her talking with Leo Salmon? Because she hadn't rescued him from police custody? Because he didn't know how she had tried to find him throughout the day?

How silly-Willie-infantile of Charlie to simply disappear, not to be here to hear her out, resign his jealous fit so they could kiss and make up the way they had so many times before.

I can't see you anymore.

Polly burst into tears, balled the note and tossed it aside.

Had second thoughts.

Retrieved it from the floor and clutched it to her breast.

Impulsively, she fled the apartment and raced downstairs to her car, determined to see if Charlie had retreated to his old place over by Westlake Park. She remembered urging him to keep paying the rent, in case things didn't work out between them.

He agreed, but needed to assure her, as he had other times, "I can always do better with where and how I live while waiting for my break. I'm penny-wise, but absolutely no Scrooge, making do on a modest inheritance from an eccentric maiden auntie I never met, who died aged eighty-nine while on a South African safari hunting white lions, rhinos and warthogs." Said in a way that left Polly wondering if it was only his writer's imagination at play.

She switched on the ignition, threw the gearshift into reverse, and—

Changed her mind.

"I can't see you anymore, Charlie Dickens, not the other way around," she shouted, forcing out the words between breaths as heavy as her heart was hammering. "I'm the one who's calling it quits." Charlie might be the writer, but Polly meant to have the last word.

CHAPTER 4

A week later, Charlie was still missing Polly, angry with himself for abandoning her with only that silly sentence after caving in to Sarah's demands, Sarah insisting it had to be done if Max Moonglow was going to buy *Showdown at Shadow Creek* and give the public the kind of quality spectacle so absent nowadays in America's bijous.

Quality spectacle.

How could Charlie argue with logic like that?

Besides, there'd be a day when he'd be able to apologize and explain to Polly, with hopes she would understand, take him back into her heart and her home.

For now, though, he was resident in a level of luxury he could only afford in his wildest dreams, a sprawling French country-style home nestled in a wooded bluff behind an electrical gate off Benedict Canyon, five minutes from the Beverly Hills Hotel, posher even than the Moonglows' home on DeMille Drive—

A reflecting pool lining the courtyard, a natural amphitheater dressed in tall palms. Inside, a large-scale living room with cathedral ceilings; a dining room fit for an army; a master bedroom suite with an enormous walk-in closet; a party-size sauna in the bathroom; floor-to-ceiling windows wherever you looked. Down from the patio, a terraced garden leading to the obligatory Olympic-size swimming pool. Everywhere, a perfect blend of exotic and expensive antique furnishings and decorations composed by the picture-star-turned-interior-designer

William Haines.

"It's the lady's private nest egg and personal preserve, a going-away present from her second husband, some king with one-a those funny accents and no kingdom to call his own."

"Where'd he go to?"

"Hell, at least that's where the lady directed him after she caught him in bed with somebody other than herself and filed for divorce. She kept the house. He got to keep the butler he was diddling."

"So Max Moonglow is her third husband?"

"Her fourth. Number Three was easy come, easy go, if you catch my drift? They got married to climax a wild weekend down in Tijuana. The marriage was over before it began. The lady stumbled out of bed the next A.M. remembering how she was engaged to Max Moonglow and they were on tap to tie the knot that same month."

"A quickie divorce on top of the quickie marriage, like something straight out of a Carole Lombard picture."

"I wouldn't say that too loud around her, Charlie. The only actress she likes to talk about is herself. Even Shirley Temple is taboo, the lady convinced she could-a done *Little Miss Marker, Poor Little Rich Girl, Little Miss Broadway,* any of 'em, if the roles had been written taller."

They were kibitzing over beers by the tennis court, Charlie and Mad Dog Mahony, the property caretaker and all-purpose factotum Sarah won in her first divorce. His given name, Aloysius, had turned him into a battler growing up on the poverty-stricken streets of South Boston. A reporter at the *Herald-Express* slapped the nickname on him following Mad Dog's pro wrestling debut at Hollywood Legion Stadium, when he escaped defeat by biting off Gentleman Jim Larsen's left earlobe and lower lip. That offense got him a week's suspension and promotion to headline status on the wrestling circuit.

It was Mad Dog waiting for Charlie at the courthouse after the cops cut him loose from the holding pen and sent him on his way. No hassle, no comment, like he had never existed.

Mad Dog saying, "If you're Charlie Dickens, you're supposed to come with me."

"I don't know you," Charlie said, baffled by this massive slab of granite bursting out of his suit jacket, a shaved head with a receding five-o'clock shadow, dangerous eyes and what passed for a nose.

"I don't know you, either, so we're even on that score. If I say to you *Sarah sent me*, would that make the difference?" He pushed his mouth into a lopsided grin, exposing empty space and a pair of stacked gold molars.

" 'Sarah sent me'?"

"No, *me*, pal, Sarah sent *me* for you."

"Sarah Darling?"

"The only Sarah I know, but if you want to make it some other Sarah, jake with me as long as you c'mon. The lady don't never like to be kept waiting."

Any time Charlie asked a question on the hour-long drive to the Benedict Canyon residence, Mad Dog responded by breaking into song, grappling with an off-key baritone to sound like Nelson Eddy; scoring strongest with "Tramp, Tramp, Tramp" from *Naughty Marietta* and the Mounties song from *Rose Marie*, but pinned for a loss by the sweethearts' song, "Will You Remember?" from *Maytime*.

He relented once, when Charlie wondered if he was a Nelson Eddy fan. "Jeanette MacDonald, but don't let on to the lady," he said, and broke into a melancholy reprise of "Will You Remember"—*Sweetheart, sweetheart, sweetheart*—sounding like a bulldog in heat.

Charlie was struck with the concept for a new screenplay:

A Canadian Mountie dies in an accident. He's brought back to life with his memory intact, but in the body of a wrestler. He and the Mountie's fianceé meet cute, but before he can reveal his identity to her—a perfect part for Polly—he refuses to throw a championship match and is murdered by bad-guy gamblers. And then . . . and then—

He'd have to work on it some more.

Sarah was sunbathing poolside, nude except for slices of lemon covering her eyes. "Welcome to Freedomland," she called, when she heard Charlie and Mad Dog approaching on the cobblestone path.

They averted their eyes while she undulated off the chaise lounge and reached for her terry cloth robe, laughing at them and taunting, "Please, boys, nothing you haven't seen already, a body to behold and be held." Did a showy little pirouette before slipping into the robe and thumbing Mad Dog to disappear. He nodded to the signal and retreated.

Sarah pointed Charlie to a bottle in the bucket stand by her lounge table. "Moet on ice, kiddo, so we can celebrate your Get Out of Jail Free card in style. Pour us some, *por favor,* before the ice melts any more than it has already anticipating your arrival."

"I need to know what's going on, Miss Darling," he said, filling two goblets and handing over hers. "One minute I'm heading to court and the next—"

"Saved at the last minute, free as a fart in the wind. Exciting, wasn't it? Like in a Saturday kiddie matinee serial. I was in a couple at Universal before my star quality was fully recognized and rewarded. *Captain Flyboy and the Air Rangers?* Twelve chapters. Me the good girl who's really the evil Voice of Disaster. *Jungle Jack and the Lost City of the Zombies?* Me Jungle Jack's ward, kidnapped by insane Dr. Scorpio." She pushed out a sigh and offered a toast. "To the bad old days, but those days are gone forever." Looked off and smiled at some memory she clearly didn't intend to share with him. "I couldn't count on you pleading not guilty, kiddo, so I used up an old favor. Your record's as whitewashed as Tom Sawyer's fence."

"What now, Miss Darling? Now you can show my screenplay to Mr. Moonglow?"

"If only life were that simple," she said, wagging her head. "First things first. You need to lick some problems I discovered reading your brilliant words through for a second time last night."

"Problems?"

"The role of the girl, it's not entirely there yet. It should fit me like a Chanel."

"Fit you?"

"Always an incentive for that bastard. Any doubts he might have had before will be offset when I tell him that. He knows his greatest successes have been with me starring in a script I cared madly and deeply about." She inched a neatly sculpted eyebrow up. "You do want me to care madly and deeply, don't you?"

Sarah was two decades too old for the role.

"I can do that," he said.

"And I want you to move in here while you mold your descriptions and dialogue to perfection, without any distractions from the outside world at large, me within easy reach anytime you have a question about how I might say something, where another of my close-ups might be placed or simply for a relaxing time-out with your conspirator-in-arms." Up went her eyebrow again. "It will be our little secret, known only to the two of us, and my sweet, loyal Mad Dog, of course. Any reason this will be a problem?"

Polly.

Mentioning Polly now might be a problem.

He would have to explain who she was and about their relationship, how he had come to think of her as perfect for the girl's role in *Showdown at Shadow Creek*.

Sarah should know about Polly, should be told, but Charlie's sixth sense cautioned this would not be the best time.

"No problem," he said.

"Then a celebration's certainly in order," she said.

She drained the goblet of champagne and tossed it aside. It crashed and splintered on the patio deck as she took him by the hand and guided him to the sauna.

By nightfall he had been to Polly's and back, packed his belongings, including the precious Royal Quiet Deluxe portable typewriter he'd scratched and scrimped to purchase after reading it was the kind Hemingway used to write *The Sun Also Rises* and *A Farewell to Arms,* choked on his regrets writing *I can't see you anymore,* and taped the note to the bathroom mirror.

He crawled into bed and tried pushing Polly out of his mind by concentrating on a story idea inspired by the day's events:

An aspiring, down-on-his-luck screenwriter is rescued from the cops by an aging actress who takes him into the palatial home she shares with a devoted manservant. And then . . . and then—

He fell asleep before he could work on it more.

"There you are, my merry men." Sarah had found them at the tennis court.

She gave Mad Dog a pat on the head. Pried away his bottle of beer and emptied it in a single swallow. Tossed the bottle aside and angled over to plant her drenched lips on Charlie's mouth. Let them linger for what seemed to him like a decade before pulling back and announcing, "We'll have to postpone our usual fun time until later tonight, kiddo, after Max Moonglow meets you."

It took a moment for the news to sink in.

She'd had him working and reworking the screenplay all week, adding scenes for the girl, giving her more dialogue, more close-ups; pushing his hero more and more into the shadows as it evolved more and more into the girl's story.

"You're telling me you're satisfied my screenplay's ready for him to see?"

"Not the screenplay—you, Charlie Dickens. I said it's time for that bastard husband of mine to meet you."

CHAPTER 5

Seeing Charlie's elation dissolve into disappointment and rebound into ecstasy, then confusion—a catalog of emotions in a matter of seconds—Sarah almost felt sorry for the poor sap, almost guilty for boosting his hopes and dreams another notch, *almost* being the operative word. He was a nice guy, a talented guy, but she couldn't let that blind her to the fact he was her fall guy for Max's murder. Even if she wanted to change her mind, too late for that.

"What did you tell him that made him want to meet me?" Charlie said.

"Max doesn't know he's meeting you."

"I don't understand, Sarah." He looked around the tennis court like the explanation might come easier from thin air than from her.

"One of Max's quirks. He deals better when it's with someone he knows and trusts, screenwriters especially. He doesn't trust agents. He doesn't trust studio brass higher up the totem pole than he fancies himself. He certainly doesn't trust me, and sometimes he doesn't even trust himself. Screenwriters, a different story. He'll get introduced to you tonight and that'll set the stage for me to give him the screenplay tomorrow." Spoken with such passion she almost believed it herself.

"What if he doesn't like me?"

"Charlie, Charlie, Charlie." She skewered him with a look that shamed him for the thought. "What's not to like?"

He thought about it. "Friends tell me I have a wimpy handshake."

She reached for his hand. "Squeeze."

He squeezed.

His handshake was wimpy.

Max despised weak handshakes, even from screenwriters. He believed handshakes measured strength of character and revealed the truth about a person as much or more than a person's ability to look someone squarely in the eye.

Never mind that his own handshake was a tragedy and it was impossible for him to look so much as a dead tuna fish in the eye.

Or correctly judge a handshake.

Over the years Sarah had learned the hard way it was easier for people to find the fault in others that they never could see in themselves.

"I feel Popeye the Sailor in your grip," she said, "and so will Max. He'll trust you after that."

"You mean it?"

"Mad Dog, shake hands with Charlie."

They shook.

"Popeye the Sailor," Mad Dog said.

"I do like spinach," Charlie said.

Maybe he was joking.

Sarah couldn't tell.

She left him in Mad Dog's care, explaining, "I'll see you there."

"Where's there? You haven't said."

"Moonglow Manor, of course. Another one of Mad Max's parties for a few hundred of his nearest and dearest friends. Remember to pretend you're seeing the place for the first time."

And the next-to-last, she told herself.

★ ★ ★ ★ ★

Sarah made two stops on the way back home, the first at a converted barn on De Longpre in Hollywood, on the substantial ranch property owned by William S. Hart, the aging, stony-faced cowboy actor who'd moved to a larger spread, *La Casa de los Vientos,* in Newhall after his stardom waned. Hart had donated the barn to Pet Savers, a volunteer organization that rescued and sheltered stray and abandoned animals, provided they never refused to take in a horse in need.

There currently were a hundred or more animals in residence, a mélange of dogs and cats (along with two horses and a Shetland pony) that sent up a cacophony of noises every time they sensed her arrival.

She dropped by once or twice a week for an hour or more, eager to return their true and unconditional love with treats and affection, guided by the memory of Muttsy, the pet pooch taken from her, never to be seen again, the same day her life became a living death.

Sarah couldn't forget that part either.

She had tried in years past, but it was her own Big C, an incurable disease she was doomed to carry to her grave.

Frankie was her favorite, an elegant short-haired Basenji black-and-tan hunting dog of Central Africa stock, whose almond-shaped eyes always seemed to plead, *Sarah, please take me home; I want to be with you, Sarah; I love you, Sarah,* accompanied by a yodeling sound that made up for her lack of a voice. Basenjis were nicknamed "Barkless Dog" for a reason, and that also was part of Frankie's appeal. They were sisters under the skin, Sarah forced to be silent—or else—for days on end before she was rescued from her pimp once and for good those many years ago.

She'd been tempted to take Frankie home on several occasions, but Max would not allow it, always claiming any dog, a

43

pet of any sort, would bring on an asthma attack that could send him to the hospital. His asthma was only that bad when she raised the subject, and she'd tell him so, igniting an argument that would last for hours, or until he clutched his throat, began wheezing, hacking and coughing, pleading for her to hurry up, fetch his lifesaving inhaler, performances that could get him Academy Award nominations if they ever were captured on film.

Afterward, days would pass where they pretended the other didn't exist.

Now, finally, the day was nearing when she wouldn't have to pretend anymore.

She worked the aisles of double-decker kennels—spending extra time with eight dogs that were new to the barn, cooing over a litter of collies feasting off Sunshine and playing toy toss with Frankie—before stopping at the director's cubby hole of a Spartan office to drop off a donation.

Sister Mary Magdalene studied the personal check. "You are far too generous, Miss Darling, more so than ever," she said, clucking away in her flighty Irish brogue.

"In case the Depression decides to make a big comeback, sister."

"God will surely bless you as He blesses the beasts and the children."

Sarah liked the idea, but she wasn't counting on it. Any blessing God had to give, she needed a long time ago, when her life was one unanswered prayer. She'd been on her own too long ever since to be taken in by any of that religion bunk. If God had a blessing for her, better He should pass it on to Sister Mary Magdalene and the other nuns running Pet Savers.

Lately she'd been dreading her visits with Barney Rooker.

More and more he'd been showing signs of getting closer to

glad-handing the Grim Reaper, worn down by his battle with death over the almost three years since she deposited him to die at New Dawn, a sanatorium tucked discreetly among homes of inconsequential architecture or charm on a palm-tree-lined street behind the Fox location lot at Sunset and Western.

Barney was a gnat of a fellow, maybe an inch or two over five feet, but a giant in Sarah's eyes after he rescued her from herself and a different kind of life than the one that let her become Sarah Darling.

She was tricking in San Diego when they met, fifteen and already a veteran of the streets, a glossed-up doll who'd fallen into the life after running away from a father who'd taught her how, beat her when he wasn't satisfied, and a mother who had turned her back on the truth and buried her head in a bottle—caricatures of people who supposedly existed only in cheap pulp fiction.

Her pimp was another caricature.

Andy Cream.

Ex-Navy.

Dishonorably discharged after he was caught hustling on the naval base and served some brig time.

He roped her in on smooth-talking lies of love, taught her new tricks of the trade and beat her worse than Daddy ever did whenever she failed to meet his "high standards," measured by the number of tricks she turned in a night, how much long green she brought in for them.

For them.

Andy always cooing it was for them.

Playing her for a dummy, but she knew better. She chose to believe him because Andy was all she had going for herself until Barney.

Barney was working the sixteen-millimeter Bell & Howell on a stag film being shot in a two-bit motor court in Old Town,

45

where Andy had signed her on to do the nasty with a pair of colored hookers from Whiz Bang John's stable. She was okay with that. It wouldn't be the first time. She knew the ladies from before and they'd always treated her fine, so not so big a deal. It's when the money man behind the shows brought a scabby Saint Bernard into the bungalow and Andy told her how the next reel was going to play out.

She remembered like it was yesterday how she had stomped off in tears, screaming, "I ain't doing no dog act, not again, not now or ever."

Andy chased after her, dug his nails into her arms, drawing blood. Lifted her off the ground and shook her until she thought her head would break loose from her neck. Sprang a rattlesnake in his voice, saying, "You giving the orders now, Sadie?" Sadie. That was her true name. "You know what that gets you, right?"

She knew.

He'd lock her in the closet when she wasn't out working, on a diet of stale bread and water, his version of the brig. Belt-spank her until her welts had welts or, depending on his mood, whack her silly with the telephone book to keep the hurt from showing and turning away potential customers. Make her keep her yapper shut, not so much as a peep, for days and weeks on end, or else.

Or else.

Always threatened, never explained.

He'd figured out early her fear of the unknown was worse than any words he could lay on her.

She said, "I can't do it a new time, Andy. Puke my brains out like the time before."

"Maybe better with a horse?"

"No, God no."

"A donkey, a sheep or maybe a pig? A pig for a pig?"

"I'm gonna be sick, Andy. Gonna throw up."

She did, spraying him with vomit before she could turn away and mask her mouth, painting puke on his hand-tailored, fifty-dollar, three-piece gabardine suit.

Andy cupped off a handful and smashed her face with the puke, like Jimmy Cagney did with a grapefruit to Mae Clark in that movie.

Slapped her hard enough on the cheek to knock loose a tooth.

Was getting ready to test his fist on her when Barney said, "I wouldn't do that I was you, mister." He had trailed them outside and was watching from the porch with the money man and Whiz Bang John. "The girl said no to the dog, that's that. Over and out."

Andy did a quick study on Barney. Andy was a head taller and fifty or sixty pounds heavier than the cameraman; nothing adding up to a fair fight Barney had any chance of winning, it came to that. He called to the money man, "The squirt speaking for you, Pete?"

The money man thought about it through a cloud of cigarette smoke. Finger shot the butt into a mud puddle on the dirt parking lot. "What you got her looking like now is ripe for certain of my clientele what like to watch it rough and such, dog or no dog."

"Good enough for me," Andy said. "Get your dinky ass back in there, bitch."

Sarah started for the porch.

Barney stopped her from entering the bungalow. He handed off the Bell & Howell to the money man. "Finish up with one of Whiz Bang John's fine colored ladies, Pete. The girl and I are leaving."

"Over my dead body," Andy said, flashing the switchblade he'd pulled from some hiding place behind his back.

"Fair enough," Barney said. He revealed the .22-caliber handgun he wore under his belt in the small of his back. "You think you can work that pigsticker faster'n I can get off a shot, go right ahead."

"I bet you wouldn't be so brave you didn't have that gun."

"You'd win the bet," Barney said.

He told Andy to drop to his knees and toss the switchblade over his shoulder.

Andy studied Barney's steady gun hand and obliged.

"Don't try nothing frisky while the girl and I skedaddle," Barney said. He pointed Sarah to a banged-up Chevy that had seen better years, lots of them, about fifteen yards to Andy's left, alongside the money man's pristine dollar-green Duesenberg.

"Owe you one big time, brother," Andy said, sounding like the devil's handyman. "You also, bitch. Get yourself ready for what's coming your way down the pike once this damn game's over and done."

Barney said, "You got me quaking in my shoes something fierce, hotshot."

Sarah shared a scream with the sky, changed direction, and charged after Andy. She pulled up behind him, scooped up the switchblade and drew it deep across his throat. Dead before he knew it, Andy fell over face forward and over onto his side, painting the dirt with his blood.

Barney had seen what was coming and called out, "Don't!" but there was too much distance and not enough time to stop her. Frozen in the moment and exploring Andy with something akin to satisfaction, she respected Barney's soft-spoken request to hand over the switchblade. He trapped her eyes. "You know how to drive?" She nodded. "I want you to take my car and scram from here. You unnerstand me? Key's in the car. Get in the car and take off. Go. Don't look back. Land somewhere you can put the life behind you and start clean and fresh."

"What about Andy?"

"He's staying."

"What about you?"

"Christ's sake, girl, you got enough worries worrying about yourself to worry about me or the rest of the world. Git."

"Why are you doing this for me?"

"Been meaning to palm off that junk buggy on someone the longest time," Barney said, the best answer she could get out of him before she climbed behind the wheel of the Chevy and took off.

It would be years before she saw him again.

Barney didn't acknowledge her arrival when she tapped on the door of his private room at New Dawn and entered. He was at the window, absorbed by something happening outside, his back to her. She gave it a minute before calling over, "Hey there, angel mine, your girl's come a-calling."

No response.

Sarah gave it another minute and tried again.

Barney managed an arm in the air and waved her quiet.

She crossed to the bed and sat down with her legs dangling over the edge. Kicked off her pumps to give her toes breathing room and smiled back at her unsmiling kisser in the framed Hurrell portrait that broke the monotony of pill bottles on Barney's nightstand. It was the one personal touch in a room that smelled of urine and worse.

Sarah was forking over a monthly premium to give Barney the dignity of his own room. The thirteen other rooms were shared by two or three guests, the frame of reference New Dawn preferred to patients, as if they were running a hotel, not a sanatorium. Barney called them inmates, same as he called New Dawn Death Row.

"You see it when you got here?" Barney said, maneuvering his wheelchair around so that he faced her, the late-afternoon light casting his face in a whiter shade of pale. "The ambulance, I mean."

"Yes."

"They come and they go from here as regular as the Red Cars. That one just took off with old Cliff Yentz, feet first. A butter-and-egg man. Not by a long shot the pinochle player he fancied himself. Left owing me a couple Ben Franklins I don't stand a chance in Hell of collecting, seeing as how I don't expect to find him there when I take up residence."

Inevitability sounded in the remnant of his once-commanding voice.

Barney always did know where his life would be taking him in death.

He said, "Old Cliff, he was a first-class do-gooder, especially with old Mrs. Lamb down the hall in Six. Doing her good every chance he got. She'll be up for grabs again, me out of the running this time. Get it?" He slapped the arms of his wheelchair. "Out of the running."

Barney laughed like he meant it.

She laughed to be polite, wondering how many more visits before an ambulance came to collect him, crying inside at the concept.

"Making friends around here is easy, a snap," he said. "Keeping them? Impossible."

"Come to you and me, Barney, my money is on forever."

"And a day," he said. He wheeled over to take her hands, struggled out a squeeze while he memorized her face.

Sarah leaned forward and kissed him, pretending away the cool of his forehead, the cold of his lips. "Is there anything you need, angel mine? Tell me."

"Just to know you're all right, Sadie. That's the tonic that keeps me going."

"I'm fine."

"And this plan of yours?"

"Max is throwing one of his parties tonight. He'll meet Charlie Dickens."

"The writer you're setting up for the kill."

"Him."

"Explain to me again how it's going to work," Barney said.

He had fallen asleep before she finished.

Not that it mattered.

Barney already knew everything worth knowing.

CHAPTER 6

Charlie felt adrift in a sea of people he didn't know, among them familiar faces from the silver screen and a few giants from behind the camera. Josef von Sternberg was easy to recognize, so was Frank Capra; King Vidor and Howard Hawks less so; George Cukor only because he had paused to smile hello while cruising the crowded living room, mistaking Charlie for George Reeves, who'd been cast as one of the Tarleton twins in *Gone with the Wind*.

No sign of Sarah in the hour since Mad Dog dropped him off at Moonglow Manor and he joined a couple hundred people in fancy dress who were rubbing shoulders, kissing cheeks, pumping hands, grabbing hors d'oeuvres off dozens of platters being passed around by serving girls busting out of skimpy costumes fit for a René Clair farce, and storming the buffet tables piled high with enough fancy foods and treats to feed Skid Row into the next century. Service bars struggled to keep up with demand. Champagne fountains everywhere offered a bubbly alternative to the premium wines and hard stuff. Strolling musicians vied for attention from party guests far more interested in trading the latest industry gossip than anything the violinists, marimba bands or adrenalin-fueled accordionists had to offer.

It was the kind of spectacle Charlie only knew from the gossip columns and movie magazines.

He poured himself a fresh flute of champagne and was gliding his way through the den back to the living room, on the alert for Sarah, when he thought he saw Polly moving out to the patio; only a glimpse, but looking too much like Polly to be anyone else. Polly! A chance to apologize, defy Sarah's edict by telling Polly enough to earn her forgiveness. A wise move? No, but his heart and the champagne were ruling his head. Afterward he'd come up with something to appease Sarah, or—

Maybe not.

And what would that mean for *Showdown at Shadow Creek*?

First things first:

Showdown at Moonglow Manor.

He chugalugged the champagne and wobbled toward the patio, pausing en route at another fountain to refill his glass. Spun around to resume pursuit. Banged into a little guy decked out like Fred Astaire in white tie and tails, spilling the champagne all over him.

The guy gave him a hard stare and a curse in some foreign language that sounded German, or maybe Jewish; Hollywood was full of both. Was sweeping himself off when Charlie noticed the dueling scar carved on his cheek and realized it was Max Moonglow.

He sputtered out his regrets and began dry-patting Moonglow's chest, so hard he threw Moonglow off-balance into a guest and, like a pinball, forward into the lake of the champagne fountain. He hurried to help Moonglow out and almost toppled in himself as Moonglow unleashed an evil eye and threw fresh curses at him in German or Jewish.

Somebody perfectly cast as a butler showed up with towels.

Moonglow wrangled free of Charlie and stood patiently while he was toweled off, encouraging the guests who had gathered to get back to enjoying the festivities, making a joke of it, declaring, "I hear Mack Sennett started this way."

The guests laughed.

"Actually, seltzer bottles and pie shells topped with shaving cream came first," Charlie said, his habit of reciting Hollywood history getting the best of him when he should have been disappearing into the crowd, delaying any introduction to Moonglow until the odds were better that Moonglow would have forgotten his face.

"Not you. You stay," Moonglow said.

Charlie froze in place.

"How'd you get in here? Do I know you?"

"Not yet, Mr. Moonglow. I was going to talk to you about—"

"Forget about yet. I don't talk to anybody I don't know. You somebody's guest, a walker, maybe? A lot of the crones who ain't what they used to be or never were—widow ladies, lesbos like that Gertie Stein over in Paris or that Radclyffe Hall—they like to have pretty boys like you at their arm. Why in Hell not? Make-believe, pretending to be what you're not is a universal sport in this town." He laughed. "Not just Universal. Paramount, Metro, Fox, Columbia and even Republic and Monogram, for Christ's sake. I could name names, but that would take me all night."

"You're doing it now, Mr. Moonglow?"

"What's it I'm doing? You saying I'm pretending?"

Sarah said, "Talking to someone you don't know, dummy," giving him the answer Charlie had in mind. She'd materialized from somewhere and was gliding her arm around his. "He's my guest, Max, so does that make me one of the old crones you were telling him about?"

Moonglow looked at her dismissively. "I got better names to call you."

"Like what, hotshot?"

He told her, his voice barking the words loud enough to draw a startled reaction from nearby guests and attract others into the room. The audience grew even larger after Sarah laid some choice words of her own on him, larger still by the time their screaming threatened to become physical, Sarah's fist shaking with anticipation, Moonglow leveling his chin and challenging her to throw the punch.

Charlie trapped her in his arms, lifting her a foot off the parquet floor, to prevent that from happening. She struggled against his grip, demanding to be set free, reducing Moonglow to derisive laughter and asking in a stage whisper that carried outside to the patio, "She that violent when she has you in bed, Casanova? You wouldn't be the first to need patching up after she's finished bouncing 'em on the bedsheets."

"He's a better lover than you ever were or ever will be with me or any of the starlets who buy into your bullshit and your casting couch," Sarah said. "And you know what else?"

Charlie clamped a hand over her mouth before she could shout her next thoughts. "I am no Casanova, sir. I am a screenwriter."

"A screenwriter, huh? What do you have to your credit besides my wife? . . . Wait!" He held out his hand like a crossing guard. "Don't tell me! Go tell it to the Marines, sonny boy." With that, he turned and strutted away, parting the guests like Moses parting the Red Sea. Most trailed after him, as if too embarrassed to remain in the company of Charlie and Sarah.

He set her down, adjusted his dinner jacket while she tugged at her gown, fussed with her Ella Cinders bob, and sent smiles to the few lingering guests before leading him out to an empty corner of the patio.

"I guess that finishes me with Mr. Moonglow," he said, choking on the thought.

"Finished? You silly boy, it couldn't have gone better," Sarah said, rewarding him with a coronation kiss.

He studied her for the joke, but she appeared serious inside a grin broader than the one he remembered from what's his name? In that picture, whatever it was called. He was too disheartened now to think about anything but the future that was surely past happening.

"I'll let you in on a little secret," Sarah said. "Max and I, we fight all the time over anything and everything. It's our way, always has been. You dig deep enough, you might even find the remains of something remotely resembling love or, at the least, a lingering affection. It doesn't make sense, but what in Hollywood does? He uses me. I use him. We use each other. And neither of us will ever admit defeat at anything in a town that thrives on success and is stocked with people who enjoy the spectacle of failure, so long as it's not theirs. You understand?"

"Not exactly."

"I'll spell it out. Max always feels guilty after one of our blowouts, especially when it's happened in front of an audience. He's ready to do whatever it takes to make it up to me in private, whatever it takes, because the poor sap doesn't want to risk losing his movie star meal ticket. In other words, if you hadn't accidentally launched Max's temper to the moon, I'd have done it myself. Later, when he comes pawing around, asking what he can do to put the ruckus behind us, I'll tell him, *Maxie, sweetie, there's nothing would make me happier than having you read Mr. Charlie Dickens beautiful screenplay, with a wonderful part in it for me.* He'll read it, and we're in business."

"What if he hates the screenplay?"

"There's always another party or the next premiere, like a week from now at the Egyptian, something or other with that adorable Mickey Rooney. I'm always at my best worst at premieres, playing to my adoring fans in the crowd." She drew him closer and rubbed her body against his, made a purring sound more intoxicating than the smell of Joy by Jean Patou, her perfume, advertised as the most expensive perfume in the world, the one preferred by the Queen of England, she told him the first time she poured half a bottle into their bath water. "Now leave, go," she said. "Mad Dog will be parked outside waiting for you. Your work is done here, and a fine night's work it's been, kiddo."

The fear that, contrary to Sarah's assurances, Max Moonglow would want nothing to do with him dogged Charlie's every step down the marble path to DeMille Drive, where cars were lined up on both sides of the street, the drivers passing time in lazy conversations inside clouds of cigarette smoke or playing card games on car hoods.

At the same time a new screenplay was building in his mind—

An aging but beautiful woman, while professing love for her husband, takes on a younger man as her lover, a Mickey Rooney type, but better, more rugged-looking, like that newcomer John Garfield—and taller than Mickey. Together they plot to deceive the husband in order to do . . . to do something or other, or—

That's as far as he got before he spotted Polly at the foot of the driveway, heading through the gate to a double-parked late-model Hudson tooting its horn.

Charlie started after her, calling her name.

If Polly heard him, she didn't let on.

The driver slipped out of the car and came around to open the passenger side door for her. He looked familiar, with good reason. It was that guy, that Salmon guy, from the Nickodell.

Charlie called, "Polly, wait!" Picked up speed as that Salmon guy helped her into the car. "Polly, hold on!"

That Salmon guy was climbing back behind the wheel of the Hudson.

Charlie ran faster.

A patent leather Oxford toe caught in a mislaid marble tile and spilled him forward into a failed balancing act.

He somersaulted over the low-slung brick wall onto the sidewalk.

Settled on his haunches, dazed, shaking free from blurred double vision in time to see the Hudson racing down DeMille Drive.

Charlie assumed it was one of the drivers offering him a hand up, telling him in a gravel pit of a voice, "A darn nice gag you pulled off there, sonny. Don't know I could've pulled it off any better when I was still at it, your age."

The face was familiar. He recognized it belonged to Buster Keaton, the great stone-faced comic of the Silent Era, and did a double take to go with his recurring double vision. He said, "Nobody could ever take a spill or anything better than you, Mr. Keaton."

Keaton shrugged off the compliment and headed off across the street.

Keaton's feet slid out from under him, as if he'd wandered onto an oil slick.

On the verge of falling backward, he somehow defied gravity with a body roll that landed him on his feet and spun him forward.

He crashed against a Cord Phaeton, onto and off the hood of a Pierce-Arrow and back onto the street.

Dusted himself off.

Resumed crossing as if nothing out of the ordinary had happened, paused to let a Bugatti cruise by and, at the last second, grabbed hold of the window frame, hopped onto the running board and waved good-bye as the car continued down to Los Feliz Boulevard.

"You see that?" Charlie asked Mad Dog, who had materialized at his side. "That was Buster Keaton."

"I'm a Chaplin man myself," Mad Dog said.

★ ★ ★ ★ ★

The phone call the next morning woke Charlie from a dream as obvious as a bullet in the brain, him trying to outrun a Bugatti barreling down DeMille Drive, Max Moonglow behind the wheel, Polly in the passenger seat, urging Moonglow to drive faster, hit the son of a bitch, put an end to his misery.

The call did that, Sarah on the line telling him, "We have a three o'clock at Max's office at RKO. Don't be late."

Chapter 7

Max motioned this Charlie Dickens person into his office, extending the old razzle-dazzle smile like he meant it, and pointed him to the conversation area where Sarah already had tucked herself into a corner of the casting couch she'd helped him christen his first day on the RKO payroll.

Max didn't like him any better now than he did last night, Sarah's latest discovery, this Charlie Dickens person, for the same reason he could never tolerate any of the young dreamers and schemers she was continually bringing around, all of them pains in the ego, especially the actors who couldn't act their way out of a nursery rhyme.

He wondered if this one was better in bed than any of the others may have been.

Really, though, wondering if he was better than Max Moonglow, however unlikely, no matter what she'd claimed during their shouting match at the party, the latest exchange in the ongoing "Battling Moonglows" saga that by noon the Tinseltown gossips had spread like manure.

He could never worm a real answer out of Sarah about any of them, any more than she was ever able to pin him down about his own protégés, many of whom actually turned out to be as talented off the casting couch as they were on it.

Only two, if he cared to be truthful with himself, but neither a million miles close to Sarah, who grabbed this Charlie Dickens by the hand before he could settle down on one of the antique armchairs and yanked him down onto the cushion beside her.

She gave his knee a motherly squeeze and shot Max an impatient stare that ordered, *Let's get down to business,* followed with a question delivered like she was not responsible for the answer she knew would be forthcoming, damn her.

"So tell Mr. Dickens and me what this meeting is all about, Max," she said. "Please. We're dying to know, aren't we, Mr. Dickens?"

"Dying," this Charlie Dickens said, stumbling over the word while avoiding Max's dissecting stare, his own eyes searching the office for a safe landing spot in the clutter of furnishings drawn from scenes in movies Max had made here since Pandro Berman lured him away from Fox with an offer he couldn't refuse, worth a lot of money, but more than that a universe of freedom in picking and choosing his productions and the contractual guarantee they'd go out billed as:

MAX MOONGLOW PRESENTS

A MAX MOONGLOW PRODUCTION

Max wasn't fooled, though. He understood the inner workings of the business well enough to recognize Pan knew he'd be getting Sarah as part of the deal, in a sense two for the price of one, and a stronger hold on his job as supervising producer, number-two man under head of production David O. Selznick, who'd been systematically clearing the lot of veteran talent he felt unworthy of his patronage.

Sarah was a bridge to the level of prestige Selznick coveted and felt was lacking at RKO. Realistically, what was there between the cotton candy fluff of the Fred Astaire and Ginger Rogers musicals and the glut of western and crime programmers? Not much. Some star-making, box-office potential with Cary Grant and Katharine Hepburn, granted, but no one as established and surefire as Sarah Darling.

That made them a package deal, like Lunt and Fontanne on

Broadway, Sarah queen of the lot and Selznick's prize pet her first day through the Gower Street entrance.

Whatever else went on when he invited Sarah in for closed-door creative sessions that could last for hours, Max didn't want to know about, and he wisely stayed quiet when the studio breached his contract, first changing the on-screen credit to—

MAX MOONGLOW PRESENTS

SARAH DARLING

In

A MAX MOONGLOW PRODUCTION

Then—

SARAH DARLING

In

A MAX MOONGLOW PRODUCTION

Was he bothered?

Certainly he was bothered.

But his name was still above the title, in a town where credit on the screen was the ultimate measure of a person's worth, for better or for worse, and so what if people sniped behind his back, whispering that everything he was he owed to Sarah?

Was it any worse than what one newspaper headline reported about Selznick after he married Irene Mayer and quit RKO to work for his father-in-law, Louis B. Mayer: *The Son-in-Law Also Rises?*

Besides, he loved Sarah.

Didn't he?

As much as he loved his status.

Sometimes more.

Sometimes less than more.

Sometimes, after they'd fought, before they kissed and made up, he thought about wanting her dead, how he'd kill Sarah if he could, but reality and common sense prevailed. Killing the goose that laid the golden eggs would have the net effect of cooking his goose.

Yet, here he was thinking it now as Her Royal Highness waited for his answer to her question. "Why I called for this meeting?" he said. "An excellent question, right to the point, so let me get to the point."

"In our lifetime, darling?"

So smug, that one. So self-righteous. "Without further adieu, my precious one," he said, and hurried around the desk to plop onto the armchair across from the couch, aim an expanded version of his hustler's smile at this Charlie Dickens, and announce, "Apart from urging you to forget about our trifling disagreement of last night, as I have, and let bygones be bygones . . ." He put some hurt in his eyes. "Can you do that, fella?"

This Charlie Dickens seemed tongue-tied. Sarah gave him an elbow in the ribcage.

"I can do that, sir."

Max blasted him with a Chevalier smile. "Call me Max. Max to you forevermore, Charlie, is it?"

"Charlie Izit? Actually, sir, Max, it's Charlie Dickens—like in Charles Dickens? My mother happened to be reading *Great Expectations* right before I was born, and that inspired her, especially since our last name also was Dickens and she always felt related somehow."

Sarah banged his ribs again, before he could get another sentence out.

"Mothers know things like that," Max said, building into a laugh. "They have this sixth sense. Perhaps that's why you became a writer, just as *Great Expectations* has now brought us together. I resist imagining where you'd be at this moment if your mother had been reading *A Tale of Two Cities.*"

"My father was, just before he disappeared," this Charlie Dickens said, his chin sinking onto his chest, his expression dripping despair. "He left us a note saying it was a far, far bet-

63

ter thing he was doing than—"

"Enough!" Sarah said. She pushed onto her feet and exaggerated her annoyance. "Can we quit with the book reports and cut to the chase?"

This Charlie Dickens looked to him for the answer.

Max threw open his arms wide. "Charlie, I have decided to produce *Sundown at the Creek* as my next Max Moonglow Presents. Congratulations."

"*Showdown at Shadow Creek,* sir. Max."

"What?"

"The title of my screenplay? *Showdown at Shadow Creek.*"

"Of course." Sarah dodged the look Max was giving her and reclaimed her seat on the couch. "And a fine title it is, Charlie, to go with a fine screenplay."

"You read it and liked it, then? You really liked it?"

"Even better. Sarah read it and liked it. Liked it? She couldn't quit raving about it or the great acting opportunity it offered the great Sarah Darling. Her endorsement was good enough for me. Who needs reading when he has Sarah? She has never steered me wrong, have you, my precious one?"

"Only because we breathe the same air, darling man." She bowed in false modesty.

"And she had a sensational idea about her leading man." Max waited the length of a drum roll. "Gary Cooper."

"Gary Cooper? Starring in my movie?"

"Starring with me," Sarah said.

"A Max Moonglow movie," Max said. "Coop will recognize this as the positively perfect follow-up to his last two westerns—"

"*The Plainsman* and *The Cowboy and the Lady.*"

"You do know your movies, Charlie."

"They wanted to borrow me for *The Cowboy and the Lady,*" Sarah said.

Max nodded confirmation. "They wouldn't agree to change

64

the title to *The Lady and the Cowboy,* so that ended that. Like fate. Like Divine Providence taking a hand. Like the powers that be knew there would be a superior *Sundown at the Creek* heading down the pike."

"Gosh. Gary Cooper in my movie," Charlie said. "Who'd have thought?"

"Me," Sarah said.

Max said, "Pan will welcome the suggestion, given all the B westerns he's been obliged to turn out, not that George O'Brien is a lousy leading man."

"For somebody else, maybe, but not for me," she said. "Darling and Cooper—an overdue blockbuster pairing if ever there was one. Why I threw out his name at Max last night."

Charlie said, "Gary Cooper," blushed at hearing himself sound like a high-school kid suffering his first crush, froze in the aftermath wondering, "But what if Gary Cooper says no?"

"And the moon is made of green cheese," Max said.

"You busy?" Pan Berman said, strolling unannounced into Max's office, Max on the portable massage table, getting his daily late-afternoon pounding from Nicky Hands, his regular guy from the Paramount Studios gym next door.

"Never too busy for you, Pan. To what do I owe the pleasure?"

"This script you sent over this morning?" He withdrew it from under his arm and flashed it at Max. "I had one of my girls read it. She says it makes the leading lady out to be a lesbo and turns the hero into a pansy."

"Nobody's perfect."

He laughed.

Pan didn't. He studied Max with the kind of intense focus that followed everybody in the business who'd started out as a film editor. "And Sarah wants to do it?" His words similarly clipped, direct and to the point. Not a wasted second, like

Warner Bros. chips at scenes—snip a frame here, snip a frame there—to keep the running time tight and the story whizzing along like Jesse Owens.

"Her idea. She brought the screenplay to me, insisting it had to be her next picture."

"And you agreed after reading this pile of dreck?" He pulled a pipe from his breast pocket and propped it between his teeth.

"Of course. We're talking Sarah Darling, you and me."

"We're talking disaster, this turkey gets made." Trenches formed across his broad forehead. He ran a hand over his receding hairline. "It would do for Sarah's career what's happening lately to Hepburn. The exhibitors, they're calling her box-office poison."

"Not if the picture gets made with Sarah and Gary Cooper."

"Coop? What's Nicky Hands been doing to you? Slapping your head around the way he's been slapping your ass?" Nicky Hands got the joke and cackled, slapping Max's ass for emphasis. "What you got here, my friend, I'd wager George O'Brien would breach his contract before he'd mount this horse."

"My contract says I can pick and choose without objection or interference."

"But it doesn't say the studio has to release what you make," Pan said, without an ounce of emotion.

Snip.

"What do I tell Sarah?"

"What do you think you tell her? You tell her Gary Cooper comes on board, the picture gets a go-sign."

Snip.

"And if Coop won't do it?"

Pan dropped the script on Max's desk and strolled out of the office as casually as he had arrived, like his silence was all the answer necessary.

Snip.

Sarah wasn't home when he called to tell her about Pan Berman.

The housekeeper didn't know where she was or when she'd be back. "Nobody here has heard from Mrs. Moonglow since she went to meet with you, Mr. Moonglow."

"Mrs. Moonglow checks in or she shows up, tell her I said to tell her I'm stuck in a meeting came up suddenly with some money men and I'll see her when I see her. Got that, Hilda?"

"Maisie, Mr. Moonglow."

"What?"

"I'm Maisie, remember? Hilda is who you fired two months ago, right before you went and promoted me in her place."

"Oh, yeah," he said, hardly remembering at all. The help kept coming and going in an endless cycle. Some even deserved to be fired, but usually it had to do with something petty that riled Sarah on one of her badder-than-bad days, which could be any day of the year. Hilda was a looker, except for the cleft palate that distorted her speaking, especially words that contained the letters *p, b, t, d, s, sh, ch,* and *f.* That's what bothered Sarah, she said, but only after she got wise to the heavy review he gave Hilda every time she came around and figured out the cleft palate might be a turn-on for him. If she had one herself, Hilda might still be around. Without it, Sarah marked her as unfair competition.

Maisie, on the other hand, looked more like one of those abandoned pooches from the dog shelter Sarah was always visiting and bringing home pictures of this hound dog or that flea-bitten collie. Shoving them under his nose. Crying crocodiles when he put his foot down again, reminding her his asthma was already too bad to get any worse, all that damn pollen in the air from the night-blooming jasmine and whatever other triggers that gardener of theirs had growing out in the damn garden, on top of everything forever gliding in from that damn Griffith Park.

Max replaced the receiver on the nightstand and rolled out of bed, padded across the room to the picture window and immersed himself in a moonlit sky bright enough on this cloudless evening to provide an unrestricted panoramic view clear to downtown from his Sunset Plaza Drive hideaway a half mile above the Strip.

The one-bedroom apartment in the nondescript set of bungalows set back from the winding road was his playground, his refuge from the realities of a make-believe world that didn't deserve him, Max Moonglow, a Sergei Eisenstein forced to work alongside inferior talents who controlled his destiny. Dependent upon the kindness of Sarah and the dictates of Pan Berman to survive through the present and maybe find a future that fit his genius.

He caught his reflection in the picture window, checked his face for signs of age, patted his dueling scar for comfort, and said, "Max Moonglow is who I am, who no one else can or will ever be." His declaration roused Dixie Leeds from the catnap she always took midway through their usual playground of gymnastic delights.

Dixie was his current discovery, a sparkling fountain of youth who captured his eye when she roller-skated over to take his order at the Skate Burger Drive-In on Melrose.

He asked for the cheeseburger, Swiss instead of American, no onions and light on the mayonnaise, a side of French fries, and a chocolate shake; afterward he left her a generous tip and one of the engraved business cards he used for special occasions, his Producer title as prominent as his name, the phone number handwritten, given he changed it regularly as he changed his discoveries.

Dixie called the next day, asking, "Are you truly a producer, Mr. Moonglow?" He rattled off some of his credits. "Oh, *that* Max Moonglow? The one who's married to Sarah Darling, that one?"

Max grimaced. How much he hated people thinking of him as Mr. Sarah Darling, but this looker was too good to pass up. "Yes, that one."

"I dream a lot of becoming a big, big star like her. Why I've been working overtime shifts at the Skate Burger, especially weekends, for money enough to take my classes at the Stardom School of Dramatic Arts with Mr. Felix Untermeyer himself. You know who that is? Felix Untermeyer?"

"He knows who I am. Listen, dear girl. When I noticed you last night, I sensed in you the same qualities I sensed in Sarah that allowed me to catapult her to international stardom. You served me my cheeseburger and the accoutrements with a grace and dignity I'd never experienced before at the Skate Burger, even remembered I asked for mustard as well as extra ketchup. You had me convinced you were a skateress, although I knew from the onset, instinctively in my theatrical bones, there was more to you than that."

"I rehearsed before I applied for the job. I pawned the diamond wedding ring my mama bequeathed me in her last will and testament and used the money to buy a pair of Whirlwind Wheels, the twin-speed ankle-clutch shoe model with the built-in brakes and extra-strength laces, better than the plain speed rotos Skate Burger expects you to bring to the job. *Practice makes perfect* is my motto in life. A job worth doing is worth doing well, Mr. Moonglow, don't you think so?"

"*Well?* In my world, you draw water from a well. You draw *stars* from the sky."

"Oh, my—" The line went quiet. Max thought she might have hung up on him, but she was back after a few more moments. "I'm so ashamed, Mr. Moonglow. What you said just then was so inspiring, got me so excited, I wet in my panties."

"You—?"

"Soaking . . . I suppose I shouldn't have told you that, but Mr. Untermeyer teaches us that half-truths are no truths at all and sharing opens the inner self to every possibility life has to offer."

Max wondered what Bible this Untermeyer was stealing his sermons from, the First Book of Baloney? "Dear girl, stardom is a possibility I'm prepared to offer you. Would you like to meet with me to discuss that?" It was a half-truth, Max already visualizing what else he could bring to her panties.

"Golly, jeepers, yes, Mr. Moonglow," she said, "but—" Followed by silence, as if she were reconsidering. She wasn't. "I don't want to sound ungrateful or anything, but we'd have to do it around my shift schedule at Skate Burger."

After they settled on a weeknight and time, Max said, "Do you know where Sunset Plaza Drive is?"

Max broke away from playing with memory when he turned and spotted Dixie easing up into a sitting position, resting on her elbows, the covers fallen away to reveal enough of the perfect body he'd been feasting on a half hour ago to get his jungle juices flowing again. She scouted the room until she located him and launched her irresistible Delilah smile. "Hey, there, honey pie," she called over. "Your Dixie is ready to give it another go."

Chapter 8

Charlie escorted Sarah to her car after they left the meeting with Max Moonglow, buoyant about his future, his dream for *Showdown at Shadow Creek* so close to becoming reality, his optimism endorsed by Sarah; telling her how thankful he was for making it all come true.

"I'll take a rain check on you proving to me just how thankful," she said, running a hand up and down his forearm. "Right now, I got me some other business needs attending."

"Would you like me to go with you?"

"Out in public? Get tongues wagging like sabers, more than they already are since the party, or didn't you see the morning papers, my name spread like manure in the gossip columns, especially Hopper in the *Times,* but the *Herald-Express* did run one of the terrific portraits Steichen took of me for *Vanity Fair,* the year I broke out big-time."

"And the stories mentioned me?" Charlie said, excited by the possibility.

"Not by name. Only as some mystery man who had a run-in with Max, a shouting match that ended with him coming between the Battling Moonglows starring in their own shouting match."

Charlie shielded his disappointment. "Your husband didn't seem at all bothered."

"They spelled his name right."

She gave him a shielded grab in the crotch after he opened

the door of the LaSalle convertible she was driving today and glided behind the wheel, blew him an air kiss and sped out of the lot.

He had second thoughts heading to his car.

Polly.

She was an easy walk away, three blocks across the boulevard, at Raleigh Studios making her Hopalong Cassidy movie.

The urge to see her, strong last night, was stronger now.

He headed off on foot, working on his apology, the words that might win her back, especially when she heard the news about his meeting at RKO and—

A problem.

How exactly would Polly take the news about *Showdown at Shadow Creek*?

About Sarah in the starring part he'd told her how many times she, Polly, would be perfect for. How he'd rewritten the screenplay to Sarah's specifications as the trade-off for getting it produced by Max Moonglow.

She'd understand, of course.

She was that kind of girl.

He'd promise not to let that happen again, next time, after *Showdown at Shadow Creek* was a big hit and he had a reputation that let him master his own destiny, less the usual ten percent for Roy Balloon, who'd agent him into cushy deals that didn't require him to parade around town like some gigolo for hire, the word Available tattooed on his cock.

No.

Better leave that part out.

That part Polly wouldn't understand.

It did have the makings of a good picture, though—

The Scarlet Tattoo.

Hector Prynne's illicit affair with a preacher's wife is exposed after she gives birth to their love child. Heck is branded with a scarlet A on his . . . on his forehead. He suffers one indignity after another, but his sin leads to repentance, his salvation and a gloriously happy ending that—

—that . . . the Breen Office would never allow to reach the silver screen and taint the innocent minds of the moviegoing public.

He'd have to work on it some more.

At the Bronson gate, Charlie couldn't get past the guard, who looked like a refugee from a war movie, one of those stiff-backed MPs, a glass-chewing voice like Barton MacLane, telling him, "You need a visitor's pass. No visitor's pass, no admittance. Rules is rules."

"But I'm a personal friend of Miss Polly Wilde."

"Who?"

"She's an actress, in *Bar 20 Justice.*"

"Mr. Boyd's new one. Never heard of her."

"You will someday."

The guard gave him a closer inspection. "A personal friend, huh? Something going on between the two of you, like lovebirds, maybe?"

"Something like that."

"Don't tell me. On the outs right now and you looking to get back in."

"Something like that."

The guard slapped his thigh. "Knew it! I can smell a spat a mile away. You seem like a nice enough fella. Not like some what come around here trying to crash the gate and get a gander at the stars, maybe steal a little squeeze."

"Actually, I'm a screenwriter."

The guard sized him up again, unleashed a caterpillar smile that crept up the side of his face. "Me, too. I should-a known. Got a script right now I'm getting up nerve to ask Mr. Boyd to have a look. It's titled *Hopalong Cassidy in Old California,* where he chases after this Zorro kind of stagecoach bandit, who robs from the rich and—here's the twist—he keeps all the loot for himself. Whaddaya think?"

"Great title," Charlie said. "Good luck."

"Yeah. I hear you. Getting attention in this business is like trying to catch water in a net, I always say." The smile crawled up his face again. "What was her name again?"

"Polly Wilde."

"As in *Call of the?*"

"With an *e* on the end." Charlie spelled it out.

"Stick around a minute, and mind the red line," he said. Retreated to the guard hut and got on the telephone. Was there for the length of time it took Charlie to think the script could really take off like Lindbergh if Hoppy wound up exposing Zorro as a fake Zorro, by the way he mishandled a saber, something like that. "You're outta luck, friend."

"She said no?"

"She's not there. They're striking the set and she's been released for the day."

Charlie thanked him and turned to leave, leaping back from the driveway as the Hudson honked madly and sped through without braking, that Salmon guy at the wheel and Polly seated alongside him.

Taking the walk back to RKO and his car, feeling like Preston Foster as "Killer" Mears in *The Last Mile;* "Killer" Dickens walking his own last mile; knowing who he'd like to kill.

Mad Dog was setting the dinner table for two when Charlie got back to Benedict Canyon, Gilbert and Sullivan echoing full blast through the speaker system, Mad Dog in pursuit of the right notes to "When I Was a Lad" from *HMS Pinafore,* singing *I cleaned the windows and I swept the floor,* barely beating a chorus echo to *And I polished up the handle of the big front door.*

He waved greetings, stepped over to the record player and snapped off the music.

"Soothes the savage beast, music does," Mad Dog said.

Actually, Congreve had written how music's charms soothed the savage breast, not beast, but right now Charlie was a savage beast who needed soothing, so he didn't bother to correct Mad Dog. He wanted to pour his heart out about Polly, explain how he had to see her again no matter what Sarah wanted, listen to any suggestions Mad Dog might offer. He knew Sarah better than anyone.

Mad Dog said, "Pretty good, my singing, huh, Charlie?"

"You definitely have a voice all your own, Mad Dog."

"You can say that again. I probably would-a tried it full-time after I cracked a few heads and sprung myself loose from the orphan asylum, but the sidewalk is a tough climb up for gutter boys like me. You learn to live by your wits, and if you learn long and good enough, you live to tell."

"And here you are."

"Talking too much. I helped myself to a few nips of Jack earlier, so that accounts for that. Easier to do these times, than when the lady's first ex ruled the roost, before she got her lawyers to give him the bum's rush out the front door. He marked the bottles so he could always know if any of the help, we were helping ourselves to his precious schnapps. You got found out, you got fired."

"But he was good to you, didn't you say? He took you in after you retired from the wrestling ring, gave you your job here, a roof over your head and cash in your pocket."

"Something like that, but nothing comes for free, Charlie."

"What exactly does that mean, Mad Dog?"

He shook his head. "It means I'm talking too much and not all talking's good for the soul. . . . Soup's on. The lady said

75

when she called not to expect her; we should go and start without her."

"Sarah say why?"

"No. She didn't say, I don't ever ask."

"Straight home, maybe?"

"She didn't say, I don't ever ask."

"Doesn't curiosity ever get the better of you, Mad Dog?"

"What it does for cats I don't want it doing to me, Charlie, something you should keep in mind for yourself."

"You make it sound ominous."

"Maybe, if I knew what that word meant," he said. "Be back in a sec. Time to yank our T-bones from the broiler. Coming up with creamed spinach and a giant baked potato, a new kind of salad from the recipe the lady got from Mr. Robert Cobb, owner of the Brown Derby. He's a first cousin to Ty Cobb, how about that?"

"One of the first five players voted into the Baseball Hall of Fame two years ago, along with Honus Wagner, Christy Mathewson, Walter Johnson, the 'Big Train,' and, of course, the one and only Babe."

"My way of thinking, the one and only Babe is the lady of the house." There was no mistaking it for a joke, the way Mad Dog spoke the words—solemnly, adoringly and what Charlie again heard as ominous.

This was no time to talk about Polly, not now, now that he recognized talking to Mad Dog was like talking to Sarah herself.

Charlie steered the dinner conversation to baseball and kept it there.

The salad wasn't half bad.

CHAPTER 9

Sarah said, "Don't be silly, you animal." She had finished dressing, was pampering her hair and freshening her makeup in the bathroom mirror, watching him watch her from the tub and enjoying the vicarious thrill that came to her in front of any type of audience. "I guarantee you there's no way in Heaven or on Earth that Coop will agree to do the picture with me, not after I turned down *The Cowboy and the Lady*."

"You mean after they turned down your demand the picture be retitled *The Lady and the Cowboy*."

"Alphabetical billing wouldn't have worked. Besides, I thought Coop might be a gentleman about it."

"Since when has the picture business been a business of manners? Revenge, more like it."

"What I'm counting on now with Charlie Dickens's script— tit for tat."

"Won't that be tat for tit, or even here are you insisting on top billing?"

"There's only one way I'd ever allow Coop on top of me."

"He should ever be so lucky, like me. In fact, I'd love to be there again now, if you don't mind a new round of rub-a-dub-dub in the tub."

His eyebrows weren't all that had elevated. She answered his hungry smile with a polite nod, but that was all he was going to get from her now. To leave them craving more was a surefire way to guarantee an open bedroom door and the rewards available across the threshold. She needed to keep him around until he made good on his promise to scrub Max out of her life, only she always spoke in terms of their lives, how they would be able to be together, out in the open, once and forever, after Max was dead and buried. She'd said it so often she was beginning to believe it herself.

"Coop turns down the picture and after a few halfhearted attempts to cast the part with a leading man equal to my box-office standing, that's that. I tell Max we should move on to something else," she said. "He tells Charlie the production is history, he's exiting the picture, so good-bye and good luck."

"And that's when it's time for Max to exit the planet."

"The way we've gone over a million times, so it looks like Charlie is furious about being rejected again and takes out all that frustration on Max. People will have seen them behaving badly at the party, making it a snap for me to testify that he was also crazy mad over me, how I had to fight off his repeated advances, and how that only added fuel to the awful fire raging inside him."

"Not the way he'll tell it."

"You're the police, you're my adoring public—who are you going to believe, me or a screenwriter whose career would be crashing, he had any career to speak of? Meantime, there's nothing to link you to the proceedings, so fade to a happy ending. You and me, you animal—happily ever after."

"I wish there was some other way than me having to—"

"Don't say it or even think it anymore." She turned to face him and opened her robe, revealing her lavender-scented body in all its glory. "Keep your eye on the prize," she said, and left him to his own devices.

CHAPTER 10

"I am not going to sleep with you, if that's what this is all about," Polly told Leo Salmon when he caught her during the lunch break and invited her to join him for drinks after the day's shoot ended. They'd seen each other on the lot in the week since the Max Moonglow party, of course, but this was the first time he'd done more than nod and wave her a greeting.

"I manage my eight hours a night without you," Leo said, his laugh as genuine as his piano-keys teeth, the feature that distinguished his otherwise good-looking face until Charlie cracked his nose, covered now by a modest bandage instead of the mountain of gauze and adhesive in place as late as yesterday.

"I apologize if I came off as a little snot. It's just that I've learned a girl can't be too careful nowadays, especially in the picture business."

He settled beside her on one of the picnic benches set up between the soundstage and the buffet tables stocked with a variety of hot and cold dishes, some of them actually palatable. "You sound like you've had some experience in that direction, or is that just my imagination working overtime?"

"Mine to know and yours to find out," she said, hiding an honest answer behind the coyness she'd brought to her modest role in the Hoppy picture, one of the qualities Leo had said led him to proposing her for the part.

He let her see he knew she was making a game of it—fine, let him believe what he wanted—but gave her a no-nonsense response she had him repeat, to make certain she had heard him correctly the first time.

"Good news, is that what you're saying?"

"I said great news, Polly." His eyes were housing a mischievous glint.

"Tell me now. Please?" Like a little girl, another quality he had admired. "More Hoppy movies, like you said you'd try getting for me. That's it, isn't it?"

"No. Better."

Better? What could be better? "Don't make me wait, Leo. I could use some good news—great news."

"Something putting a frown on that farmer's daughter face of yours? Fess up."

She hadn't wanted to share her news with anyone, but now she'd gone and opened her fat yap. Better to tell him the truth than feed him a bunch of malarkey. "I've lost my job at Contento's Guaranteed Garden Fresh Fruits and Vegetables over at the Farmers Market. They said the picture work was getting in the way and I'd have to choose. So, what do you think I chose? Meaning I need to give up my place and find somewhere cheaper, whatever else anymore it takes for a girl to keep her hopes up in this business."

"I've met quite a number of girls in the same predicament. Some gave up, fell by the wayside, but there were others who stuck it out, are still sticking it out, and making a go of it."

"Like the one from the hospital?"

He appeared baffled. "The one from the hospital?"

"The one who I was told came and picked you up, that one?"

He thought about it. "Like her, yes."

"Some actress trying to get on your good side, I suppose."

"I have two good sides. She's been on one of them for quite some time."

"And now are you going to tell me I'm on the other?"

He turned as pious as a tent pole preacher and held the pose for several moments before breaking out his keyboard smile again. "That's for me to know and you to find out," he said.

Polly didn't want to give him the benefit of the laugh welling inside her, but she couldn't help herself. He liked seeing that, just like a man. "So, she's my competition for more Hoppy movies?"

"Not anymore." He turned away from her. "She's been cast."

Polly couldn't hide her dismay. She leaned over and put her food platter on the concrete, no appetite for what was left of her chicken breast, slice of medium-rare roast beef, sweet potato, creamed corn, and toasted bagel buried under a blanket of butter and cream cheese. "I need to get back," she said, rising.

He got up, too. "So, I'll come by the soundstage and fetch you when the shoot shuts down for the day, somewhere around six."

"Don't bother, Leo, okay? I've had about all the great news I can stand for one day."

"Farm girl, that was her great news, not the great news I have for you."

"Then tell me now."

"I'll catch you around six," he said, wandering off without a backward glance.

Polly expected Leo to escort her across Melrose to the Nickodell.

He surprised her.

He guided her to his Hudson, parked outside the modest office space he rented in the railroad train of a two-story Craftsman-style building there since the studio was built and opened as Clune Studios in the Twenties, saying, "Great news demands nothing less than a great setting."

An hour later, after a drive full of his small talk, they were attacking champagne cocktails at Jack's at the Beach, an out-of-the-way show-business refuge at the end of the Ocean Park amusement pier in Santa Monica.

He had slipped the maître d' a five spot to get a picture-window table for two that gave them a majestic view of the Pacific Ocean, what was left of it now that darkness had rolled in with the waves slapping the shoreline beneath them. A few motor and sailboats cruising in the distance, outlined against the sinking slice of orange-peel sun illuminating the horizon line.

Leo took a deep swallow of the salted air seeping through cracks in the slat wood flooring, raised his glass and invited her to join him in toasting her future.

"*Cento anni di salute e felicità.* A hundred years of health and happiness," he said. "An old Italian toast taught me by my *nonno,* my grandfather, before he died." He made a throaty noise that passed for a laugh. "Well, he couldn't have taught it to me after he died, could he now?"

"What about the present, Leo? This great news of yours you keep promising me, or did you get me out here under false pretenses?"

"My pretenses are as real as anyone's in Hollywood, freckle face." The humor went out of his expression. "I got out here from Jersey looking to build on a dream I'd had since I was a kid spit-shining shoes in Tutti Romano's pool hall, to make it big-time in the picture business, somebody who calls the shots. Big house. Big bankroll. Big car. The respect that comes with all the trimmings. I'm a fast learner. One of the first things that I learned—you don't ever need to break your back or strain a muscle getting a job done when you can get to the top climbing up on the backs of people with talent, where you can make their talent your own. Use it until you bruise it, then move on. I may be a casting director today, but I got plans working that'll hopscotch me up to the next level quicker'n anyone can say Jack Robinson. I'm a wop in a world of Jews, but watch my speed."

"Why are you telling me this, Leo?"

"So you'll understand the great news I have for you is also great news for me, part of my plan for me, myself and I. Helping you succeed, I'm helping myself. My generosity begins at home. *Kapish?*"

"And you're helping me succeed by getting for some other actress the new Hoppy movies you were talking to me about, raving about what they could mean for my career and all the while undressing me with your eyes, like some front-row pervert at the Follies Theater downtown. Don't tell me you weren't."

"I was, yes. Sure I was, but getting you in bed ranks second to getting you cast in movies that can make a difference for us. The Hoppy movies made sense until they quit making sense."

"And when was that?"

"When my out-of-work friend from the hospital babbled her good news to me, how her agent had her up for roles in George O'Brien's next two westerns, I knew what I had to do, and fast—sidetrack her so I could sell you. I got on the horn and got her set for the two Hoppy pictures, clearing the way for me to use my magical mumbo jumbo to promote you into the O'Brien pictures. And presto!—they're yours, farm girl. Congratulations."

He settled back in his chair like a stage actor waiting for applause.

"That's your great news?" Polly said, her expression a portrait in disappointment. "I get to go from B westerns to B westerns?"

Leo turned his palms to the peeling wood-beam ceiling, shaking his head, and gave the air a *Can you believe this girl?* "You're not seeing the big picture, freckle face."

"I'm seeing B westerns, Leo. Where's the big picture in that?"

His sigh could be heard all the way to New York. "Here's how this plays out," he said, leaning forward now, elbows settled on the table, laced fingers supporting his fragile chin. "First, it's not another Harry Sherman indie production, one of Harry's typical quick flicks. You move across the street to RKO and a studio deal, seven years with options and a weekly paycheck. People interested in grooming you for bigger parts in pictures where a horse doesn't get higher billing than you. And something else you might want to classify as great? My friend from the hospital said RKO would be looking at her for something being cooked up for Cary Grant, Victor McLaglen and Douglas Fairbanks, Jr., a take on *Gunga Din*, the old Kipling poem. I've started moving you in line for that, too."

"You're joking, putting me on!"

"I'm no Bob Hope."

"That is great news, Leo. I don't know how to thank you."

"Of course, you do," he said.

"But I won't, so what do you say to that?"

"I'm in no hurry," he said.

They strolled along the pier after dinner.

It was brightly lit now, crowded with people escaping the realities of everyday life at the game and concession booths, who cheered with delight over every game toss victory and every time somebody caught the brass ring on the arcade merry-go-round; shrieked at every bottomless drop and dangerous curve of the ominous wooden Hi-Boy roller coaster rising seventy-five feet above the concrete surface.

He scored at the baseball toss and let her pick a chalk Mickey Mouse from the third shelf, got her a miniature teddy bear from the second shelf at the balloon darts game, played the graceful loser when she outscored him at the rifle shoot, apologetically explaining that her daddy had taught her how to use the family rifle when she was eight and she'd gone on to win junior girl county fair blue ribbons and 4-H competitions every year she entered.

"Lots of us farm girls got to be pretty handy with rifles and shotguns," she said, "in case we came across predators on the prowl, foxes aiming to break into the chicken coops, like that. Daddy bought me my own handgun as a going-away present when I was packing for Hollywood, saying he'd heard there were lots of predators roaming around the picture business and better safe than sorry."

"A wise man, your daddy."

"Never yet come close to having occasion to use it, but the gun's right there under my pillow, there's ever cause. See for yourself, I ever give you the chance."

She blushed, thinking how that must have sounded, like an invitation.

Maybe it was, she realized.

She found herself liking Leo more and more, not only for what he was doing for her career, the RKO pictures and all.

She felt comfortable in Leo's company.

Leo had made no secret with her of who he was, what he was, what he was after, and honesty wasn't something she had experienced a lot since striking out for Hollywood, then striking out in Hollywood until she managed to get that first meeting with Leo.

Two of Leo's favorite rides, Shoot the Shoots and the Aerial Swing, were closing down for the night, so after the bone-cracking Whip he led her next door to the Fun in the Dark ride, where the rail tracks glided by ghoulish apparitions that sprang out of nowhere, causing couples in the cars ahead and behind them to shriek and draw closer together.

Leo could have thrown a protective arm around her or given her hands a comforting squeeze, but he kept his gentlemanly distance, mostly laughing away the noisy spooks, one after the next. She was appreciative until his inattention turned annoying; she'd never liked being ignored, not even in high school, where she'd won senior class president and the May Day Queen title by campaigning for the boys' votes inside their pants.

A fierce-sounding Dracula emerged as their car navigated another sharp curve. She cried out and threw herself against Leo, inspiring him to reach for her. His hand grazed her breast accidentally. He pulled it away. She peeled it off the car's safety rail and put it back. "It makes me feel safe with you," she said, and leaned over to reach his ear with her tongue before starting a campaign for his vote.

"Not here, not now," he said, barely able to whisper the words.

He took her to the Toonerville Fun House, a walking tour of dimly lit corridors and narrow stairways that led to and through dark rooms and finally to a steep slide down to an exit through a giant rolling barrel. There was no escaping the putrid smell of sea water and urine or the empty beer and whisky bottles that littered the walkways. After ten minutes of blind walking, satisfied they had temporary privacy, he braced her against a wet and sticky wall with the urgency of a dog in heat.

Polly didn't resist.

Leo was a lousy lover, at least here under battlefield conditions.

She'd had better under the football field bleachers.

She shut her eyes and wondered what it might be like under the pier, at the ocean's edge, clinging to a pillar wrapped in seaweed, her feet buried in the wet sand of a million tides. Maybe some stumblebum happening upon them and stopping to watch and applaud, judging her performance and—

Leo gasped his first and last.

She seized the moment to think of Charlie Dickens.

She released herself to Charlie's image.

Wondering if she should feel guilty.

Wondering why she didn't.

Meaningless sex, that's all this was.

Not the first time.

Not the last time.

This time—

A thank-you present to Leo for RKO, the contract, the George O'Brien movies, and maybe even *Gunga Din*. Daddy would be proud of her when she got around to telling him.

Leo stepped away from her wondering, "How was that, farm girl?"

"Great," Polly said.

CHAPTER 11

To no one's surprise, least of all Sarah's, Gary Cooper turned down the opportunity to costar with her in *Showdown at Shadow Creek,* his agent claiming he was off westerns for the duration, instead would be doing *Beau Geste* for Wild Bill Wellman at Paramount, in the title role, joined by Ray Milland, Robert Preston and Brian Donlevy.

She watched Max stalking his office, demeaning Cooper first, then Wellman, then a bunch of names from the German film industry he always dredged up when things weren't going his way, always leading off with Dr. Joseph Goebbels, Hitler's rabidly anti-Semitic propaganda minister.

He complained, "What's *Beau Geste* anyway?" and answered his own question: "A western with more sand than the Mojave Desert. Cooper and the others wearing Foreign Legion uniforms and talking with lousy French accents instead of lousy western drawls."

"So, Max, that means Pan Berman will be giving *Sundown at Showdown Creek* to the George O'Brien unit?"

"Gave. Pan already gave it to O'Brien, and he was right. Word in this town travels faster than a refugee escaping Hitler's Germany. O'Brien said he'd take suspension before he took one of Gary Cooper's leftovers."

"So he's being suspended, what Pan said would happen."

"Of course not. He's the only western star on the lot. He's got a following left over from his caviar days, costarring with

Janet Gaynor, being directed by Murnau, one of my old mentors, for Christ's sake. All his pictures are cheaply made, reliable programmers that make money for RKO."

"So instead of insulting O'Brien, they insult us by canceling the picture and we let them get away with it," she said, with just the right touch of indignation, inwardly pleased at how well her plan was playing out.

"Not yet. Not if I can land a leading man equal to Coop; make you and the studio happy at the same time. I'm already calling around. Warner Bros. got back to me at once, suggesting they loan out Bogart."

"Bogart? Is that some joke? He's been typecast as a mobster for so long people get scared when he walks into a bank; at best Bogie's a second-rate featured player who has as much star quality as Guy Kibbee. I'm surprised they didn't offer you Eddie Robinson."

"They did."

"And who did Metro come up with, Lionel Barrymore?"

"I asked about Bob Taylor and Franchot Tone. No answer yet."

"That delicious Ty Power at Fox would be acceptable to me."

"I figured, so I asked. He's going straight into *Jesse James,* him as Jesse and Henry Fonda as his brother, Frank, after production wraps on *Suez.*"

Max's asthma was acting up.

He retreated behind his desk and slumped into the chair, wheezing heavily while he opened a drawer and found his inhaler. She sat quietly, watching him recapture his breath, thinking how soon it would be before he'd need more than an inhaler to keep breathing, something along the lines of a miracle.

In her mind, she'd have Max dead and Charlie Dickens under lock and key, charged with his murder, any day now.

The miracle came first.

Pan Berman had given Max a week to come up with an acceptable male lead.

The best Max could do was Lew Ayres on an expensive loanout from Metro, the high asking price Louis B. Mayer was demanding based on rave comments for Ayres on preview cards for *Young Doctor Kildare* that had sparked rumors of a new MGM series in the making.

"My personal physician comes cheaper than that," Pan said when he got the news, pipe smoke streaming from both sides of his mouth. "The old junk dealer should pay us if he wants our help building a bigger box office for his boy Lew." His eyes wandered over his uncluttered desk from Max to Sarah, who had insisted on joining Max for the meeting in Pan's office. "What would you say if we take a leaf from Louie's tree and use the picture to boost the career of our own Tim Holt, Jack Holt's kid?"

"Not at my expense," she said. "You're thinking like that, Pan, my dear, maybe it's time for you to call your personal physician."

"Max?"

"You heard her, Pan. Our star has spoken."

Pan pulled an invisible plug from the air. "Done," he said. "No Sarah Darling, no *Showdown at Shadow Creek*."

"Where is he?" Sarah asked Mad Dog when she got to the Benedict Canyon house.

Mad Dog snapped a thumb over his shoulder. "He wanted to drown himself in the pool after you called and told me to tell him it was Max's secretary got me on the phone to give him the bad tidings. I steered him to the bar, where he's now drunk as Cooter Brown."

She tracked after Charlie.

He was behind the counter, using the surface for support while he poured himself a Glenfiddich that overflowed the highball glass. He put down the glass and briefly studied the mess he'd made, shrugged and began drinking straight from the bottle. "Hey, you," he called across the room, raising the bottle like the Statue of Liberty's torch. "Peeps a boob, I seize you."

He hurried around and aimed for her, was halfway across the room when he tripped over his feet and stumbled forward, missing her by inches as he sailed into the wall, hitting a small Picasso oil and knocking it off the wall onto the intricately patterned red, gold and orange, sixteenth-century Tabiz Medallion rug her ex often bragged about smuggling into the country under the nose of customs officials.

Charlie worked his way into a sitting position. Somehow he'd managed to hold onto the Glenfiddich bottle. "Cheers," he said, emptying the bottle in a swallow before he broke out in tears. "But there's nothing to cheer about, is there, you wonderful, glorious you? You know what I mean? You heard?"

"I was there when word came down from the executive office," Sarah said. "Max seemed pleased, almost as if he'd helped get the production killed, getting even for some hostility he still feels toward you, although he'd told us otherwise."

"That SOB."

She scooped up the Picasso, breath-blew it free of dust and carefully put it back in its place on the wall. "I was just as shocked as you and rushed here hoping to be the one to tell you in person, explain how I fought for us to keep going with *The Creek Shadow,* but I was shouted down by Max, told by him in no uncertain terms to shut up, because my vote didn't count."

"Bastard, him."

"It's a tragedy, Charlie, but it's not the end of the world."

"Your world, maybe, not mine, Sarah. I voted for Roosevelt,

so where's my New Deal coming from? Tell me that, can you?"

She settled on the floor beside Charlie and draped a comforting arm around his shoulder.

"Charlie, get hold of yourself," she said.

He gave her an obedient nod and locked onto his crotch.

"You need a drink to settle your nerves," she said, and called out for Mad Dog, who'd been standing invisible guard in the hallway. "Mad Dog, make us something nice and soothing, please."

"You got it," Mad Dog said, indicating with a nod he understood it was time to oblige the instruction Sarah had given him when she phoned. He crossed to the bar and poured two double bourbons over ice, lacing Charlie's drink with a heavy dose of chloral hydrate.

Charlie downed the bourbon like a child attacking a candy bar.

Within minutes, the Mickey Finn had done its job.

His eyes shuttered and his slurred speech quit entirely.

He drifted into a fetal position after Sarah gave him a peck on the cheek and a poke on the shoulder—dead to the world.

Mad Dog helped Sarah back onto her feet.

She thanked him with a smile, adjusted her skirt and jacket, brushed at her hair, and said, "Try not to get caught, Mad Dog."

"The Invisible Man got nothing on me," he said.

He scooped up Charlie from the floor, tossed him over a shoulder like a sack of potatoes and left.

Sarah took a sip of her bourbon, set the glass aside and padded over to the Picasso. She hadn't got it quite straight enough before. She remedied that now, took a step back to verify she had corrected the problem and, satisfied, proceeded to the telephone and dialed. Her call connected on the fourth ring.

"I've taken care of Charlie Dickens," she said. "Get ready to go do your part."

CHAPTER 12

Max at first thought the noise that woke him and caused him to bolt upright in bed was a different ending to his recurring nightmare, this time the damned Nazi bastards and their vicious hunting hounds chasing him through the woods, determined to keep him from fleeing the country.

Last time it was the sound of gunfire whizzing past his ears, before that the sound of rifle butts crashing open the door to his bedroom. Never the same disturbing noise twice in a row, but always the same result, his prayer for a night of peaceful, uninterrupted sleep unanswered.

Sweating like a pig, lungs congested, phlegm clogging his throat, he shook his head clear, reached over for his inhaler, and—

Max heard the noise again.

From the garden.

Growing louder as it sailed in with the breeze through the open bedroom window.

Somebody on the prowl?

He finished spritzing, tossed the inhaler aside and hurried across to the window, positioned himself to see without being seen, saw—

Nothing.

Heard what sounded like grass being crushed underfoot, then footsteps treading lightly on the veranda.

A burglar?

More than one burglar?

He knew better than to play sitting duck.

He hurried from the window and worked his way downstairs to his office, where he kept the Walther PPK .32 he'd learned to use before fleeing Germany. He gripped it with confidence, eased to the private door that gave him a direct link outdoors and listened hard for new sounds or signs of movement.

Almost at once they closed in on him in a rush, the voice calling his name, urging him not to fire.

A Nazi trick, that.

Don't shoot, so we can shoot you first.

How many friends had he lost that way?

He only remembered losing count.

Max waited until the advancing hulk of a figure was less than ten feet away.

Fired.

The impact spun the hulk around and into a series of zombie steps ending when the hulk fell forward, splat, head cracking on the imported marble decking.

Max froze, momentarily stunned by his action.

Waiting out the possibility of a second burglar.

The asthma clawing at his throat and lungs again, worse than ever.

He retreated after the inhaler he kept at his office desk, returning with a flashlight after relieving himself and putting in an emergency call to the police. Pitched the beam at the body resting on a pillow of blood. Stepped over for a better look and recognized who he had killed.

Threw up.

Perry Lieber, RKO's head of publicity, found Max hiding in the maze in a near-comatose state when he arrived at Moonglow Manor a good twenty minutes before the police got to the hilltop residence, pumping himself with his asthma medicine like some gas station jockey filling an empty tank.

Max threw himself at Lieber, tearful and wide-eyed, babbling out fears of being arrested and convicted of murder, doomed to the electric chair, or—worse—deported to Germany, where a different kind of death sentence would be waiting for him.

"My career, also at a dead end, Perry," he said, his wail carrying over the hedges, igniting a symphony of howls from neighborhood dogs and what could have been a pack of free-ranging coyotes that often wandered over from the Griffith Park side of Los Feliz Boulevard.

Lieber shook him still. "You'll be fine, Max, everything will be okay. It's all taken care of. . . . Do you hear me, Max? Are you listening? It's all taken care of."

"I don't understand," Max said, swimming in despair and confusion.

The soft-spoken Lieber, trying to inject Max with his own unflappable demeanor, said, "You wisely called Pan Berman and told him what occurred. Pan immediately called in a favor from our ex-boss, Dave Selznick, who got on the horn to his papa-in-law, Louie Mayer, who called Mayor Shaw on his private line. Shaw called the chief of police, and Jimmy Davis sent word to his boys on how to handle this situation."

"Handle?"

"You'll see when they get here. An out-and-out case of a burglary in progress, the burglar shot and killed when you saw he was armed and leveling a revolver at you. Self-defense, plain and simple."

"But it's not the truth."

"It will be, Max."

"He wasn't armed. I saw no revolver."

"Of course you did—the revolver that'll be noted in the official police report."

"Even after they learn who it is laying there dead in my backyard? My connection to him?"

"You leave that worry to me, Max. That's what I'm here for. It's my job. I'm good at what I do, why Pan's second call was to me. I geared up, got my boys working. By the time the birdies are welcoming in the sunrise there won't be a better kept secret in the world. No press. No radio. No rumors sailing up and down the gossip line. Guaranteed. Like it never happened."

"Sarah's got to know."

"We'll tell her together, explain how to play the game. Anything else, you come to me first. When the cops get here, you stick to the story and leave any other talking to me."

Max thought about it. "I'm not telling you your business, Perry, but would it hurt any if, maybe, there was a story out that said only how Max Moonglow, famous producer and director, bravely thwarted a burglary at his mansion?" Lieber appeared lost for words; dug out a deep sigh. "Including mention of RKO, of course. Louella would be fantastic."

"Let me think on it, Max."

"Hedda, if you decide she'd be better."

Police were swarming the backyard when Max and Perry Lieber exited the maze. Lieber took him by the elbow and steered toward two men engaging in deep conversation in an isolated corner of the rose garden.

Both greeted Lieber like an old friend, warm handshakes all around.

In turn, Lieber introduced Burt Cobbler and Jerry Lee Swaggart to Max.

"Burt's the LAPD detective who'll be running this show," Lieber said. "Jerry is—"

"Mayor Shaw's man," Swaggart broke in, giving Max a campaign-trail handshake, his melodious voice soaked in southern honey. "Mayor Shaw extends his best wishes and wants you to know he understands the situation and is concerned for your continued well-being, why he dispatched me with specific instructions to personally look after your best interests."

"And his," Burt Cobbler said, earning a brief, contemptuous frown from Swaggart.

"Like you're the poster child for honesty, my friend?"

"It's the best policy, even when we're ordered not to practice it," Cobbler said, his answer as sharp as an executioner's axe.

Swaggart let the remark pass. "I'm right here if you need me, Mr. Moonglow," he said, and wandered off.

Appearances are deceiving, Max reminded himself. If he hadn't learned better, he would have pegged Cobbler as the mayor's man. The detective, a ruggedly handsome six-footer in his mid-thirties, wore his stylishly cut charcoal-black double-breasted suit with broad-shouldered elegance. A fresh red carnation graced the buttonhole of the wide lapel and echoed his oversized carnation-red bowtie. Piercing green eyes and regulation-length almond brown hair under his broad-brimmed black fedora completed the outward picture of a man used to being in control.

On the other hand, Swaggart was a roly-poly bundle of average everything, from his shock of unkempt white-streaked gray hair flapping over his overgrown ears to a pair of scuffed patent leather shoes. Mismatched off-the-rack sports jacket and wrinkled slacks struggling to disguise his pork-packed body. A heavy vacation tan full of crow's-feet and wrinkles that put him somewhere in his late forties to early fifties. Penetrating steel-gray eyes hiding secrets under sleepy lids—missing nothing and, like the political pro he was, filing away everything he saw for possible future value.

Max suspected Swaggart's boss, the mayor, was going to be owed big-time for what was happening here, the kind of debt worth collecting in an election year and the heated battle for votes Shaw currently was fighting with reform-minded Fletcher Bowron.

If Bowron won, it would have a negative impact on James "Two-Gun" Davis's run as chief of police, heading a force Hearst's newspapers were constantly portraying as the most corrupt in the nation, where the cops were often more criminal than the criminals they put behind bars.

"So, Mr. Moonglow," Cobbler said, drawing Max's attention, "what can you tell me about what happened here beyond what I've already been told happened here? I'm excited to hear your version." He was wearing his sarcasm on his sleeve, like a corporal's stripe.

Perry held him back with a gesture. "It'll be the same story you already got, Burt."

Cobbler smiled. "I've always liked you, Perry, but I'd probably like you more if I ever saw you with clean hands."

"Me, too," Perry said, laughing off the remark.

A scream cut into their banter.

They turned toward the mansion.

Sarah Darling was standing over the uncovered corpse, her face and arms raised to the hovering three-quarter moon, shouting, "My God! Dear Sweet Jesus! God. God, God! It wasn't supposed to happen this way!"

Cobbler said, "Sounds like she's the one I should be talking to, gents."

CHAPTER 13

"Damn!"

The words had spilled from Sarah spontaneously, in the heat of the moment, her emotion overtaking all the cool calculation she'd put into the planning of Max's murder. She recognized she'd have to proceed cautiously answering the detective's questions. He was not a good enough actor to fool her into thinking he wasn't smarter than he let on.

He coddled her with compliments as she led him inside to a corner of the den that gave them privacy from the crime scene hubbub and, to Sarah's relief, temporary escape from Max's angry, accusatory stare, as if he knew why Willie Frankfurter was prowling around Moonglow Manor in the middle of the night.

He'd be right, of course, but only as far as his suspicions went, not the lethal rest; nothing at all she planned to admit to the detective now or to Max later, if he was foolish enough to start another shouting match that wasn't a lovers' quarrel so much as a quarrel over lovers.

"I let out a whoop and did a little dance that night I heard they gave you one of those Oscar acting awards," the detective said, easing into an easy chair across from hers. "That's how much of a fan I am, Miss Darling."

She smiled like she meant it, a hand over her heart. "I admire your taste, Detective Cobbler, but you do understand that nobody *gave* me the Oscar for *An Appointment with Tomorrow.* I *won* the Oscar for *An Appointment with Tomorrow.*"

"Exactly. No offense intended. . . . I'm hoping to get your autograph before I leave. The boys back at the plant would be jealous as all get-out."

"A signed photograph, how does that sound to you?"

"Like I died and went to Heaven," Cobbler said. He shook his head in disbelief.

"For now, you said you had some questions for me?"

"Yes, if you don't mind?" Spoken like the decision was hers to make. She turned up a hand, inviting him to begin. He pulled out a slim notepad and pen from an inside jacket pocket. "I understand from Mr. Moonglow that both of you knew the victim, Mr. William Frankfurter, that correct?"

"Willard, actually, not William, but everyone called him Willie at the studio, RKO, where he was one of the producers turning out budget movies, the B-pictures, so called."

"Not what I suppose are the A-pictures that you star in for Mr. Moonglow?"

"Ours are the A-Plus pictures."

"Of course."

"Of course. Mr. Moonglow had no inkling what brought him here. Do you?"

"Yes and no."

"How about you explain the yes part first?"

"Willie was always out there promoting himself, hungry to join the big boys, like Pan Berman, Dave Selznick, Merian Cooper, Max, of course; always racing around the lot buttonholing anyone he figured could give him a leg up, waving a screenplay in their face, proclaiming it surefire box office. You know the type, Detective Cobbler?"

"The department's full of 'em."

"He'd try for attention with musicals by cornering Rogers or Astaire. Ginger would send him off to her stage mama, Lela, who makes all the decisions. The only thing Freddie reads with a critical eye is the *Daily Racing Form.* Willie tried worming his way to Max with a script or two, but Max wouldn't give him the time of day, so he came onto me next. I told him straight out, *Kid, you ever fall into a genuine diamond, not the phony ice more fit for Hepburn than me, let me know and I promise I'll personally give it a read, take it to Max if I decide it's fit for a queen."*

"Mr. Moonglow said Mr. Frankfurter was a pest, who bothered him more than his asthma."

Sarah snatched a Gitanes from the Tiffany sterling silver cigarette box on the coffee table and waited for Cobbler to light it for her. Sent a shaft of smoke sailing to the wood-beamed ceiling. "The other day Willie caught me coming back to our production office from lunch at Lucey's. He said he was close to getting his hands on a script with the role of a lifetime for me—guaranteed. He asked if he could deliver it to me at Moonglow Manor. I thought that was curious, but had never seen Willie so excited. I got caught up in his enthusiasm. I told him oke, but to call first." She donned a doleful expression and studied the red glow of the Gitanes. "He never did."

"And I don't suppose, if he had, you would have had Mr. Frankfurter coming over at such an ungodly hour."

"Of course not."

"Or entering the premises unannounced."

"Of course not."

"So why do you suppose that's what Mr. Frankfurter did?"

"I wouldn't suppose anything, detective."

"Or why we found no script on him or around the crime scene."

"You're the detective, detective, so you tell me. Like you may have heard me say earlier when I realized it was poor Willie dead on the ground and now can understand—it wasn't supposed to happen this way."

There!

She'd worked it in, given him meaning that made sense to her suspicious burst of honesty.

Damn Willie!

If it happened the way it was supposed to happen, Max would be dead now, not Willie, and she'd be playing the grief-stricken widow for the detective, salting her tears with memories laced with motives that linked Charlie Dickens to the nasty deed and left her free as the wind to begin the next chapter in her life.

Later, once the police were gone and Max had stormed off for RKO, wordlessly, his fierce look telling her he didn't buy for a minute the story she'd sold to the detective, Sarah showered, dressed in one of the tailored Dietrich-style trouser outfits she'd stolen from the wardrobe department after the last shoot and headed off for a visit with Barney Rooker at the New Dawn sanatorium.

Barney made no secret of being less than thrilled as she wheeled him out for a trip around the neighborhood, reporting what had happened away from the possibility of being overheard. "It turned out being a fiasco with this Willie guy, this plan of yours, so why risk it again, maybe get caught the next time, angel mine? You got everything you ever wanted. Leave well enough alone. Leave Max alive and get on with the wonderful life you've built for yourself."

"Nobody ever gets everything, darling, not after they see there's more out there than the everything they have. As long as Max is around, I'm tied to him same as I once thought I was tied to that bastard Andy Cream—forever."

"As it is, you're leading separate lives."

"Private lives, yes, but outside that I'm another Max Moonglow production, bound to him by contract. I'm in Max's pictures until he's out of mine. Only then can I graduate to big-

103

ger pictures with bigger producers, bigger directors, bigger—"

"Enough!" Barney said, slapping the arm of his wheelchair. "I've heard all of this from you a million times already. Just push."

They circled the Fox lot, not as busy since the studio relocated to the west side of LA about ten years ago, to rambling acreage that had been the personal ranch of cowboy hero Tom Mix. Only the low-budget pictures were being made now at Western and Sunset, she'd read in the *Hollywood Reporter*, currently a Mr. Moto picture from the B-unit of Sol Wurtzel. It had started out as a Charlie Chan movie, but was rewritten for Peter Lorre after Warner Oland, the actor who played Charlie, died unexpectedly just before production got underway.

"I need a drink," Barney said, finally.

"You're not supposed to drink, darling."

"Any more than you're supposed to murder anyone. . . . A smoke then?"

Sarah dipped into her handbag and filched a Gitanes from an etched gold-and-silver case, lit it for Barney with a matching lighter and took a heavy drag before handing it over. He broke off the filter tip and tossed it away. "Damned nuisance, those," he said. He took a deep suck and swallowed the smoke, breathed out the residue through his nose. "You ever try real cigarettes instead of these sissies?"

She ignored his complaining. "It'll be better the next time," she said, studying one of the outdoor sets rising tall above the planked wood fencing topped with coiled barbed wire that guarded against break-ins on the Fox lot.

"Next time, what? Camels, my first choice, but I'm game for anything that comes without a filter and is made in the U-S-of-A, aside from menthol. I want a flavor, I'll order Jello."

"You know I mean the plan, darling."

He made a clucking noise with his tongue. "Who's the patsy

going to be now that your Willie boy is unavailable?"

"My gardener. I've told you about Earl Stanley."

"You said the poor sap was about as smart as the weeds in your rose garden, better between the silk sheets than behind a lawnmower. He doesn't sound to me like anybody's idea of someone who can pull off a murder and get away clean."

"The only person I know who fits that bill is you, darling."

"And you see what that got me. I got sentenced to the chair anyway," Barney said. He cranked the wheels free of her grip, sped along Sunset past a sprinkling of pedestrians, several in turn-of-the-century costumes, and disappeared around the corner.

Earl was waiting for her at the bar when she got to Don the Beachcomber's about twenty minutes late, delayed by an extended stop at Pet Savers, where she came close to leaving with a Chihuahua that had jumped into her lap, whose soft purr and bold, begging eyes pleaded with her for rescue.

He was toying with the little bamboo umbrella in his drink, a Tahitian Rum Punch, and picking at a platter of pupu appetizers. There were two empty cocktail glasses in front of him on the bar counter. His eyelids were at half-mast and his eyes lit like Christmas tree ornaments, far less inviting than the Chihuahua's had been.

She let a hug and cheek kisses serve as her apology and settled on the wicker chair beside him, signaling the bartender for her usual. He promptly abandoned a conversation in progress with two tourist types in Hawaiian shirts at the end of the bar to mix and serve her a Zombie cocktail, waving off the cost when she wondered how much.

He said, "Compliments of those butter-and-egg men, Miss Darling."

She sent them an appreciative wave.

"Okole Maluna," Earl said, raising his glass to hers. "Cheers! Bottoms up!" He gave her a sly look. "Your calling and wanting to see me, it mean what I think it means?"

"Depends on what you're thinking."

"You know." His voice dropped shy of a whisper. "Your husband, he's—you know, what we talked about before, so I could come back into your garden full-time?"

"No. Not yet." Disappointment distorted his face. "I've been missing you something awful, you big lug, that's why. I couldn't get through another day without seeing you." She reached over and touched his cheek.

He pressed his palm over the same spot and looked at her like he'd been blessed. "I'm hungry for ya, baby, big-time. Can we get outta here, go somewhere?"

Sarah reached for him under the counter. "I can tell. Finish your drink, and hurry."

His Tahitian Rum Punch disappeared in a swallow. He slipped off the stool, almost stumbling as he took his first rubber-legged steps toward the front entrance while she fished a five spot from her handbag and left it as an overripe tip, a show of generosity being one of the pitfalls of stardom. No star ever got far being called a cheapskate, except maybe Jack Benny.

"Miss Darling, can I trouble you for an autograph before you leave?" The man had stepped away from the phone bank in the entrance alcove. He was in his fifties, wearing a baggy suit and soiled Panama hat, hopeful blue eyes blinking madly behind thick eyeglass lenses. "I'm one of your biggest fans," he said. "I've seen all your pictures and loved you in every one of them."

"Then how could I possibly resist," Sarah said, putting on her public face. She took the napkin and pencil he offered, propped the napkin against a wall. "Who should I make it out to, dear man?"

"Kurt would do nicely, Kurt with a K." He spelled it for her.

Sarah wrote: *To Kurt, Sincerely, Sarah Darling,* adding the date and a little heart wounded by Cupid's arrow below her signature.

Kurt took the napkin and pencil from her and studied what she'd written. "Gonna treasure this forever," he said, bowing, backing away and out the door like some loyal and obedient servant leaving the presence of royalty.

Outside, Earl had disappeared.

Sarah ran a check up and down McCadden Place.

Surveyed the restaurant's parking lot.

No Earl.

Was he so drunk that he'd wandered off, forgetting he was leaving her behind?

If he remembered seeing her at all?

So much for the scenario she'd worked out, how she'd steer him on the short walk over to Grauman's Chinese and into a pair of those posh, oversized leather loges. She'd do him there, good and plenty, softening him up for any defense he might want to raise after she told him she had a new, improved plan that called for Earl to get rid of Max for her.

For them.

For their future together.

Well, anyway, that's what she'd tell him.

"Hey, baby, look here!" He had stepped out from behind a residential hedge across the street. "Had to answer the call of Mother Nature real bad," he said, zipping his trousers. He howled an *Owww!* for the ages. He'd neglected to park himself back inside.

Sarah crossed the street and took him in tow.

Ten minutes later they were stepping over the cement hand and footprints of DeMille, Jack Barrymore, Doug Fairbanks, Wally Beery and others Sid Grauman had immortalized in the Chinese forecourt.

She navigated around Natalie Talmadge, Mary Pickford, Marion Davies, Norma Shearer, and Jean Harlow, treating them like sidewalk cracks, unwilling to give anybody watching the idea she was stepping into their shoes.

She was, after all, Sarah Darling.

Sarah Darling deserved to be in the forecourt, in cement, in her own shoes, and damn that Sid Grauman for not yet extending her the invitation.

A Tyrone Power picture was playing.

Not that it mattered.

"Come to Mama," she told Earl after they'd settled in the stuffed leather loge seats in an empty side section at the extreme rear of the house.

Later, Sarah explained what else she had in mind for him.

For them.

For their future together.

CHAPTER 14

At first, Charlie had no idea where he was, then—

How he got here.

Here being a park bench, stretched out like he was rehearsing for a casket, watching marshmallow clouds lumber past him in the blue-and-burnt-orange sky, driven by the same cantankerous wind stinging his face.

He was sure he heard a time bomb ticking inside his head, toward the moment his skull would explode and put an end to his misery.

Every bone and muscle in his body ached.

His legs refused to cooperate after he struggled into a sitting position and tried to stand. He fell back onto the bench his first two tries, his equilibrium in desperate need of a tune-up.

Last he remembered, he was at Sarah's place, drinking away the lousy rotten news about *Showdown at Shadow Creek* with Sarah and Mad Dog, and—

That was it.

He struggled to his feet and managed to stay there, chose a direction at random and wandered down a rutted concrete path lined with tall palms and sweet-smelling cedars, in a valley setting framed by mountain ranges. After about ten minutes of lonely wandering, he spotted the first signs of life at a shuffleboard court and a turf area where old men in bulky sweaters and berets were on the attack at chess, checkers, dominoes, and backgammon.

A hand-carved walnut sign planted by the entrance walk welcomed him to:

Weston Park
Est. 1921
City of Hemet
Hemet.

He recognized the name from the picture *Ramona* a few years ago, Loretta Young and Don Ameche sort of acting the Indian equivalents of Romeo and Juliet, like something he was working on at the time, *Juliet of the Mountains,* only not exactly. He was setting his screenplay in Kentucky and West Virginia and making the lovers members of two feuding hillbilly clans, the Hartes and the McPeaks. It was still a saleable idea, maybe one he'd get back to one of these days, maybe Polly playing the desirable Annarose McPeak, his Juliet of the title, if they ever got back together.

Hemet.

That put him in Riverside County, at the base of the San Jacinto Mountains in the San Jacinto Valley, but still didn't tell him how he got here or how he was getting back to Los Angeles, a good ninety or a hundred miles away.

He asked around, got mostly silence and the kind of stares reserved for strangers until a thin-skinned chess player, tired of hearing Charlie announce the question, called over to him, "The A-T-and-S-F got its regular freight load of oranges heading down to Union Station in an hour or less, you can get over there by then, grab yourself a hobo squat."

"Where's over there, sir?"

"What do I look like to you, young fella? That *Information Please* what's new on the radio?" That earned him a laugh from his bony-faced opponent. "You ever gonna make another move, Peachy?"

Peachy cackled. "Buster, gonna teach you against taking your concentration from the game," he said, and did something with his white knight.

"So's your old man," Buster said, moving his black queen. "Checkmate."

A stoop-backed shuffleboard player who'd shuffled his last, Peachy said, "You seem like an honest young man to me. C'mon. I'm heading over that direction." He led Charlie to a Ford pickup in a line of wagons and vans parked fifty or sixty yards away, its doors painted with the image of wooden crates labeled "Hemet Peachy Peaches."

"That's me and mine," Peachy said, bursting with the pride of ownership. "Been in the family since nineteen hundred and ten, right when they put in the railroad spur making Hemet the San Jac Valley's trading center for agriculture. Citrus, apricots, olives, walnuts and the like. You come visit some other time, you'll leave with a trunk full of our Peachy Peaches finest."

The freight train was pulling off the spur onto the main line when the pickup pulled up. Charlie got off a quick thank-you and dashed after it, searching for a stock car he could hop onto before the train picked up speed and left him behind.

It was six down the row, a car with an open door.

He got a one-handed grip on a ladder step handle and struggled to hang on until he caught the handle with his other hand. Pulled himself up one sweaty palm grab at a time. A couple times came perilously close to falling away from the train, now charging along the main line at a million miles an hour.

Finally high enough to try jumping from the step handles to the platform lid of the freight car, he took a deep breath and leaped. He landed awkwardly and angled backward, off balance, nothing to grab onto and save himself from falling off the car, breaking a few bones, or worse.

Charlie was starting a prayer when a hand clamped onto his wrist.

Pulled him into the car.

Swung him around.

He banged hard against a wall of wooden citrus crates bearing a variety of colorful product labels, flopped forward, and landed on the ice-cold metal floor staring back at the broad-shouldered, muscular woman in overalls and worn leather chore boots who'd saved his life. She answered his grateful smile with a guarded look on a leathered face that spoke of too much sun over too many years.

"Thank you," Charlie said, once he'd regained control of his breath.

She nodded acknowledgment, ran a hand behind her neck, under a tight boyish cut of sun-bleached blonde hair, and continued studying him. He figured her to be a migrant field hand, probably ten years younger than the early to mid-forties she appeared. A six-footer, give or take an inch; somewhere around a hundred and seventy or eighty pounds.

"So, what's your story anyway, mister?" Her voice gutted to a growl by one too many cigarettes that also defiled a modest Southern accent. "You dress up too good and you're way too clumsy car-hopping to be one of our breed or one of them stinking railroad bulls, so answer me that."

Charlie told her the story in broad strokes, while she fished out a pouch of Prince Albert cherry vanilla tobacco and rolling paper from a breast pocket and fixed herself a smoke; lit up with a stick match she ignited with the snap of a dirty, chewed thumbnail; took a hungry drag.

"Now it's your turn," he said, declining her offer of the butt.

"Not much to tell," she said. "I pick what other people grow, earning enough to get by. Been doing it for years, since my mam and pap lost everything back home and set out to find a new life for us. An early grave is what they found, going on six, seven years now. Me, I still got my dreams."

"Dreams like what?"

She pulled a folded newspaper page from a hip pocket and handed it over. "Right there, down at the bottom," she said, tapping a small advertisement for a World Series of Amateur Wrestling at the Hollywood Legion Stadium. Spread over the weekend, the ad promised a grand prize of two hundred and fifty dollars for the man, half that amount for the woman. All comers welcome.

"Gonna win me that money, yessiree, and you can bet your bottom dollar on that," she said, savoring the future she imagined for herself while staring outside at the passing scenery, an occasional stretch of homes and storefronts breaking the monotony of vacant acres of farmland. "Works out, I get me a reputation and a career in the ring. There's a lot of easy money to be made in wrestling, you ever get a step on the ladder."

"And if it doesn't work out?"

"It's back to the grapes and the groves, I suppose. But it will." She threw a glance over her shoulder. "Ain't that right, Brother?"

"You say so, it will, Sister," answered a voice from behind the mountain of crates across the way from Charlie. "Never known you to lose out once you got your mind set on something," Brother said, stepping into view. "Someone thinks otherwise, someone's got a new think coming."

He was half her size, but about the same weight, wearing a stained, red-and-blue-buffalo-plaid lumberjack shirt and poorly fitting overalls, boots that appeared too large for his feet and gave him a Charlie Chaplin kind of walk. Raccoon eyes. Matted black hair that fell past his shoulders. Maybe fifteen or sixteen years old. Tapping a length of lead pipe in his palm like a cop working a night stick.

"We're not really brother and sister, me and Kenyon," she said. "We call each other that to keep us from getting separated on the job calls, ever since I promised his dear ma to look after him in that final hour before she went off to meet her Maker."

"We stick together, me and Nance," Kenyon said. "They choose one of us, they get both of us."

"Most bosses have a soft spot for family, but there are some, you got to ante up on payday to stay in their good graces," Nance said.

"They try for more with Sister, that's where I look after her good as she looks after me, mister, if you know what I mean," Kenyon said, pounding his palm with the lead pipe. "What's your name, anyway?"

"Charlie. Charlie Dickens."

"Charlie Dixon."

"Dickens, like the writer."

"Whatever that means. . . . You carrying any lettuce on you, Charlie Dixon?"

"Lettuce? I don't understand."

Kenyon's eyes narrowed. His outsized scorched lips took a nasty turn. "Lettuce as in cabbage. Folding green. Money. You got it, I want it. Hand it over if you know what's good for you."

"You're kidding, right? This is some kind of silly little joke you're playing on me." Charlie looked to Nance for confirmation.

Her expression had hardened and was telling him otherwise. "You come across like a right guy, a decent gent, not like the usual body-sockers we run into, so make it easy for us and we'll keep it easy for you."

"Or else I'll have to do some irrigating on you with this," Kenyon said, wagging the lead pipe in Charlie's face.

"Gosh, all you had to say was you were short on money and

I'd have been happy to help out, not that I have much myself."

"We don't go for handouts, Charlie Dixon. Beggars do that. Me and Sister, we seen enough beggars around to know we'd rather be thieves. Now you see us, now you don't, so you can't laugh on us, point your finger and say, *Look there at them beggars.*"

"It's a matter of pride," Nance said. "You go to the picture shows, you see how the gangsters get more respect than the bums."

"The gangsters always die in the end. Robinson. Cagney. Bogart."

"We all gotta die sooner or later," Kenyon said, "so do us all a favor and make with the lettuce already." He swung the lead pipe like a baton.

Charlie felt the sweat irrigating his underarms, his forehead, everywhere, going after his billfold.

Kenyon swiped it away and handed it off to Nance.

She pulled out what bills there were and tossed the billfold aside. "Eight dollars," she said, rolling her eyes. "Would have expected better from the likes of you, Charlie."

"I'm also a disappointment to my mother," he said, immediately wishing he hadn't.

The remark drew a growl from Kenyon, who stepped closer, apparently intent on putting the lead pipe to work before a change of mind halted the pipe in mid-flight. "You got a watch on your wrist should bring a few at the hockshop. Gimme."

"Please. It was my father's, my grandfather's before that."

"It'll be close as I ever come yet to knowing a father."

Charlie freed the watch from his wrist. Kenyon tried it on. It hung loose. He undid the strap and gave the watch to Nance, who dropped it into a pocket.

"Something you should know," she said. "That wrestling business I told you about? Nothing more'n yakety-yak while I softened you up, so don't bother sending over the cops to look for me and Brother at the Hollywood Legion Stadium."

"But sure as God made little green apples you would make one damn fine wrestler, Sister."

"One Mildred Burke's already one too many for my taste," she said, seating herself on a stack of apple crates. She pulled a plump greenie from a crate that had been cracked open and tossed it to Brother. Sent a greenie to Charlie. Took one for herself. "A woman's place is in the fields," she said, a hollow sound to her words.

Conversation lapsed into silence for the next half hour, until the train slowed and slipped onto an auxiliary track at a modest brick depot and water tower in the middle of nowhere, interrupting Charlie's thoughts about a screenplay that tracked a poor girl's rise from backbreaking field work to breaking backs in a wrestling ring, climaxing with her defeat of the woman's world champion. And, maybe, she'd move on to claim a crown in another sport or two, amassing a fortune along the way, guided by a devoted manger who is secretly in love with her and along the way rescues her brother from a life of crime, or something like that. Check out this Mildred Burke, maybe write in a juicy role for her, or for Babe Didrickson Zaharias, something like that.

He'd have to work on it some more, he was thinking as the train finished taking on water and began inching forward on rusted wheels that screamed the news. Nance, who'd moved to the door and pushed it open wider, summoned Charlie. "You need to come and see this," she said. "You, too, Brother."

Charlie joined her at the door and surveyed left and right, saw nothing but shrubs and the ubiquitous Burma-Shave red metal signposts decorating the two-lane dirt roadway running parallel to the rails, one after another a hundred feet apart, their

four-line couplets followed by the product reminder, this batch
telling him:

Romances are ruined

After they begin

By a hair on the jacket

Or a lot on the chin

Burma-Shave.

Charlie felt his chin, ran his hand around his face, was thinking how good a shave would go around now, also a shower, too,
when Nance said, "Time for us to part company, Charlie."

Before he could interpret her meaning, Kenyon clamped onto
his shoulder blades and shoved him hard enough to send him
flying out of the boxcar and sliding down to the roadway.

He landed sprawled out, barely conscious, in the path of an
oncoming humpback panel truck, its horn blasting a warning
that roused Charlie. He rolled out of the truck's path with only
a few yards to spare, scrambled onto his feet and made it to the
roadside in front of a speeding flatbed approaching from the
opposite direction, bouncing into one of the Burma-Shave signs,
the line reading *Don't lose your head,* as if it were expecting him.

He looked around, trying to get his bearings in the rise and
fall of empty land that reminded him of someplace Bob Hope
had described on his Pepsodent radio program as "miles and
miles of nothing but miles and miles."

Wherever that was, he was there now.

He spotted the tag end of the freight train shrinking in the
distance.

Los Angeles had to be that way.

He headed off, hopeful of finding a gas station, a farmhouse,
a Howard Johnson's, anyplace with a phone, before his feet gave
out on him.

Kept himself company alternately working on his wrestling

117

screenplay and trying to put a melody to the Burma-Shave couplet:

Don't lose your head
To gain a minute
You need your head
Your brains are in it.

A fresh idea came to Charlie after a few miles.

Surefire.

Original as all get-out.

What if he structured the wrestling story as a musical for Fred and Ginger, maybe Ruby Keeler and Dick Powell over at Warner Bros., or Jeanette MacDonald and Nelson Eddy at Metro? He discarded his working title, *Glamour Girl of the Wrestling Ring,* and rechristened the screenplay *Singing in the Ring,* never more excited than now, overjoyed, wondering if Babe Didrickson Zaharias could carry a tune as well as she wielded a golf club.

Dusk settled in—after how many miles, Charlie didn't know—revealing the flickering light and smoke of campfires rising from a ravine. He shimmied down the narrow slope and into the first Hooverville he'd ever seen outside of a newsreel, a shantytown of tents, lean-tos and cardboard tenements occupied by Depression victims—tramps, rail-rovers, entire families bound together by homeless poverty and an instinct for survival, maybe a hundred in all.

The air smelled of soups and stews simmering in cast-iron pots and rabbits roasting over open flames, setting off a hunger pain in his stomach, a reminder that he'd had his last real meal a day ago.

"You look lost, friend," the man said, his basso the only rich thing about him, out of place on a skeleton-thin frame somehow strong enough to support the three- or four-year-old boy with the gap-tooth smile riding his broad-boned shoulders. "We ain't got much, but enough for sharing you need to stick for a while, especially seeing as how gosh-darn dog-tired you look, ain't that so, Scarlett?"

"A-men, Daddy. A-men to that." The boy was a girl. Charlie had been fooled by the castoff short pants that exposed her matchstick legs, but mostly the silly tilted bowler hat a size too large that made him think of Kayo in the Moon Mullins comic strip, the boy who slept in a dresser drawer.

"A-men," Charlie said.

Scarlett said, "How's that, Daddy? How I do?"

He reached over and patted her bruised kneecap. "Y'all did right fine, Scarlett. Your mommy'll be right proud of you when I tell her so."

Scarlett beamed. "You hear that, mister? Mommy'll be so proud. A-men. A-men to that."

"Name's Holliman," her daddy said, offering his hand after wiping it clean on his patchwork pants. "People mispronounce it like holy man, maybe because I'm a preacher, so it makes sense doing that. Good for a smile or anything if it gets them a step closer to God. Y'all a God-fearing man, Mister—?"

"Dickens. Charlie Dickens." Charlie thought about the question. "Most of the time."

"An honest answer, so hallelujah that," the preacher said. "Always room to improve in every blessed one of us. I often cast a suspicious eye on him what claims perfection as a virtue and not as the vice it truly is."

"A-men," Scarlett said. "A-men to that."

"We was getting ready to settle down for supper when I noticed your arrival and sensed you was a man in need, Mr. Charlie. Perhaps you'll enrich us with your presence, frugal repast though it may be?"

"A-men," Scarlett said. "A-men to that."

The Hollimans' home was a freestanding lean-to, three walls and a slope roof built from box wood, cardboard and scraps of abandoned metal, by the base of the ravine, some distance removed from all the other makeshift homes. A cast-iron stew pot made bubbling noises on top of a mound of stones heated by newspapers, tree branches and tumbleweeds.

"Hope y'all have a hankering for rabbit and chicken bone stew, plus some potatoes and carrots acquired by our neighbors, the Mosbys," Emma Jane, the preacher's wife, said. She gave a wave to the two adults and four young children among the dozen people armed with cheap eating utensils and metal cups who were politely waiting for the preacher to say grace. "Them's the Mosbys, that bunch there," she said. "Sammi Jo Mosby already working on her fifth blessed event, Chet not knowing how to let well enough be."

"God's little miracles not Chet's to decide," the preacher said. "Every one-a them children is nothing less than a blessing in disguise."

Emma Jane disputed him with a look that contradicted her modest size and a plain face sporting a hawkish nose and hollow cheeks. "You got a hungry flock waiting on you, Mr. Holliman, so kindly deliver our heartfelt thanks to the Lord while Scarlett shows Mr. Charlie to a place of welcome around our table."

Scarlett said, "Not really any table, Mr. Charlie. Mommy only says that because we once had a table, she says. Now we got our laps and that's just as good, she says, 'cause we can take our laps wherever we go, ain't that so, Mommy?"

"A-men to that," Emma Jane said, forcing a quiet smile, removing Scarlett's bowler to apply some loving pats to her scraggly mop of soup-bowl-cut, auburn-colored hair.

Reverend Holliman was leading the dinner circle in what seemed to Charlie like a prayer without end, every thank-you and request to God layered in heavy resonance and dramatic gesture, when sounds emanating from the road up above—noisy brakes and cranky motor engines quitting, undecipherable conversation punctuated by noisy affirmation—captured his attention.

He quit speaking and gestured everyone to patience while he gave the sounds a closer listen. After a few moments, he shook his head in despair. "Disperse for now," the preacher told his flock. "I'll tend to this business heading our way with expectation of the same happy result that the dear Lord willed us two times before, giving us added reason to rejoice in His name when we resume."

All looked hungrily at the stew pot before they wandered off far less happy than they'd been a moment earlier.

The preacher said, "You, also, Mr. Charlie. Shouldn't take but a minute or five to satisfy this unexpected interruption, so not to worry."

"Worry? What's going on, Reverend Holliman?"

"Local farmers and merchants come to call again. They want us out of here, though it's fair-and-square squatter territory, saying our little village gives the area a bad name and ain't good for growth. Saying we scare their children half to death, making them fearful of using the road. They made demands the first time around, threats when they showed up the last time, but I talked them off explaining how we're all God's children and how He put us on this path for good cause they needed to respect, whatever else they thought, same as we respect the path He put them on."

"A-men to that," Scarlett said, moving in to clutch her daddy's leg, her hazel eyes growing with alarm as more than a dozen began navigating down the hillside, all of them toting baseball bats, makeshift clubs, a weapon of some sort; several angling rifles and shotguns in the crook of their arms, fingers on the trigger. All of them wearing white bedsheet robes and pillowcase hoods, like they were fresh off the set of Griffith's *Birth of a Nation.*

One of them stepped forward and inched his masked nose closer to Reverend Holliman, playing the leader of the pack.

He said, "Preacher man, it's obvious you didn't take our warning serious last week or none of you would be here now." His words carried more weight than his featherweight voice. "No more games. Get off our land right now or you and everyone here get ready to suffer the consequences. Kick your asses from here to Kingdom Come."

Reverend Holliman held up the worn Bible he had been packing under his arm. "Your land, hardly," he said. "The Good Book tells us many times that the land belongs to God and no one else, that He created the land with the purpose of serving and benefiting every human. We may not be here forever, sir, but we're here because of Him and we'll leave at His direction, not yours, just as you should leave us in the same peace we wish upon you."

The leader of the pack laughed derisively and turned to his masked cronies. "Hear that, boys?" They mimicked his high-pitched laughter. "Lemme have a look at that Good Book of yours."

Reverend Holliman freed himself of Scarlett, stepped up and handed over the Bible.

The leader of the pack leafed through its pages, pausing here and there to mumble through a sentence or two. "You know what, preacher man? This don't begin to compare with *God's Little Acre,* what I call a good book, a real good book," he said, stretching the word *real* and adding a wink.

He held out the Bible like he was returning it to Reverend Holliman, but stepped back before the preacher could take hold and launched it to the clouds, calling, "Target practice, Delbert."

One of the bedsheet invaders raised his rifle, sighted the Bible and fired. The shot caught the Bible dead center before it landed. The other bedsheets applauded. "He's surefire to win this year's Thanksgiving turkey shoot like he has the last eleven times," the leader of the pack said. "Just as soon put a bullet in you, you don't get on to moving your sorry ass out of here, preacher man, this time for sure, and any others thinking otherwise."

Reverend Holliman stooped after the Bible, brushed the cover free of dirt and said, "I forgive you and your friend this transgression, as I'm sure our Good Lord would have me do."

"Ain't you the kindly one," the leader of the pack said. He stepped forward and gave the preacher a backhanded whack on the face. "Now get on moving while I start a count to ten, you know what's good for you."

"Daddy!" Scarlett called, frantic with alarm, and managed a couple steps before her mother grabbed her, saying, "Hush, baby girl, Daddy gonna be fine," not entirely sounding like she believed it herself.

Reverend Holliman rubbed his cheek and stood his ground. "Our Good Lord exhorted us in his Sermon on the Mount not to resist an evil person. If someone strikes you on the right cheek, turn to him the other also, He told us."

The leader of the pack took it as a dare and connected a fist to the preacher's other cheek that resounded with the sound of bone cracking. The preacher hung motionless for a moment, dropped the Bible and followed it down, blood spilling from inside his mouth.

Scarlett broke free of her mother, screaming, "Don't you hurt my daddy!" and lunged after the leader of the pack.

He swatted her away like a fly.

She picked herself up and went at him again.

He hit her harder this time.

Some part of Scarlett snapped like a twig.

She landed yards away, motionless.

Her mother swooped over and dropped to her knees, pressed Scarlett against her moaning, "Baby girl, you all right? You all right, baby girl? Baby girl, answer me. Say something."

One of the bedsheets was carrying a megaphone Charlie recognized as the kind Rudy Vallee crooned into. "Gimme that thing," the leader of the pack said and shouted into it, "Everybody, time to git, unless you want some of the same what we just dished out to your preacher man. You got five minutes before this sin of a city of yours gets torched down to the ground."

The sight of Reverend Holliman and, especially, Scarlett being battered had injected Charlie with the stratospheric level of fury and resentment he reserved for all the brain-dead picture-business morons who rejected his screenplays. These morons hiding inside cloaks of anonymity were far more dangerous— lethally dangerous. The smart thing to do would be to run, flee, get out of their way before the Hooverville squatters massing behind him did something stupid that could only end in violence, bloodshed, and—

"Why don't all of you turn tail and get the hell out of here?" Charlie heard himself saying, astonished to realize he was addressing the leader of the pack and his bedsheets, not the squatters. He started for Reverend Holliman, intent on helping him to his feet.

"Stop in your tracks, young fella, or I'll help you do so," the leader of the pack said.

Charlie kept moving.

The leader of the pack said, "Delbert, shoot him."

CHAPTER 15

A week had passed since Max shot and killed Willie Frankfurter, Sarah unable to get her mind to shut down and let her sleep through the night. One night. Was that asking too much?

She was increasingly anxious that Charlie Dickens was gone, missing, nowhere to be found when Mad Dog went looking to retrieve him.

She needed Charlie in tow as much as she was struggling to come up with a new murder plan he could be tagged for.

The old murder plan?

As dead as she still wished for Max.

She recognized how stupid it would be to have Earl duplicate the strategy she had mapped out for Willie Frankfurter, not least because it didn't work.

Sequels were fine for the pictures, but something like that in real life could have the boys in blue sniffing at her heels faster than Rin Tin Tin, questioning her absence from the mansion on two different nights her husband was targeted for murder by someone sneaking through the garden.

Jeez-o, it even sounded fishy to her, so how would it sound to a detective like Burt Cobbler, who already had given her the shady eye, like he wanted to ask but was too much the gentleman?

He'd have gotten the stock answer, of course, how she and Max lived separate lives, thank you very much, but that would open a can of worms.

How separate?

Why separate?

Where separate?

You have another residence, Miss Darling?

Did Mr. Moonglow know about your other residence, Miss Darling?

Your houseman, Mr. Mahony, did Mr. Moonglow know about him, Miss Darling?

Did Mr. Mahony, perhaps, look after more than the house for you, Miss Darling?

Were you and Mr. Mahony together earlier that fateful night, Miss Darling?

On and on and—

No question where Cobbler or any detective worth his badge would run with that line of reasoning. Maybe get Mad Dog arrested, accused of the killing and half a murder plot hatched by the two of them. Definitely cut her career short, censor her straight out of the picture business when the bluenoses of the Breen Office reminded RKO of the morals clause in her contract.

She rolled out of bed, tossed on a robe, and padded across the room, thinking, No, no, no. There had to be a new plan, a plan that was foolproof and had no links to the old plan, except for Charlie Dickens, a neurotic screenwriter—weren't they all—on the brink of success until production on his picture, *Showdown Creek,* is cancelled. He wrongfully blames Max and, seething with anger, kills him and disappears. Resurfaces in time to be arrested, Sarah despairing over a talented young man who'd been driven over the edge by disappointment.

She could hear Cobbler saying, *I understand he was residing at your place, Miss Darling. What was that all about, Miss Darling? And your husband, Mr. Moonglow, he knew you were keeping Mr. Dickens there, Miss Darling?*

She'd give him a withering look.

He'd know better than to pursue that line of questioning.

And this time, Earl having succeeded where Willie failed, she would be able to say, *If Max were alive I'd tell you ask him, detective. He needed a helping hand, and I was only too thrilled to be in a position to extend mine, detective.* That would send Cobbler off with his tail between his legs.

Sarah was on the balcony watching the sun sneak up behind the distant hilltop cross overlooking Forest Lawn Memorial Park, humoring herself with the thought that the cemetery already had more stars under ground than MGM claimed were in the heavens, when Max wandered out. He gripped his gorilla arms around her and mashed his hairy belly against her, complaining, "You know how disappointed I was when I rolled over in bed, thinking to give you a good morning *zetz* and you weren't there to be *zetzed?*"

"So you solved the problem by taking it into your own hands."

"You know how old that gag is, Mrs. Moonglow?"

"Older than the combined age of your last two mistresses?"

"Three, but who's counting?" He released her. "Are you ready to tell me yet?" he said, the playfulness gone from his voice.

"What now?"

"What now? What I've been asking you for a week. Willie Frankfurter. What was he really doing here? Delivering a script at that time of night? Nonsense. Sneaking over to see you is more like it, right? Expecting to be welcomed with open arms, right? Open legs more like it, right?"

"Except I wasn't home, right? Really, Max darling, maybe he was planning to join you between the sheets?"

"He was only a B-picture producer, for Christ's sake."

"A Frankfurter who definitely was no wiener, but maybe with a hot dog he thought you'd relish?"

She'd always been able to derail their arguments, no matter how serious, with the sense of humor that had saved her hide more than once in her old life and ever since. Now was no different. Max burst out laughing and pulled her to him. "George S. Kaufman got nothing on you, funny lady."

"Play your cards right, Max darling, and in a minute I'll have nothing at all on."

She guided him back into the bedroom.

"If sleeping powders don't work for you, there's a doctor I've heard about who they say performs minor miracles," Pan Berman said, inching up an eyebrow. "I'll have my girl get you his name and particulars before you go."

"How thoughtful of you, you're a dear," Sarah said, not that she had any intention of ever using sleeping powders or anything stronger. Even aspirin powder was a problem for her, had been almost since Barney Rooker helped rescue her from her old life and the drug habits drilled into her by that pimp bastard Andy Cream.

She was clean as a whistle the day, years later, when Barney materialized on her doorstep with Pete, the money man who was bankrolling the stag film she refused to do with a dog or any other animal on more than two legs, leading up to her slashing Andy's throat.

He made it seem like only yesterday, smart enough not to call them *the good old days,* and talked in glowing terms about the pictures he'd seen her in. He named them one by one, all of them, in the same order they'd hit the screen. It seemed like he'd never get to the point of his surprise visit until Pete clipped his ribs with an elbow and said, "We're not here to join Sadie's fan club, Barney."

Sadie.

She couldn't remember the last time anyone had called her that.

She corrected him. "It's Sarah now, if you don't mind, Pete. Sarah Darling. Changed nice and legal-like even before I graduated from bit parts to something bigger."

"I'm here to talk about Sadie," Pete said, indifferent to her explanation, a false smile filling a cherubic face that no longer reminded her of an overgrown angel. His cheeks and chin had become chicken wattles and his once spotless pink complexion was riddled with wrinkles and creases. Fifty, give or take.

He stood well over six feet, but there was a slight stoop she didn't remember from before. He was dressed pricier than she remembered, a stylish suit that must have set him back a pretty penny, matching Princess Mara tie and pocket handkerchief, two-tone Italian leather shoes, steel-gray fedora. Only, on him everything looked cheap and ill-fitting. Some men were not meant to be fashion plates, no matter how hard they tried, how much cash in the bank they had to back up the effort, and Pete was one of them.

"So, what exactly about Sadie?" Sarah said, turning to Barney. "What's going on? What brings you here?"

Barney shrugged. "I turn around while I'm shooting a stag over in the valley for Naughty Nooky Productions and there's Peter Peterman, giving me the glad hand after a long time no see. Turns out Naughty Nooky is another one of his companies. We get to reminiscing and he says where he's seen you done pretty good by yourself in the movies and maybe I could put him with you to talk a business proposition easier than he could do it by his lonesome. I get a lot of work from Naughty Nooky, so . . . ya know? What's a feller to do?"

Something about the way Barney explained it had her thinking there was more to the story than he was letting on. "You could have called or come over first, Barney. Tipped me off. I'd never be able to say no to you, and you know it."

"I was counting on that, even though it's been a couple or more winters since we traded faces here, so what say we go ahead and give a listen to what Pete has on his mind."

Sarah said, "Your turn, Pete."

"I'll keep it brief and to the point," he said. "You got a picture career that's going places, but it could be over before you can say Jack Robinson if word ever got out about you doing the stag circuit and worse if some of the stag reels you made for my companies found their way to the press."

She knew a blackmail pitch when she heard it. "You saw this coming, Barney?" He answered her with a shrug. "How much you asking for all the reels and your silence, Pete?"

"Real gentle since we go back a long time, Sadie."

"It was too long the same day I met you."

"Just enough to cover some gambling mistakes I made with certain unsavory types and a bit more to keep me solvent until my new stags make it into circulation."

"A number, Pete. Give me a number."

He told her what he had in mind.

"Do I look like the United States Mint to you? That's more than I score in a year. Two years."

"You've always struck me as being smarter, tougher and more resourceful than the run-of-the-mill whores Andy Cream was always bringing my way, so I'm confident you'll figure out something, Sadie, seeing as how it's an investment that'll help keep the twinkle, twinkle in your little star."

"And if I can't?"

"I've got me some dandy reels to share with the world, and something more." He turned cold as death itself. "Wouldn't it be horrible, the cops down San Diego way got an anonymous tip about Andy and who and what might have happened to him?"

"You would, too, wouldn't you?"

"Let's not put it to the test, oke? Take the next twenty-four hours to come up with the cabbage. Let Barney know when he phones and he'll pick you up, deliver you to where we'll make the exchange. That so, Barney?"

"I'm good with it if she is."

"I can drive myself."

"No, you can't," Pete said. "Barney's my cushion against you trying to pull some stunt, like bringing someone with you, some uninvited guest out to make life difficult for me; you get my meaning?"

"What's your piece of the pie, Barney? How much you stand to make?"

"I got no complaints," Barney said.

Exactly twenty-four hours later, Sarah's phone rang.

She said, "I don't have it, Barney. I couldn't make it work."

"Hold on," he said. She heard a muffled conversation, as if he'd put his hand over the mouthpiece. Nothing said was clear enough for her to understand before he was back telling her, "Have the payment ready in a suitcase or something like that, Pete says. He'll do likewise with the merchandise."

"Barney, I said I couldn't put the cash together."

"I'm on my way over in an hour."

"You gone deaf on me? I don't have the money, Barney. Twenty-four hours wasn't long enough time."

"It don't matter what plans you already had for tonight, you get me? Cancel them, and be ready to shake a leg when I get there."

Sarah hung up the receiver thinking, *I'll be ready, all right. You can bet the farm on it,* and headed for the bedroom closet, where she kept her Colt .38 Detective Special parked in a shoebox on the overhead shelf.

The snub-nosed double-action revolver was a half-forgotten relic of her days on the street, her protection against johns who got a little too frisky or heavy-handed, picked up at a pawnshop in an under-the-counter trade for a blow job.

Seeing the gun usually was enough to either frighten the john or convince him to cough up extra bucks as an apology, except for that one time she put a bullet in a whisky-dipped pervert's thigh, missing her intended target by inches.

She'd use it on Pete, it came to that.

She parked the .38 in her clutch purse and went after her overnight case, weighing it down with back issues of *Motion Picture, Modern Screen* and *Movie Mirror.* Waited for Barney over four fingers of vodka from the bottle she kept in the icebox, working out how to keep him from examining the case before they took off. Was still fighting to invent a believable excuse when he arrived carrying a satchel of his own.

He gave Sarah's overnight case a glance. "What's that about? You said you couldn't come up with the cash."

"Don't ask, Barney." It was the best she could do.

"I already asked."

"I need to get my hands on those films, Barney, one way or the other."

"What'd you pack in there? A knife? You plan on pulling another knife trick, since it worked out for you once before?"

"No." It wasn't a lie.

"Swell, so let's go with my way." He tossed his satchel at her feet. "Check it out." The satchel was stuffed with packets of tens and twenties. "On a short-term loan from my nest egg," he said. "What Pete's expecting, down to the penny."

"Whose side are you on, Barney? Why are you doing this for me?"

"Doing it for myself as well as you, kid. I don't cotton to people messing with other people's lives. Pete sucker punched me into this action, saying he'd blab to the cops about how I disposed of Andy Cream's body, accessory after the act, I didn't get into the ring and go the whole ten rounds with him. If he kept his fat yap shut, made only the stag films his bargaining chip, let me in on where he had 'em stored, this business wudda been over and done with long ago, you none the wiser."

"You're a regular Sir Lancelot, Barney, shining armor and all."

He deflected the compliment with a hand wave. "Let's get moving," he said. "You drive."

Sarah followed Barney's directions south past the undeveloped flatlands of Baldwin Hills and up La Brea, west on Stocker to one of the many dirt service roads in the jungle of rusted, bobbing oil derricks that multiplied after Standard Oil drew the first gusher in 1924. About four hundred were still active, filling the night air with a pungent smell, but not the inactive well in the field of shut-ins where he told her to park.

There was no sign of Pete or anybody in the dark gloom of the petroleum field, lit only by a smattering of lamps hanging from the pumping mechanical monsters.

Barney checked his pocket watch. "He should be here any minute," he said. "You go along with what you hear and nothing stupid, we'll get through this with flying colors."

They sat in the car and waited, talking nothing in particular, mostly nothing at all, Sarah too antsy for conversation, Barney silent after explaining why he suggested the oil fields for the trade.

"I knew around here would be nice and cozy around this time, safe from prying eyes, from before, back in thirty-two, when I shot some reels not too far away, over on Stocker where they built a village for the summer Olympics," he said. "It was for the men only, a hundred buildings, a post office and telegraph office, an amphitheater, even a hospital, a fire department, and a bank. Whoosh, all torn down afterwards. You think your reels are something sassy, kid, you should see what I got on film with the jocks who couldn't keep their rods in their jockstraps. Topped only by some of the stuff with the girlies, who were put up at the Chapman Park Hotel on Wilshire. Gave new meaning to whoever it was first said stick it to your own kind."

The sound of an approaching car churning dust cut him off while he was describing some of the films, like a proud father sharing photographs of his children.

It was an old-model, steel-black-and-ruby-red Rolls-Royce 20, the "baby Rolls" for owners who'd rather take the wheel than leave it to a chauffeur.

Pete parked it alongside Sarah's car, hopped out and waved them over. "You show me yours and I'll show you mine," he said, rubbing the chill from his hands.

Barney moved forward toting the satchel, Sarah six steps behind him, a firm grip on her purse, ready to go for the .38 in case of—

What, she wasn't sure, only that right now she didn't trust anyone but herself.

"On the fender's fine," Pete said. "Down gently, though. Atta baby." He unzipped the satchel, spread it open and nodded approvingly.

"It's all there," Barney said. "Counted it myself."

"Now it's my turn," Pete said, and began checking the packets, lips moving to his silent tally. Finished, he said, "Outstanding," zipped the satchel and passed it through an open rear window. He headed to the rear of the Rolls and raised the trunk lid, revealing a steamer trunk. "There you are, Sadie. Barney, give me a hand moving it on over to Sadie's car."

The steamer trunk was heavy and took some struggling before

135

they had it settled.

"My turn," Sarah said, easing the lid open. All the film cans were marked with the titles and a production date.

"The original masters," Pete said. "Good to my word. A deal is a deal."

"How many copies are out there?"

"Not many, if they're around at all. None on my shelves. Besides, you've changed enough that nobody's likely to recognize you unless someone tells them."

Barney said, "And you're not one to do that, are you, Pete?"

"Who ever knows for certain what the future holds for anybody?"

"I know about yours," Sarah said, her voice rising. She had pulled the .38 from her purse and was aiming it two-handed at Pete. "You're the snake in my Garden of Eden, and that's one snake too many."

"A snake sure, but never a snitch, so you can please put that thing away."

Barney stepped between Sarah and Pete.

She said, "Get out of the way, Barney."

"You got what you come for, so don't do anything you'll regret later." He held out his hand. "C'mon, kid, don't be a dope. It don't look good on you."

Sarah debated with herself what to do. Given what he knew, Pete would always be a threat, nothing to prevent him showing up down the road with a fresh demand for money to keep his lip buttoned. She'd be better off with him dead, so shoot him. *Now,* she ordered herself, but her finger froze on the trigger. Barney was rock solid in the line of fire and not about to budge.

Sarah reluctantly loosened her grip and surrendered the .38 to him.

"Good girl," Barney said.

Pete said, "Thanks, Barney."

Barney said, "Don't mention it," and—

Wheeled around and fired.

The shot hit Pete in the chest. He sailed backward, banged into the side of the Rolls and rocketed face forward into the dirt.

Barney stepped to him and fired again.

Pete's head split open like an overripe melon.

Barney said, "Now you still got clean hands, kid, and we got nothing to worry about from him." He stuffed the .38 inside his belt. "C'mon, there's housekeeping to do before I send you on your way."

With her help he pried open a wooden cover at the base of the well and pushed it aside. Dragged Pete over and dumped him inside, waiting for what seemed like forever before the body landed with a bone-cracking thud. "That's that," he said, making the sign of the cross. "Nobody's ever gonna check down this duster."

The film cans went into the abandoned well next, one and two at a time, followed by the steamer trunk and Sarah's .38. "Now let's get the cover back in place," Barney said. "Then you drive home, forget you were ever here or any of this ever happened."

"What about you?"

"I got Pete's Rolls to get rid of, somewhere, but not here."

"Call me afterward and let me know."

"I'm not one for long good-byes."

"Good-bye? Why good-bye?"

"Got places to be, kid."

"Stick around instead, Barney. You're great with a camera and I'm getting to know some producers in the business. I could put in a good word for you, help you catch on as a cameraman somewhere legit, out of stags, to where you could be making real pictures for real money."

"I'm where I belong right now. Gave my word as a down payment on unfinished business, so how about a rain check?"

"Whenever," Sarah said, "but answer a question for me before I scram. Why are you so good to me, that first time down in San Diego and now here?"

He played the question in his mind before answering. "Probably it's because you remind me of the daughter I once had."

"Once? What happened to her, Barney?"

"I ever find out, I'll let you know, kid."

It would be years before Barney came into her life again, but he had no answer for her then or ever since, or so he told her whenever she put the question to him.

"So, shall we get down to business?" Pan Berman said, snapping her out of the past.

Based on his tone, his mechanical smile and the way he used his pipe to orchestrate his words, Sarah knew she wouldn't like what she was about to hear.

"Please do," Max said, expressionless, his way of masking his personal discomfort with situations over which he had no control.

"Suffice it to say, I wouldn't have asked the two of you over on such short notice if we weren't confronting a situation vital to our mutual best interests and basic to your future with RKO," Pan said. He wheeled around in his chair, putting his back to them. "You have to make that damn awful *Showdown at Shadow Creek.*"

"Did Coop change his mind, or, unlike Max, have you found me a costar worth my time and talent?" Sarah said.

"Sorry, no."

"Then my words exactly, Pan—sorry, no."

"I don't make George O'Brien or Tim—what's his name?— Tim Holt westerns, so you got another think coming, you think that," Max said, rising as if to leave. "Time to go, my precious one. Meeting adjourned. Let us know whenever you have brighter news, Pan."

Sarah got up to join him.

Pan turned back to them and slammed the desk with his fist. "Sit down, the both of you," he said, with uncharacteristic force displacing his usual passion for calm persuasion. "You leave this office before I say the meeting is adjourned and both of you can finish out the day packing your things and checking off the lot for good."

"You would defy my contract?"

"No, but the studio has a dozen lawyers who will—and keep you tied up in court long enough to empty your piggy bank, while Perry and his publicity boys keep planting the kinds of stories guaranteed to keep either of you from catching on anywhere else once the dust settles."

"And all along I thought I escaped from the Nazis when I left Germany."

"Don't go so melodramatic on me, Max. This isn't my doing. You know I love you like a brother."

"And Cain loved Abel," Sarah said, settling back down in her visitor's chair, hands clasped firmly, legs tightly crossed, as if she were protecting her virtue.

Max pushed out a ton of breath and resumed his seat. "What's the story, Pan, that all of a sudden this western picture takes on such importance, like it could be another *Stage Door* or even *The Informer?*"

Pan anchored his elbows on the desk and formed a pyramid with his fingers, leaned forward and dropped his voice, like he was entrusting a state secret to them.

"Orders from on high," he said. "The big boys back east turned to jelly worrying that Willie Frankfurter's death might somehow turn into a scandal that could bring down the value of the stock and cost them millions in corporate and personal profits. They got the idea of turning a sow's ear into a silk purse by filming the script he was bringing over to Sarah as a tribute to Willie's memory. And who better to produce and direct than Max Moonglow, of course—the brilliant filmmaker, making up for accidentally killing Willie by making the picture Willie so passionately believed in and now will serve forever as a tribute to a great talent cut down prematurely."

"Who writes your speeches, Pan? The Brothers Grimm? I haven't heard a fairy tale like that since I was in knee pants, growing up in Germany."

"Almost a word-for-word Western Union from New York. They expect to hear from me before the day is over."

Sarah said, "What happened to the idea of sweeping Willie's death under the rug?"

"Turns out Willie has an uncle on the RKO board, who landed him his job here in the first place and carried enough weight to demand more and better than that. Add to that somebody tipped off Winchell, who's been calling around ever since. Perry says Winchell told him he's leading with the story, for better or for worse, on his Sunday-night broadcast. He couldn't be persuaded otherwise."

"So I'd get to be a hero on Winchell?"

"To Mr. and Mrs. North and South America and all the ships at sea."

"So maybe the *ferkakta* script isn't as bad as it is. What do you say, Sarah?"

"If I can't have a Jimmy Stewart or a Hank Fonda, the picture introduces an actor brand-new to the silver screen, a Max Moonglow discovery, how's that sound, Pan?"

"Sweetheart, whatever makes you happy makes me happy."

"So, first things first, I got to discover somebody who'll make magic and chemistry with my favorite leading lady, like it always was with Gable and Harlow."

Sarah said, "Maxie, dear, I thought you knew by now—give me any actor at all and I'll supply the chemistry," but she was thinking something else. She was thinking how Pan Berman's ultimatum had unexpectedly led her to the new murder plan she'd been straining to find.

She waited until she was certain Max was asleep, his snores vacuuming the ceiling, before slipping out of bed and downstairs to the telephone extension in the den.

Earl came on the line sounding groggy until he recognized her voice. He cleared his throat of sleep. "Hey, baby, hearing your voice this time of night, it's better than a wet dream."

Sarah cupped the mouthpiece with her hand and whispered, "It's oke to come back to work tomorrow."

"Swell. Mr. Moonglow be around, or can we celebrate?"

She let his question slide. "Anybody asks where you been, you were out of town visiting a sick relative, something like that."

"Matter of fact, my uncle Jerry up Oxnard way, runs charter fishing boats, a bait-and-tackle shop, he's been under the weather lately. You'd like him loads, you ever meet him."

"Tomorrow, Earl. You can tell me all about him tomorrow."

Hanging up, she thought she heard that clicking sound again, like someone had been on the line with them. She eased the receiver off the hook, covered the mouthpiece and waited, not sure, for what.

Her curiosity was answered two or three anxious minutes later.

Another click.

Followed by a number being dialed.

Followed by a busy signal.

Followed by that clicking sound and—

Silence.

CHAPTER 16

Max looked at Sarah across the breakfast table like she was crackers.

He said, "He's a gardener, for Christ's sake. What makes you think Earl could be an actor, not to mention an actual movie star?"

"That's his dream, Maxie. He's told me that more than once in the past, so why not give a break to somebody who's almost like a member of our family?"

"Because maybe his dream is one thing and the truth is something else, like he has no talent?"

"I have more than enough talent for the both of us. Besides, it's me people will be paying their quarters at the box office to see."

"In a Max Moonglow Production that deserves better than a cheap western."

"In your hands it'll look like a million dollars, Maxie."

Max took a gargantuan bite of cherry strudel, got up from the table and, coffee cup in hand, crossed to the bay window.

Earl, shirtless and sweating, was shoveling dirt in the irrigation trench that ran the length of the maze hedge. He caught Max studying him and paused to answer with a bright smile and a wave; stretched his excessively muscular six-foot frame, ran a hand across his brow and threw the sweat away; got back to work.

He wasn't exactly another Errol Flynn, more rugged-looking

than pretty boy, but he could catch on with the ladies, given half a chance. Max had to admit to himself that Sarah might be on to something, probably Earl himself, given how she'd suddenly turned into his champion, a fairy godmother interested in more than trading coins for baby teeth left under a pillow.

"What the hell," he called over his shoulder. "If Earl's who you want, my precious one, so be it. I'll phone and break the news to Pan so he can break the news to New York."

There was another call to make, but he needed to save that one for the office, out of her earshot.

"So what did you discover about her? Don't hold back."

"God's honest truth, Mr. Moonglow—this lady of yours, if she's cheating on you, it's only in her dreams and your imagination."

"You're certain of that, Mr. Duff?"

"On a Bible. Rinso couldn't get her any cleaner than she already is. In all the years I been carrying a private investigator's license, seventeen years on the force before that, I've seen more cheating at Holy Saints of Mercy bingo. There any gentleman in her life besides you, he's Claude Rains from *The Invisible Man*."

"Excellent news, Mr. Duff. Thank you. I'll look forward to your next report."

"You sure you want me to stay on the case, Mr. Moonglow? It'll be like throwing good money after bad."

Max said, "I have plenty to throw, Mr. Duff," and disconnected.

He switched to the red phone, his direct line out, and dialed the Sunset Plaza Drive apartment, anxious to hear Dixie's sweet voice, relieved the investigator's report contained nothing that would have caused him to evict her from his hideaway and his heart.

"Hey, honey pie, been missing you something awful," she

said. "Was truly hoping to see you and you know what else before it got to be time to head over to Skate Burger."

"Honey lamb, your Skate Burger days are about to be behind you," Max said. "Call in sick, put a bottle of Dom on ice, and be ready to celebrate when I get there."

"Celebrate? What, what, what?"

"It's a surprise."

"Golly jeepers! I love surprises almost as much as I love you," Dixie said. "Hurry, I'll be waiting and you know how."

Max stopped by Rudy Bundsman's office before leaving the studio and caught his attention with a cough.

The casting director looked up from the stack of photos he was sorting, adjusted his half-moon specs and answered Max's grin with a condescending smile. "Don't tell me, let me guess," he said, his tone dispelling the notion he'd guess wrong. "You've got a girl you want me to put in *Showdown at Shadow Creek.*"

"Maybe I just dropped in to say hello to an old friend."

"Maxie, Maxie, Maxie. You know how many years I been casting for RKO? Since there was an RKO. The only time I ever see or hear from a producer or a director anywhere but in an interoffice memo or on the phone is when he needs a favor, and the favor usually involves two long stems and titties. So, what's her name already, this time?"

"You sly old dog. . . . Dixie Leeds."

Rudy closed his eyes, ran a hand over his thinning strands of silver and white hair and repeated her name a couple times. "Never heard of any Dixie Leeds. She new in town or only on your couch?"

"She's a real find, Rudy. Trust me on that. More than a close-up and a kiss-off."

"And that's what Sarah also thinks?"

"I'd like this kept strictly between us, Rudy, you and me."

"I got you. Like it's better Sarah doesn't know what the tomcat dragged in. . . . You want your Dixie Leeds for what, one of the gambling casino hoochie-koochers? The school marm, what would give her two or three lines of dialogue to screw up?"

"Editor of the *Shadow Creek Sentinel.*"

Rudy pushed back in his chair and made a whooshing sound, his surprise written all over his face. "Third lead, billed third or fourth depending on who gets cast as the bad guy. Right now I'm partial to that young fellow, Ward Bond."

"I trust your judgment, Rudy."

"Bond, he's going places. Maybe Harry Carey as the rancher, but that would push down your girl's billing."

"Put her last. Introducing Dixie Leeds as so and so— whatever the editor's name. . . . I'll arrange for Dixie to come by and see you, and you can judge for yourself how right I am about her, Rudy."

"Chill Wills, he'd be good for comic relief if he's off the new George O'Brien in time," Rudy said, and went back to sorting his photographs.

Max saved the news until after he'd survived his first tussle with Dixie and fed his wheeze with his asthma inhaler, Dixie sitting beside him in bed, her breasts as naked as her grief, blaming herself for bringing on the asthma attack.

"I come to care silly for you, so you shouldn't scare me like that," she said, raining tears on her words. "Nobody's ever treated me good as you, honey pie. I don't know what I did to deserve you, but I love you more than the world."

He wrapped her in his arms. "Believe me when I say I feel the same about you," he said, surprised by the truth of his words, an outward display of affection alien to his nature and rarely exposed since he was a young man starting out at UFA and smitten with Esther from the secretarial pool.

Esther seemed to enjoy the way he joked around, her ribald sense of humor a match for his own, rewarded him with a hug and a lingering kiss on the cheek when he surprised her with a two-pound box of hand-rolled milk chocolates and a dozen red roses fresh off the vine for her birthday, didn't hesitate to accept that day he finally mustered up enough courage to invite her out on a date—the cinema; Valentino.

As the picture show progressed, Esther, audibly swooning over the so-called great Latin lover like all the other young women in the theater, reached for his hand and moved it onto one of her ample breasts. Her nipple pressed hard against his palm through her silk blouse. Max froze, unsure how to react beyond the reaction growing between his thighs, an area Esther took as her own a minute or two later, unbuttoning his fly and grabbing hold of his *zuckerstange,* his candy cane.

His response was immediate and made her giggle before she attacked him with her mouth and drew satisfaction out of Max a second time. She ran her tongue around her thick lips and whispered in his ear, *Es schmeckt nach salz, It tastes of salt;* freed her breast of his hand and went back to watching Valentino as if nothing untoward had happened.

Impulsively, he sought out her breast again and aimed a kiss at her cheek, blurting out with unexpected bravery, announcing, "I love you, Esther."

She shoved him away and demanded he stop.

"I said I love you, Esther."

"So what? Not the first one, not the last, so mind your manners."

After that, Esther found somewhere else to look, some way to avoid him, whenever she saw Max approaching her station in the secretarial pool. He wound up with somebody else the several times he requested Esther by name and quit trying the day of the Christmas party, when he saw her disappear with one of UFA's hotshot producers, her hand playfully squeezing the producer's elephantine ass.

It was not until many years and many women later that Max realized on reflection he'd never said *I love you* to any one of them, even though a few might have qualified for those words if he hadn't dumped them from his life for real or imagined cause, or simply because he felt it was time to move on.

Yes, he supposed he loved Sarah, given how long she'd been his wife, serving him as well as he served her, but had he ever told her, *I love you.*

Yes, he could hear the words, but always in Sarah's voice, not his, just as they were now in Dixie's voice, not his. *I love you more than the world.* Maybe the day would arrive when he could do better than *I feel the same about you,* but today wasn't that day.

He said, "Honey lamb, time to cheer you up with the good news I told you about."

"First tell me you're oke and promise not to scare me like that anymore," she said, pampering his dueling scar.

"I'll do my best. . . . Honey lamb, have you ever thought about doing a western?"

She looked uncertain how to answer his question. "Is that anything like a sandwich, you know, a three-way?" she said.

CHAPTER 17

Chet Mosby saved Charlie's life.

It cost him his own.

Chet had been one of the gang of Hooverville squatters massing off-center of the bedsheets and preparing to counterattack
when the leader of the pack ordered Delbert to kill Charlie.

Before the sharpshooting Delbert could squeeze the trigger
and most certainly cut Charlie down for keeps, Chet had flown
at him like he'd been shot from a circus cannon and thrown
Delbert off-balance.

The shot caught Charlie in the arm in the seconds before the
bedsheets plowed into Chet, wrestled him down to the ground
and batted and boot-stomped him to death, cheering themselves
on like partisan fans at a baseball game while drowning out the
unholy screams of Chet's missus, Sammi Jo, and her four kids.

That put an end to the squatters' uprising.

Within hours, they had dispersed, taking with them whatever
they could carry, their Hooverville reduced to rubble and ashes
by the locals, who headed home to celebrate their victory at a
festive barbecue awaiting their arrival in the town square.

Charlie was huddling with Robin Moon in the back of Ernie
and Millie Keyes's '28 Chevy Stakebed as it plowed along an
unlit stretch of highway, trying to pretend away the pain radiat-
ing from his wounded left arm while Robin, a potato-faced girl
in her twenties with the dark-brown, sun-dried skin and defeated
look of a migrant field hand, held tight the tourniquet she'd

fashioned for him from a length of clothesline rope.

Robin and the Keyes had dragged Charlie to the truck and sped off while the bedsheets were savaging Chet, Robin shouting to be heard over the din, "They're sure to get back to finishing the job they started on you once they're finished doing their worst with that good man."

After about two hours of bumpy going, Ernie pulled off the road, down a narrow embankment onto a flat patch of land that had the remnants of a campfire and other signs of recent use. "We'll camp here till sunrise and then figger out what's what," he said, his pronounced Okie accent a match for Robin's, and set about rebuilding the campfire, using scraps of wood and sagebrush.

Millie dug out a woven wood picnic basket with swing handles from the back of the truck and set it down by the fire. "Not much by way of fancy pickin's, but sure beats starving," she said, her voice a sweeter version of Robin's, as delicate as bone china. She used a discarded newspaper for her tablecloth and covered it with beef jerky, sections of baked potato, a modest selection of fresh vegetables, hard bread, a hunk of moldy Swiss cheese, and a military canteen of water.

They gathered around the campfire, and Ernie said, "Join hands and let's us pray." Charlie managed easily enough gripping Millie with his right hand, but struggled against the pain taking Robin's with his left. She recognized his discomfort and made a sour face that disappeared quickly inside a false smile.

"Dear Lord," Ernie said, "We give our humble thanks to You tonight, as always, for all the blessings You have bestowed on us, and grant us another day to serve with all Your other faithful servants as messengers of peace on earth to men of good will. A-men. Millie, pass on over some of that bread and cheese."

The prayer gave Charlie a puzzle greater than his pain:

He wondered how any person in his right mind could be

thankful to God for the Dust Bowl and the nation of poverty-stricken nomads it created, yet there were Ernie and Millie, benevolent smiles almost too big for their sunken cheeks, their bodies illustrating hard work and harder living; as joyous as characters out of books by his namesake Charles Dickens.

Later, after they had retreated to the cabin of the Stakebed and he and Robin were sharing what was left of the campfire, he put the question to her.

"God knows," she said, and changed the subject.

They settled for the night in the back of the Stakebed, sharing the warmth of an old shabby quilt, close enough to pool their own body heat against temperature dropping into the twenties. He woke in the middle of the night to her arm around his midsection, her face nesting on his shoulder, her breath warm on his face, her sensuous mouth near enough to capture with his own. She saw he was awake and closed the distance; a lingering kiss that stirred them both to maneuver inside the privacy of the quilt, suppressing any noises that might wake up Ernie and Millie.

Her grin of satisfaction when they were finished spoke miles. He answered Robin with one of his own, not entirely meant. There had been an early moment when he erased her body from his mind, substituting images of Polly, and struggled to keep from shouting Polly's name.

Robin said, "I don't remember the last time I had it so good, even though it wasn't my idea, that awful Luke Doolin deep into his shine and caring for me more'n a damn hoot and a holler than he ever gave my way when he was sober. How was it for you, city boy? I don't get to hear it so often from anyone that hearing it now from you wouldn't be an act of kindness."

"Do you even have to ask?" Charlie said, pushing out the grin again, as far as he could. Robin broke into tears, gushing like a broken fire hydrant. It made Charlie feel like a louse. This was, after all, the woman who had helped save him from the murderous bedsheets.

He thought, maybe, give Robin another pump, a deserved and gentlemanly act of kindness, but was stopped by her saying, "Why it makes me hurt real bad all over for what I have to do next to you." She indicated his wounded arm. "The tourniquet, it can't be there forever, especially not with you carrying the bullet inside you."

"What do you mean?"

"We don't get the bullet out, you're looking at infection, gangrene setting in, getting bad enough to cost you your arm and probably even your life. The answer's get that bullet out soon as possible, before it's too late."

"So I need a hospital."

"You see any hospital around?" She checked over her shoulders. "I don't. Besides, you think any doctor or hospital's ripe to help us through any emergency looking the way we do? If we were any lower on the ladder, we'd be halfway to China." She shrugged and turned her palms to the sky. "Best you can get these circumstances is me."

"You're going to take out the bullet?"

"With some help from Mr. and Mrs. Keyes, they're up for it."

"And you know what you're doing?"

"Done it more times than you can shake a stick at, when my kin and our neighbors were making and running shine. The law any better with their weapons than they were at catching my people, I'd-a had hardly no practice at all."

Robin prepared Charlie for his truck-bed surgery with a liberal dose of sour mash from Ernie Keyes's dented metal canteen, reserving an equal amount for use in sterilizing the wound before and after she'd removed the bullet. She plugged his mouth with a foul-tasting wad of coarse cotton fabric ripped from one of Millie's two spare summer dresses, sour mashed Charlie's left arm and—with Ernie and Millie holding him down—cut into Charlie's skin with the largest blade of the Boy Scout knife Ernie sterilized with wooden matches. Blood spilled out as Robin stretched the skin wide enough for her to reach inside the opening and probe for the resident bullet with her thumb and two fingers, indifferent to Charlie's pain-infused eyes and muffled cries before he passed out.

He wasn't sure when he lost consciousness, but thought it was around the time he began wondering about Chet Mosby's wife, now widow, Sammi Jo, and their four kids, wondering if his vision of them being spirited to safety while Chet was being beaten to death by the bedsheets was something he saw or was inventing now. He prayed they were safe, that he wouldn't have to carry the burden of responsibility for Chet's death for the rest of his life.

Chet died saving me, he told Polly, who'd sprung out from somewhere to cheer him up, forgive him for whatever it was that had fractured their relationship, only to be shoved aside by Sarah Darling, who ordered the spotlight turned on her while she insisted he stay with her, not Polly. *For what?* Charlie screamed at her. *So you can shatter my dreams all over again by telling me Max Moonglow will not be making* Showdown at Shadow Creek?

It hurt, oh, how it hurt, but there was balm in his fresh idea for a different kind of screenplay, one he'd fashion around the army of displaced Dust Bowl survivors battling cruelty and wanton oppression while pursuing their dreams of a new and better life. No, no, no. What was he thinking? What was he drinking? The Dust Bowl? Okies? Arkies? Hoovervilles? Far too downbeat, far too depressing to make the leap from script to silver screen, where Happily Ever After is what sells tickets and

the truth is always trumped by make-believe. *That's reality,
Charlie, so wake up to it,* he told himself, *wake up to Robin telling
you,* "We got the bullet out, stitched you up, and you'll be good
as new in no time, Charlie."

"—as good as new in no time, Charlie."

He was conscious, and she was there—Robin—slowly emerg-
ing in focus, Ernie and Millie angled behind her, all three looking anxious for some sign of recognition from him. "See?" she
said, leaning over to give him a closer look at the bullet she held
between her bloodstained thumb and index finger.

He wanted to thank her, but he couldn't make himself speak
past the layers of pain that had outlasted Ernie's sour mash and
the operation. His mouth was broken. Any thanks would have
to wait. All he wanted now was to sleep. For as long as it took
the terrible hurt to go away.

Charlie woke to the distant howl of coyotes and dogs running
wild in the unsettled wasteland. The heat of the day had given
way to the heat of Robin's plush body pushing against him, her
melancholy brown eyes illuminated by a full moon dodging in
and out of thick cotton-candy clouds floating in the night sky.

Sadness tilted at the corners of her mouth, asking, "How are
you?" like she already knew the answer and dreaded hearing it
from him.

Unsure of his voice, Charlie answered with a smile and finger
printed THANK YOU on her bare shoulder in bold capital letters. She responded increasingly to each, as if the letters were
sending charges of electricity through her body. She pressed a
hand over her mouth to bury sounds that might otherwise rival
the coyotes and wild dogs.

She pulled the quilt all the way over them and asked short of
begging, "Do it with me again, can you, Charlie? One last time?"

He found his voice. "One last time?"

"You and me together, it's not like we're gonna be forever; like we might not even last out another day now that you've been patched up. You'll be aiming to hurry on back to the city, while us others head on over to someplace or other good for getting a dime a day pickin', plantin' or whatever's needed."

There was no reason to lie. "Yes, and that includes trying to find out how I came to be here in the first place, but I'll miss you, Robin, I will, and I'll be forever grateful."

"You do it with me, I'd like for you to mean it, not like you're helping some poor critter out of her misery the way you would some flea-bitten old hound dog begging for a belly rub. That possible, Charlie? It ain't, tell me so, and"—Robin hesitated a moment—"Lord knows, I'm game for us to go and do it anyway. . . . When you can't have honesty in your lovin' and can't settle for no lovin' at all, you take the leftovers and the bread crumbs and use your imagination to fill in the rest."

Mid-afternoon, Charlie parted company with the Keyes and Robin at a T-junction. One road would be taking them inland after work in the orange groves, apple orchards and vineyards of Southern California, while he would follow the railroad tracks along the other road a mile or so to a station siding where the freight trains heading to Los Angeles paused briefly to take on water or hitch additional boxcars.

There were handshakes and hugs all around before Ernie and Millie climbed into the Stakebed cab and Ernie struggled getting the motor to turn over. Robin lingered long enough to share another hug and steal a kiss, telling him, "I'm gonna miss you something awful, city boy."

"You ever get to town, look me up." He recited his address. "That doesn't work for any reason, try the phonebook."

"Hearing about all your stories come to mind for the pictures, I expect you'll be too big and important by then to ever have time for a nobody like me."

"Always time for someone like you, Robin."

She'd always been stingy with her smiles, but broke out a big one now, exposing a mouthful of broken and missing teeth, gums gone sour through neglect. "Then I got a favor to ask, you don't mind. . . . "You know Mr. Clark Gable, the actor? Opportunity ever comes around, I'd surely like to meet up with him."

"Count on me to see what I can do," Charlie said.

Ernie was honking for her.

Robin gave Charlie's makeshift arm sling a last adjustment, turned and hurried over to hop onto the Stakebed, hung over the side rail smiling and waving good-bye. He waved back and waited for the truck to disappear over the horizon line before heading down the road, the smell of wildflowers occasionally lost inside exhaust fumes from the few motor cars that sped past his hitchhiker's thumb, with only the Burma-Shave signs for company.

Lickety-split

It's a beautiful car

Wasn't it?

Burma-Shave

He liked that one, liked even more the one farther down the road—

If you don't know

Whose signs these are

You can't have traveled

Very far!—

Where he shouted out the refrain—*Burma-Shave!*—before he reached the post, as if the answer would get him a prize on "Professor Quiz" or "Uncle Jim's Question Bee," the two radio quiz programs sponsored by George Washington Coffee. And, boy, oh, boy, what he wouldn't give for a cup of steaming hot java right now.

Charlie was about two hundred yards from the station when he saw a freight train inching from the siding onto the main track in slow motion, wheels grinding and grunting, steam hissing out from under the engine, the engineer leaning out from the cabin, yanking the whistle chain to warn he was under way.

Charlie picked up speed, anxious to hop an open boxcar or flatbed before the train got beyond his reach, but stumbled to a halt when he heard clanging noises and saw they were being made by the Billy clubs a pair of railroad bulls were pounding on cars as they passed by, looking to scare out any hoboes.

What to do now?

Take his chances, risk slipping past the bulls and boarding a car?

Stake out and hop the next train, however long the wait, hoping the bulls would be gone by then?

Safety first. That made more sense, but he shuddered at the possibility of having to spend another night out here in the middle of nowhere, this time without Ernie or Millie or, especially, Robin for company.

What the hell.

The bulls were closing in on the rear cars.

Charlie began racing in the opposite direction, toward the head of the train, running parallel to the tracks, then at a diagonal, aiming for an open-top car about three back from the engine. The train was picking up speed faster than his legs were taking him there. His lungs were near bursting. No way he could make the last ten yards and grab on to handrail. There was an empty platform car three cars farther back. He still had a chance to catch that one if his body didn't break down first.

This wasn't the movies.

He was no Douglas Fairbanks, his boyhood idol.

His legs gave out.

The race was over.

The train had won.

He slumped forward, supporting his weight with the hand of his good arm clamped to his knee, fighting to catch his breath, and watched the freight train fly down the track, unaware he was about to be joined by the two railroad bulls until the crunch of loose gravel under their metal-toed military boots signaled their arrival.

They were twin brutes in their thirties, big and beefy, six-feet-something, their no-nonsense black marble eyes staring down at him over misshapen noses, one busted in two or three places, the other shattered almost out of existence. Thick five-o'clock shadows that could do with some Burma-Shave.

The heavier one by about thirty or forty pounds said, "Miss your train, my friend?"

"Yes, sir," Charlie said, sensing no lie would work. They already knew better and had him marked as a candidate for their Billy clubs.

"Whaddaya know, Pud? We caught ourselves an honest fish for a change."

Pud made one of those *so what?* faces. "See you got your wing in a sling," he said, in a matching sandpaper tenor. "You caught your train and we caught you, by now you would have your ass in a sling, compliments of Sparky and me."

"So, I'm not breaking any law, that right?"

"As rain, only you notice it ain't raining right now, that right, Sparky?"

"As rain, Pud," he said, and shared a hyena's laugh with his partner. "In fact, my friend, you are trespassing on railroad property, punishable by a fine or jail time or both, depending on Judge Truby's mood when we bring you up in front of him."

"His mood?" Charlie said.

"He starts off the morning with a good bowel movement, you could get off with a slap on the wrist. His digestion acting up, it's usually anywhere from three to thirty days in the hoosegow."

"Don't remember the last time the judge had a good bowel movement," Pud said.

"And God forbid if it's a day when his lumbago's acting up. That's a certain thirty days and a fifty-dollar fine, the least," Sparky said.

"Fellows, isn't there some other way to settle this, maybe—"

"Hold it there!" Sparky narrowed his eyes and spit out the words: "You looking to bribe us, my friend?"

"No, no, no. Absolutely not."

"Shame," Pud said, easing into a grin. "Sparky and me, we're always fair game for trying to ease the burdens of Judge Truby and the court."

"Then yes, absolutely yes," Charlie said. "How much would it take to forget I was ever here?"

Pud said, "Hear that, Sparky? Our friend's talking like he got himself a pot o' gold buried somewhere."

"What's a train tramp like you got to offer?" Sparky said. "You look and smell like death warmed over. Any bucks to spare, you'd be traveling on a passenger ticket, not out here haunting a freight yard."

"Help me get back to Los Angeles and you'll see. You won't regret it."

"What's back in Los Angeles?"

"A swell reward from someone who's been looking for me since I disappeared." It wasn't exactly the truth, but it might be.

Pud and Sparky exchanged quizzical expressions and pressed Charlie to explain.

He gave them an abbreviated *March of Time* newsreel tour,

beginning with Sarah bringing him the rotten. news about *Showdown at Shadow Creek* at her place in Benedict Canyon. Getting drunk with her and Mad Dog, then waking up in Hemet, no idea how he got there. Hopping the freight and riding the rails until Nance and Kenyon put an end to that. The Hooverville, the Hollimans, the invasion of the bedsheet brigade and his narrow escape from death, thanks to Chet Mosby. Ernie and Millie Keyes. Robin, and—

"Now you fellows," Charlie said.

"You sure packed a lot of lifetime into a few days," Sparky said, shaking his head in awe, "but tell me something else—this Sarah Darling you told us about, she really the movie star?"

"One and the same."

"And the first since Harlow hot enough to set my gonads on fire," Pud said.

"If your movie's deader'n a doornail, why would she even want to get you hurrying back home to her or pay us a reward for delivering you safe and sound?"

Pud rolled his eyes heavenward. "To set his gonads on fire, you damn fool. Ain't that so, my friend?"

"They're heating up already," Charlie said.

Sparky inclined his head and studied Charlie from the corners of his eyes. "Well, let's us go and check up on that," he said. "C'mon."

With Pud bringing up the rear, Charlie trailed Sparky about a quarter mile inland to a one-room wood frame shack sparsely furnished with bunk beds, a coal-burning potbelly stove, an upright two-door ice box, a scarred kitchen table and two mismatched chairs, and a slab of wood resting on sawhorses that served as a desk.

Sparky pointed him to the chairs, stepped over to the desk, put down his Billy club, and plowed aside stacks of paperwork to get at the phone.

"What's her number?" he said, as Pud stepped in hugging the small pit bull that had been stretched out asleep by the door and sprang up when they reached the porch, barking with all the ferocity of a rusty hinge after Pud flashed him some sort of hand signal.

"Brutus, he says he missed us," Pud said, stroking the dog. "I told Brutus we missed him, too, didn't I, Brutus, you darling boy?" Brutus gave an affirmative hum that turned into a nasty growl when he cast his inquisitive eyes on Charlie. "Sparky, you get Sarah Darling on the phone, you be sure and tell her I'm her A-number-one fan."

"More important things than that to put to her," Sparky said.

Pud turned to Charlie with a resigned expression. "What else would you expect of someone thinks it's Mae West ever going to tell him to go on up and see her sometime?"

Sparky dialed the number of Sarah's Benedict Canyon house and waited out four rings before he got an answer.

He listened intently and, without a word, hung up.

Reached for his Billy club.

Told Charlie, "That was an operator come on telling me there's no such number as the number I dialed. . . . What's your game, my friend?"

Brutus, sensing the change in atmosphere, aimed a series of angry barks at Charlie and tried to struggle free of Pud. "Calm down, boy, calm down," Pud said.

Charlie gripped the edges of his chair, wondering who was more dangerous, Brutus or Sparky, who said, "You got an answer for me?"

The best he could do was to urge Sparky to try the number again.

Sparky dialed.

Listened.

Hung up and shook his head.

"Looks like we'll be giving you a taste of our own reward before hauling your sorry ass over to Judge Truby," he said.

"Once more," Charlie said. "Please. Let me try it."

He started up from the chair reciting the number.

Brutus roared and bared his teeth. Pud released his hold. The pit bull leaped onto the concrete floor, intent on attacking Charlie before Sparky two-fingered a whistle that caused him to quit into a sitting position.

"Brutus, stay," Sparky commanded. He cocked an eye at Charlie. "That wasn't the phone number you gave me before," he said, reciting the number he'd been dialing. He had transposed the second and third numerals.

Charlie wasn't about to correct him. "Sorry, my mistake," he said.

"Let's us hope the third time's the charm for you," Sparky said, dialing the number. He counted aloud the rings, gave Charlie a grim look after passing four and was moving to hang up after announcing, "Six," when he hastily returned the phone to his ear, and—

"Hello?" Sparky said. "This the residence of Sarah Darling?" He gave Charlie a smile and a thumbs-up. "Doesn't matter who's calling. Calling about Charlie Dickens. . . . Not *for* him—*about* him. . . . What about him? We got him here, that's what about him, and we were thinking you might like to buy Charlie back. . . . You heard it right, *buy* him back. . . . Kidnapped? Yeah, you could say that, only I'm thinking it's more like paying a reward for finding him. . . . Lemme put it to you this way—we know how much Charlie is worth to us and, for his sake, we hope he's worth the same to you. . . . Whaddaya think happens, he's not? I gotta spell it out for you?"

CHAPTER 18

Mad Dog told Sarah about the call from Charlie's kidnapper.

"What else? How'd you leave it?" she said.

"I said he should call when you're here, that all's I could do was replay the message when you got home. He wasn't happy about that, started giving me a load of lip, so I said for him to go ahead and keep Charlie for all I gave a wooden nickel and hung up."

"I bet that showed him more moxie than he was used to. How different was his tune when he called you back?"

"He didn't. He hasn't. I been worrying myself sick ever since that maybe I put the kibosh on Charlie with that hard-nosed SOB."

"This is not good, Mad Dog, not good at all." Sarah kicked off her heels and sank onto the sofa. "I go and steer his dumb script back into production, because I still can use him as the patsy for Max's death, and Charlie goes and does this to me."

"The nerve of him," Mad Dog said. He plopped down beside her and reached for his half-finished Steinie bottle of Schlitz on the end table next to the phone. Took a deep swallow and wiped his mouth with the back of his hand. Passed off the bottle to Sarah.

"You mocking me, Mad Dog?"

"Me and the kid, we always got along just fine and dandy," he said, avoiding the question. "I blame anybody, I blame myself for him getting heisted, seeing it was me who dropped Charlie in Hemet in the first place, then couldn't find him."

"Losing him, that was clumsy, definitely not like the Mad Dog I trust with my life." She drained the bottle and tossed it at him. "Any more where that came from?"

"Be back before you know I'm gone," he said, rising.

The phone rang while he was out of the den.

Sarah leaped for the receiver and shouted her name into the mouthpiece.

The gravel-pit voice that Mad Dog had described said, "You know who this is?"

"No."

"But you know what it's about?"

"Yes. How is he? How's Charlie?"

"Except for a shot he took in the arm, no problems. He sends his regards."

"Why'd you go and do that—shoot Charlie in the arm? Just because you got a little guff from my guy here when you called before?"

"My skin's thicker than that. Charlie said it was some guy dressed like the Ku Klux Klan, and this not even close to being Halloween. World's full of nut jobs, you know?"

"Put Charlie on the phone. I need to hear him tell me he's fine."

"First I need to know from you we're on the same wavelength."

"We will be after I hear from Charlie."

"Lady, don't you understand who's in charge here?"

Sarah hung up.

At once regretted the move and snatched the receiver.

Too late.

A dial tone.

Mad Dog returned with the beers.

She grabbed a bottle and had it half gone before he'd settled back down. "I just did something stupid," she said, and told him.

He pulled his mouth into a grin. "He called back once, he'll call back again. Count on it."

"What makes you so sure?"

"What happened with me in the long ago." He nodded confirmation with himself. "The boys come around wanting me to toss a match, me favored five-to-one, a shot at the championship riding on the outcome. Make it worth my while, they said. I told 'em back how my reputation was worth a lot more'n any while they cared to shell out for and, besides, no one or nothing was gonna cheat me out-a my chance at the championship. A couple or three days later they caught me on the phone, asked if I'd thought over their offer. I gave them the old skidoo and hung up. They called back, warning me what could happen I still refused to go along." He zipped a finger across his bull neck. "Hear what I'm explaining? They always call back, they got bread riding on it. Always."

"You're talking about your match with Iron Mike Pendleton?"

"That one, yeah."

"I remember you telling me you won, took him in straight falls, but you never said anything about any championship match after that."

"Because one never came off." He took his finger to his throat again. "They killed me before it could happen," Mad Dog said, and stretched a thunderclap of laughter across the room.

The phone rang.

"See? What'd I tell you?" he said.

"They want two hundred and fifty bucks," Charlie said. He was on the line after the caller verified it was Sarah's number they'd reached again. "They said that's how much they got when they returned Gypsy Rose."

"The stripper?"

"Somebody's pet cat. A Persian."

"Enough," the caller said from the background. "Gimme that phone." Now he was telling Sarah, "We're only asking a fair price. Good enough for Gypsy Rose, good enough for Charlie, don't you think so?"

"How about a hundred?" Sarah said. "Gypsy Rose was named for a star. He's only a screenwriter."

They haggled for a few minutes, the caller reluctant to lower his asking price until Sarah threatened to quit negotiating and hang up again. "Okay, okay, okay. A pair of Ben Franklins, two hundred smackers, but first my partner needs his say."

"Hello, Sarah? Miss Darling?" The voice not as gruff or demanding as the other guy's; almost timid.

"If you think you can squeeze more money out of me than your friend already has, you got your head on backwards, mister."

"Not that," he said. "I'm your biggest fan, so I wouldn't dream of doing that. I got some demands of my own, though." A breath that sounded like he was trying to swallow the receiver. "I'm demanding you personally deliver the reward money and also bring with you an autographed picture." He emptied his lungs. "Maybe not really a demand. A request is really what it is. Did I say yet how I'm your biggest fan?"

"Sure, but the photo's going to cost you a hundred."

"That's my entire half."

"Your half of Gypsy Rose was a hundred and twenty-five, so you're still ahead of the game. Or maybe we should just forget about the picture."

"No, no, no. Fine. A hundred. But maybe you could also make it out to me, not just your name?"

"For my biggest fan? Sure. Who should I make it out to, the

autograph?"

"Pud. Make it out to Pud."

"What kind of a name is Pud?"

"It's a nickname, really. Short for Puddle, because I always used to like splashing around in rain puddles on rainy days, I was a little kid. Real name's Grover. You can make it out to Grover, if that's what you'd rather."

The other guy erupted in the background again, saying, "Gimme that, damn fool, saying your name like that." A scuffle, and the other guy back on the phone telling her, "Folding green, no checks or funny stuff. You got pencil and paper? I'll tell you how we're gonna do this."

Four hours later, Sarah and Mad Dog were in Chinatown, standing under the dim light of a lamppost by the west gate entrance to Gin Ling Way, Sarah fidgeting nervously in a high-collar alpaca coat, wide-brimmed slouch hat and oversized dark glasses intended to disguise her against recognition by the flow of tourists overrunning the sidewalks, Mad Dog chain-smoking, on guard for someone in the crowd wearing a black derby with a red feather stashed in the hatband.

"How much longer?" she said.

Mad Dog checked his pocket watch. "Twenty minutes late now."

"You know how I hate that, being late." She kipped his cigarette, took a heavy drag and handed it back, released a tunnel of visible off-white smoke into the chilly night air. "I give it another ten minutes before I figure they played me for a fool."

"Then what? We leave?"

She scoffed at the notion. "Of course not. Then we wait another ten minutes."

"Good to see you haven't lost your sense of humor."

"They want their money. I need our Charlie."

"Excuse, missus lady." The kid tugging at Sarah's coat couldn't be more than seven or eight. Chinese. Wearing a one-piece silk mandarin gown like someone out of *The Good Earth*, his toothsome smile all aglow. "You a movie star, missus lady?" His pronounced accent straight out of a Charlie Chan movie.

"Scat, little boy, no autographs," Sarah said, too on edge to make nice.

The kid was undeterred. "If you a movie star, you supposed to see this, what I'm showing you." He revealed the black derby with a red feather in the hatband he had been holding behind his back. "So, you a movie star, missus, like Missus Anna May Wong and Missus Soo Yong?"

Mad Dog answered for her. "Yes, she is, sonny."

"And she got the stuff with her?"

"What stuff?"

"I don't know what stuff, only to ask. Did you, missus?"

"She did," Mad Dog said.

"Oke doke, then. You come with me to where I got take you." He skipped off, gesturing them to follow.

Sarah said, "I don't know about this."

"Of course, you do," Mad Dog said. "And a little child shall lead them?"

They followed the boy about a mile, on poorly lit streets and alleys that took them east of Alameda Street, past a confluence of railroad tracks to the edge of a construction site where a new Union Station was nearing completion on six acres of Old Chinatown that had been acquired by railroad interests. Most of the restaurants, shops and business offices had moved to New Chinatown, along with a bean-cake factory, but lost to what was widely heralded as civic progress were an opera house, a self-contained phone exchange and three temples that once served a population of more than three thousand landed Chinese.

"You got to stay right here," the boy said when they reached an intersection of abandoned commercial storefronts, their doors and display windows boarded up against vandalism, other windows shattered behind iron pull gates, the only light from a crescent moon in an otherwise coal-black sky. "You don't go nowhere," he said, did a dervish whirl and disappeared into an alley, leaving them to the uncertainty of their empty surroundings, not so much as a stray dog prowling the sidewalks and no cars except for one parked at an awkward angle across the way that looked as abandoned as they were.

The sudden bursts of air whistle signaling the arrival of a train at the Union terminal across the construction zone startled Sarah. Mad Dog gave her a wave meant to calm her. She quit fidgeting, answered him with a smile, and hugged herself as a defense against a cold breeze sweeping down the street.

"Hey!" The kid was motioning for them to join him at the alley entrance. "Come on and follow me to where I go," he said, retreating into the alley.

Sarah sent Mad Dog a questioning look. He pulled back his jacket to show her the .45 he was packing in a shoulder holster, patted the weapon like a faithful pet, and issued a reassuring grin, gripped her by the elbow and charged after the kid.

After about a hundred yards, the kid disappeared into a doorway. Was waiting for them when they reached him. Pointed up a narrow flight of stairs. "Door up there. Knock twice, like this." He rapped out four notes on the sidewall. "Show 'em hat so they know it you." He handed the derby to Mad Dog and scooted away, his steps echoing on the pitted concrete until they faded along with the rest of him inside the dark shadows of the alley.

"What do you think?" Sarah said.

Mad Dog tilted the derby on his bald head and romanced the jacket bulge over his shoulder holster. "I think we go up there and knock twice," he said, easing her behind him. "Me first."

CHAPTER 19

The metal door at the top of the stairs was out of place in a building that appeared likely to collapse around it any minute. Mad Dog knuckled the code and stood inspection after a peephole slid open. It closed within seconds, and the door was swung open by an Oriental in his early twenties, who had five inches and fifty million pounds on Mad Dog, wearing a king-sized version of the mandarin gown the kid had on.

"Good evening, sir, ma'am. Welcome. Mr. Fong will be with you in a moment," he said, expressionless, his mouth a mine-field of polished gold, his voice bearing little trace of an accent and better suited to a midget.

He stepped aside and motioned them in, quick to close the door behind them.

An odor slight and barely noticeable on the climb up the stairs was stronger now and stung Sarah's nostrils. The smell was familiar, from her Sadie days. Mad Dog showed her he also was welcoming an old acquaintance.

A minute passed, then another, before an Oriental in an elegant tuxedo rounded a corner at the rear end of the corridor and hurried toward them, arms extended like he was preparing to embrace family members. A benign smile playing on his handsome, early-thirties face under a slick, midnight-black pompadour. Wire-framed eyeglasses a half inch thick.

He pulled up alongside the doorman, clasped his hands below his neatly trimmed goatee, and paying the barest attention to

Mad Dog, said, "I couldn't believe my ears when they told me to expect Sarah Darling, but it certainly is you under that disguise. My eyes never deceive me." He bowed gracefully. "Welcome to my humble business establishment, Miss Darling, and you, too, sir."

"You look familiar," Sarah said.

"All Chinamen look alike," he said, and gave her a wink. "Better, maybe, you saw me in *The Good Earth* or *The Adventures of Marco Polo*? *Shanghai Express,* maybe? I won't mention my appearances in those outrageous Mr. Motos or Charlie Chans, but, oh, there, now I've gone and done it, so much more the shame."

"You're an actor?"

"In a manner of speaking, but not really and not often. Certain of my clients here at my Pleasure Garden from time to time reward the special favors I extend them with a small role in their current production. Maybe a line or two, uncredited, but I am a card-carrying member of the Screen Actors Guild." He reached for his wallet. "I'll show you."

Sarah held him off with a palm. "Don't bother. That's not why I'm here."

"Oh, yes, why you're here, the fortuitous circumstance that inspired this meeting. I believe you have something for me, Miss Darling?"

She drew an envelope from her outsized Cartier handbag, a gift years ago from a Poverty Row producer anxious to show his appreciation for her uninhibited performance during their weekend romp in a garden cottage at San Ysidro Ranch.

"The money's all there," she said.

"And a signed photograph, which I was led to understand is part of the arrangement you entered into? Ah, yes, so I see, here—and a lovely photo indeed, beautifully inscribed. I wouldn't mind having one like it for the wall of my herbal shop in New Chinatown."

Mad Dog said, "Right now I believe you have something to give Miss Darling in exchange."

"Of course," Mr. Fong said. "You have my sincere apologies for delaying our little transaction. I can understand how anxious you are to be reunited with your friend. If you'll please to kindly follow me."

He led Sarah and Mad Dog down the corridor and into a cavernous room stuffed with curtained wooden bunks on both sides of a central aisle, the closeted air saturated with the sweet, pungent smell of opium thick enough to see and taste. Female attendants wearing skimpy cheongsam robes monitored the room, ministering to the needs of two dozen or more reclining patrons clutching long pipes over oil lamps that vaporized the opium so it could be inhaled and transport them to another world.

"I apologize if you and your gentleman friend are shocked by what you see, Miss Darling."

"Don't bother," she said. "It's old hat to me."

"That's what I was once led to believe," Mr. Fong said, "or I certainly would have been more discreet in conducting this business for my two friends there." He pointed to one of the curtained nooks.

Mad Dog stepped over and pulled back the curtain.

The two men facing one another on a shared bunk were too lost inside their pipe dreams to recognize they had visitors.

"Who are these crumbs?" Mad Dog said.

"They work for the railroad and have patronized my modest operation for many years now, often sending me other customers, so I couldn't very well refuse them their request to serve on their behalf with Miss Darling while they took pleasure in relaxation, could I, now?"

"My friend," Sarah said. "How about let's get to him? Where is he?"

"Yes, of course. Across the way, behind that curtain."

She crossed over and opened the curtain, reared back at the sight of Charlie.

He was propped upright against a bunk post, inanimate, expressionless, bloodshot eyes trapped in a blind stare, lost inside an opium wilderness.

"Jeez-o, he's bonkers."

"Not as my friends intended for your friend to be," Mr. Fong said. "He was meant to wait upstairs in my office or, perhaps, choose a suitable companion from among one of the lovely ladies in my employ who reside on the floor above us."

"Charlie, can you hear me?" Sarah said, leaning over him. "It's Sarah, Charlie, and Mad Dog's with me. We come to take you home." No reaction. She backed away, repelled by the stink from his dirt-infested body and clothing.

Mr. Fong said, "My two friends and I cautioned him against experimenting, but he was excited by the idea of taking his firsthand experience and making it into a screenplay, like *I Am a Fugitive from a Chain Gang*, he said, only it would be *I Am a Fugitive from an Opium Den*. Perhaps with a modest part for me."

"Mad Dog, let's get him out of here," Sarah said, bothered by how the opium was beginning to intrude on her. Old habits die hard. She wasn't about to get suckered back into a relationship with Auntie Emma. It came close to killing her once. Once was enough.

Mad Dog said, "We taxied down to New Chinatown, Mr. Fong. How's about you kindly ordering up a cab to get us away from here?"

"I don't think so," Mr. Fong said.

"Why's that?" Mad Dog said, his hand inching inside his

jacket after the .45.

"I have my car and driver waiting outside," Mr. Fong said, hands clasped and bowing slightly, his magnified eyes dancing between them. "He knows to take you to wherever you specify. My sincere compliments, to compensate for any inconvenience caused you by my friends."

The doorman and another of Mr. Fong's overgrown bruisers lifted Charlie off the bunk, gripped him by his underarms and struggled steering him from the den to the stairs, Charlie indifferent to the world around him, his legs dragging like an unstrung marionette.

The bruiser took the lead in angling them down the narrow stairway, one hand on the rail and the other around Charlie's waist, the doorman matching him one step at a time the first few steps until a shoe somehow wedged between Charlie's useless feet.

He lurched forward, out of control, taking Charlie and the bruiser with him.

The bruiser landed on his back, Charlie on top of him, the doorman completing the sandwich.

"Clumsy oafs," Mr. Fong shouted after them. "I warned you after the last time what the consequences would be if this happened again." He gripped the rail and hurried down.

Sarah and Mad Dog, paralyzed momentarily beyond shouts of alarm, made it safely downstairs and pried the doorman off Charlie, still as content as a corpse.

The bruiser had hit his head on the concrete flooring and was unconscious.

Mr. Fong quickstepped to the door, yanked it open and called for his driver. "Help my guests get their friend into the car," he said.

The doorman pulled himself up and joined Mad Dog and

the driver in maneuvering Charlie to Mr. Fong's cherry-red Cadillac Fleetwood, parked outside the Pleasure Garden.

"That's far enough, gents." The command belonged to one of three Chinese kids in their teens who had stepped out of the alley shadows aiming automatic pistols, their grim expressions meant to underline they meant business. "Keys in the car?"

"Yes," the driver said, barely able to get out the word.

"Idiot," Mr. Fong said, giving a backhand to the driver's shoulder. "You, boy, do you know who I am?"

"Do you know who I am?"

"No."

"Then we're even," the trio's spokesman said. His buddies squealed with laughter.

Mr. Fong didn't share their amusement. He studied their faces with resignation.

The spokesman said, "None of you move, none of you do nothing stupid and none of you going to get shot dead." He snapped his fingers.

The kid nearest the Cad double-timed over, climbed behind the wheel and triggered the ignition. The car purred like a contented kitten. The kid backed up parallel to the alley. The other kid rushed over and opened both doors on the passenger side before hopping into the backseat. He closed the door, rolled down the window, kept his gun aimed at Mr. Fong and the others while the spokesman angled onto the front seat and shut his door.

The Cad roared off and disappeared around a corner.

Mr. Fong shook his head. "If you ever wondered why some boys never grow up to be men, now you know the answer," he said.

"Meaning what exactly?" Mad Dog said.

"Meaning my brand-new Cadillac automobile is well known in our community," he said, "so those foolish boys won't be getting too far, most definitely not far enough away to escape punishment for their ill-advised prank." He turned to Sarah. "My sincere apologies, Miss Darling. It appears I will be obliged to order you a taxi cab."

"And forget we were ever here," she said.

He nodded agreement. "Of course, Miss Darling. Discretion in all things has been and remains the cornerstone of my modest success in a most challenging business."

An hour later she and Mad Dog had Charlie back at the Benedict Canyon house and were rewarding the cabbie with a tip double the meter for helping them haul him inside and stretched out on the living-room sofa.

"What do we say when he's back among the living?" Mad Dog said.

Sarah thought about it. "For openers, that he smells worse than a fart factory. We save the good stuff for later."

CHAPTER 20

Charlie couldn't tell what ached more, his head or his body—a migraine to end all migraines, muscles begging for absolution—in the first minutes after finding himself back at Sarah's place in Benedict Canyon, not the opium den in Chinatown, no memory of the time in between.

He eased into a sitting position on the couch, sat stone-statue still until a numbing dizziness passed, then eased onto his feet and made a slow, stiff-kneed march toward the hum of conversation coming from the veranda.

Sarah and Mad Dog turned to greet him as he stepped outside into the garden-fresh air that was pleasant, but didn't approach the saintly, transporting smell he'd tested at Mr. Fong's Pleasure Palace.

"Come join us, sleepy head," she said, pointing him to a chair at the glass-topped table covered with the remains of a late communal lunch, tuna fish and cucumber sandwiches on white bread shorn of crust, an assortment of fresh vegetables, a bowl of chocolate chip and sugar cookies, and a Tiffany pot of coffee.

Mad Dog said, "You had us scared for you, Charlie. What's the story?"

Charlie tested the pot for warmth, poured himself a cup and emptied it by half in a giant swallow, nodded approvingly and knocked back the other half; then, poured himself a refill and emptied the cup with equal greed.

"I'm hoping you can tell me," he said, reaching for a sugar cookie.

"One minute you're here, the next you disappear without a word," Sarah said. "Next we know, days later, we get a call from kidnappers that sends us racing after you to New Chinatown, where we wait and wait and—nothing. Nobody shows up. You're nowhere to be found. We left fearing the worst for you."

Mad Dog nodded confirmation. "I wake up this morning and there you are on the couch, looking and smelling like a fugitive from a garbage dump," he said. "I phone her pronto with the news, and here we are."

Sarah finished munching a radish and picked at residue trapped between her teeth. "Your turn to fill in the blanks, Charlie. Last we saw of you, you were running up a storm of emotion, boozing it up good, like there was no tomorrow."

"They're my blanks, too," he said. He tore off a corner of a tuna fish sandwich and washed it down with coffee, aimed for a chocolate chip cookie and rinsed his mouth clean with more coffee. "I got the bad news about our movie. I got blind drunk. Next I knew, I was in Riverside County, Hemet, no idea how I got there or how I was getting back."

He explained about the railroad yard, hopping the freight; described his encounter with Sister and Brother, Nance and Kenyon, and how they booted him from the train. He told them about the Hooverville, about Scarlett, Reverend Holliman and the rest of her family, about the Mosbys, how Chet Mosby saved his life and was killed by the bedsheet boys; about Ernie and Millie Keyes and dear, sweet Robin Moon; about the two railroad bulls, Sparky and Pud, trying to cash in on him, catch a nifty reward from Sarah for returning him home.

"Their doing, that pair, how I came to wind up at Mr. Fong's Pleasure Palace over by Old Chinatown, not the new one where you were," Charlie said. "It was an opium den, that Pleasure

Palace, and I asked permission to try some." His bloodshot eyes grew wild with excitement. "I mean, I could write a screenplay based on my firsthand experience. A straight ace of a guy gets kidnapped into an opium den and becomes an addict, for cripe's sake. He escapes. They come after him and—" He paused, perplexed. "I still have to think on it from there."

"Sort of like *I Am a Fugitive from a Chain Gang*?" Sarah said.

"Exactly!" Charlie brightened and shook a victory fist. "I've been calling it *I Am a Fugitive from an Opium Den.*"

"Nice," Mad Dog said, throwing Sarah a look.

Charlie started working on a sugar cookie. "Something else? I was thinking after it's written you could show the script to Mr. Moonglow as being right up his alley for his next picture? The frosting on the cake? Instead of Mr. Fong, it would be Mrs. Fong, and you know without my saying who'll be perfect to say my words."

She knighted him with a Queen Victoria smile. "Except for one problem, Charlie, darling."

"Oh?"

"Max is about to start his next picture?"

"Oh?"

"It's a western, *Sundown in the Shadows.*"

"Huh?"

Mad Dog said, "It's your script, pal. Sarah here got it turned back on at RKO."

"Congratulations, dear boy. You're about to have your first picture made, a Max Moonglow production starring yours truly. Casting is almost finished, except for a few minor parts, and Max is off scouting locations with his key people."

Charlie's eyes clouded over. He brushed at them, too choked up to push out more than a barely audible thank-you, but recaptured his voice after a minute. "Please, tell me again," he said. "Tell me it's not the opium. Tell me I'm not still dreaming."

A week later, the sweet taste of reality had turned sour for Charlie.

"Everyone's shutting me out, like I don't know a hill of beans about *Showdown at Shadow Creek*," he was complaining to Rudy Bundsman over lousy coffee in the casting director's office. "It's like I don't even exist, Mr. Bundsman, you being the one exception."

"Maybe it's because you don't," Rudy said, looking up from the *Academy Players Directory* he had been browsing, pausing to tap an actor's photo and jot down the name of the industry contact listed on a legal-size yellow pad, in precise, microscopic handwriting. He put aside his pencil and closed the directory. "You the producer, Charlie?"

"Of course not."

"The director, maybe?"

"Please, Mr. Bundsman. You know that's also Max Moonglow."

Rudy moved a two-inch stack of file folders closer, rifled after the one he was seeking and displayed it for Charlie. "I know you're not one of the actors been cast, or I would have you in here, so what does that make you? Don't tell me. Let me guess. You must be the writer."

Charlie tilted up his chin and rolled his eyes. "As if you didn't already know."

"Something else I know," Rudy said. He leaned forward, pushed his half-moons tight against his face, and angled a hand against the side of his mouth. "My friend, you don't matter anymore," he said, his stage whisper aiming for the ceiling. "Over and out after you signed your name on the dotted line. The studio got what it needed from you. You became as expendable as a used rubber."

"But it's my picture."

"No. It's your script, but it's RKO's picture. You want more and better? You want a parking space on the lot, instead of the lot outside across Gower? Do something to make a splash in this town and move up the food chain, something like Bobby Wise is doing."

"Who?"

"Bobby, he wants to direct. He's in the sound department right now. Worked on *Top Hat, The Informer, Gay Divorcee,* after starting out as an apprentice on *Of Human Bondage.* Angling to become a film editor. From there, it's an easier leap to directing. Remember the name, Bobby Wise, and where you heard it first."

"All I ever want to do is write for the movies, Mr. Bundsman."

Rudy feigned cheerfulness. "Well, you'll always be welcome to a cup of java here," he said. "What else can I do you for?"

"Maybe you're doing it by just being my friend, Mr. Bundsman."

Rudy's eyes narrowed with suspicion. "Nobody ever drops by just for me to be his friend, so what else? Make with it. I got business needs getting back."

Charlie raised his arms in surrender. "I was never much good at lying."

"So much for any hopes of you ever succeeding in the picture business."

"I have this girlfriend—"

"I take it back."

"She's not only beautiful, she's talented."

"Aren't they all?"

"There's a part she'd be perfect for in *Showdown at Shadow Creek,* but I haven't been able to see Mr. Moonglow and—"

"The grapevine has it you're tight with Max's missus and

she's who helped get the picture onto the production schedule, so why not take it to her to take it to Max to bring to me, or is your beautiful and talented girlfriend someone you'd rather not kiss and tell about with Sarah?"

"Sarah helped about my screenplay and I'm indebted to her, but that's all it's ever been between us," Charlie said, no intention of telling stories out of school—out of the bedroom, actually—that might sully her reputation. Or that he'd tried going to Sarah, but she never had time for him, one excuse after the next, since he'd moved back to his place over by Westlake Park. "Besides, she's always known about Polly and me."

"Sure," Rudy said, not even pretending to believe him. "Polly, that her name?"

"Polly Wilde. She's working across the street on a Hopalong Cassidy."

Rudy's face registered puzzlement. "That's not right, my friend." He scrambled through his stack of files, found and flipped open the one he wanted, and ran his finger down the top sheet. "Not right at all." Tapping the sheet. "The girl's here with us now, working in a new George O'Brien programmer and down for the one after that, a two-picture deal putting in gear a basic seven-year contract."

"Polly Wilde? You're sure?"

"Can't be two actresses using the same name. Against Screen Actors Guild rules. She's also being talked about for the female lead in a picture on George Stevens's slate, a western done up in Indian drag, *Gunga Din*, with Cary Grant, Vic McLaglen and Doug Fairbanks, Jr., heading the cast. My money's on Joan Fontaine, Olivia de Havilland's kid sister, who's been building quite a rep for herself." He slid the file across the desk. "Have a look-see for yourself."

A small head shot was stapled to the top sheet. It was Polly. Charlie pushed out a sigh of regret. "She would've been so damn perfect playing the editor of the *Shadow Creek Sentinel.*"

Rudy hid a snicker behind his palm. "My friend, that piece of casting would never have happened, even if your Polly Wilde were Garbo herself." He found the *Showdown at Shadow Creek* file and the page he was after. "Here you go, here's your newspaper editor. Check her out."

"Dixie Leeds, huh? She looks more like a town hooker than a newspaper editor. I don't see what made you cast her in the role."

"Not what, my friend—who."

"Huh?"

"Max Moonglow himself. Sat where you're sitting and ordered me to cast her. That made Miss Leeds absolutely perfect for the part, you know what I mean? Second-guessing the Max Moonglows of the business buys you a one-way ticket to the breadline."

"You think there's something going on between them, Mr. Bundsman?"

"I'm not one to gossip," Rudy said. "You want to know bad enough, ask Max, not me."

The O'Brien unit was filming on the outdoor western street at "40 Acres," the old DeMille studio in Culver City that RKO had acquired about ten years ago and used most notably for the jungle scenes in *King Kong.* In fact, it was only about twenty-nine acres of land and a large chunk of that now belonged to David O. Selznick, who would be shooting scenes there for his forthcoming production of *Gone with the Wind.*

As a parting favor, Rudy had called ahead and cleared Charlie for a drive-on.

The trip west from the studio took him about half an hour along Venice Boulevard, paralleling electric trolley line tracks running along the middle of the wide boulevard from downtown to the beach. He veered left at the Culver Boulevard intersection and left again onto Ince Boulevard until he reached Gate Two of "40 Acres."

A uniformed guard with Gable's mustache and outsized ears found his name on the visitors list and directed Charlie to a dirt parking lot halfway between the Old New York and Old West streets. The New York set stood silent and empty, unlike the Old West set, where the crews seemed to be racing against a fleet of ominous rain-barrel clouds drifting in from the Pacific, repositioning and adjusting lights and microphones outside the corner saloon Charlie recognized from a thousand movies.

George O'Brien was engaged in spirited conversation over by the camera dolly with two men Charlie took to be the director and the cameraman. His was the only familiar face. A dozen or so costumed townspeople were massed by the horse pen about a hundred yards away, killing time by reading, playing gin or solitaire, playing chess or checkers; no Polly among them.

Charlie asked around after her without success until he tried a woman studiously manicuring her nails at the bank of makeup tables, who directed him to a private dressing room near soundstages eleven and twelve. "Joe Kennedy had it built exclusively for Gloria Swanson while he was running things around here," she said, sounding like it was a story she enjoyed sharing. "Made it easier for them to do the nasty regular-like and away from prying eyes, but nobody was ever fooled."

"It's unlocked, come on in," Polly said. She lost the smile in her voice when she saw it was him. "You're not who I was expecting," she said. "Please leave."

"Not until I get some answers," he said. He closed and locked the door behind him and settled on the sofa across from the vanity table where she was studying her face in the three-way mirror; except for the boots, her cowgirl costume hidden under a shaggy pink bathrobe.

"Make it snappy, then," she said, her eyes never quite connecting with his.

"I've been calling you, but only get the answering service. I leave messages. You don't call me back. I've dropped by your place at all different times. You're never there. I went over to the Contento's stand at the Farmers Market and they told me you quit. They made it sound like you were no longer there when I went over to Raleigh and got nowhere there, not for the first time and not only once."

"Because I'm here now, Charlie, and as for the rest of it— I've started a new chapter in my life and it doesn't include you. I know about *Showdown at Shadow Creek*, so what's the beef? You're doing fine without me. Now, please leave. Go. Good-bye and good luck."

"Now I get it," he said, palm-whacking the side of his head. "You're mad because you didn't get a role in the picture and you're making it my fault. Will it make a difference to hear I was trying to get you cast in an important role when I thought you were still over at Raleigh doing the Cassidy and this could be your big breakthrough at RKO?"

"No," she said. "Something wrong with your ears, Charlie? It's over between us, now and forever. I have my big breakthrough at RKO, and I did it without you. I do not need you anymore, Charlie. Can I say it any plainer than that?"

"This isn't the Polly I know talking. The Polly I know would never talk that way."

She wheeled around in the chair and shot him an insincere smile. "The Polly you knew doesn't exist any longer. Maybe she never did."

"I don't believe you."

"Same old Charlie," she said, and turned back to reviewing herself in the three-way mirror, humming a tune he didn't recognize while toying with several stray strands of hair until interrupted by a knock at the door, a half-familiar voice calling her name. "Good-bye, Charlie," she said.

He'd intended to tell her about everything he'd gone through, how she was uppermost in his mind during even the darkest moments, but he recognized this was neither the time nor the place. He blew her a kiss and headed out.

Leo Salmon was waiting to be let in.

He gave Charlie an indifferent glance angling past him to Polly, who bounced up and threw herself into a tight embrace and an open-mouthed kiss that appeared to last forever.

Charlie wandered off convinced she'd staged the kiss for his benefit, but grew less certain as he headed back to town. Halfway there, he changed his mind, reversed direction and aimed for Culver City again. He found street parking with a view of the Ince gate and waited for Polly to exit, determined to trail her home for another go at convincing her they belonged together.

About six-thirty her car pulled out, swung a left and braked to a sudden stop when Leo Salmon came running onto the street waving and shouting for her attention. She cut the motor, stepped out of the car and traded a few minutes of conversation and a brief hug before Salmon helped her back behind the wheel and headed back the studio.

The scene vindicated Charlie's judgment—

No generous embrace—

Hardly a hug at all.

No eternal kiss—

Not even a peck on the cheek.

Hah!

She had staged the dressing-room scene.

She wanted to make him jealous, make him plead for forgiveness before relenting and welcoming him back into her life. He couldn't remember what had driven them apart in the first place, but it didn't matter. He was wise to her game. They'd be together again, that's what mattered.

Boy meets girl.

Boy loses girl.

Boy gets girl back.

A story as old as the motion-picture business itself.

Overflowing with romantic notions, instead of tracking Polly's shadow, Charlie sped off intent upon finding a flower shop. If he was fast enough, she'd get home to find him waiting with an orchid corsage. She had told him once or twice how much she loved orchids. It would be an irresistible peace offering.

He busted the boulevard speed limit, barely braked for stop signs, and got stopped by a traffic cop, who took his sweet time writing him a ticket.

Finding a florist open at this late hour chewed up more time.

It was closing in on eight o'clock when he got to Polly's and cruised past her garage spot behind the apartment building. Her car was there. He circled around and glided into a space across the street. Caught his breath, steeled his nerves and headed for the apartment, clutching the cellophane-wrapped orchid corsage like a life preserver while he climbed the creaking stairway to the second floor and headed for her door at the end of a corridor that smelled of dinners, cigarettes and odors of time that clung to the walls and the threadbare carpeting.

Charlie pasted a smile on his face and rapped a melody on the door.

No answer.

He tried the melody again and this time got a response—

A door latch being thrown, the doorknob turning, the door opening wide enough for him to recognize a shirtless Leo Salmon staring back at him, Polly deeper inside the room wearing a skimpy dressing gown and a surprised look that instantly dared him to challenge what he saw.

Charlie fled.

Used the back stairway down.

Tossed the orchid corsage into a garbage can.

Halfway to his car spotted Leo Salmon's Hudson.

Headed for it after pulling a tire iron from his trunk. Used the tire iron to smash the windshield of the Hudson. Crack both the headlights. Cave in the driver-side door. Letting the world know what he thought about Leo Salmon with every blow.

Residents were coming outside to see who and what was causing the racket.

Charlie quit.

Dashed to his car and took off before any cops arrived.

Feeling good about what he'd done.

No regrets.

Except about Polly.

Wondering what it would take to get her back.

Once home, he flopped into bed and wrestled with the question through the night, woke to a bunch of impossible answers never meant to survive his dreams.

CHAPTER 21

"I've met more than my share of loony writers, but this Charlie Dickens ranks as the worst of them," Leo Salmon said. "Showing up that way, unexpectedly, after you told him it was over between the two of you—he's got me scared for your safety, freckle face."

"Charlie is all noise and confetti, Leo. I'm guessing that finding you here just now, you half-undressed and me like this, is all it took to finally convince him that I've moved on, that you're the new man in my life, lover boy."

"You didn't see the look in his eyes, borrowed from Cagney, like he was about to pop me in the nose again."

"But he didn't. He saw you and he took off."

"What if he does turn up again, only this time I'm not here and you're alone? How do you feel about your nose, or worse?"

"I keep a gun under my pillow and I know how to use it, remember me telling you that?"

"He scares the pants off me."

"He could've done a better job of it," Polly said, giving him a hungry look as she sashayed over and worked at unbuckling his belt. "I think it's time for us to finish what we were starting before we were interrupted, don't you?"

He answered by lifting her into his arms and carrying her into the bedroom.

It was over in a matter of minutes, Leo no better a lover in bed than he'd been the first time, when he didn't add much fun to the Toonerville Fun House.

She'd made all the necessary howls and yowls, begged him for more, poured on flattery that kept his body raining sweat until he let out a gasp-encrusted sigh, rolled off her, posted an angelic smile, and almost at once fell asleep.

Polly threw the blankets over Leo, retreated to the bathroom and made herself a bubble bath. She luxuriated in its strong orchid scent, her find filled with Technicolor visions of the stardom he'd promised her. Why else would she be playing this game with him? Helping her succeed was helping himself, Leo had freely admitted that night at Ocean Park. His generosity began at home, he said.

She could have told him she was playing the same game with him.

She didn't bother.

Men were creatures of confession, where the wisest of women knew how to make silence speak whatever words were necessary to control a situation. She put herself in that category, one of the wisest among the wise. She would be Leo's consort, his willing partner in Hollywood intrigue, until he'd outlived his usefulness to her.

Morning came and so did Leo.

He seemed distracted afterward, as if there were something playing on his mind that he wanted to share with her, but wasn't sure how.

She fed him the old-fashioned country breakfast her mom had taught her to make, fresh orange juice, eggs and pancakes, bacon and ham, blueberry muffins straight from the oven, hot apple pie, always reminding Polly that the way to a man's heart was through his stomach.

It wasn't until the coffee had finished perking and she'd poured him a cup that she backed into the subject, wondering,

"Did I do something wrong, Leo?" The question drew a quizzical expression. "I'm thinking maybe I made the bacon too crisp this time, knowing how you like it, but it wasn't on purpose and I'm sorry."

He gave her a loving look. "The bacon was fine. Everything about breakfast was fine; simply swell. You're swell, too, for caring that much about how I like my bacon."

"Well, it's something else, then. I can feel it about you. Tell me, please, Leo, so I can do better next time."

He weighed her request behind closed eyes. "Here's what," he said, passing a hand over his coffee cup, measuring the steam for heat before taking a cautious sip. "After that business last night with Charlie Dickens, and so what if you have a gun under your pillow, I'm afraid for your safety, freckle face. Truly scared, no matter how brave a front you put up trying to convince me otherwise. What do I have to do or say to convince you to move in with me?"

Polly let the question hang in the air for a minute.

"How about, just ask?" she said.

CHAPTER 22

Barney Rooker gave her one of his wide-eyed little-boy innocent looks, insisting, "It's not like I went and squealed on you to the law, Sadie. Hell, Fong's running an opium den, so he's never gonna be one to go around spilling the beans to anybody about your old habit. Besides, the way you tell it, he was only reacting to something you said."

"He could have just let it slide," Sarah said, "Instead, his eyes lit up like maybe I might want to revisit Dreamland before Mad Dog and I scooped up Charlie Dickens and scrammed. I knew at once the only person in my life he could have heard it from was you, and how do you come to be dredging up yesterday's news?"

"Because the conversation was a million yesterdays ago, while I was shooting one of Naughty Nooky Productions' nudie cutie one-reelers up at Fong's place. He-said-I-said or I-said-he-said. It just happened. That one time and not again, so forget it, Sadie. It's only Chinatown."

She wasn't in a forgetting mood. "Maybe right now Fong is telling somebody who's telling somebody and on and on. It's a fire I don't need at this time in my career, when I got so much else at stake."

"You mean like making another stab at bumping off your husband and pinning the rap on this poor schnook Charlie Dickens?"

"Jeez-o, there you go again, shooting off your mouth. Why

don't you shout it from the rooftop?"

"Because I can't get to the rooftop by myself," Barney said, "but your slightest wish is my command." He spun around in his wheelchair and aimed for the door of his room at New Dawn. Quit at the doorknob. "You coming, or will you settle for my shouting it out the window?"

He had turned little-boy cute. She couldn't resist laughing. He always knew how to diffuse her. She threw up her arms in surrender, stopped pacing the floor and settled on the edge of his bed. He wheeled over to her, popped a Gitanes into his mouth from the pack in his pocket. "Got a light?" he said. "I mean besides the fire burning in those beautiful eyes of yours."

"You really shouldn't," Sarah said, fishing her lighter from her bag. "At your age, it's not good for your health."

"At my age, what is? Lemme know when you come up with something, will ya?" He turned serious. "Not that going after Max again is necessarily good for your health, Sadie. Tell you what—I'll give up smoking if you give up the idea once and for good."

"My mind's made up, angel mine."

His grimace added more wrinkles and furrows to his ghostly complexion. "Oke, I'm listening. Spill the rest of it," he said, and sent a tube of gray smoke sailing to the ceiling.

"We begin filming next week, on location at the Paramount ranch over in the hills between the San Fernando Valley and Malibu. Outdoors, in that canyon area, anything can happen, understand?"

"Help me out."

"Max is going to have an accident, a fatal one, and he's going to disappear, never to be seen again."

"Then what do you need Charlie Dickens for?"

"Charlie's our patsy, our fallback, in case Max gets found before we can disappear him. Everything will point to Charlie, same as last time, only this time there won't be any Willie Frankfurter to mess up the works."

"Mad Dog's good with all of this?"

"He works for me, angel mine."

Sarah watched the doubt rise on Barney's face as he extinguished what was left of his Gitanes on the burn-scarred arm of his wheelchair and deposited the butt into a robe pocket. "I give," she said. "What don't you like about the plan?"

"What plan?"

"What I just explained."

"I don't like the part where your screwball ideas go south and I'm not there to help rescue you, clean up your mess, like in the old days." He went after another Gitanes. "Light me."

Sarah was loitering in the tub, full of self-righteous indignation, defending her plan against Barney's dismissive attitude—treating her like the child she'd stopped being years ago—when she sensed Max's presence. He was in the doorway, his arms laced across his chest, studying her with hungry eyes.

"I was just thinking about you," she said. It wasn't a lie.

"A penny for them," Max said.

"Free of charge," Sarah said. "How I was trapped inside a block of stone until you came along and freed me to become the Sarah Darling I am today."

His smile outshone hers. "Your own Michelangelo, who would explain to admirers of his brilliant statue of David how David was always there, the sculptor no more than the instrument of his release." It was a comparison Max worked into conversation whenever he wanted to impress someone, anyone, delivered with a false modesty designed to underline his self-proclaimed creative genius.

"And something else, Maxie?"

"What's that? Tell me."

"I'll never be able to thank you enough."

"How about a little thank-you right now? I'm sticky from sweating like a pig all day looking after locations in heat the devil would despise and could use a good soak, so a little thank-you right now would go a long, long way."

"Always room for one more," Sarah said. "C'mon in. The water's fine."

It wasn't until they moved to the bed and after a go at lovemaking less cramped than in the tub, where Max pulled a thigh muscle or something trying some stupid position that had her choking on bubble bath and afraid for a minute she'd drown under his weight, that they got to talking about the picture, Max describing some of the locations he'd worked out at the Paramount ranch.

"Even with the Old West town sets, I figured some camera angles that will make that tired place fresh again," he said, throwing a finger kiss to the ceiling. "Wait and see, Sarah, we got trapped into this silly picture, but it will look like a million dollars when I get finished with it. And you? It will only happen because of what you never fail to bring to the screen."

"Because you and only you know how to draw that kind of performance out of me," she said. Her response came naturally, nothing forced, because it was true. Max Moonglow did have that impact on her, so why so determined all of a sudden to get rid of him? What guarantee was there that any other producer or director could raise her star higher than he had already taken it? Where was the sense in disposing of a proven winner to chase after greater glory on chance? Maybe it wasn't her plan that was the screwball idea Barney said it was. Maybe she was the screwball for ever thinking it. Maybe—

"And the surroundings? Nature has provided me with an opportunity to advance the cause of Expressionism in film, bring

to the screen magic beyond anything created by that damned
Kraut countryman of mine, Fritz Lang, with *M* and *Metropolis*
and *Das Testament des Dr. Mabuse, The Testament of Dr. Mabuse,*
before he packed his monocle and escaped to America."

Fritz Lang again, Sarah thought. Max had this obsession
with Lang, admiring him some times, despising him other times.
Complaining he was more due the glory Lang got in Germany
and now in America, with *Fury,* the Spencer Tracy movie he
made at MGM, *You Only Live Once,* the Henry Fonda movie
for Walter Wanger, and now *You and Me* at Paramount, with
George Raft. So intense was this rivalry, at least as Max
practiced it, he never put Lang on the guest list for any of their
social gatherings.

If she had any complaints about Lang, it was his choice of a
leading lady for Tracy, Fonda and Raft—Sylvia Sidney in all
three instances, that little Jewish New York nothing with the
saucer eyes and trembling lips, who owed a lot of her success to
her not-so-secret affair with Paramount boss B.P. Schulberg.
There. That was it. That's what Sarah Darling needed in her
life, a studio boss, who could do for her what B.P. Schulberg
did for Sylvia Sidney, outside the reach of a producer or director like Max Moonglow. Give her a Tracy or a Fonda or a Raft
as her costar. Make it impossible for a Gary Cooper to turn
down a picture with her. Give her roles worthy of her talent, not
a silly little western like *Sundown in the Shadows.* Yes. Don't lose
sight, Sarah. That's why Max has to go.

"You hearing me, Sarah? There's one scene in the canyon
where you'll be framed and lit like an angel at Heaven's gate, so
magnificent that audiences will want to erect a shrine to your
beauty, the industry will need to give you another Oscar. That's
what you inspire in me. You and only you, my precious one and
only."

"And you mine," she said, running her hand down his body

until she found what she was searching for, inciting him to riot.

Max was gone when a shaft of morning light cracked through a modest opening in the drapes and landed on her face, its warmth pulling her from the bottomless sleep always brought on by one of their marathon frolics. He was one of the few men who could satisfy her among the many who tried and failed, although she always left them feeling they were her incomparable conqueror.

Sarah often wondered about her ravenous appetite for indiscriminate sex.

Given the ugly past she'd survived, the men who had brutalized her mentally and physically, she'd have thought herself immune, more a candidate for the cloistered life in some remote convent somewhere—

A nun who got none, she often joked to herself.

Instead, quite the opposite.

She was addicted to screwing, but always with a purpose beyond sheer pleasure, giving to get whatever her needs of the moment. Her husbands were an example of that, replaceable once they had outlived their usefulness; same with gullible soft touches like Earl Stanley and Charlie Dickens, who would be out of her life soon enough, once she'd cried at Max's funeral and shoveled dirt on his coffin.

Next?

Sylvia Sidney had B.P. Schulberg wrapped around her pinky, but maybe Cecil B. DeMille? Louis B. Mayer or his son-in-law, David O. Selznick? Darryl F. Zanuck over at Fox? She'd heard he was quite the player. Or maybe Harry Cohn over at Columbia? He stood out among the others for a dumb reason. He was the only big shot without a middle initial. She fancied approaching him one of these days and popping the question. *Hey, Mr. C. Your family too poor to give you a middle initial or what? Hey, Mr. C., you ever think you might have pulled Columbia out of Poverty Row if you had a middle initial like all the others?* Conversation openers, and who knew what could happen between them after that. Might even get her a shot with his fair-haired boy, Frank Capra, someone else who scored without a middle initial.

She rolled into a sitting position and lit up when she saw the Tiffany's blue gift box on her nightstand. She knew it was Max's doing, and not because it wasn't there when they tumbled into bed last night.

Before the start of their first picture together, *Mrs. Quasimodo*, he'd given her a Tiffany's twenty-four-karat gold charm bracelet and a one-of-a-kind charm representing Notre Dame Cathedral, made to his exacting specifications.

A tradition was born.

It was Cupid aiming his bow and arrow for *Daydreams.*

For *An Appointment with Tomorrow,* it was a miniature Oscar, so confident had Max been of the performance he would drag out of her.

Sarah yanked off the powder-blue ribbon and dove into the box after the treasure waiting for her in the royal-purple gift bag. The charm symbolizing *The Showdown Creek Showdown* was a cowboy in a tall Stetson toting a pair of six-guns.

Max wasn't always the most subtle of men, but he certainly ranked among the most thoughtful and charming, a romantic who understood that the way to a woman's heart was through her jewelry.

She padded over to the dressing table, fished through her jewelry box for the charm bracelet, latched on the cowboy, and slid the bracelet onto her wrist. Studied it admiringly before crossing to the window and drawing back the drapes, hoping to spot Earl Stanley in the garden.

He was turning over the soil and layering a flower bed with a sack of manure, had already worked up a sweat. She chuckled at the sight of her future leading man shoveling shit, not the kind of shit she associated with most actors, but Earl wasn't ready to consider himself an actor.

"It's what I been doing best and have proven myself at," he had told her. "So I'll just keep on gardening until this acting job you got me works into something real serious, turns me into a movie star."

"You'll do absolutely great, you big lug. Remember, Mama will be around to help get you through every scene."

"Especially the one you got me doing for you with your husband?"

"Especially that one. You're not having second thoughts, are you?"

"Hell, no, it means you and me got a future together."

She sensed doubt undermining his brag.

"It's all I ever think about lately," she said. "Us."

"Then what're we waiting for, sweet mama? Time's a-wastin'."

"Soon, you big lug. Soon."

Sarah opened the window and called out Earl's name.

He looked up, found her and waved.

She signaled him to join her, her naked breasts adding meaning to the invitation.

A few minutes later he stepped into the bedroom, a smile cutting his face in half, his tongue rimming his lips while he examined her by the inch.

"Man, oh, man, been thinking about you all morning and for days before," he said.

She patted the mattress. "There's a time for thinking and a time for action, big boy."

"Dirty as a kitty-litter box and smelling like a buzzard, so I need to shower down first," he said, kicking off his boots. He unhinged his overalls, tossed them onto the bed and littered the carpeting with the rest of his clothing on the way to the bathroom.

Sarah waited until she heard the water running before she joined him in the shower stall. He welcomed her with open arms and more, was soaping her down when he spotted her charm bracelet and asked, "What's that about?"

She'd accidentally neglected to take it off. "A charm bracelet, one of a kind," she said, dangling it at him. "I put it on this morning, when I was getting ready to make a wish. The bracelet always brings me good luck."

"What'd you wish for this time?"

"You're here, aren't you?" she said, drawing her nails across his hairy chest.

CHAPTER 23

Max spent the morning in his office at RKO engaged in the busy work that always precedes the first day of actual production. He checked the last location reports. Reviewed a fresh batch of revised storyboards. Approved some additional set and costume designs. Grudgingly signed off on a front-office directive to use a standing saloon interior set when the George O'Brien unit finished with it.

Everything was budget-budget-budget, but he intended to show them all how his greatness was in part measured by what he could do under the worst of conditions, which this most certainly was.

"Christ only had to turn water into wine," he said to Rudy Bundsman while they were reviewing some minor casting additions. "Me they got turning dross into diamonds. Can you answer why I put up with it?"

"They're treating you like a god and you're complaining?" Rudy said, waving off Max's complaint. "Listen to me, *bubeleh*. Hear what I'm telling you. You're doing them a giant favor over this Willie Frankfurter business, so they'll owe you down the line. That's how it works around here. Sarah, too; them knowing she's bigger and better than a two-bit western. What I don't understand? How you convinced her to let a complete unknown with no credits be her costar."

"Not completely unknown. He's our gardener."

"Of course. Now it makes sense. Cheap is cheap, Maxie, but

maybe next time just pay his bill and let me handle the casting, like always?"

"He was Sarah's idea, Rudy, not mine."

"No. Your idea was Dixie Leeds."

"Not the same thing, Rudy."

"Did I say different? It's none of my business anyway, so don't look so bothered." He got up from his visitor's chair and turned to go. "What is my business—we're looking fifty-fifty on pulling in Chill Wills for your grand epic. If he's no-go, I have us a tentative offer out on Andy Devine. You good with Andy Devine?"

"Either. Did you lock up Ward Bond for the villain?"

"Yes and no."

"That's a maybe? A week before I start shooting and a maybe is the best you can give me on a key player for a key role?"

"We got him we want him, but I been thinking three other names to throw into the hopper, fresh faces from New York who could fit the bill."

"Throw."

"Howard Da Silva, Lee J. Cobb, Mladen Sekulovich, all from the Group Theatre's production of *Golden Boy*."

"I already got enough fresh faces and none of them from that bunch I hear tell are all communists anyway. Let them stay back in New York. We have enough commies here already."

"Warner Bros. got big plans for another one of them, John Garfield. He's got a lead in *Four Daughters*."

"I heard. They played their cards right, they could have had Earl Stanley."

About an hour later, this guy he didn't know from Adam sprinted after Max as he hurried from his office to his car, late for his rendezvous with Dixie at their Sunset Plaza love nest, to work with her on her lines once she finished working her special brand of magic on him.

"Only need a minute or two of your time," the stranger called, and a few seconds later had covered the distance between them. "I guess you weren't aware of me sitting in your outer office."

Max increased his speed. "You had an appointment?"

This guy, younger and in better shape, easily kept pace, after another moment was in front of Max and trotting backwards. "Not really. I was hoping you'd spare me—"

"I don't talk to anybody I don't know, and I don't know you. Call my girl and ask for an appointment. Then, maybe, but don't count on it." He sped up, tried and failed to dodge around the pest.

"We actually did meet, Mr. Moonglow, although it was brief and certainly far from memorable, at your beautiful home on DeMille Drive."

They had reached Max's car in a bank of marked parking spaces reserved for the producers. Max caved over, hands clamped on his knees, his breath labored, feeling the early onset of an asthma attack, thanks to this damned whoever he was. He fumbled after his car keys to get at the inhaler in the glove compartment.

The guy waited him out and picked up where he'd left off. "A lovely party and I felt honored to be included on your guest list, Mr. Moonglow."

"My guest list was full up only with people I know."

"I confess. I called in a favor from a mutual friend who was invited. I introduced myself and shook your hand not ten minutes before there was that awful ruckus between you and the writer Charlie Dickens, whose script it turns out you are now producing and directing."

"I remember the night and Dickens better than I remember meeting you."

"Leo Salmon's the name. I'm a casting director, but that's

only right now. I have my sights set much higher."

"Congratulations and now good-bye. You want to talk casting, that's what the studio keeps Rudy Bundsman for."

"I was with Mr. Bundsman earlier today and got nowhere with him, but I'm not one to quit when I have my mind set on something. He told me I'd be wasting my time trying to convince you my client, Polly Wilde, would be perfect for the role of the newspaper editor in *Showdown at Shadow Creek*, but I took it as a challenge."

"I'm sure Rudy meant wasting *my* time. I commend you for doing a good job."

"If there'd been a chance for you to meet Polly at your party, you'd know without my telling you that she's going places, Mr. Moonglow."

"Same as I'm trying to do, so move out from my way."

"Imagine, I'm driving off and he's calling after me that this Wilde girl, his client, should have your role in my picture. That's *chutzpah* for you."

"Who?"

"Not a who, honey lamb. *Chutzpah* is the Yiddish word for nerve. I give him that, this guy Salmon. He had a lot of nerve approaching me like we were equals, but I put him in his place quick enough. I let him have it both barrels, how I already got the absolutely perfect actress for the part, who, if anybody, will be going places in this business."

It wasn't entirely the truth, but Max wanted Dixie to know how much he believed in her. That was the truth. They'd been running lines now for two hours and he had difficulty holding in his excitement. She was a natural, putting life into dialogue that was flat on the page and would have stayed there if spoken by someone less gifted. He was excited for the first time about producing and directing this piece of shit. Sarah would do fine in a role she was too old for. But he would have to restrain himself from throwing to Dixie the scenes they were in together. Sarah could count, so he'd have to be especially careful about doling out the close-ups, filtering hers through enough Vaseline and gauze to tone down her age and lend believability to her romance with Earl Stanley.

"I don't know what I ever did in my whole life to ever deserve someone like you," Dixie said, growing emotional.

"Maybe reminding me how there still are some real people with real talent left in the business of make-believe."

Tears rolled off her cheeks and onto the pillow. "I don't ever in this lifetime want to disappoint you, honey pie."

"Impossible." He swiped at her cheeks and kissed the wet patches. "I'll be back in a minute," he said, eased from the bed and aimed for the living room, returned secreting his hands behind his back. "I brought you a very special gift," he said, sighing over her beauty as she sat up, her head cocked with curiosity."

He built in several seconds of suspense before revealing what he held—

A Tiffany's blue gift box.

Her eyes widened and her breasts heaved with excitement as she carefully removed the ribbon, lifted the lid in slow motion, dug into the purple bag, and removed the twenty-four-karat gold charm bracelet holding a single charm, a newspaper's front page engraved *Shadow Creek Sentinel.*

"The charm was created to my specifications," Max said. "It's one of a kind, and not only because you're one of a kind. It celebrates your role in what I know will be only the first of the many pictures we will go on to make together, just as there'll be lots more charms in your future."

Dixie's eyes flushed tears again. She held the bracelet out for him to help her slide it onto her wrist, claiming, "I don't ever need you to give me presents to get me to love you more than I already do, honey pie. You're already now and forever my Prince Charming."

"And you are my Cinderella."

She pulled him to her.

Later, on the way home from Sunset Plaza Drive, Max stopped briefly at Schwab's to make a phone call. He'd been bothered since his conversation with Rudy Bundsman, by the leer in Rudy's voice, in his eyes even, when they talked about Sarah and Dixie.

Rudy had made a good guess about Max and Dixie that led to his innuendo about Sarah and Earl Stanley, or did Rudy know more than he was saying?

Did Max really care?

No more than he cared about other men in Sarah's passing parade of indiscretions.

Curiosity, that was it, wasn't it, and maybe a little ego, too, especially now that he was growing better, stronger and more confident about the depth of his relationship with Dixie, fresh clay for him to mold into greatness?

That was it despite affection for Sarah he couldn't and doubted he ever would be able to shake.

The pharmacy was relatively empty except for the soda-fountain cowboys with nowhere better to be, trading gossip and job leads. He charged for the bank of telephone booths at the back of the store to avoid being approached by any of the at-liberty actors with their résumés and photographs. It wouldn't be the first time.

"Mr. Duff, it's me, Max Moonglow," he said into the receiver. "I'm wondering if you have anything new to report about my wife, specifically about her and our gardener, Earl Stanley."

"The one I hear tell will be costarring with your beautiful

wife in that new western picture of yours? No ride 'em, cowboy, going on there. He's pruning your roses and that's all, Mr. Moonglow. You sure you still want me to rack up the hours?"

"You rack," Max said. "Whatever it takes."

CHAPTER 24

Polly had a seven-bone pot roast cooking under a low flame on the stove and was setting the dinner table when Leo got home showing off a smile as bright as summertime and a bottle of Dom Perignon. She had spent her first day off the call sheet trying to add a feminine touch to his modest Cape Cod cottage on Emmet Terrace in Whitley Heights, the not-quite-chic steep hillside oasis overlooking the Cahuenga Pass.

The day she moved in, Leo described it to her as his last stop before a place more grandiose in a glittery neighborhood like Los Feliz or Beverly Hills that would signal his rising stature in the show business. "All the way to the top, and you are going to help me, us, get there," he had promised her, carrying her across the threshold like he was marrying her to his future.

Except for some flowers collected from his English-style garden and settled around the rooms, there was not much of a feminine contribution she could make to the place. Leo had furnished it simply, kept it cleaner than Mary Pickford's reputation and neat right down to canned goods in the kitchen, lined up in orderly fashion with their labels facing forward, positions outlined in chalk to help guarantee that their replacements would fit exactly.

"Good news?" she said.

"Yours truly is, indeed, the bearer of good tidings as well as a great champagne to celebrate with," Leo said, his overgrown teeth on full display. He breezed her lips with a kiss and spent the next minutes popping the cork and filling the two Waterford flutes he had fetched from the stemware shelf. "Cheers!" He emptied the flute and poured himself a refill. "What's it? You're not drinking?"

"Waiting to hear your good news first," she said, unable to figure out what she read as a forced quality to his enthusiasm. "*Gunga Din,* is that it? You got me the part in *Gunga Din?*"

Leo dropped his smile, almost immediately shoved it back into place. "Afraid not, freckle face. It's looking more and more like they're going with Joan Fontaine."

She was unable to disguise her irritation. Up to this minute, he'd talked like she was close to becoming a shoo-in. She hadn't moved in with him to suffer disappointment. She'd already endured enough disappointments to last a lifetime. What good to her was Leo if the best he could deliver was bad news?

He thrust out a hand. "Before you say what you're thinking, hear me out."

"I'm listening," Polly said.

"I have something better than *Gunga Din* cooking on the back burner for you," he said, his hand over his heart like he was getting ready for the Pledge of Allegiance.

"I'm still listening."

"I had a sit-down with Max Moonglow earlier today, filled in all the blanks about Polly Wilde. Showed him your pictures. He remembered seeing you at the party he and Sarah Darling tossed. He wasn't a pushover, but I convinced him you'd be perfect for the newspaper editor in *Showdown at Shadow Creek.*"

"Come on, Leo. I've seen the production reports in the *Hollywood Reporter.* I know his picture rolls next week with someone named Dixie Leeds in the part, while I'm moving from this movie with George straight into his next one, so why feed me a bunch of hooey? A lie will never be an acceptable substitute for the truth if this relationship of ours is going to continue working."

"Not hooey," Leo said, quietly, his head sashaying left and right. "Max told me the same thing about the scheduling conflict and demanded, *What are you really after me for with this actress of yours? Tell me, Leo. No more games.* He wasn't fooled any more than you are." He sniffed the air. "Lots of onions and garlic in that pot roast you're cooking up for us?"

"Don't change the subject."

He bought more time rinsing his mouth with a load of Dom Perignon.

She submerged her amusement, waiting to hear how Leo would try squirming his way out of the hole he'd dug himself into, seriously wondering if she had made a mistake buying into his brag and hitching herself to his wagon. It had hardly begun, but maybe get out now while the getting was good?

"I was saving the best for last, but it has to be a secret," Leo said.

"Try me."

"Seriously. I told Max what I had in mind for bringing the two of you together and he went monkey nuts. He wants to meet with you and me after he finishes the *Showdown at Shadow Creek* shoot, and soon after make the announcement at a big press conference he'll have RKO's publicity boss, Perry Lieber, arrange." He framed the air with his hands and his words turned dramatic, like a *March of Time* narrator. "At exactly the right moment Max will introduce you"—he made a trumpeting sound—"Polly Wilde, the icing on the cake, ladies and gentlemen of the international press corps."

He eyed her for approval.

"Go on."

"You know how word spreads in this business, like wildfire, and that's why Max made me promise to keep what we'll be doing a secret from everybody, including you, in order to keep it an event instead of becoming two lines in a Winchell or Parsons column. I promised, but I already knew in my heart I couldn't not tell you, seeing as how you're the one really behind it all. God, what a great team we make, farm girl."

"Damn it, Leo. Tell me already."

He told her, finished with a canary-eating smile.

It became her turn to push out a ton of air. "And this isn't a bag of bullshit you're handing me?"

"All the way to the top, freckle face."

Was it that she believed him or that she wanted to believe him?

Either way—

Polly reached after her champagne glass.

"All the way to the top," she said.

CHAPTER 25

Max needed his ritual massages more than ever, plagued by bad weather that had delayed filming by more than a week, caused a reshuffling of the shooting schedule from the outdoor locations to a soundstage, added hundreds of dollars to the meager production budget because of below-the-line overtime labor costs, and led to casting disruptions.

A scheduling conflict cost him Lowell Sherman, but Rudy Bundsman did a bit of sleight of hand and pulled in Onslow Stevens to replace Sherman as the disreputable town banker.

While he could live with that, he also had to live with the casting of Susan Hathaway and Marcia Nesbitt as the Bart Black Saloon's stellar attractions, although neither could sing nor dance as well as the two girls they were replacing.

In fact, at all.

He'd told Rudy, "I sat through their screen tests, like you asked. Four left feet in all and voices that could put a scare in Frankenstein and Dracula combined."

"All well and fine, but they came to me highly recommended from up on high, where they had performed with flying colors, if you get my meaning," Rudy answered, illustrating with hand jerks that told the rest of the story.

"So, the screwing he got is responsible for the screwing I'm getting?"

"Why do you sound so surprised?"

"Why do you answer my question with one of your own, like

it's the Eleventh Commandment?"

"Why do you think? You ever meet a Jew who doesn't?"

"That's two questions right there."

"I'll owe you one, how's that?" Rudy said.

Max was mentally replaying their conversation while Nicky Hands hammered the stress and frustration from his body, Nicky's thumbs deftly locating every pressure point, turning pain into pleasure with every knot he worked out of every muscle, when the door to his outer office burst open. A half-naked Indian in war paint whooped inside wagging a tomahawk and aimed for the massage table, Max's secretary in screaming pursuit.

At once, Max's body converted to one giant spasm, undoing all the good work by Nicky. He cried out in pain as he instinctively rolled away from the oncoming blade, lost control and rolled off the table, crashing onto the floor hard enough to throw his vision out of focus.

Nicky froze, uncertain how to protect Max from the aggressive Indian, but Max's secretary showed no indecision, throwing herself onto the Indian's back, her arms locked around his shoulders as she wrestled him to the ground and onto his belly.

She was a large, olive-skinned woman, maybe twice the Indian's size and weight, looked far more fit for the wrestling ring than for the RKO secretarial pool.

She squatted on top of the Indian and beat on him with her fists, treating his back like her personal war drum, the tune harder and fiercer than any Nicky had ever tried on Max; answering the Indian's appeals for her to quit with a shouted series of swear words in troubled English that suggested European roots, maybe one of those Balkan countries with the unpronounceable names. Her name was also a mouthful, so Max had taken to addressing her as "Sugar" since she materialized earlier this morning and introduced herself. She liked that, he knew, when she started answering the phone as "Miss Sugar." For now, however, there was nothing sweet about her.

She angled off the Indian, rolled him over and stripped him of his war bonnet, shaking its feathers loose as she flung it aside; shoulder-bounced him alert and warned him to stay put with a look as menacing as the words in whatever the language she threw in his face; looked to Max for instructions.

"Something familiar about him," Max said, wrapping himself in a towel and rising from the floor. "Nicky, go scrub the Max Factor from his face. Let's have a better look."

Nicky drew a bottle of water and a sponge from his supply kit and approached the Indian with caution, making certain Miss Sugar had him under control before Nicky hunkered down and got to work washing away the war paint decorating high cheekbones, an aquiline nose and copper-colored skin, revealing a young man in his early to mid-twenties.

He signaled he was finished.

"Not who I was thinking, nowhere close," Max said. His mind had been fixated on a blurred vision of that crazy pest Leo Salmon. He stepped over for a closer look. "I'll say this much for you, whoever you are—you definitely look like the real thing, honest Injun." He laughed at his little joke. So did Nicky. Miss Sugar stayed as stone-faced as the Indian while guarding against any surprise moves by him.

"I am an Indian," the Indian said, pride studding his every word, delivered in a rich baritone. "I am Wahanassatta of the Cheyenne nation."

"Wahaha—who?" Max said, wondering whatever happened to real names that rolled off the tongue. First, Sugar from the steno pool. Now, this nut case.

The Indian pronounced his name again. "It means *He Who Walks with His Toes Turned Outward* in my native tongue."

"You coming after someone with your tomahawk, shouldn't

it be a chiropractor who did you dirt, couldn't fix the toe problem, not some movie producer and director like me, who doesn't know you from Sitting Bull?"

"I was playacting, meant no harm. Auditioning and protesting at the same time. I needed to climb over the wall of the cemetery that's behind the studio after guards refused me entrance at the gates and otherwise made me to feel unwelcome."

"What set you on the warpath, He Who Walks, etcetera, etcetera and so forth?"

"My woman, Abequa, and me, we come here from our home in the Black Hills of South Dakota, my eyes fixed on acting in the movies. Lots of cowboy and Indian movies, so why not? Far better than laboring in the mines day in and day out. Only I never can get farther than this Central Casting of yours. Sorry, they tell me, no work. I tell them, *Look, I see Indians in a lot of the movies, only they're not real Indians like me, not even Iron Eyes Cody. He's Espera de Corti, a Sicilian from Louisiana. Why not hire a real Indian like me?* They have no answer except for me to try again, but the next time, it's the same as the last time and the time before that."

Max gestured for Miss Sugar to let the Indian up.

The Indian eased onto his moccasins, stepped after his headdress and adjusted the war bonnet squarely atop coal-black hair that matched his probing eyes and flowed down past his shoulders.

"What do people call you in real American talk?" Max said. "You have another name?"

"Ronald. Ronald Wahanassatta."

Max raised his eyes and grunted. "It's a start. You need something catchier, short enough to fit on a marquee, you ever going to make something of yourself in the picture business, like Iron Eyes Cody's done. John Wayne. You think he'd be so tall in the saddle under his real name, Marion Michael Morrison? Marion, for Christ's sake—a sissy girl's name. You think women would be swooning over Cary Grant he was still Archie Leach? Thanks all to God I was put here on His green Earth a Moonglow. Max Moonglow. Max Moonglow Presents. Magical on a marquee, because moviegoers know I fill my pictures with the truth."

"Why I came hunting after you today, Mr. Moonglow, sir, not anyone inferior who is making other western movies here, hoping you would see the injustice and take pity on my sad situation. Put me in your picture and prove to the world that an Indian can portray an Indian as well as any Sicilian from Louisiana."

"Except for one thing," Max said, heaving a noisy sigh. The Indian's hopeful smile turned upside down and he braced himself for what he sensed as bad news coming. "There are no Indians in my picture, Ronald, my boy."

Ronald's chin sank onto his chest and he dabbed at his eyes, reminding Max of the pain he felt in the old days in the old country, before his genius was recognized, whenever he was derided and denied work for being a Jew. That was his only crime, not being one of them. It might have stayed that way— his career destroyed before it was any career to crow about— except for Herr Professor Schmidt at UFA, who bravely employed him on features where he would not be noticed at first, guiding him later on to more responsibility on films that showed off a creative genius that made him acceptable to all but the most dedicated of Nazis.

Herr Professor Schmidt.

Max hadn't thought about him in years, since their correspondence ceased abruptly, his benefactor's last letter spelling out dreams of finding his own way out of Germany and to America; no reply to Max's offer of assistance in any and all ways necessary.

Rumors surfaced that Herr Professor Schmidt had disappeared after he was placed under arrest for being a homosexual, in violation of Nazi party policy, but other rumors attributed his disappearance to the discovery the professor was not a Schmidt at all, but a Schwab, a Jew. Max kept meaning to ask the drugstore Schwabs if they were related, but had yet to do so; maybe now that he'd been reminded by Ronald here.

Maybe now was payback time.

"There could be," he said, like some Caesar on the balcony. "Yes! There could be an Indian in my picture. There will be an Indian in my picture, and you will be my Indian, Ronald whatever-the-hell-your-last-name until we change it." Caught up in his rhetoric, Max raised a victory fist punctuated by an uplifted thumb. It happened to be the hand holding up the towel draped around his midsection. The towel fell to the floor, exposing more of Max than he ever put on public display.

Nicky Hands scrambled to rescue the towel for Max, who had formed a modesty cup with his hands, while Miss Sugar, at first mesmerized by the sight, her mouth agape and eyes wide with admiration, turned and fled the office.

An overjoyed Ronald sprang ear-blistering whoops that bounced off the walls, and, possibly confusing the accident with some sort of contractual ritual, dropped his buckskin britches to seal the deal from his end and began a wild song and dance around the room.

He didn't have the budget to pull in a new writer on *Showdown at Shadow Creek* from RKO's stable of contract hacks, who specialized in pumping out the B-programmer screenplays, and, of course, it would be too embarrassing to ask an A-list friend to work for nothing. Under the circumstances, Max reluctantly summoned Charlie Dickens to his office the next day and spelled out the changes he wanted in Charlie's script.

Charlie listened intently and grew increasingly agitated, his foot tapping noisily, as if adding an Indian would be tantamount to restaging Custer's last stand. He let Max finish talking before he erupted like Vesuvius with a gargantuan belch of a word: "No!"

Max resisted the urge to call in Miss Sugar to have her expel the ungrateful writer from his presence. Instead, he made like a desperate Dutch uncle, a variation on the role studio boss L.B. Mayer played at Metro-Goldwyn-Mayer sometimes, if that's what it took to win his way with someone.

"It's not what I wanted either, an Indian," he said, choking on his words. "The order came down from the very top of the totem pole, my boy. A banker on the studio's board of directors in New York, whose only talent is making money, not movies, but he saw ours as a way to pay overdue tribute to a distant relative who was an Indian and fought against the sale of Manhattan Island."

"Inserting an Indian would upset the symmetry of the story, couldn't he see that?"

"Apparently not, damn him all to hell, doing this to us on the eve of our going into production, but I told him that Charlie Dickens was a miracle worker and could make this happen, in honor of his relative and for the good of the picture. I meant it, too, Charlie. We have had our little differences, but your glittering talent, however fully recognized it's yet to become, has never been cause for argument or complaint. Never, my boy. Never." Max pressed a palm to his heart, but hard as he tried he couldn't get a tear out. "This picture will be only the beginning of what I foresee as a beautiful relationship."

Charlie bit.

Believing he now had the upper hand, he stalked the office like an absinthe fiend, substituting his vision for Max's ideas.

Max had pictured the Indian sweeping floors and washing dishes at Bart Black's Saloon, getting drunk the way Indians do and causing the barroom brawl that leads to the showdown at Shadow Creek. Somewhere in all that, a line or two of dialogue.

"We'll call him Raging Bull," Charlie said. "He's constantly raging against the evils that befell his people because of the paleface devils. He's the only member of the outlaw band to survive the showdown, who recognizes the sins of his ways before the vigilantes break him out of jail and take him to be hung over the objections of Sarah's character, who pleads for his life and mercy and, in that last scene at his grave on Boot Hill, proclaims, *It is a far, far better thing you did than you or any other Indian has ever done, Raging Bull, and it is a far, far better rest you've gone to than you ever would have known.* What do you think, Mr. Moonglow? Pretty damn fine, if I do say so myself."

"Yes, yes, brilliant, my boy," Max said, applauding; at the same time wondering to himself if this second-rate second-rater recognized all he'd done was substitute the Indian for the Gringo Kid character already in the script. Good news for Ronald Whoozit. Not so good for Douglas Fowley, who was set to play the Gringo Kid. "I'll need your new pages by tomorrow, my boy, and meanwhile I will sleep well tonight knowing you'll be working with all the genius you've now demonstrated here, yes?"

"Maybe not," Charlie said.

"Maybe not?" Max didn't like the fire he saw burning in Charlie's eyes. He clutched his heart, as if he sensed an oncoming heart attack. "What's to maybe not?"

"The screenplay is my baby, yet everyone's been treating me like an outsider, Mr. Moonglow—"

"Call me Max."

"Everyone's treating me like an outsider, Max, like I'm a bad parent who doesn't deserve to be with his child."

"How dare they!"

"I hate saying it, but that seems to include you, Max."

"How dare I!" He hammered his desk. Pressed the intercom key and ordered: "Take a memo to all parties, Miss Sugar. Effective immediately, from now on Charlie Dickens is to have complete and total access to soundstage and location filming for our picture."

"And meetings," Charlie said.

"You hear that, Miss Sugar? Add 'and meetings,' and get the memorandum typed, duplicated and out to everybody post haste." He aimed his best Barnum smile at Charlie, who was now all puffed out, like he'd won a major battle. He had, too, at least until he left the office and Max could instruct Miss Sugar to forget about the memo.

CHAPTER 26

Charlie left Max Moonglow's office and aimed straight for home, intent on getting to work on the script revisions, reluctantly scuttling any thoughts of chasing down Polly, impressing her with the news and, maybe, hopefully, reigniting their relationship.

First things first. He needed to prove to Max how his ability to turn on his creative juices, make them flow with brilliance, could survive any deadline, even the one Max had imposed on him, only—

It didn't work out that way.

Pulling up to his garage apartment, he recognized the '28 Chevy Stakebed he was parking behind even before he saw Ernie and Millie Keyes, Millie seated on the running board, deep into her Bible, Ernie relaxing against the fender, studying a fleet of pigeons that had settled on the telephone pole wires across the way.

He stepped from his car calling Ernie's name. Ernie traded in a gloomy expression for a smile and charged over to Charlie for a double handshake while Millie called, "Praise be the Lord you're here, Charlie."

Charlie surveyed the Chevy, expecting to see Robin Moon. She wasn't there or anywhere else he looked up and down the street. Ernie answered his question before he could ask. "Robin's why we come looking for you, Charlie. The girl's in serious trouble. We're hopin' for your help."

"Prayin' for your help," Millie called over.

"What's going on? Where is she, Ernie?"

"Hell on Earth, close as Millie and me, we can figure it out."

Charlie steered Ernie and Millie inside the apartment, settled them over reheated percolator coffee on his Salvation Army couch, pulled over a chair from the secondhand dining table that doubled as his writing desk, and sat down across from them. "Tell me the rest of it," he said, his expression as troubled as theirs.

What he'd already heard was beyond alarm, past his ability to provide help, but he knew he had to do something once he learned more, not to repay Robin for removing that bullet from his arm before infection could set in—he gently rubbed the spot, still tender to the touch—and certainly not as repayment for their lovemaking, remarkable though it was, since that had been her inspiration, not his. Why, then? Maybe because, like the Keyes, she offered unconditional friendship at a time of great need, much like her need was great now.

They'd picked up what little day labor was available in the vineyards, orchards and groves of Riverside and Orange counties and decided to take a crack at the San Fernando Valley. Passing into Los Angeles last night, police pulled them over because of a broken taillight. Ernie, worn out and grumpy, gave the cops a sour lip for picking on decent, God-fearing folks who worked hard to earn survival money in these tough times.

The cops were anything but sympathetic, causing Robin to unleash an unladylike barrage of insults and lash out at them with her fists when they moved on her. She caught one on his shoulder, the other on his chest with ineffective blows they laughed off before they shut her up with a punch that split her lip and drew blood and a nightstick to her belly and back that sent her sliding off the road, down a narrow embankment into a muddy field of overgrown weeds.

They ordered Ernie to climb back into the cab and move on. Millie, who had sat silent and petrified with fear as the incident played out, worked up sufficient nerve to ask them to help get Robin back to the truck. That wasn't going to happen, the cops said. You want her, they said, come claim her and her fat mouth in the morning, after she spends a night cooling off in the cooler at the Hollywood Division station.

They spent a sleepless night parked on an industrial side street, in a service alley between rows of loading docks, worrying over the possibility it would take cash money they didn't have to pay any fine it might cost to spring Robin from the hoosegow.

They had more than money to worry about after they found the Hollywood station. *We ain't finished processing her,* the desk sergeant told them. *Come back later, in two or three hours.* On the way back to the truck, a disheveled woman came chasing after them, urging, *Hold on a minute. I got something needs telling you.* It was clear from her tawdry dress and overdone makeup, the defeat showing in her deep-set, drug-weary eyes, that she was a working girl.

She said, *You friends of Robin, I heard right. That's who you were asking after just minutes ago with that bully desk tender Fat Freddy, a brain smaller than his eenie-meenie-teenie weenie?*

What about her? What about Robin? Ernie said. Something about the way she put the question had set his nerves on edge.

She's been getting initiated ever since Murphy and McCracken brought her in last night. The whole precinct's been taking turns on her, every bonehead in blue with a boner. She won't be there when you get back. They'll have handed her off to another precinct, then another, another after that, until they've finished up with her and are ready to toss her out with yesterday's garbage.

Millie clutched her chest. *But they're police officers,* she said, *and our Robin, she's no, no, not a—*

You can go and say it, lady. She's no two-bit like me. Maybe she wasn't when she got here, but like it or not, she's been initiated into the sisterhood by now. Who can tell? Maybe it'll turn out she likes it. Lord knows, that's how it worked out for yours truly. She crossed herself, gave them a wistful smile and trotted off in the opposite direction on her three-inch heels.

That's how much of the story Charlie knew so far.

"It gets badder'n that," Ernie said, finally, responding to a nudge from Millie. He reached over for her hand and looked up from his coffee cup. "We waited out the time driving around, but mostly parked, to conserve on the gas, until two hours passed. The desk sergeant told us Robin was still being processed, so we left, too scared to tell him anything we had heard tell from that woman. After all, what if she'd only been looking to make ourselves as miserable as her life was already become? We gave it another hour. This time there was a different desk sergeant on duty. He shuffled a lot of papers before he told us how there was no Robin Moon ever been brought into his Hollywood Division station. I knew better'n to argue, and that's when I thought of you, Charlie, and how Robin said you told her to look you up in the telephone book she ever was around."

"Can't you help us, Charlie, can you?" Millie said, a whimper coloring her question. "I'm as fearful for Robin right now as I ever was over anything we've ever been through on the road, and that's sayin' plenty."

"I'm going to do my darnedest, starting right now," Charlie said, pushing himself up from the chair. He crossed to his desk, dug out the phone directory from one of the tall piles framing his Royal Quiet Deluxe portable typewriter, and a minute later was dialing the Rampart Division station.

The conversation was brief and unproductive. He got the

kind of answer given the Keyes. *Robin Moon? Nobody logged in here by that name. Maybe try another station.* He spent the next hour trying every station listed, every time the same result; every time his question answered in the same flat, firm unemotional manner, two or three times with what sounded like a snigger, like the cop knew a secret he had no intention of sharing with Charlie.

It was as if Robin had fallen off the face of the earth, if she ever existed at all.

Charlie grew increasingly frustrated, came close once or twice to losing his temper.

Ernie sat quietly, patiently, occasionally rising to work the kinks out of his legs or to walk the room, the look on his face growing less hopeful every time Charlie concluded a call and dialed again.

Millie took comfort in her Bible, her finger tracking the lines, closing her eyes to passages she knew well enough to recite to herself from memory.

After striking out with the last station listed, Charlie tried a call to County Jail, got the same perfunctory Civil Service tone and no better result.

No Robin Moon on the books.

Charlie tossed the directory aside and dialed the next number from memory.

Mad Dog answered on the second ring.

Finally, a friendly voice.

"Maybe you can give me some help with this," Charlie said, and explained the problem.

"She important to you, this Moon dame?"

"I owe her, Mad Dog, and some special people sitting here right now, worrying along with me."

"Good enough," Mad Dog said.

The phone went quiet for several moments, except for a

steady hum that told him Mad Dog was thinking through the situation. "Charlie, I need you to stick to home while I make a call or two."

Maybe ten minutes passed before the phone rang. Charlie scooped it up. "Mad Dog, how we doing?"

"Not Mad Dog, Charlie Dickens. Calling at his request. Rooker's the name. Barney Rooker."

"Do I know you?"

"No, but I know all about you. Come see me. Now, Charlie." A command, not an invitation. "I should have some good news about your friend Robin Moon by the time you get here," Barney Rooker said.

Charlie hadn't expected Barney Rooker to be this small antique of a person sitting in a wheelchair in a smell-infested room at a nursing home full of frail-appearing residents who had studied him with curiosity as he traveled the corridor, backing away the closer he came, as if he were an emissary of the Grim Reaper.

Rooker's vigorous voice over the phone had suggested otherwise. Even now, his manner was full of an inner strength while he surveyed Charlie from across the room. He wheeled to within a few feet and ordered, "Don't turn away. I ain't through searching into your eyes."

"For what?"

"Your soul."

"You're kidding."

"Squat before my neck gives out." Charlie squatted. "That's better. . . . Quit it; I'll tell you when to move." After an uncomfortable minute: "Oke, you can stretch it now, Charlie. I saw what I was looking for. Nothing I didn't like." He fell silent, wheeled to the window, turned his gaze to the street.

Charlie let a minute pass. "About Robin Moon, Mr. Rooker. You said you might have some good news for me."

"I said I *should* have, Charlie. Not might. *Should.* I do, but I'm afraid you're not going to like how it comes dressed." He pulled a packet of Gitanes from a pocket of his bathrobe, pointed to the nightstand. "Lighter's over there. Grab it and flame me."

Charlie found the lighter among Rooker's collection of pill bottles, but a greater discovery was the framed photograph of Sarah Darling decorating the nightstand.

Rooker must have noticed his double-take. "She's been talking to me a lot about you lately."

"You know Sarah Darling?"

"How the hell else would she be able to talk to me, I didn't?"

"What's she say? She tell you about our movie?"

"Manner of speaking, yeah, but what's it going to be, talking about her or talking about the situation that brung us together?"

Charlie averted his eyes, embarrassed that he'd let his ego momentarily overtake his concern about Robin.

Rooker cracked off the filter tip and tossed it away before allowing Charlie to light the Gitanes. At once the air filled with the cigarette's strong, distinctive odor. Rooker took a deep swallow, shot a rail of smoke out the window, and coughed into his fist. "You gotta hand it to the Frenchies," he said. "They know how to roll a smoke." He took another drag, let the smoke float out from the corners of his sunken lips. "Where were we? What was I saying?"

"About Robin."

"Yeah." He picked at a bit of tobacco glued to his tongue and flicked it away. "You know what I'm talkin' here, I say Ridin' the Banana Boat? . . . I can tell you don't. It's a game some of the boys in blue play sometimes with stray dames they pick off for the hell of it, and I don't mean streetwalkers theirs for the go-down anytime they want. Good-looking or ugly, built like a pencil or a bulldozer, makes no difference to those bozos. The cops take 'em, make 'em and pass 'em along from precinct to precinct, up for grabs by any cop with a hard-on and an urge to merge."

"Not Robin!"

"Who do you think we're talkin' about here, Little Bo Peep? Way the story comes to me, she got roped by two horny cops who are veterans at the sport and often start and steer the Banana Boat Ride, Murphy and McCracken by name. They hauled her to the Hollywood station, personally broke her in, and kept the ball rolling before they deposited her, the way it always ends for these poor souls."

"Deposited?"

"At a porn palace over in the valley, where they endure more of the same, only with pay-for-play rough trade, get their pictures took and perform stunts in stag reels I wouldn't wish on my worst enemy's mother. By then, they're swooning on the needle and hungry for more at any price or too far gone to be of further value and dumped in some back alley or empty lot a thousand miles away, no links to the valley and definitely no links to the cops."

"My God! You're telling me that's where she is now?"

"No."

"Where, then?"

Rooker glanced out the window. "Come see for yourself."

Charlie hurried over. Two white-frocked New Dawn orderlies were struggling to lift someone from the backseat of a midnight-black Rolls-Royce Phantom parked with its motor running in front of the building. They got her to the sidewalk, and at once the Rolls took off with a roar.

Charlie shouted Robin's name and raced out of Rooker's room, nearly tripping over a few residents wandering the corridor in slow motion before he reached the main entrance ahead of Robin and the orderlies. They were holding her up, her feet barely touching the ground as she struggled on shaky legs with one step after the next.

He slipped his arms around her and whispered her name like he'd found gold.

Robin's eyes were dead. They showed no recognition. Her broken lips twisted into an ugly scar before she began hammering on his chest, screaming, "Leave me alone, leave me alone, leave me alone," like a chorus in some private nightmare.

"It's me Robin, Charlie, Charlie Dickens."

"No more, no more, no more," Robin pleaded, the words descending into a whine, begging, "No more, please. Enough. No more." Her fists quit and her arms dropped to her side in surrender. She slipped from the orderlies' grip; stumbled backwards and sank at an angle onto the tiled walkway; rolled into a fetal position, her pleading reduced to a guttural moan.

"The doc does decent work," Barney Rooker said. "He'll patch the girl up nice and good, you got no worries in that department. It's the mind, not the body. There's never any guarantee about with the ones manage to get away, so good luck on that."

"She's a strong girl," Charlie said.

"*Was.* She *was* a strong girl. That was before Murphy and McCracken punched her ticket on the Banana Boat Ride. What's working in your favor is my being able to pull her out of the valley before she started sailing in that shit storm. You like to hear how I got it done, maybe write it up for the movies one of these days?"

Charlie could tell the old man was anxious to brag. "I would," he said.

Rooker fished out the Gitanes from his robe, flipped one between his lips and torched it with his lighter, sent a string of smoke rings sailing into the doctor's waiting area. I'll give you the *Reader's Digest* version, going back more years than I can count, when you were still in knee pants," he said, staring off into the past. "I was a cameraman, made a solid living specializing in stag reels and worse, pictures that would make Polly Adler turn her head in shame, if you get where I'm going. My clients included names you would know I said them out loud, which I won't"—he fingered his nose to one side—"who liked how I put the artsy-fartsy in even the most basic of camera setups, aiming the lens where no lens ever went before, so I was always in demand. That's when I learned about the cops and their Banana Boat Ride, filmed a lot of the girls they turned over once they were done with 'em." He smashed the Gitanes on the arm of his wheelchair and pocketed the butt, replaced it with a fresh smoke. "Go ahead, make a face and think what you want. To this day I'm not proud about being part of that dirty business, but I won't make excuses, neither. None of that history behind me, I wouldn't-a been no help rescuing your girl Robin after Mad Dog caught me on the horn and spelled out the situation, knowing I could help."

"Mad Dog knew about your past?"

"We got a lot in common, Mad Dog and me, yeah. So, he spells out the situation and I call around, starting with the cops."

"Murphy and McCracken, you know them?"

"I know them. Met 'em when they were young snots fresh out of the academy and already into banana boats. I went higher up than them pricks, headquarters brass who owe me favors for favors received, their word as good as their memory. That got me the valley address, where I used to do some of my best work, and the inside phone number. The place is now run by the son and daughter of a decent family man, who counted on me to deliver him winners. More than a couple of times I turned out stags on the cuff that put bread and butter on his dinner table, kept him afloat during periods when the business went soft as a priest's dick. The daughter got on the phone immediately, remembered me and how nice I treated her and her brother whenever they hung out around my sets. I explained why I was calling. She didn't hesitate for a second telling me I'd phoned just in time and where would I like her to have their driver deliver her."

Charlie supposed he should have been shocked by what he was hearing, words like "decent" pinned to somebody who operated so despicable a business and even brought his children into it, but the only emotion running through him now was gratitude. He said, "I can never repay you enough for helping rescue Robin, Mr. Rooker."

Rooker tossed away the declaration with the back of a hand. "You don't owe me a plugged nickel, boy. Mad Dog, he'd tell you the same about himself and his part. It's what friends do for friends, where we got it all over the people who live their lives only out for themselves. It's what you went and done for your Robin."

"Where is she, how is she?" Ernie Keyes said, urgency in his voice entering the waiting area steps ahead of Millie, whose anxious expression added fright lines to a face already overloaded with wrinkles.

"Safe, she's safe," Charlie said, rising. "We're waiting to hear from the doctor. He's in with her now."

Ernie said, "A doctor? Why? Why a doctor, Charlie? What didn't you tell us when you called up on the phone and said for us to head on over?"

"Oh, dear Lord," Millie said, and burst into tears. "What's happened to our darling girl?"

"What's happened is that you get her back all in one piece," Rooker said. "More'n that you don't need to know. It's over and done with. It's history, unless and until she decides it's something to tell."

"She's family, mister, whoever you are, and sitting in a wheelchair don't give you no right to be talking to my wife like that." He stroked Millie's face and kissed her on the forehead, guided her to a chair and helped her settle.

Charlie waved for attention. "This is Mr. Barney Rooker, whose phone call brought me here, Ernie. He's responsible for getting Robin out from under."

At once, Ernie's anger melted, defenseless against the truth.

"Also nothing they need knowing," Rooker said, abruptly wheeling around and out of the room.

"Somebody should have said something before I opened my big yap," Ernie said.

Charlie roused to the heavy smell of disinfectant stinging his nose, opened his eyes to a cleaning lady navigating her mop and scrub bucket over the worn linoleum, unsure of how long he'd been sleeping. He checked his watch in the half-baked light of the waiting room. Not quite four A.M. He was alone. No sense of Ernie and Millie, when they had left or where they had gone.

Last he remembered, the three of them were keeping vigil, waiting to hear from the doctor or, better, be told Robin was up for a visit. His muscles ached. He pushed himself onto his feet, did some leg stretches and knee bends to work out the stiffness. The cleaning lady offered a toothless smile and went about her business, under her breath humming a tune he didn't know.

He headed for the information counter in the lobby, passing early risers among the elderly residents who were taking careful steps along the corridor, some using walkers or canes to avoid a fall that might cause their fragile bones to break or fracture. He'd learned all about that a year or so ago, researching old people for a screenplay he never got around to writing past the title, *Old People*, convinced by agent Roy Balloon it wasn't commercial. *You know who's interested in old people?* Roy had said.

Nobody, not even old people.

The young guy at the information counter looked up from his comic book when he realized he had company and forged a welcoming smile. "You here to visit, visiting hours don't start for another three hours," he said.

Charlie explained the situation.

"Oh, yeah. You must be Mr. Dickens. They left hours ago, when I was starting my shift. Hold on." He reached under the counter for an envelope and passed it across. "They left this note for you."

It was from Ernie, written in a neat, cursive hand, every letter meticulously formed:

Dear Charlie,

You got to sleeping and were so when the doctor at last came with news we could see Robin. She cried at us right away the minute she saw us and said we had to get her from this place even though the doctor said he wanted to keep her here for observation for a few days more. So we are going and taking her with us, Robin always being very strong-willed and knowing her own mind better than anyone. Thank you and God bless you for all you done for her and for Millie and me.

> *Very truly yours,*
> *Ernest Keyes, Jr.*

Charlie told the information guy, "I need to speak to the doctor who was on duty yesterday, who took care of Robin Moon."

"Sure, easy as pie when he's on duty again, which'll be in about six hours, his shift starts."

"Now."

"Sure wish I could help out, but it's against the rules."

"You never learn that rules are made to be broken?" Charlie fished a five from his billfold and passed it across the counter.

The information guy pocketed the bill, picked up the phone

and dialed a number. After a minute: "Dr. McNichol, this is Ira at New Dawn? Sorry to wake you, doctor, but the gentleman here is claiming it's an emergency. Thank you, sir." He handed the receiver to Charlie.

Charlie explained the situation, heard alarm growing in the doctor's voice while he described Robin's condition and the potential consequences of her being moved too soon. "It's nothing I approved or can condone," the doctor said. "That poor young tortured girl could die as matters presently stand."

Charlie tossed the receiver to the information guy. He scrambled out of New Dawn, ignoring dozens of stoplights and stop signs racing home on mostly empty streets, morning sun just beginning to show on the horizon, hoping to find Ernie, Millie and Robin there.

They weren't.

He settled at the Royal Deluxe and forced himself to concentrate on reworking the *Showdown at Shadow Creek* script to Max Moonglow's specifications, all the while hoping they'd show up before he finished and left for the studio.

They didn't.

CHAPTER 27

The limousine took Sarah to the studio and the empty, half-lit soundstage two hours before her wardrobe, hair and makeup calls.

There always was something about the first day on a new production that had her apprehensive: the size of her portable dressing room. It had to be bigger and grander than any other cast member's. Max knew this. Max always took care to make sure it was so, but she was the type of person who needed to personally confirm the square footage, why she always made sure to have a tape measure in her handbag.

She was using it now to verify the measurements she got from Ace Berland, Max's AD on all his pictures, in spite of Ace's assurance it not only was the largest in the row of dressing rooms lining a wall of the soundstage, it also was the dressing room closest to the set, another of Sarah's requirements.

It's not that she doubted Ace; he was always true to his word. But her eye had told her the dressing room three down, the one assigned somebody named Dixie Leeds, might be the same size. That wasn't about to happen, absolutely not, especially with some dame who, as Max explained it, had been forced on him by the studio brass, same as the Indian who had cost Doug Fowley his role as the Gringo Kid.

She'd be measuring that one next, also checking how it was furnished, Sarah not one to be outdone in that department, either. Everything here was familiar, of course, all her favorites, the sofa bed, the dressing table, the wardrobe closet; hers exclusively, a match for anything Ginger Rogers's overbearing mama, Lela, insisted be stored away for her darling daughter whenever Ginger was between pictures.

That was nice.

That was good.

At RKO that put her in the same league with Ginger Rogers.

Maybe one day she'd tackle a singing and dancing role, prove she belonged in a bigger, better league, the Sarah Darling League, adding to the army of actresses already envious of her rank.

Meanwhile, she had this dreary little western to make, leaving those creatures to gossip if, maybe, Sarah Darling's career was on the downslide. Hah! As much chance of that being the case as Marie Dressler winning Miss America. So much malarkey, but she couldn't very well explain how it was the price she was paying in order to get rid of Max once and for always, so she could move onward and upward with a director like Lloyd or Borzage or Milestone, who could guide her to her second Oscar, prove again that Garbo had nothing on her. She knew the business thought otherwise, so fine and dandy—where was Garbo's Oscar?

Nowhere, that's where.

Hah!

She was on her knees navigating the tape forward from the back wall when the knock on the door interrupted her. Before she could rise or respond, the door opened a crack and Earl peeked in.

"Looks like you were expecting me," he said.

"I wasn't, but there's no reason to waste the time," she said, interpreting the sly grin working up one side of his face. She tossed aside the tape measure. "C'mon down, big boy, the weather's fine."

It happened fast, furiously, no wasted time or energy, as easy as cracking a bottle of champagne to launch a ship; their every move familiar, practiced and welcome; ending in a swamp of sweat; both out of breath and giggling like school kids.

"Sure beats gardening," Earl said, stepping back into his cords, "although yours is one garden I never get tired of watering, baby."

"And don't you forget it," Sarah said, wrapping herself in a shantung silk robe she fished out of the wardrobe closet.

"Why would you even say that?" He made a face. "I only have eyes for you, now and especially later, after—you know—that thing you want done on Max."

"It's not your eyes worries me, you big lug. There's a lot of temptation floats around the studios, especially those Tillie the Toilers who think they can upgrade their situation by spreading 'em for a big movie star."

"I'm no John Wayne, baby."

"You will be once *Sundown Shadows* gets finished and released and the public gets a whiff of Earl Stanley. Even if you couldn't act your way out of a paper bag, you got what it takes to make the grade. That square jaw for one thing. And another thing— you got me to help get you through the picture, making sure you're lit good, making sure you get close-ups that I would scream bloody murder about if they were going to any other actor had the chance to break in opposite me on the silver screen."

"You'd do that for me?"

"For us. When the picture says The End, it'll only be the beginning for you and for me, living happily ever after—after Max, when we can settle down in a cozy nest of our own, like all lovebirds are meant to do." She let her robe slip open to emphasize the point.

Unnecessarily.

He already had her nailed with a hungry look, his tongue dog-lapping his lips.

"Again?" she said, growling.

"What do you think?" he said.

Sarah shed the robe. "Come to Mama," she said, mindful of keeping him happy and satisfied until Max was out of the way and she could let Earl down gently, get on with the rest of her life.

Sarah was on the slant board in full costume and makeup, waiting for Max to finish lighting the set and positioning the camera to his satisfaction, puffing away furiously on a cigarette, anxious to get the first take out of the way. She had expected more speed out of Max, given the mediocre budget and the tight shooting schedule, but he was his usual self, in pursuit of perfection, what he called "the Max Moonglow touch," as if that were enough to pair him with Ernst Lubitsch; only "the Lubitsch touch" was one of lighthearted sexual innuendo, where Max was compelled to pull the light out of darkness, the same way Lang did, digging deep down into the roots of every truth, however menial, to uncover the evil lurking there.

And, of course, there was yesterday's traditional Moonglow nonsense, his gathering key cast members around a table as a means of pumping them full of team spirit, creating a family feeling during his slow line-by-line read of the script, Max acting out every line so there could be no misunderstanding of what he wanted to capture on film, prepared to shut down any of the actors who might speak up, propose another way to play the scene, and earn his menacing glare and standard invitation: *You don't like what I'm telling you to like, there's the door.*

Sarah noticed Onslow Stevens and Ward Bond struggling more than once to keep their opinions to themselves. The Indian who had replaced Doug Fowley was braver, but smart enough to challenge the dialogue, not Max, when he wondered, "I get shot, I don't know I would say, *You got me, paleface.* Maybe I would say nothing at all, only fall dead?"

It sparked a thunderous guffaw from gravel-voiced Andy Devine. "First actor I ever heard ask to *lose* a line. You wouldn't be trying to set a bad example, would you, Tonto?"

"What do you expect from a redskin anyhow?" Bond said, unlike Andy, no humor in his words. "They've been rising up like that ever since Custer and the Little Big Horn."

"Since before," the Indian said, quietly, looking at Bond like he was measuring him for a scalping.

Bond looked like he'd welcome the opportunity to avenge Custer. He started up from the table mumbling about wampum and teepees and firewater and how the Indian should learn to mind his place the same as Iron Eyes Cody.

Harry Carey, who was sitting next to him, clamped a hand on Bond's shoulder and pushed him back down, his head steering left and right, controlling the tense situation the way he had playing hero in dozens of cowboy movies going all the way back to the silents.

Everyone else remained frozen, waiting for a reaction from Max, except for the girl playing the newspaper editor, who said, timidly, her voice dipped in honey, her fingertips tucked between her lips, "Maybe you could film the scene both ways, Mr. Moonglow, and decide after which way works best?"

It was the first time she'd spoken in the three hours since the group assembled. The others looked at her like she'd cast herself in a tragedy of epic proportion—daring to make a suggestion to Max without invitation, same as the Indian had done. Sarah wouldn't have been surprised if Max ordered them gone, off the picture then and there, but he delivered a surprise totally out of character.

"Excellent thought, Miss"—running a finger down the cast

list—"Miss Leeds, and that's exactly what we'll do." Her smile answered his, paving the way for smiles and nods of approval from the others, except for the Indian and Ward Bond, who resumed trading daggers, and Sarah.

There was something about how he'd answered her, the coo in his voice coupled with a fire in Max's eyes that argued against his ability to remember her name. Sarah had seen and heard it all before from him with other sweet young things.

Sweet old things, too.

Not all of them natural beauties like this one.

Some uglier than sewage.

Sarah imagined Max drew the line between the living and the dead, although it was nothing she could swear to under oath.

One thing for certain, though:

Dixie Leeds was no ingenue pushed on him and the picture by Rudy Bundsman, on irrevocable orders from the front office—the story he'd laid on her when she questioned his choice of an untested unknown for a part more suited to a contract player like Irene Hervey or Laraine Johnson, who was now going by Laraine Day.

Sure, she played around too, but so what?

That wasn't the issue now.

Max was the issue.

Still.

But not for much longer.

Funny, for all his shortcomings, she would miss Max when he was gone.

But not as much as she would welcome the freedom his death would buy her.

Damn it all, her body was on the verge of cramping from too much time trapped on the slant board, watching the crew dance to Max's barked commands, no sense how much longer it would be before he'd satisfied his every mercurial change of mind and was ready to shoot the first scene inside Bart Black's saloon, transformed from someone else's saloon in the George O'Brien western currently shooting exteriors on the "40 Acres" lot in Culver City.

The way Max had plotted the shot, the camera would glide down from an overhead angle that took in Ward Bond and the Indian at opposite ends of the bar, braced to shoot it out, and ease over to a medium shot of her leveling a double-barrel shotgun at them from the saloon stage, warning, *You draw your six-gun, either one of you, you get a deadly taste of old Bubba here, so better think twice about making a bloody mess inside my place.* Bond and the Indian were locked on their marks, but—one of the perks of stardom—her stand-in was suffering the hot kliegs in Sarah's place.

"No, no, no, no, no," Max shouted from the camera crane. "Too much light where I want more dark and shadows." He put the actors on standby until the lights were adjusted and hurried over to her wearing one of his apologetic expressions. "I'm sorry you have to be waiting like this for so long," he said, throwing out his hands. "I should have seen it coming. You do a low-budget picture, you wind up working with low-budget talent." He gave her an air kiss to avoid damaging her makeup. "What do you think so far?"

"Much longer trapped here and my ass is going to fall off."

"After this comes your close-up, so I only have to be worried about your face, not your ass, and how beautiful I'll make you look for the camera." He patted her hand, threw her another air kiss and hurried back to the camera.

The Indian materialized from somewhere moments later. "Begging your pardon," he said. "Got a minute?"

"That's the least of it," Sarah said.

"Been waiting for a chance to pay my respects, Miss Darling. Also to thank you."

"Thank me?"

"For yesterday, that business with Ward Bond—supporting me the way you did."

"I didn't say or do anything."

"Not that the others could tell, but I saw—how you were giving him the evil eye for his derogatory, uncalled-for remarks about me."

Sarah suppressed a smile. "You're quite the observant one. A good thing for me you don't also read minds; you might've discovered what I was thinking."

"Actually, your eyes told me all that I needed to know, how you would think kindly of underdogs because you were once an underdog yourself. Isn't that so?"

She should have sent him packing, but she was intrigued. "In a manner of speaking, maybe, before I made the grade in pictures."

"No. Before that. I see your pain still, embedded in your memory in a way that can never leave a person who has suffered at the hands of others or escape notice of one who's suffered similarly." He held out his hand. "I'm Ronald. Ronald Redman."

"Redman? You're listed by some tongue twister of a moniker on the cast list and call sheet."

"Wahanassatta."

"You say so."

"My true name from the Cheyenne. It means *He Who Walks with His Toes Turned Outward.*"

"I noticed. I'm a little pigeon-toed myself."

Not all she'd noticed.

By any name Ronald Redman was the rugged leading-man type, along the lines of Gable, Coop, Bob Taylor and Earl Stanley. Tall, dark and handsome, but sadly, the dark part was bound to prevent him from ever growing out of bit parts.

Chances were excellent she'd have him doing war dances in bed before shooting wound on the picture. She'd never done it with an Indian, best she could remember, so that would most definitely be a feather in her cap. Hah! Little joke there, Sarah; little joke.

"My woman—Abequa is her name—she'll be pleased to learn of this conversation. She admires you greatly, as do I." Jeez-o, maybe he did read minds. "Your husband, Mr. Moonglow, he is full of invention." Full of something, that was for sure. "Like bringing all of us together, as he did yesterday, to better understand the script and the role each of us will contribute to its success as a motion picture."

Break it to the Indian? How it wasn't something originated by Max, but by another of Max's idols, the other Max, Max Reinhardt, maybe the leading figure in German theater and pictures and as an acting teacher before the Nazis took over the country, reminded him he was Maximilian Goldman, a Jew, and caused him to flee for his life to England, or so her Max had mentioned recently, suggesting he had heard it from Reinhardt himself. The truth or wishful thinking? She couldn't be sure. Max often dropped Reinhardt's name, always to boost his own credentials. Over time he had promoted himself from what he described as a *schlep* in Reinhardt's picture and stage companies to being Reinhardt's right-hand man and trusted confidant.

Sarah said, "He's a genius that way."

"And soon, a hero to the Cheyenne nation," the Indian said.

They were interrupted by one of Max's *schleps,* a pimple-faced teenager, telling them they were needed on the set. "The maestro is ready for the first take," he said, eyes washing over Sarah, otherwise treating the Indian as if he didn't exist.

Max was patrolling the barroom set decked out in jodhpurs, calf-high riding boots, wielding a mallet like he was ready for a game of polo, lacking nothing but the horse, a style of directorial dress inspired by their Los Feliz neighbor Cecil B. DeMille.

He swiped a finger across the surface of the bar counter, as if the presence of dust would wreak havoc with the scene. Created a viewfinder of his hands and framed various areas, nodding or grunting approval, except for one time, when he started moving around the dozen or so extras seated at the gambling tables.

She figured it for the kind of unnecessary last-minute fiddling Max loved to engage in, to remind everyone who was boss, until she saw how repositioning the extras gave the camera a clear view of Dixie Leeds seated behind them on the piano bench, looking as out of place as a eunuch in a whorehouse.

There was nothing in the script or anywhere that put Dixie Leeds in the scene.

Nothing, damn it.

Sarah double-timed over to Max. He saw her coming, smiled broadly and held out his arms in welcome. She stayed outside his reach. "What the hell's this about?" she said, her voice loud enough to reach the catwalk.

"What, sweetheart?"

"Don't *'what, sweetheart?'* me. Her. There."

"The newspaper editor? Think about it and you'll understand."

"I have been thinking about it. Tell me anyway."

"The faceoff between the bully and the Indian. The newspaper editor learns about it. She races over to write an eyewitness account for her newspaper. What any newspaper editor worth her salt ration would do. My inspired notion."

"My ass."

"I got my girl tracking down Charlie Dickens, so he can write it into the script."

"I have my own inspired notion for him to write into the script."

"Tell me. I want to hear."

"Better. I'll show you."

The players and the crew, caught up in the confrontation, watched as Sarah crossed the set and stepped up onto the stage, struck a pose and called to Max, "My mark, right?"

"As rain. Always in the frame, and after we do a close-up on your beautiful face."

"And after my close-up—" She stepped down from the stage and marched to the piano, explaining en route, "I'm not happy to see the newspaper editor and I want her to hear from me she doesn't belong in my saloon."

"Where does it say any of that in the script, my precious one?"

"Wherever you tell Charlie to write it." Sarah leaned into Dixie Leed's face, close enough to recognize her perfume. She'd smelled it often enough on Max in recent weeks. She'd dismissed his latest shack-up, whoever she was, as a condemned prisoner's last meal, but it was different now that she had a face tied to the odor, especially one so pretty and so present. And so young. Here where the shack-up had no business being, in a Sarah Darling picture, confirming what Sarah had sensed yesterday at the cast meeting.

The shack-up misunderstood her smile and smiled back.

Such pretty picture-perfect teeth.

Paid for by Max maybe?

Probably.

Sarah punched Dixie Leeds in the mouth. Slap-wiped her hands and headed away declaring, "I'll be in my dressing room until you're ready to shoot the scene as originally intended, Max, my darling."

The force of the blow split Dixie's lip and slammed her back against the keyboard. She pitched forward, landing on her hands and knees, then used the piano bench to drag herself onto her feet. Spit out a bloody tooth as she charged after Sarah.

She caught Sarah by the shoulders, wheeled her around and pushed her onto the ground. Sarah pulled her down with her. They rolled around trading punches and noise, pulling hair and tearing at their costumes, egged on by hoots and hollers from the crew. Earl Stanley tried separating them and received a swift heel in the groin for his failed effort.

Max shouted over the roar of the crowd for Nicholas Musuraca, his cameraman, to roll the camera. "I want all of this on film. It's going in the picture, all of it. You hear me? Roll the camera, Nicky. Roll the camera. Is the camera rolling? Are you getting this? This is magic we got here. Magic! The Moonglow Touch!"

Hearing that, Ward Bond and Andy Devine jumped into camera range and teamed to pull Sarah and Dixie apart, ignored their screaming, kicking demands to be set free, and turned to Max for direction.

Sarah managed to struggle loose from Ward Bond and launched herself at Dixie.

Bond turned and gave the camera a grim, determined glance before heading after her again. He lifted Sarah off her feet, her legs flailing madly as he took steps backward, not quick enough to prevent one of her kicks from connecting with Dixie's shin; the sound of bone cracking instantly drowned out by the damn shack-up's pitiful scream, something straight out of a horror movie; startling Andy Devine into releasing her. She hit the floor unconscious. The Indian called for someone, anyone, to go for medical help. Sarah limped off for her dressing room, motioning for Earl Stanley to follow her.

CHAPTER 28

Nothing Max said could convince Pan Berman to let him delay the start of filming until Dixie Leeds recovered from her injuries, the swollen, purple-hued face, the missing tooth, especially the cracked shin that had her in a thigh-high cast and on crutches. "Max, for Christ's sake, it's a Max Moonglow Production starring Sarah Darling, not an ingenue nobody's ever heard of, someone who's easily replaced," he said. "No more delays."

"What's a week or two?"

"A month, the very least, according to the studio doctors who patched her up. Also, a cast and crew being paid to sit around and wait. We're not after an Oscar award with this picture, remember? It's a lousy B-programmer we're trapped doing for reasons I don't have to remind you. A ten-day shoot you're expected to bring in on budget or less; over and out."

"Dixie Leeds has star quality that together with Sarah can make this an A-plus-plus production," Max said. "That's what you'll be denying me and my picture."

"And your bed, according to the story going around the lot."

Max slapped his heart and feigned shock. "I'll pretend I didn't hear that, Pan. That kind of gossip is beneath you. Besides, Sarah's got herself Earl Stanley, or isn't that a story also making the rounds?"

Pan made like a school crossing guard. "Something else," he said. He pulled a pipe from its desk cradle and went through the precise ritual of filling, tamping and lighting the bowl of tobacco, sent a line of sweet-smelling smoke rings floating across the office. "She cornered me, Sarah did, and let me have it straight out. If Dixie Leeds stays in the picture, she's o-u-t out." More smoke rings. "Sarah walking is not an option. She goes, the picture goes bye-bye, too, and with it the tribute to Willie Frankfurter by the esteemed producer-director who shot Willie dead."

"I can talk to New York on the long-distance, explain."

"They already have legal fine combing your contract for deal breakers." He let the news sink in. "Give it up, Max. The screwing you're getting isn't worth the screwing they'll give you." He drew a file folder from the top drawer and slid it over. "Here's a girl we want you to take on in the part."

Max flipped open the file folder and studied the photograph. "Polly Wilde. What's it with this dame?" He told Pan about his parking-lot encounter with some casting director touting her as the best thing since sliced bread.

"That would be Leo Salmon, a hustler who knows how to work all the angles," Pan said. "He made some connections high up that helped him get her over here from some Bill Boyd Cassidys across the street and cast in one of our George O'Briens. It's a one-plus-one deal, with a seven-year start-up contract if she comes across as something special. She was in line for *Gunga Din,* but Olivia de Havilland's sister, Joan, got in the way of that casting, so Perry Lieber said to stick her in *Showdown at Shadow Creek* in place of your injured girl, see how well she does for a director of your quality and stature."

"Save the soft soap. I don't like her already," Max said.

He broke the news to Dixie that evening, while recovering from a torrid session in bed that left him gasping for air and on the edge of an asthma attack threatened less by the sexual pyrotechnics than by the anticipation of what he'd say and how she'd respond.

She took it well, further deepening the depression he had carried with him out the door of Pan Berman's office and throughout the day. Somehow, over their time together, Dixie had become far more than his current *schtoop.*

What had started out as lies meant to inspire her to unreserved performances in the bedroom had turned his lust into what might be actual love.

Love, a word he used often, but rarely more than as another word in his vocabulary, not in his emotions.

He supposed he loved Sarah, but that was less for what she brought to his life than what she meant for his career.

It wasn't the same for him with Dixie, that much he knew for certain, but not what made it different.

Unless—

Love?

The newness, the freshness, the uniqueness had gone out of their clandestine affair a long time ago, yet here they still were, here he still was, as hungry for her as he was the night she skated into his life at the Skate Burger Drive-In on Melrose.

"You sure you're okay, honey pie," she said, cuddling closer to him, nibbling at his ear, fingers rummaging his chest hairs. "I don't want you to feel bad for something wasn't your fault in the first place. All you ever were trying was to do good for me by the career I can still hope to happen one of these days soon."

"And it will, honey lamb. I promise you. I swear to you. This isn't my last picture, only my last picture without you being in it."

"You don't have to promise or swear," she said. "I believe you because you're you, and I never expected I would meet anyone as good and sweet and kind and honest as you, not in Hollywood, not in the show business."

She patted his cheek, kissed his dueling scar, moistened his lips and chased after his tongue with hers while locking a hand onto his pulsating pogo stick.

He responded urgently, but only briefly before he pulled free and nudged her away, pleading, "Wait. Not yet. There's something I have for you."

"I already have what I want, honey pie," she said, reaching for him as he rolled out of the bed, but not quick enough to catch him.

He padded in double-time across the room to the clothing she had stripped him of and tossed into a corner. Found what he wanted in a jacket pocket. Dashed back to her and patted a place for her to sit beside him.

"Close your eyes," Max said.

"You're such a director," she said, making light, but she did as commanded.

He took her hand and seconds later told her, "I meant to go and do this a long time ago. You can open up now." Dixie recognized what he'd placed in her palm—her mother's wedding ring—and exploded in tears to go with the crybaby sound bursting from the back of her throat. "I almost forgot the name of the hockshop you told me," he said. "Good thing I didn't, wouldn't you say?"

"I'll show you instead," she said. She saddled him, gave him a hard kick with her leg cast, and rode him like Eddie Arcaro whipping home a winner at the Santa Anita racetrack.

He started wheezing and coughing, struggling to breathe, his chest closing in. He tried telling her to stop, quit, get off him, but could not put together a complete sentence. What words he managed sounded like gibberish. Not enough strength to push her off him. Abdominal and neck muscles straining, and—

She quit the ride, her eyes wide with alarm. "Jeepers, honey pie, what's going on? Your lips, they're turning blue." She rolled off him and onto her feet. "Maybe I should call a doctor or something?" All he needed—desperately—was his inhaler, but she couldn't make sense of what he was trying to say or where he was pointing her to with a finger as steady as a willow in the wind. He found the strength to struggle onto his feet and took a step toward the pile of clothing; the inhaler in the same jacket pocket where he'd kept her mother's wedding ring. His shoulders hunched. He lost his ability to concentrate. He grew confused. Forgot where he was headed or why. Fell down.

"Dear Lord, it's the asthma," Dixie realized. "Your breathing thing, where is it? I need to get it for you." She dropped beside him. "Where is it, lambie pie? Lambie pie, can you hear me?"

CHAPTER 29

Max was stretched out on his back under the bedcovers, locked in a deep sleep, his breathing normal, his snoring the usual ghastly noise that put a bull elephant's trumpeting to shame, when Sarah got there with Mad Dog, and Dixie led them into the bedroom.

"I found him his inhaler and just in time from the looks," Dixie said.

"Who else knows about this?" Sarah said, taking charge. "You phone anyone else?"

"Only you. I wanted to phone for an emergency ambulance, get him to the hospital, but he said no, to phone you; you'd know what to do. He's been like this ever since."

"And you like that?" Sarah meant her hair a mess, her makeup a disaster zone, her chemise exposing enough body to catch Mad Dog's interest and cause him to overlook her missing tooth and the purple swell under one eye. Dixie crossed her arms over her picture-perfect breasts and answered with a guilty expression that further revealed her for the two-bit tramp she was. "Exactly how long have you been sharing this cozy little love nest with my husband?" Sarah stressed the word *husband*. "How much does Max pay you for services rendered? I can't believe for a minute your kind of person would give it away for nothing. Was the part you no longer have in our picture the price, tootsie, or maybe only the down payment?" Arms akimbo. A look of utter contempt.

"He loves me," Dixie said.

"Which explains why he had you call me?" That stopped the tramp cold. "You hear her, Mad Dog? She sounds like she believes in fairy tales. Who are you, really? Little Red Riding Hooker?"

"This is who I am," Dixie said. She stepped forward and showed off the diamond ring she was sporting on her left hand. "You're his wife now, but not forever. He gave me this ring tonight, just before he got so sick with the asthma. You got me out of one picture, Miss Darling, and soon I'll be getting you out of the other, his real, true life."

"Over my dead body," Sarah said.

Her temper snapped beyond control.

She did a quick side step and seized a pearl-handled stainless-steel cuticle pusher from the manicure set neatly laid out on the vanity table.

Mad Dog recognized where this was heading, shouted, "Sarah, don't!"

She was at Dixie before he could prevent her from plunging the diamond-shaped point of the cuticle pusher into the side of Dixie's neck and jamming it up into her throat.

Dixie looked at her in disbelief, the light draining from her eyes as she grabbed the cuticle pusher and yanked it loose. Gushers of blood soaked her chemise a Technicolor red. She did an awkward pirouette and fell onto the bed, landing facedown beside Max, whose sudden grunting noise from the back of his throat briefly interrupted his snoring.

Sarah backed away, braced herself against the wall, her adrenaline in overdrive, and studied the two of them. It had been a long time since she killed anybody, for revenge that first time, this time out of anger. That other time, when dear Barney would not let her pull the trigger and did it himself, she could have done it without so much as a second thought, putting an end to blackmail that could have destroyed her career. Funny, all three murders different, except for her feeling of self-righteous, exhilarating relief; deaths in the service of her life.

If it made sense, she'd get rid of Max right now, forget about the plan in the works to make it look like an accident. Stuff a pillow over his face until he quit breathing, and—

Stage it to look like a lovers' quarrel—

Max kills Dixie Leeds, bringing on the asthma attack that kills him.

Tempting, yes, but one false step and it could lead to precisely the kind of scandal that could put a permanent dent in her career—

Sarah Darling's husband and his mistress found dead under the same roof.

No.

Better to stick with the plan—

Sarah nowhere near the scene when Max dies by accident or at the hands of a disgruntled screenwriter named Charlie Dickens. A period of mourning for the grief-stricken widow. Afterward—

"How are we gonna handle this mess?" Mad Dog said, bringing her back to the reality of the bedroom. "Here's the last place in the world you need to be right now."

"Or them," Sarah said, a solution taking root in her mind. She found the phone and dialed Earl Stanley's number, drumming an impatient melody on the table surface before he picked up. "It's me. An emergency's come up and I need to see you." She gave him the address.

By the time Earl got there, every trace of Dixie had disappeared, her bloody corpse, the crimson blankets and bedsheets rolled into a rug from the living room and ready to be taken away; the bedroom rinsed and scrubbed clean using a bottle of Lysol

Sarah found in the bathroom cabinet.

She ran to him acting the rescued damsel in distress, wrapped onto him and dotted his face with wet kisses, explained the situation and what she needed from him in a voice cracking with desperation, her lips trembling. "So, can you, will you, or what, darling?"

"This is nothing like what we ever talked about," he said, easing her aside. He sank into a lounge chair and appeared to lose himself in prayerful thought for a few minutes. He called across the room to Mad Dog, "This is nothing like what we ever talked about, her'n me, you know?"

"Or her and me," Mad Dog said, entering the game with a mirthless grin. "I hurried over when I got her emergency call for help, because that's what good friends do, and now you're here, more than her good friend from everything I ever heard out of her mouth."

"You know about us?"

"Sarah trusts me, has for years, but not as much as I swear she trusts you."

Earl looked to Sarah for confirmation.

She crossed her heart. "And hope to die," she said.

"Never no way," Earl said, rising. "Let's us get to doing what's got to be done."

Something hit her shoulder and dropped onto her lap, startling Sarah awake. She'd fallen asleep on the satin lounge chair she'd moved nearer to the bed, the better to monitor Max's breathing. He had managed himself upright and reached one of the dozen or so pill bottles on the nightstand.

"This can't be Heaven because I feel like Hell," he said, his voice chunky with phlegm.

"You look it, too."

"Also because you're here."

"My master's voice."

He coughed into a fist and tossed aside the residue. "Where's Dixie?" His eyes roamed the bedroom and stopped at the door to the living room. He mustered enough breath to try calling for her, but couldn't raise more than half a whisper. It stuck to his throat. He tried again, with worse effect.

"She's not here, Max."

"Where is she? Where'd she say she was going?"

"She didn't say. She called me sounding frantic, saying it was an emergency, an asthma attack and you wanted me here. The front door was wide open. You were alone, stretched out unconscious down on the floor. I found your inhaler, pumped the life back into you, broke my ass getting you up into bed, and here you are, so we can live to fight another day." Max looked hurt, like the little tramp had meant more to him than a steady lay. She almost felt pity for the two-timing bastard. "So lucky you told her to get me over here, wasn't it, Maxie dear?"

"More than that," he said. "I knew you would know what to do, no matter what, but there was something I needed to confess." His eyes strayed from her and he fussed with the bed-covers while working out whatever he intended to say, revealing a spot of blood she'd missed earlier. A speck, really, but, if he also noticed, that's all it might take to start him asking questions she didn't want to hear.

She flew from the chair and over to him, readjusting the covers to bury the stain while telling him, "My darling man, what I don't know about you and Dixie Leeds I don't have to know. It doesn't matter. You're alive. That's all that matters."

"Not her—you," he said, and drew silent again. Collected his breath and coughed his lungs clear. "When I thought I was dying, thought any second I'd be reaching the light at the end of the tunnel, my only other thought was of you, Sarah." Another pause. "I told myself I did not, could not die; refused to die without seeing you one final time to tell you how much I love you. That's why I told her, Dixie, to call for you."

"Thank goodness she did."

"And now I promise you, she's out of my life forever."

"You don't have to promise," Sarah said, leaning over to settle a kiss on his dry lips. "For better or for worse, in sickness and in health, till death do us part."

Next morning, it was business as usual on the set, Sarah back on the slant board as Max, all hustle and bellow, overcompensating for his brush with mortality, rehearsed Dixie Leeds's replacement through the barroom scene. Polly Wilde, her name, definitely as wrong for the part as Dixie Leeds had been. Too youthful, too fresh-faced, a big-boobed body that one day would turn to cow; entirely lacking enough sex-appeal fizz to ever become a threat on-screen or off, although crew whispers were making her out to be someone's pet project, Howard Hughes the name most often mentioned. She could buy that. The stuttering flyboy loved Mount Everest boobs as much as he loved the cockpit, dreary Kate Hepburn being the only exception Sarah knew about. Pancakes had more oomph than Kate Hepburn.

Max called a break, and aimed toward her towing Polly Wilde and some guy in a spiffy three-piece black silk suit out of *Esquire Magazine*—broad shoulders, narrow waist, cuffed trousers, decorated with a splashy Countess Mara tie and matching handkerchief in the breast pocket; black patent leather pumps; a slightly off-center nose and rabbit teeth on a boyish, freshly laundered face behind a layer of toxic aftershave; strutting like an agent or a gangster or a pimp, not that she'd ever found much difference between those species.

The closer they came, the more familiar he looked. She knew why by the time they reached her, Max in his gracious host mode, telling Sarah, "People I know you've been as anxious to greet as they've been anxious to meet you, my precious one."

"Miss Wilde, isn't it?" Sarah said, holding out a hand. Polly clutched it in both hers. "I've heard many good things about you. Max has been praising you to the sky."

"I'm humbled in your presence, Miss Darling."

Max said, "And we owe your presence to Leo Salmon here, the first to bring your amazing talent to my attention and convince me I needed a better, stronger actress in the demanding role of the *Shadow Creek Sentinel* editor than casting had delivered to me, my dear Polly."

She pressed his words to her heart and did a half curtsy, like he was some king.

Leo Salmon said, "Only the messenger, sir, ever grateful that a man of your great stature would take the time to hear me out."

"You have a way with words, young man, a gift, impossible to ignore."

Leo lowered his head and humbled himself. "In all due modesty, who am I to argue with a proven genius like Max Moonglow?"

"Indeed," Max said.

They shared a brief Hollywood hug, pats on the back and what passed for affectionate laughter, like that was supposed to disguise the lies passing between them.

Sarah understood Max's motive, but not the game Leo Salmon was playing.

She turned her brightest smile on him. "I believe we met briefly at a party Max and I threw at Moonglow Manor."

"I'm flattered you'd remember, Miss Darling. A simply lovely evening disrupted by some fellow who traded loud, ugly words with Mr. Moonglow."

"Charlie Dickens," Sarah said. "A screenwriter. Maybe you

know him?"

Polly and Salmon traded blank looks and shared them with her.

Who did they think they were kidding? Positively another lie from one or both of them. Polly keeping secret from Salmon exactly how well she did know Charlie? And what did that say about her relationship with Salmon? Sarah smiled inwardly at the only answer that came to mind. Polly Wilde was a user, working her way up one Tom, Dick and Harry at a time, emphasis on the dick. She'd bear watching.

"Like I ever need to be reminded about that night," Max said, rolling his eyes, "yet here I am doing a picture from his screenplay. Only in Hollywood."

"One more example of your generosity, Mr. Moonglow. So rare in this town."

"Talent is talent, Leo. Dickens wrote a script too good to ignore and provided a new challenge for me, opportunity to again turn hamburger into top sirloin with my Moonglow Touch."

Polly clapped her hands appreciatively.

Sarah said, "You're Polly's agent, is that it, Leo?"

"Her manager, yes, but until recently no more than an independent casting director who'd struck oil with this remarkable gusher of talent."

"And you've been pumping the well ever since?"

Salmon caught her meaning. The humor went out of his smile. He turned to Max for rescue.

"Time to get back to work," Max said, taking Polly by the hand. "My precious one, we'll be ready to bring you on and roll film in ten minutes."

Even that sounded like a lie to Sarah.

Almost an hour passed before they came for her.

★ ★ ★ ★ ★

The day went smoothly, Max showing his usual efficiency once he was satisfied with the setups. He bought the second of two takes on the long shot, ordered all three of her close-ups printed, and framed a new shot that had Sarah asking, *What's she doing in here?* before angrily tearing after Polly at the piano bench.

"From there we go straight into the fight footage, cut so no one can ever tell it was a different newspaper editor," Max said beforehand, taking her aside to explain and request her approval. "I won't be happy or satisfied unless you are, too, my precious one," he said.

"Since when did you need my approval for anything, Max?"

"Since I'm still alive, thanks to you," he said.

Earl trooped into her dressing room during the meal break looking every inch a man of the west in fringed shotgun chaps over bull denim trousers, two hawg-leg holsters hanging empty from his gun belt, and scarred leather boots that announced years of riding dusty trails, their first time alone since he and Mad Dog carted Dixie Leeds out of Max's Sunset Plaza Drive hideaway last night.

"I don't know how long I can stand the pressure," he said, tossing his sweat-stained Stetson onto the sofa bed and settling down. "More than I ever would have dreamed up in my worst nightmare, worse than how a year without rain can harm the best-kept lawns and gardens." He fiddled with the neck tissues guarding his shirt collar and checkered bandanna against the makeup hiding every pit and blemish under a rich desert tan.

"The girl is gone, out of our lives forever, and that's that," Sarah said. "We have our whole future ahead of us once Max has his tragic accident. Think positive, you big lug of a lawman."

"Not her or that," Earl said, staring at her with bloodshot

eyes he could barely keep open, his shoulders as defeated as the grim edge to his voice. "I'll tell you what it is. It's my first big scene coming up, where I actually have to say words. I ever knew how hard it was to learn words, I never would-a thought to become a movie star; would-a stuck to being a damn fine gardener."

Sarah threw her hands out at him. "And you are going to become a damn fine movie star, so stop your silly talk, sheriff; Mama right there to help out, you need any helping, like right now, helping you relax away all your worrying." She settled beside him on the sofa bed, bit his earlobe, and whispered, "We have to be careful about our costumes, so the next best thing will have to do for now."

"The next best thing?"

"I'll show you," she said, and in moments had him begging for more.

In the calm that followed, Sarah asked Earl about last night.

"Mad Dog didn't tell you?"

"We haven't had a chance to connect. Max and I drove here together, straight from the bungalow."

"It went just the way you wanted it to happen," Earl said, grinning like a Boy Scout who'd just helped someone across the street. "Mad Dog and me, we lugged the, y'know, the rug out to his buggy, stashed it in the trunk and drove off for Oxnard and my uncle Jerry's bait-and-tackle place. Got the spare dock key from his emergency hiding place and loaded the, y'know, the rug onto one of his small motor boats. Took it slow out of the harbor into the open waters, where we mummy wrapped the, y'know, the rug with anchor chains and slipped it over the side. I said a little prayer of thanks that we didn't run into the Harbor Patrol or the Coast Guard, and that was that. Out of there and back to LA without a hitch."

"You're certain?"

"Sure as I know my flowers from A to Z, acacia to zinnia, and you wanna know something else? Acadia means *secret love* and zinnia means *lasting affection*. What could be more A to Z than that?"

Earl was a natural.

He maneuvered the scene with an easy, hip-shifting gait and delivered his lines with an honest Midwestern clarity that gave fresh life and meaning to Charlie Dickens's run-of-the-mill dialogue for Sheriff Long John Brooks.

Cast and crew rewarded him with applause that made him blush.

Max, who had expected problems with Earl and the need for multiple takes that could throw the production schedule and the budget out of whack, added his own praise.

Sarah recognized that Earl could steal the movie out from under her if she wasn't careful, and something else—

Polly Wilde saw it, too.

She was on Earl like white on rice the minute Max called *Cut!*

Marking him.

Getting ready to trade up from an agent to a movie star in the making.

Dangerous, that one.

Dangerous and cunning.

So what?

She was welcome to Earl.

But not until Sarah was finished with him.

And that would be soon.

CHAPTER 30

Charlie somehow had managed to get through the script revisions Max Moonglow wanted, but it was a struggle, his mind never clear of Robin Moon in deteriorating physical condition, on the road somewhere with Ernie and Millie Keyes, although the doctor at New Dawn said she belonged in bed under intense medical supervision until her wounds healed and she'd regained her strength.

He needed to find her and take her back there.

He owed her that much, didn't he?

Why was it a question?

It wasn't.

It shouldn't be.

Plain and simple, it was something he had to do. How had Barney Rooker put it to him? *It's what friends do for friends*, he'd said, *where we got it all over the people who live their lives only out for themselves.*

The starlet-hopeful at the RKO reception desk, all smiles, her resolve as firm as her curvaceous body, refused him admittance and threatened to summon security guards when Charlie made a move past her. His claim to the contrary, there was no interoffice advisory from Max Moonglow Productions. As a courtesy, she dialed the Moonglow office, entered into a brief hushed conversation and reported, "No one is available now who has an answer for us." Rather than waste more time arguing, he gave her the new script pages for bicycle delivery by a messenger boy.

A half hour later he was downtown monitoring the Union Terminal freight yard from a vantage point outside the authority of the railroad bulls, where he figured to spot anyone hopping off a flatbed or out from a boxcar, with any luck a familiar face from his plague-ridden time riding the rails home from Hemet.

There was a lot of hobo and migrant family traffic, but nobody he recognized.

He chased after three or four rail riders, who looked like they might be itinerant field hands—they were—and loosened their tongues with a couple greenbacks apiece.

None knew the Keyes by name, but one remembered a couple who matched his description of Ernie and Millie.

"Did they have a young girl with them?" Charlie said, hoping the man's answer would be the one he was desperate to hear.

The man narrowed his eyes to the possibility and scratched at the stubble on his sunbaked face. "Lotsa young girls with lotsa people stoopin' to survive, mister."

Charlie described Robin.

The man thought some more. "Yeah, sounds about right. Comin' yesterday when I was gettin' ready for goin'."

"Where?"

"I ain't no roadmap, mister."

Charlie got the hint and handed over another two bucks.

The man stuffed them in his pocket. "Out Yucaipa way it was, up in the Oak Glen country, hoping to score at one of them apple orchards there. Can't say what happened after that. Lots of growers in the market for cheap labor one day to the next."

"They'd be in an old beat-up Chevy Stakebed."

"Yeah, rings the bell. Like you was talkin', older couple and the girl, stop and go in a Stakebed."

Getting to Oak Glen took Charlie almost four hours of bump-and-grind driving on serpentine roads, past miles of undeveloped acres, dairy farms and vineyards separated by a half dozen communities with less than a mile between their Welcome and You Are Now Leaving road signs.

Redlands possibly the one exception.

Barely.

He grew weary and knuckle-sore knocking on doors. None of the growers he spoke with recognized Ernie, Millie and Robin from his description. None remembered seeing a Chevy Stakebed during the week. All said they were weeks away from the hiring season, their Delicious and Rome Beauty apples not yet ripe for picking and packing.

Daylight was running out of time and he was too worn out by failure to make the long drive back to LA.

"Sure sounds like you were flimflammed good," said the cherub-faced woman showing him to his room at Apple Annie's Pioneer Ranch and Historical Hotel, a plump, motherly type in an old-fashioned green-and-red gingham dress, gray and silver braided hair neatly piled in a bun on top of her head, her voice as soothing as cough syrup; Annie herself. "If your friends were already over in LA, why come back up this way when the San Fernando Valley's closer and ripe with groves ready for the pickings right now?"

At once Charlie confessed to himself, *I'm a fool.* He'd forgotten hearing that when Ernie was describing how the police had hauled Robin off to jail, too consumed by fear for Robin's safety and the need to rescue her from custody. The realization made for a restless night, an on-again, off-again nightmare about finding Robin before her health disintegrated beyond repair. He was back on the road shortly after sunrise, half asleep behind the wheel, occasionally trapped in pockets of traffic that added another hour to the monotonous drive.

He stopped home briefly for a quick shower and shave and a change of clothes. An interoffice envelope from the studio had been slipped under his door, containing a memo from Max Moonglow, who wanted another new scene written for *Show-down at Shadow Creek*. Maybe two. Drop everything. Come at once to the Paramount ranch.

Charlie balled the memo and tossed it into the wastebasket.

An hour later he was combing valley ranches for Ernie, Millie and Robin, having no better luck than he'd had in Oak Glen. By the time he reached the Ventura County line he was worn out and frustrated, wondering if it made sense to keep up the search. If they had come in this direction, somebody would have seen them by now. Yes? No? It was a mystery in the making, *The Search for Robin Moon*. Nothing he was about to turn into a screenplay, not without the kind of happy ending movie audiences demanded. Where was his happy ending? Farther north? Somewhere in Oxnard? Montecito? Santa Barbara? Or was he on another empty trail? Had Ernie changed his mind and direction, maybe headed south in hopes of finding work in one of the beach cities along the coast? Hell. He'd stop for a quick bite and a latrine; think it through, how to proceed; maybe by the flip of a coin. Ready to call it heads or tails, but not quits.

Charlie pulled off the highway and navigated through a shallow dirt parking lot packed with commercial trucks and panel vans fronting a faded red barn, a sign mounted on the gabled cedar-shake roof announcing Sutton's Truckline Café—Rich Food at Poor Boy Prices—Open 24 Hours.

He squeezed between an overgrown freight transport and a one-ton, was about to head for the entrance when he saw it—

Ernie Keyes's Chevy Stakebed.

Parked across the lot.

No mistaking its scratches and dents, the chipped engine cowl, the sloppy green-over-black paint job.

He hurried inside Sutton's and was immediately struck by the cumulative stink of griddle grease and tobacco smoke that hung over the poorly lit café, making it impossible to identify anybody at the booths that rimmed the busy counter. A jumble of conversation drowned out the jukebox, Bea Wain's searching vocal on "Where in the World" with the Larry Clinton orchestra giving way after a minute to Bob Willss' western swing version of "San Antonio Rose."

Charlie shouted for Ernie over the din. Nothing. He tried again, calling for Millie and Robin when that failed. All he got in response were customers yelling for him to shut up, a request echoed more politely by the bald-headed gent at the cash register, whose belly could pass for a life preserver.

Undeterred, Charlie shouted for anyone who knew anything about the '37 Chevy Stakebed parked outside. Nothing except for a disdainful look from the cash register gent. Bob Wills gave way to Bing Crosby crooning "Too Marvelous for Words." A beefy six-footer who could pass for Johnny Appleseed, beard, broad shoulders and all, stepped over wondering, "I hear you asking after my truck while I was practicing my piss in the john?"

"The thirty-seven Chevy Stakebed?"

"What about it?"

"Since when's it yours?"

"You accusing me of something?" Johnny Appleseed said, clenching his fists.

Charlie forced a smile. "Only curious, that's all. It looks like a Stakebed I remember from a friend of mine."

"Your friend, he got a name?"

"Would it matter?"

"Might."

"Ernie, Ernie Keyes." Charlie described him.

"On the road with a wife and a sick kid, a girl?"

"Yes."

"Then him, all right. Met up at the Greyhound Station in Hueneme, him scouting after anybody might care to trade the van for bus money. Too good a deal for me to pass up on. I can sell it and make a nice profit once I get to San Diego."

"Did Ernie say where they were headed?"

"He did, it wasn't to me, but if I was in his shoes it would be to the nearest hospital and fast. That kid of theirs looked sicker'n a dog. I've seen plenty sick dogs in my time, but she took the cake."

He marched off.

Charlie settled at the counter over scrambled eggs, a stack of wheat cakes and a mountain of hash browns swimming in grease, debating about what to do now. Maybe, a ticket clerk at the Hueneme Greyhound station would remember the Keyes, could tell him where they were headed. Maybe, drive straight north to the Sonoma wine country, where Ernie and Millie were likely to look for work. Maybe admit the futility of the chase, quit, go home hoping they'd see what Johnny Appleseed saw and get Robin to a doctor or a hospital before it was too late.

An answer came at him unexpectedly.

The beefy trucker next to him at the counter wheeled off his stool and left, leaving behind a well-thumbed copy of the *Los Angeles Examiner*. Charlie pulled it over, turned from the horse-racing charts to the front page, and froze at the headline that stretched across all eight columns:

MURDER VICTIM FOUND IN OXNARD WATERS
IDENTIFIED AS MOVIE STARLET DIXIE LEEDS

In gruesome detail, the story reported how Dixie Leeds was discovered by sports fishermen out for an early run after sea bass, halibut, rockfish, and yellowtail; described the ghastly condition of her body; quoted studio spokesman Perry Lieber about the tragic end to a promising career and how she'd be replaced in the Max Moonglow production *Showdown at Shadow Creek*, currently filming on location at the Paramount movie ranch, by another starlet verging on major stardom, Polly Wilde.

Dixie Leeds.

Showdown at Shadow Creek.

His movie.

He remembered the memo he'd tossed from Max Moonglow.

Was Dixie Leeds's murder the reason behind the memo?

The new scenes Max wanted.

New scenes tailored to fit Polly Wilde?

Charlie threw a handful of coins onto the counter and raced for his car, tore out of the lot and ignored the speed limit signs racing to the Paramount ranch; barely slowing for the deceptively dangerous curves of the Agoura hills; suffering guilt every second of the thirty-minute trip over quitting his search for Robin; promising himself he would pick up where he'd left off tomorrow or the next day, but right now it was his movie that needed him.

Charlie was directed to the church on the main street of the western-town set, where Perry Lieber was at the elevated pulpit addressing the assembled cast and crew members in a somber, emotionless tone. He reassured everyone that production had been shut down for one day only, drawing a noisy blanket of sighs and scattered applause that got louder after he observed, "It's carved in stone, you know, how the show must go on, and it's assuredly what Miss Leeds would have asked from all of us. So, be sure to remember Miss Leeds in your prayers tonight, even as you remember not to discuss what you know of her or of her tragic death should you be approached by anyone from the press. You advise them to come talk to me."

"And the cops, what about them?" somebody called.

"Unlikely you'll hear from the police," Perry Lieber said, and let it go at that.

He descended the pulpit and the people began drifting out, faces in the crowd that Charlie recognized—Harry Carey, Andy Devine, Ward Bond, Onslow Stevens—but not Max.

Or Sarah.

Or Polly.

Perry Lieber had aimed down the center aisle straight for him. He offered his hand, saying, "You're Charlie Dickens, right?"

"Yes, sir."

"Come along with me, Mr. Dickens. We have business to talk about."

Charlie accompanied Lieber ten or fifteen yards before he halted, announcing, "No, sir. I can't."

"Can't what, Mr. Dickens?"

"The show that must go on for me isn't here, Mr. Lieber, not right now. There's something more important that needs doing by me right now."

"Mr. Dickens, I don't know how wise this is of you," Lieber said, unable to mask his annoyance.

"I do," Charlie said.

Within minutes he was on the road heading north for Sonoma, speeding to make up for lost time.

CHAPTER 31

"You can't buy this kind of publicity," Perry Lieber said, displaying the front pages of the Los Angeles papers: *Examiner, Herald* and *Times.* "The story is being played big by AP, UP and INS here and abroad. No question audiences will flock to the box office. Why we're promoting *Showdown at Shadow Creek* to our A list of releases."

"And more time to shoot, fix the script, do what has to be done to get it right?"

That got Max's attention, the question, not all that blah-blah-blah Perry had been dishing out in the production trailer, making it sound like Dixie's murder was a publicity stunt cooked up by his press agents. Until the question, Max was deep into mourning for Dixie. Every moment, every movement had been a mental and physical struggle for him since Perry called to break the news of Dixie's murder and almost caused another asthma attack, that's how fond Max had become of that darling girl who seemed to want nothing more than to please him. And please him she did. And a big star she would have become under his guidance if she had lived.

Perry said, "A fair question, Mr. Salmon, and certainly matters that Mr. Moonglow will be considering in the hours ahead, applying his special touch to further turn a tragedy into a triumph. Isn't that so, Max?"

"What's he doing in here anyway?" Max said, recognizing Leo Salmon, who had a protective arm around Polly Wilde. "It

271

was supposed to be you, Sarah, the Wilde girl, and me for this meeting, that's all. Right, Sarah? What Perry said?"

"Where she goes, I go as her manager, Mr. Moonglow, especially in situations that might negatively impact Polly's career."

"Negatively impact? She's not the one who's dead," Max said, a sharp edge to every word.

"Max, please," Perry said. "Mr. Berman made the request on Mr. Salmon's behalf. Pan saw no harm in Mr. Salmon joining us. Neither do I."

"I do."

Sarah patted Max's shoulder. "Let's hear Perry out, darling. What's this meeting really about, Perry? You didn't ask us here to brag about the front-page news stories and what they'll mean for the picture."

"Correct, Sarah. I wanted this time to quickly brief all of you before he arrives"—he checked his watch—"in about ten minutes from now."

"Who?"

"Burt Cobbler, the LAPD detective on the Willie Frankfurter shooting. Cobbler has some questions to ask about Miss Leeds. Although jurisdiction is with the Oxnard police, I agreed to his request for a meeting as a courtesy, to protect RKO, the picture and everyone in this room; prevent any news leaks we wouldn't want leaked."

Max exploded again. "For Christ's sake, you make it sound like the two deaths are connected somehow, like somehow one of us could be responsible for Dixie's murder."

"A horrible thought," Sarah said, swatting away the idea.

"The negative impact I'm talking about," Leo Salmon said. "We never even met the young lady, Polly and me."

"Never," Polly said.

"We're leaving," Salmon said. He stood and reached for her hand.

"Sit," Perry said, a command softened by the wisp of a tight-lipped smile. Salmon sat back down. "Nothing for you to worry about, Mr. Salmon. Anything I hear I don't care for, I do some calling around to the press boys, get on the phone to certain people at police headquarters, and that takes care of it. It gets no further."

"How can you be so sure, Mr. Lieber?"

"Same way I know the sun comes up in the morning, Mr. Salmon."

"And the moon at night," Burt Cobbler said. He was standing at the trailer door, no telling for how long. "I guess no one heard me knocking," he said, removing his fedora. He stepped inside and closed the door. "Mr. Lieber can pull those strings, ever he has the need, but my visit is all off-the-record unofficial. Like the man said, I have no jurisdiction in the Dixie Leeds investigation, save for some curiosity that has my nose itching and in need of scratching." His liquid green eyes twinkled mischievously. He inhaled the fresh carnation in the buttonhole of his tailored jacket. "Shall we begin?"

"Mr. Moonglow, you're the star of the Burt Cobbler production now playing in my head," Cobbler began. "You shot and killed Willie Frankfurter believing he was a burglar, not someone from the studio endeavoring to get a script to you."

"It upsets and saddens me to this day."

"More than rumors you were provoked to murder because Mr. Frankfurter had a different reason for sneaking into Moonglow Manor in the dead of night?" He directed a look and flicked a smile at Sarah, who turned away.

"If I were to go around shooting every male in heat rumored to be carrying on with my wife, Hollywood would be a ghost town," Max said, determined not to lose his temper.

"On the other hand, I understand there were rumors about you and an attachment to Miss Leeds that transcended business."

"I was grooming Miss Leeds for stardom, that's all," Max said, his pulse starting to jitterbug.

"Maybe she got a little too frisky, made demands that turned her into a liability?"

"Poppycock! What is it, now you're inventing rumors?"

Cobbler fiddled with his tie, pampering the Windsor knot. "How did Shakespeare put it? *Rumor is a pipe blown by surmises, jealousies, conjectures . . . the blunt monster with uncounted heads.*"

"How I put it: fuck you, detective!" He turned to Sarah with a look she correctly read as lobbying for support.

She said, "I have no reason to doubt my husband, detective. We're not the perfect couple, but we are and always have been perfect for each other. It's crazy to think for one single second he'd ever commit murder." She leaned over and kissed Max on his dueling scar.

"And you, Miss Darling? I regret saying this, being one of your biggest fans, but how about you?"

Sarah arched back and clutched her throat, jerked her head left and right in slow motion, broadcasting a look that combined surprise with open-mouthed disbelief. "I don't believe what I just heard," she said. "Perry, can he talk to me that way? Insult me?"

"You have an answer for Miss Darling, Burt?"

"She and Miss Leeds got into an argument on the set that spun out of control. They traded angry words, and next thing, all captured on film, they were having at each other, Miss Leeds so battered by her there was talk about delaying the production. Maybe Miss Darling decided to take it a step further. On some pretext, she lures Miss Leeds to Oxnard and murders her; loads her on a boat; dumps her in deep waters, never expecting the body to be recovered, so she's home free. How's that?"

"Insane," Sarah said.

Max said, "You've been seeing too many B-picture potboilers, detective. Maybe you should turn in your badge and start writing them yourself."

"I don't see where any of this involves us," Leo Salmon said, rising. "Come, Polly."

Cobbler said, "But it does, Mr. Salmon."

Perry Lieber motioned Salmon to sit.

Salmon did so grudgingly.

"It's no secret that you've managed to advance the career of Miss Wilde with skill and ingenuity, Mr. Salmon, from bit parts in Hopalong Cassidy westerns to a deal at RKO and more important roles in westerns starring Mr. George O'Brien; from a swank party at the Moonglow home to a major, potentially star-making part in a Max Moonglow picture opposite the one-and-only Sarah Darling."

"As good as I am, *Showdown at Shadow Creek* was already cast with Dixie Leeds in the role I wanted for Polly. I couldn't get anywhere with Mr. Moonglow, hard as I tried."

"But if anything were to happen to Miss Leeds—there you were with Miss Wilde ready, anxious and willing to step into the part. And something did happen to Miss Leeds, and what do you know—?"

"You're putting her death on me now?"

"Or me?" Polly said, looking like she'd been slammed with a baseball bat.

Cobbler closed his eyes to her question. "Mr. Salmon asked me how this little get-together involves the two of you. I answered his question, Miss Wilde."

"So what are you saying, exactly?" Max said, his shoe tapping a furious rhythm on the trailer's carpeted floor. "That one of us

275

killed Dixie? In which case, as for it being me, you need to do something, see a doctor about the hole in your head."

"Only illustrating how there's a straight line from your party to Willie Frankfurter to your movie to Miss Leeds's death, Mr. Moonglow. Maybe it's no more than coincidence, but it keeps me interested on an unofficial basis unless or until the Oxnard boys solve the case without uncovering anything that floats it back across the county line to me."

"In which case you're one candidate short," Sarah said, all sass and smirk, like she was the better detective. Cobbler waited her out while she lit a Gitanes and shot a line of smoke at the windshield. "Charlie Dickens."

"The Dickens who wrote *Showdown at Shadow Creek*."

She thought about the title. "Right. At our party, it was him who badgered Max into a fight and had to be restrained. It was him who wanted Polly Wilde for the role Dixie Leeds got. Maybe when he didn't get his way he let his temper get the best of him and took matters into his own hands. Why isn't Charlie Dickens here being suspected by you?"

"He was on the list I gave to Mr. Lieber."

Perry said, "I was bringing Mr. Dickens over when he turned tail and took off, not so much as a word of explanation, or he would have been here, Burt."

Sarah made a triumphant noise. "What's even more curious than him running like that: when I asked Polly and Leo there if they knew Charlie Dickens, they said no. That being the case, why then was Charlie angling so hot and heavy for her to get the role in the first place?"

Leo turned red, blue veins springing from his neck and forehead. "What's going on here? Now we're accused of lying and maybe even in a conspiracy with Dickens to murder Dixie Leeds and get the part for Polly."

"I couldn't explain it better myself," Burt Cobbler said.

Cobbler sponsored another ten minutes of conversation without conclusion before he saluted everyone with a tip of the fedora and an inconsequential smile and slipped away as quietly as he had arrived, leaving behind a collection of frayed nerves and self-serving oratory that carried on for fifteen minutes more before Perry cleared the production trailer, allowing Max to weigh his own thoughts privately, pacing the trailer in conversation with himself.

Mostly, he appreciated how quickly and powerfully Sarah rose to his defense, but why, he wondered, was it necessary for her to direct the blame for Dixie's murder at Polly Wilde, Leo Salmon and even the missing Charlie Dickens?

Self-protection, to dodge the incriminating finger Cobbler had aimed at her?

As good an answer as any, especially since Sarah had to be one of the last who saw Dixie alive, a truth both instinctively had kept from Cobbler.

He ran the scene through the Moviola of his mind—

Waking up at his secret apartment to find Sarah, not Dixie, by his bedside, Dixie having summoned her to help deal with his near-fatal asthma attack.

Sarah unable to account for Dixie's absence, telling him he was alone when she arrived.

Would Dixie have abandoned him like that?

Hardly. No. Definitely not.

What then?

Either Dixie was forced to leave before Sarah arrived by someone or something, or—

Dixie was still at the bungalow when Sarah arrived.

Dixie there?

Then what?

He tried closing his mind to an answer that could help explain why Sarah had been so forceful in defending him and accusing the others:

She was deflecting the blame for Dixie's murder away from herself.

No, damn it, no.

Sarah was capable of transgressions, but murder?

Not murder?

Besides, she couldn't be in two places at one time, at his bedside and in Oxnard.

She'd have needed help.

Who?

Charlie Dickens?

She'd certainly made a believable case against Dickens with Burt Cobbler.

Why would Sarah do that?

Because she knew something she was keeping to herself, even from him?

"Where's your mind, Max," he said, throwing the question against the trailer wall. "Why are you torturing yourself this way, with a guessing game, when there's a way to get answers for real."

He reached for the phone and dialed Kurt Duff's number.

Left word with the private investigator's answering service.

Duff returned Max's call an hour later, telling him, "First chance I had to check for my messages, Mr. Moonglow. Was in the field tagging after your missus. The bird's back in her nest now."

"And before her nest?"

"Out at the Paramount location ranch, then straight back to home except for a stop at Pet Savers, the dog place run by the nuns over at the old Hart place on De Longpre in Hollywood."

"Tell me, the past week, has my wife made any unusual stops, places she's not been before?"

Duff spent a minute mulling over the question. "Only the one I'll be logging in my next report, where you already know about, sir."

"And that would be?"

"Up Sunset Plaza Drive? Apartment out back of the bungalows?"

"Why would I know?"

"Is this some joke, you asking?"

"No."

"Like this—I'm doing the night shift outside Moonglow Manor, when out Mrs. Moonglow comes, speeding down the street like she's making a qualifying run for the Indianapolis Five Hundred. I stick on her tail and stake out across the road from the bungalows. Nothing for the longest time, until you show up yourself and head in. That's it until the morning, when the two of you come out and take off for the studio. A little home-away-from-home romancing, sir? Definitely one way to spice up a marriage. Nothing I haven't run into before, even tried it once or twice myself."

"Yes, exactly," Max said, making Duff's story his own. "Good work. Keep it up." He disconnected and experienced an immediate rush of relief. Nothing Duff said disputed what Sarah told him. He could mourn Dixie without fearing that his wife had murdered his mistress.

CHAPTER 32

"Did he buy it?"

"Lock, stock and barrel," Kurt Duff said. "Besides, it was the truth, if not the whole truth and nothing but, which is why I phoned you right after and suggested getting together so you could hear face first how it went down. Better over coffee than over a party line, if you know what I mean, Miss Darling?"

Duff tilted his voice upward when he said her name, like he was calling attention to the fact he was sharing a table for two with a famous movie star. Nobody at the out-of-the-way Engineer Al's Choo-Choo Train Diner on Barham seemed to notice or care except for a pair of gawky teenaged girls at the far end of the counter sharing giggles and whispers.

"Setting me up for what you call a bonus, is that what you mean, Mr. Duff, like you meant three other times before? What other people might call blackmail?"

"Service above and beyond the call of duty, and that makes for a bonus, the way I see it, Miss Darling. Besides which, I never claim to be the most honest of men. I was, I might still be wearing LAPD blue instead of scratching out a living catching husbands and wives where they don't belong, doing the old horizontal hula with parties of the third part. Besides which, if I hadn't connected with you after your husband put me onto you and you hadn't suggested our little 'see no evil, hear no evil, report no evil' arrangement, look where you'd be right now, up the creek without a paddle."

"And if I tell you, enough is enough, no more bonuses?"

"I go fill in the blanks for your husband, tell him how I saw your man, Mad Dog, and your boyfriend, Earl Stanley, meet up with you at the apartment. How they came out later lugging a rolled-up rug and drove off. How, playing a hunch, I followed them out to Oxnard and a certain boat, saw what the rug was all about. . . . You need to hear more?"

"How much of a bonus?"

"Times before, you bought Papa a brand new pair of shoes. For this I'm thinking Papa deserves a whole new wardrobe." He named an amount.

"You're joking."

"I sound like Jack Benny to you?"

"I've never found greed anything to laugh over."

Duff rose to leave. "Tomorrow night, same arrangement like the last times." He tossed a dollar bill on the table. "My treat," he said, and ambled out of the diner like he'd broken the bank at Monte Carlo.

The teenage girls hurried to her table and asked for Sarah's autograph. She wanted to tell them *No, scoot, scat, go away, leave me alone,* but she was incapable of ignoring the love and admiration they were heaping on their favorite star. *In the whole wide world,* they said. They treated her like royalty and she responded in kind, their exuberance acting like a tonic that eased the excruciating pain trying to dig out of her stomach.

Mad Dog entered the diner and headed over, causing the teenagers to retreat as he slipped into the seat across from Sarah. He read her face and said, "What's up now with that mistake of nature?"

She told him.

He shook his head in slow motion. "Trouble finds you like a fly to honey," he said. "Exactly what I predicted the first time Duff pulled this stunt."

"Worse this time. For all of us. Me. You. Even Earl. He tells what he knows."

"Then we don't give Duff the chance, do we?"

Sarah somehow got through the next day's shoot and fled the ranch, telling Max she would be late getting home—

Barney Rooker the reason—

A call from New Dawn saying Barney's health had taken a turn for the worse and he was asking for her.

"He's a fortunate man to have a friend like you for so many years," Max said.

She'd taken Max to meet Barney once, a long time ago.

They got along well, with Barney on best behavior, recounting the story Sarah had invented to explain how they'd come to know one another, the truth pretty much limited to her saying he'd been like a father to her, Barney calling her the daughter he never had.

"I'll tell Barney hello from you; you're sending him your best," Sarah said.

Max patted her hand and shrugged indifference, still too infected by the gloom he'd worn like a shroud since learning about Dixie Leeds. She had counted on that keeping him from volunteering to accompany her.

She traveled the hairpin twists and curves of tricky Mulholland Drive cautiously, ruled by the taillights of the few vehicles ahead of her and the blinding headlamps of the cars maneuvering downhill, the drivers hitting noisy brakes to avoid overshooting a ridge and plunging into the dark, shrub-infested canyon, and reached Runyon Canyon Park half an hour early.

The park, a collection of fire roads and walking trails within one hundred thirty acres of drought-resistant evergreen trees and lush foliage, was a nighttime destination for dog walkers and couples out for a stroll or sex, as well as tourists aiming for Indian Rock, highest point in the park, with a three-hundred-sixty-degree unobstructed view to the Hollywood and downtown skylines, the Pacific Ocean and Catalina Island.

As she had for other meetings with Kurt Duff, Sarah pulled into the dirt parking area fifty yards off Mulholland, empty tonight except for a dozen or so cars and several dog owners chatting animatedly like old friends. She had dressed down, her face clear of makeup and half disguised under a broad, floppy-brim hat to deter recognition; sat half slouched behind the wheel, her elbow on the open window frame, puffing furiously on a Gitanes.

Waiting for Duff to arrive, she thought through the scheme she'd figured out with Mad Dog. It was almost too simple—a motorized version of what was coming for Max. Poor, dear Max, soon to rejoin his dear Dixie Leeds, making it possible for his precious Sarah Darling to move forward in her career unhampered by his dominating presence, a final gift to her from Max, although he wouldn't be around to know how apprecia-tive she was. The thought earned a smile and got her thinking about Max's last will and testament. His last will and *testicles*. Hah! Another smile. Dixie Leeds was welcome to his testicles. There were more for Sarah where they came from. She'd gladly settle for his other assets, like Moonglow Manor, the bank ac-count and the contents of a safe-deposit box she could never bring him to tell her about.

She was fantasizing stocks, bonds and other securities, diamonds, rubies and pearls, gold ingots, wads and wads of cash, when Duff glided his early-model Ford Tudor into the spot beside her and tooted his horn.

She reached for the thick envelope on the passenger seat and sat half out the door, waited for a dog walker exercising a pair of matched Scotties to pass, before she wandered over to the

Ford. Duff joined her, turned serious after a good-natured greet-ing and pointed at the envelope. "Looks thin. It all there?"

"Not all."

Duff didn't like that. "It's supposed to be all, like before. We talked nothing about doing this on the installment plan, Miss Darling."

"I had to clean out my personal bank account for this much. The rest will have to wait until next week." He checked her for the lie, indicated with a shrug that something was better than nothing. "Oke, next week for the rest, plus another five G for my patience, good will and understanding."

"You're awfully generous with my money, Mr. Duff."

"Look at it this way, a small price to pay for the giant favor I'm doing you, helping you to get away with—"

"Yes, thank you," Sarah said, shutting him up before he said a word she didn't need broadcast. "You're a regular good Samaritan."

Using the time Sarah, by design, had bought with her conversation, Mad Dog moved from a canary-yellow roadster four cars behind Duff to within feet of him. He signaled her he was ready.

She held out the envelope for Duff and let it slip from her hand.

Duff bent over to retrieve it.

Mad Dog was at him in an instant, tossing and tightening a length of clothesline around his throat. Duff struggled to pull the rope loose, but was unable to counter Mad Dog's strength. He coughed up a last gasp, quit battling for breath, and nose-dived to the ground as Mad Dog released the rope.

At once, Sarah opened the front passenger door of Duff's Ford Tudor and stood watch while Mad Dog moved him into the car, got behind the wheel and hit the starter button. The motor gasped more than Duff had and quit on him. He tried again with less success. Jumped out of the car and started fiddling under the hood.

"Looks like your friend could use some help. I'm a mechanic by trade." She had been fixed on Mad Dog and unaware of this portly gent in the ill-fitting blazer who had now suddenly joined her. By the way he studied her over his nose, pushing up his tortoise-style eyeglass frames for better focus, she saw that he recognized her.

"He's doing fine," Sarah said, exaggerating her smile.

"I'm around it turns out he could use the help," the gent said. Tipped his motoring cap and returned a smile brighter than hers. "I'll be right over yonder." He waddled toward a bench, waved on by a casually dressed younger version of himself who was holding tight rein on an energetic Rottweiler. They hugged and began gossiping like old maids, eyes cast on her.

Mad Dog was back behind the wheel. This time the motor held. He pointed her to her car and began easing out. Within minutes they were navigating Mulholland Drive.

A mile down from the park, he pulled off the road onto a safety siding and hopped out of the Tudor with the motor still running.

Sarah pulled in and doused her lights, waited while he moved Duff upright behind the steering wheel, released the emergency brake and, using a hand to guide the wheel, put his shoulder to the Tudor's frame and pushed.

The car didn't budge.

Mad Dog signaled for help.

She waited out a station wagon that had slowed down and seemed intent on pulling in, but instead sped away, then joined Mad Dog in pushing the Tudor.

They got the car rolling.

It crashed through the post-and-board safety rail and plummeted down the canyon, slam-bounced and echoed off ledges and boulders until it settled quietly, invisibly, in the dense canyon underbrush.

Mad Dog's car was parked about a quarter mile down the road, on a side street that fed into Mulholland. She dropped him off and blew him a kiss. "I don't deserve friends like you," she said. He gave her a look that told her it wasn't news to him.

Max was on the patio when she arrived at Moonglow Manor, a script on his lap, a tall scotch over ice in his hand, staring into the star-infested sky like he was searching for signs of life on the crescent moon. She tiptoed over, gave his bony shoulder a squeeze and planted a kiss on top of his head.

He imprisoned her hand and patted out a welcome. "How was it with your friend, Barney?" he said, trying to sound like it mattered to him; his speech slurred, revealing he was long past one too many.

"False alarm. The old rascal is too mean to die easy and keeps fighting death to a draw. He'll outlive both of us before he's through."

"Nobody lives forever," Max said.

"Barney will die trying."

"Better my pictures should live forever. That happens, even just one, I'll rest happy in my grave knowing I haven't been forgotten." He tossed aside the script and finished his drink. "Am I making sense, Sarah?"

How was she supposed to answer? Tell Max he would be resting in his grave soon enough—*that* she could predict with certainty. But would his pictures live forever? The ones that starred her, definitely, if for no other reason than because they starred her. The others? "You'll be remembered long after the Griffiths and the DeMilles are forgotten," she said, telling him what he was desperate to hear.

"Eisenstein? Murnau? Carne? Clair? Renoir? That poseur Lang?" He rattled off another half dozen names that meant everything to him and nothing to her.

She silenced him with a hand over his mouth. "All of them," she said, bringing tears to his eyes and inspiring an expression that reeked of gratitude.

Overcome with emotion, Max sprang from the chair, gripped her arm and led her upstairs to the bedroom. The liquor freed him of any inhibitions. He molded her body to his specifications, like he might never have the chance again. Once or twice she thought she heard him call out Dixie's name in a burst of ecstasy. She let it pass. What difference did it make now?

CHAPTER 33

As usual, Max had roused and pushed himself out of bed before the sun broke through the gray mist that floated over from Griffith Park most mornings and gave the birds a new day to sing about. It was his habit to be the first man on the set, to remind everybody who was boss and keep the production running on schedule and on budget.

He was brokenhearted about Dixie, mourning what might have been, but he could not permit his emotions to override his responsibilities, not now or ever or for any reason, on this production or any production, today or any day.

He spent a minute studying Sarah, who was locked in deep sleep under the covers; suffered a momentary twinge of guilt for wishing it were Dixie there, same as he had last night when he cast Sarah as Dixie and inhabited her one more time, applying his drunken fury to the thought of never having her again.

By the time the studio limo deposited him at the Paramount ranch, Max's mind was for the most part clear of Dixie and fixed on the series of scenes he'd be shooting today.

He found Polly Wilde camped on the production trailer steps.

Polly was dressed casually, her hair piled on top of her head, and shorn of makeup. It took him a moment to recognize it was her, not a new girl the studio had sent out from the secretarial pool. She bounced up, spent several seconds deciding what to do with her hands before settling on a prayer grip, and forced an awkward smile.

"Did you misread your call times?" he said. "You're an hour early for wardrobe and makeup."

"I was hoping you would spare a few minutes for me to speak to you in private, Mr. Moonglow." She appeared frightened at the prospect he'd deny the request, exactly what he intended to do. It wasn't her fault she had replaced Dixie in the picture, but that didn't take away his resentment. She could be Carole Lombard and he'd feel the same way. "It's about Dixie Leeds."

Dixie.

Now he was too curious to turn her away.

"Go ahead. What about Dixie Leeds?"

"I know how much she meant to you."

"You know nothing of the sort."

She absorbed his irritation without shrinking. To the contrary, it seemed to propel her forward, add muscle to her brittle voice.

"I'm sure you had your reasons for wanting her in the part," Polly said. "I sensed it yesterday at our meeting with Mr. Lieber and that detective, I see it now and I can hear it, so I need you to hear it from me: yes, I knew Charlie Dickens. He'd been my boyfriend, but it was already over between us when he tried getting me the part. Leo Salmon, he was only doing his job, trying to earn his ten percent."

"And here you are, so congratulations, however it happened, however wrong you are in the part."

He tried to get to the trailer door around her, but she shifted position and blocked his way, indifferent to his insult.

"I'm not done having my say, Mr. Moonglow."

"I'm done giving you a listen."

"Just this," she said, refusing to step aside. "As wrong as you say I am for the part, I hope and pray I'm able to give you at least half the performance you wanted and expected from Dixie Leeds. Please, I'm asking you—begging you, really—to, with an open mind, allow me that chance to show you I deserve to be here. Will you?"

"Aren't you overdue at wardrobe and makeup? I expect you on the set for blocking not a minute later than on time."

"Is that a yes, Mr. Moonglow?"

"It's whatever it takes to get you out of my way."

It wasn't much of a scene:

Inside the office of the *Shadow Creek Sentinel.* Editor Kate Washburn is engaged in a lively conversation with the sheriff, Long John Brooks. Tempers flare. Brooks shouts some parting words and tramps off.

Max had devised a way to give the scene his Moonglow Touch:

Inside the office of the *Shadow Creek Sentinel.* Editor Kate Washburn is engaged in a lively conversation with the sheriff, Long John Brooks. Tempers flare, but instead of the sheriff tramping off—

Kate takes a swing at him. Brooks dodges it and ropes her in for a kiss. She breaks free and delivers a roundhouse punch that rocks Brooks back on his heels. He shakes his head clear, grabs Kate and punishes her with another kiss, this one more passionate than the last. After a few beats, Kate quits struggling and joins in.

And throw away Dickens's stilted dialogue.

Let the emotions play on the screen, wordlessly.

Let the audience recognize the heat being generated between Kate and Brooks and wonder how Lola Jolly, Sarah's character, would react if she discovered the claim she has staked on Brooks was threatened.

By the time the actors arrived on the set Max had blocked out the action with the crew. He would start outside the office, the two at each other as the camera craned down and into a dissolve that would lead to a series of interior medium shots and close-ups exposing the truth of the passion stirring in both of them.

Max had more in mind than attaching his brilliance to a B-movie, of course.

He was satisfied Earl Stanley could invest a sufficient amount of reality and sizzle to the scene, but Polly Wilde? For her it would be a test, an opportunity to prove she was as good as she thought she was, capable of equaling the magic he'd have drawn from Dixie, or an opportunity for her to fail, as he expected, and show she was just another bump on the log of mediocrity.

He was wrong.

From the moment they stepped in front of the camera and faced off, like Gable and Harlow they projected an overpowering, almost erotic, explosive chemistry that Max knew instinctively would translate onto film and have audiences demanding more. The crew also knew it, whispering similar predictions among themselves after every take and rewarding Earl and Polly with sustained applause after Max sounded the last cut and print before the lunch break.

"We need to talk," Sarah said. It was his first awareness she'd been watching from the sidelines. They retreated out of hearing range. He knew what to expect, and he wasn't disappointed. "I don't know where that monkey business came from—not from the script—but I want it out of my picture, Max."

"Why?"

"Don't you play your old game with me. You know damn well why. I'm no patsy for your shenanigans."

"I did it for you, my precious one, but *nisht kefelecht*, no big deal, if that's what you want. Out. Gone." He knew when to put on the kid gloves, just as he knew how she'd react; give him a suspicious once-over before demanding an explanation.

"How for me? Let's hear it and none of your usual soft soap."

"The more the audience believes there's something romantic

291

brewing between Long John and Kate, the more breathless they'll be waiting to see what Lola does when she finds out. They'll be thinking of Lola, you, not Kate, every minute. More than that—when your moment of truth arrives, your big scene, for as much fire as her Kate has shown, your Lola will torch the entire theater. Polly Wilde's 'good' will help make Sarah Darling's 'great' that much greater. I daresay, and I'll put it in writing, it could bring serious attention and a first Oscar nomination ever for an actor or actress in a nonsensical B western, with you in line to win a second Academy Award. That's how I always make what's best for you in a Max Moonglow production uppermost in my mind, so what do you say?"

She wheeled away and left him without an answer.

Max took that as a good sign.

The afternoon shoot seemed simple enough on paper—

Sheriff Long John Brooks and Big Buck Hatton face off on Main Street. They're on the verge of drawing their Colts when Lola, armed with a shotgun, throws herself in front of Brooks and takes the bullet meant for him. She blasts Big Buck before staggering into the sheriff's arms. The sheriff comforts her and she responds in kind, neither one knowing if she'll survive or die.

Max had planned to start with the master shot under a clear blue sky, while daylight was at its best, work down to the two-shots and close-ups, when the daylight would be less critical.

Wiser to lavish his attention on Sarah, he decided.

Reinforce his predictions and promises.

Run less risk of making her a bigger pain in the *tuchus* than she normally was.

It delayed the first take for more than an hour while the crew made the necessary technical adjustments, another half hour searching after Sarah and Earl Stanley, last seen straying from the picnic benches set up by the food-wagon people.

They emerged at almost the same time from opposite ends of the street, Sarah arm in arm with the Indian, Earl chatting amiably with Polly Wilde; Earl looking flushed under his pancake, Polly taking blame—without explanation—for his being late; Sarah uncaring, as ever, making it evident time was meant to serve her whims and fancies, dismissing the Indian with an imperious wave.

She made up for her behavior with her acting, bringing her star quality and range of emotions to every take, in the process elevating the story beyond its B-picture roots. What few times there was need for a second or third take, the call came from Sarah, telling Max, "I can improve on that."

He indulged her, of course.

If Earl Stanley had held his own with her on a first take, the sexual tension between them as strong—possibly stronger—than on display in his scenes with Polly Wilde, on the next take she'd act circles around Stanley, upstaging him mercilessly, like she was teaching Stanley a lesson that had more to do with life than with role-playing.

Max would have liked one more take from them, where Sarah might take pity and strike middle ground, but he didn't have a chance to ask.

"I'm ready for my close-ups whenever you are," she said, and strolled off, joining the Indian, who had been watching the action from the sidelines. They exchanged a few words before she headed in the direction of her trailer, the Indian tracking after her.

Not a good sign, not good at all.

Sarah at it again, this time with an Indian, for Christ's sake?

Max felt shame for himself as well as for her.

Surprise that he cared as much as he did.

Was it because, having lost Dixie, he was back to settling for the next best?

Somebody better than nobody at all?

Or was it because Sarah Darling was his, she belonged to him, no matter what?

And to nobody else.

Knowing what he did or suspecting what he might, he would never accept the concept of her being with another man.

A double standard?

No.

A single standard.

His.

Consumed by jealousy and doubt, using the inhaler to fight off a threatened asthma attack, he had put aside all thought of Dixie by the time he got to the production trailer and phoned Kurt Duff.

Max had to know more about the Indian.

Duff was the man to find out for him.

The engaging voice at the answering service took the message, promising to have the private detective return the call the minute he checked in.

"When? When will that be?"

"Difficult to say, Mr. Moonglow. Mr. Duff is usually real good about checking for messages, but we haven't heard from him yet in over a day."

Max slammed down the phone and sank into his chair.

His fingers tapped out a nervous rhapsody on the desktop.

His palm moved to his dueling scar, his *renommierschmiss,* on the left side of his face. He always encouraged people to assume this mark of class, courage and honor dated from his days at the University of Berlin. In truth the scar was not earned by Max standing his ground while another student chopped away at his face with a heavy saber. He paid a doctor to form the wound, afterward, repeatedly tore it open and rinsed the wound with salt and wine, once sewing in horse hair, to cause the prominent keloid scar meant to help him pass into the upper reaches of society at the same time he was making a mark in the picture business at UFA.

That took bravery of another kind.

Informed the fiction and drama he would ultimately bring to the screen in Germany and America.

Bravery.

Beherztheit.

That's what life, real life, was demanding of him now.

Waiting for a call that might not come for hours, staying stranded on an island of suspicion and doubt—that was a coward's way. Max needed to know if monkey business was going on behind his back with Sarah and that damned Ronald Wahahah-whatever with his damned toes, and the sooner the better.

He fled the production trailer and marched to Sarah's trailer, certain he was about to catch her at it with the Indian. Then what? Banish the Indian from the lot, junk the Indian's scenes, and bring Douglas Fowley back in as the Gringo Kid? Wait to deal with Sarah until after the picture was shot, edited, and in the can? He hesitated before knocking on the door, recognizing the problems he might incite with a resentful Sarah, who knew how to delay a production and throw a budget out of whack, further threatening his unstable relationship with RKO.

Was he brave enough to run that risk?

No.

The door opened before he could turn to go.

"I thought I heard someone out there," Sarah said, startled into an uncertain smile. "I'm glad it's you. Something I need to talk to you about, a problem." She checked around. "Scoot on in so we can do this in private."

"What kind of problem?" Max said, following her into the

trailer. He settled on the sofa bed while she carefully adjusted the robe protecting her costume before easing down across from him at the makeup table and turning to study herself in the mirrors.

"Can you believe the shade of this lip gloss or the eye shadow that doesn't bring out my eyes the way they should look?" she said, her face registering dismay. "Don't you know by now it should be a Westmore for me and me alone, not any beauty school student doing her homework on my face?"

"All the Westmore boys were working or you'd have one of them for sure. I'll check again with Bud over at Paramount, see what I can do. You know how I look after you, take care of you."

"You are my guardian angel." She sent a kiss sailing to him.

He caught it and brought it to his lips. "So, does that take care of your problem?"

"Not the one I meant."

"What's that one?"

"Not *what*, Max, *who*. It's Ronald Redman, he's my problem."

"The Indian?"

She sliced her throat with a finger. "You need to get rid of him before he becomes a bigger pain in the patootie than he already is, on me wherever I turn, trying to score points by buttering me up, begging me to use my influence with you to beef up his part. I've been stringing him until I could tell you. I mean, Jeez-o, you know how it goes with Indians and booze. I blow him off, he takes one drink too many and decides to get even, come after me with a tomahawk or something." She hugged herself against a sudden shiver, looking like she meant every word.

Max hid his relief, feeling like a fool for thinking the worst. "Leave it up to me. I'll take care of it," he said.

She gasped relief and threw herself at him, smothering his face with kisses. "Thank you, thank you, thank you, thank you, my sweet darling, and you won't forget about talking to Bud Westmore, will you?"

Max's AD, Ace Berland, was waiting for him at the production trailer, wearing the grim look that always announced a new problem before he spelled it out. "You know that canyon location where we shoot day after tomorrow?" Ace said, his resonant voice deep as a grave.

"Ruggles Ridge. Of course, I know it. I chose it. What about it?"

"A problem. Was a rock slide that area this morning sent it crashing down into the ravine, resulting from the ground being weakened by all the rainstorms last year and this, so the county's closed it off until further notice."

"I want what I want, Ace. I built that location up so high with Sarah, the last thing I need is to have her *kvetching* about anything more than she's already *kvetching* about. Buy somebody off, like we've done a million times over."

"You know how there's always one honest inspector in the bunch? We got him, but I personally scouted a location almost as fine about a half mile farther west. I thought you could check it out later or even tomorrow, give it the Max Moonglow stamp of approval."

"And if I don't stamp?"

"We could move up the jailhouse exterior, the vigilantes dragging Raging Bull out to be hung and—"

"I'll let you know," Max said, pointing Ace out the door, not ready to announce the Indian was out and Fowley back in as the Gringo Kid, assuming Fowley was still available. Assuming the Indian was as Sarah had made him out to be.

Max believed her, of course, or *wanted* to believe her—that was a far more accurate way of explaining it—but there was always an element of doubt whenever she came at him for something. The Indian wanted more than he already got, he didn't need Sarah. He could have come straight to him. It worked out fine the first time. Why not again?

Max reached for the phone and dialed Kurt Duff's number again, got the answering service again. Next, he had the switchboard put him through to Bud Westmore's office at Paramount.

CHAPTER 34

"About the way you're adding fuel to the fire with Earl Stanley?"

"You complaining, Leo?"

"Endorsing. The hotter the sizzle off-screen, the hotter it'll come across on camera. Sarah Darling may be the star of this low-budget mishmash, the one who puts asses in the loge seats, but audiences will leave the theater wanting to see more of Polly Wilde and Earl Stanley. Believe me on that, my dear Miss Wilde, and keep up the good work."

"Keeping Earl up, that's a problem half the time. He wilts more often than some of the flowers he yakety-yaks about, on and on—roses this, violets that, gladiolas something else . . . chrysanthemums—like he'd rather be watering his flowers than me." She rolled her eyes. "And he stinks from fertilizer. I hold my breath till I'm blue in the face. When I let it go, he thinks it's because he's brought me to the Big O, and he lets out this stupid Tarzan sort of a yell."

"Gable, the whole town knows about the King's false teeth and breath that smells like Jesse Owens's socks, but that doesn't stop stars like Joan Crawford and Loretta Young from lining up to take a crack at his kisses and whatever. Get used to it, Polly. Before I'm through, RKO won't be the only studio fighting to sign both of you to lucrative, long-term deals."

"But not before I've helped you make Earl your client first, right, Leo?"

"As rain. Our deal. Whatever's good for Polly Wilde is also

good for Leo Salmon and vice versa."

"Then maybe we should be taking turns screwing Earl now, or are you waiting for him to sign up with you before you start screwing him?"

"You're the only client I'm keen to screw, and you can take that any way you want."

Polly glanced at the alarm clock on the nightstand. "I can squeeze you in one more time before I have to shower and scoot to the ranch for costume and makeup, so the usual way will have to do, doctor."

"Open wide and say *Ah*," Leo said, drawing her to him.

She had him saying *Ah* first.

Max was barking orders to Ace Berland, his AD, and Ace was trumpeting them to the crew when Polly arrived at this morning's location, the railroad station platform where Sheriff Long John Brooks, Lola Jolly and Kate Washburn would be waiting for the train to arrive before Raging Bull charged into the scene with "Spearfish," the character played by Andy Devine.

Ace streaked over wearing a false smile. "Sorry I didn't catch you before this," he said. "Been busy reworking setups since hours ago." He bought another minute calling out a correction to the electricians. "Don't roam too far unless or until you hear otherwise from me, same as all our other players, oke?"

"What's going on, Mr. Berland? What's this about?"

He worked his head left and right like he was watching a tennis match. "Can't say for sure. Something to do with the Indian. He's off the picture. We're waiting for Vic Jory, who's in as the Gringo Kid, like was originally written, Vic because Douglas Fowley's off doing time at Metro." Racing his words. Betraying his New York roots. Excusing himself on a flimsy excuse and racing back to the set, calling instructions into the air, before she could ask another question.

Polly retreated to her trailer, scowling as she passed by Sarah's; larger, wider than any of the others; the size trailer or larger she'd have one day soon if Leo delivered on his word. She couldn't tell Leo's lies from his truths half the time, but it didn't matter as long as he continued to deliver the goods for her, even if it meant tolerating Earl Stanley's stinky breath. She'd smelled worse, was ready to smell even worse than that, if that's what it took to make the grade.

She was turning the key in the lock when the sound of gravel crunching underfoot made her glance over her shoulder. Earl was fleeing Sarah's trailer as Sarah stepped back from the open door and slammed it shut.

He spotted Polly, quickly shifted direction and headed over wearing a grin the size of Texas. "Can I come in?" he said. "Got something I need to tell you, you should know."

"If it's about the Indian being replaced by Victor Jory, I've heard already from Ace Berland."

"Me, too. No. It's about Sarah and you and me."

"What about Sarah and you and me?"

"She knows about us."

"How'd she find out?"

"I told her."

"I thought we were going to wait until the picture finished shooting."

"Hell, Polly, it's not like people weren't already starting to talk. The gossip around here travels faster'n pussy willows. She said she overheard it being told Barbara Shore in wardrobe by Eddie Gorman, the best boy who has got a mouth on him like Joe E. Brown. He's the one what told me first day on the job: *If you haven't slept with Sarah Darling yet, you must be new in town.*"

"How'd she take it?"

"Went down like castor oil, but what's done is done, and now it's you and me, all the way. So what say we celebrate while we're waiting for them to be ready for us on the set?"

"I have a headache," Polly said.

He'd just given it to her.

The last thing either of them needed was Sarah out for some sort of revenge.

It's exactly what happened though, from the moment shooting resumed, all that day and into the next, almost every scene framed by Max Moonglow like they existed only as back-of-the-head props, dress extras, off-screen voices to the close-ups lavished on Sarah.

Dear God, you'd have thought her costars were Ward Bond and Andy Devine.

Had Sarah complained to her husband to bring this about, invented some story that ignored the truth while raising him to anger?

Of course—

As certain as Earl's big mouth had caused the situation.

Sarah said nothing to either of them, showed all the emotion of a blank sheet of paper whenever she bothered looking at them, which wasn't often. Fine, maybe she was only half the cause. Maybe Max Moonglow was still cracking at her for replacing Dixie Leeds.

Maybe Leo was telling the truth when he answered her complaining with words of sympathy and support too seriously expressed for her to care whether he was telling her the truth or feeding her an empty lie. "It's under control, I have it under control," he repeatedly answered her angry howls. "Wait, you'll see. I have as much to lose as you, maybe more, if I let something this early and this petty bring us down. You'll see, freckle face. You'll see. I need you to trust me. Do you? Can you?"

"The proof's in the pudding," Polly said.

Leo took it as a compliment.

CHAPTER 35

Sarah had reason to be disturbed when Earl told her he was tossing her over for a younger woman. The announcement soiled more than it bruised her ego, given how much Polly Wilde reminded her of the unscrupulous, calculating girl she'd once been herself and in many ways still was, but that wasn't the rub, since she planned on giving Earl the brush once they got rid of Max.

It was the rest of his declaration that struck her like a thunderbolt from the blue:

"I've decided not to help you about Max, you know what I mean?" Earl said, cool as a summer breeze, like that was that, the end, over and out, and nothing she could say would change his mind. "Don't worry, though, I won't be telling tales out of school if you go on ahead and do it without me, anymore'n I expect you to be talking about my uncle Jerry's boat and all."

"Just go," she said, pointing him to the door.

"No hard feelings?"

"That floozy is welcome to you," she said, playing the woman scorned in close-up, forcing a tear that trickled down her check, storing away for later thoughts about putting an end to Earl's picture career as easily as she had made it happen.

"And the other?"

"What choice do I have?" Another tear, down the other cheek.

"Me, too."

"Not even her, is that what you're telling me?"

"Not her or anyone, s'help me." He crossed his heart. "Something else though? I'd still like to tend your garden, if that's not asking too much? Maybe come around Sundays and any other days I get off from moviemaking?"

"Please leave, Earl. Go." She pushed up from her dressing-table perch and pushed him out the door, slammed it shut, and puzzled over what to do about Max until she was called to the set.

Max greeted her like royalty, drew her close and whispered in her ear, "That little problem with the Indian you told me about? All taken care of, my precious one, as you're about to find out. See sitting there, where the Indian won't be sitting anymore? Victor Jory. Our new Gringo Kid, and no more Raging Bull."

The Indian.

She'd almost forgotten about the Indian in the wake of Earl's little bombshell.

First the Indian, now Earl—

The Indian rejecting her when she offered herself to him, not once, but twice, the second time doing a slow strip in her trailer to illustrate the gift Sarah Darling herself was offering him— Sarah Darling herself. Carrying on about honor and his wife, like that made a difference.

She swallowed her ego and said, *Of course, honor and your wife and let's us forget this ever happened,* already counting the minutes before she could demand Max get rid of the Indian, get the Indian off the picture, get the Indian out of her sight.

The reason?

She'd have one by the time she got to Max.

Later, back in the trailer after her last scene was shot, sulking, she stripped to her skin and studied her body by the inch, recognized the signs of aging she couldn't prevent, the modest sag to her belly, the flab starting to inch under her arms, the wrinkles and the crow's feet taking deeper root in her once-flawless complexion. The hint of blue veins on the backs of her hands.

She told herself, *Face it, face it, face it, Sadie. The Indian is only the first rejection to come your way. More you'll get the older you get.*

Now, today, Earl Stanley, somebody else turning her into less and less competition for the Polly Wildes of the world. How soon before they'd be offering her the Jane Darwell and Dame May Whitty roles?

How old was she?

She refused to remember.

Other questions crept into her nightmarish concern:

How good an idea was it at this stage of the game to rid herself of Max and go after a well-established, highly regarded, award-winning pro? Wouldn't he be more concerned with prolonging his own career by attaching himself to someone newer, fresher and—yes, damn it—younger than Sarah Darling? *Out with the old and in with the old* didn't make a lot of sense, but—big but, Sadie—was there some hotshot new kid on the block willing to stake his career on a proven commodity, who wouldn't look at her like a relic from ancient Rome? She couldn't come up with a single name, brooded before what had turned into her personal Eleventh Commandment years ago pushed aside every downbeat question:

Thou Shalt Not Fail.

She'd been given it as a gift from Barney Rooker after he rescued her from herself the first time. He told her, "Take care of the present and the future will take care of itself, Sadie."

Yes, Barney, yes; yes, yes, yes.

Max would go according to plan.

Or close.

She didn't need Earl, but she did need Ruggles Ridge.

She picked at her nails, scheming how to get Max there now that a rock slide had made it off limits for the scene he'd sworn would have audiences ready to erect a shrine to her beauty, discarding one idea after the next before hitting on one she was certain would work.

She set it in motion two days later.

CHAPTER 36

The car quit on Charlie on a dark, empty stretch of highway between Sonoma and San Francisco while heading back to LA after four days of searching without success for Robin and the Keyes at dozens of wine country vineyards. Only one of the field managers remembered them, saying the old man, how he characterized Ernie Keyes back at Charlie, talked about trying their luck again in the San Fernando Valley.

"Problem was, they were on foot and short on cash," the field manager said. "I had nothing for them here, so I did the Christian thing, fed them a meal and put a few dollars in the old man's pocket before I settled them with one of our drivers trucking drop-offs down south as far as San Diego. His old lady cried buckets and blessed me like I was the Second Coming Himself while I helped her up into the rig, damn near drove me to tears myself."

"The girl, what about her? How was she? How'd she look?" Charlie asked.

The field manager adjusted his wide-brimmed straw against the midday sun and pampered the sweat off his brow with a napkin-size red-checkered handkerchief, thinking about the question. "Yeah, now that you mention . . ." He nodded and his look turned grim. "Even said something to the old man, who said she was past the worst of it and able to do her full share of work I gave them the chance. It weren't any of my business, so that was that, but all honesty—I've seen ailing dogs had to be

308

put down that looked better than that poor creature."

The image played to Charlie's worst fears while he worked the roadside with his thumb, hoping to catch a hitch to the nearest garage. He wasn't out of gas and everything under the buggy's hood was alien territory with a language he didn't speak. He had almost given up hope, resigned himself to bunking overnight in the backseat, start a tramp down the highway first thing in the morning, when a late-model crimson-colored Buick in prime condition glided to a stop in front of his car.

THE AMAZING LESLEY was splashed across the door panels in glittering gold circus sideshow letters trimmed in powder blue and blushing pink. The woman behind the wheel angled out the window and called, "You need help, fella?"

"All I can get," Charlie said, and described the problem.

"The Amazing Lesley to the rescue," she said.

"I'm Charlie. Charlie Dickens."

"Of course you are," she said, amused the way most everybody was when they heard his name for the first time.

She unwound out of the Buick and joined him, revealing a curvaceous body on an unusually tall frame, six-feet-something give or take in high heels, and a pair of unpadded broad shoulders Joan Crawford would envy inside a flamboyant silk dress in shades meant for Technicolor. A helmet of black hair framing her heavily made-up, heart-shaped Betty Boop face marred only by the beginnings of a double chin. He figured her for mid- to late twenties.

"You know about cars?" Charlie said.

"Not as much as I know about this highway," she said, her voice unable to decide between vibrant soprano and a deeper register. "It's not a safe place to be stuck, especially around this time, when traffic is light. There's a good chance of getting robbed, getting the car stolen, getting yourself killed, you try to put up anything resembling an argument." She dipped a hand into a dress pocket and revealed a snub-nosed revolver. "You get what I'm telling you?"

Charlie wigwagged his hands and reached after his billfold. "I'm down to my last few bucks, but you're welcome to them. The whole wallet, in fact. My watch? That, too."

The Amazing Lesley laughed. "I didn't mean to frighten you." She dropped the revolver back in the pocket. "I wanted you to see what you were up against, in case you turned out to be one of the bad guys, using your car as bait. I travel ready for the worst, ever since the time I was left for dead by the side of the road. I'm still around thanks to a truck monkey who spotted me and got me to the hospital before I could breathe my last. I've been paying back that act of kindness ever since."

She stepped over to the car and checked under the hood, humming a Gershwin tune as she probed and poked before rising with a verdict. "The fan belt's broken. See? Replace it and you should be as good as this old clunker allows."

"Any chance of you driving me to a garage?" Charlie said, taking the belt from her.

"That would be Todd's A-One Auto Service about five miles down, but Todd locks up early and it wouldn't be before the rooster crows he could do you any good, so how is this for an idea? I was intending to one-stop overnight at the Log Cabin Roadside Inn a couple of miles from here before heading on into San Francisco. You're welcome to bunk with me and, come morning, I'll get you to Todd's place."

"You're a peach, Lesley."

She waved off the compliment. "Get that buggy of yours locked up nice and tight and we'll be on our way."

The desk clerk, a bony, fragile-looking fellow in his thirties, looked up from his *Life Magazine* when the door opened and the reindeer bell tinkled. He aimed a nervous smile of recognition at the Amazing Lesley and gave a curious once-over to Charlie, his heavy-lidded shamrock-green eyes blinking nervously.

"Your usual room's taken, but I got one for you just as nice three doors down the row," the clerk said. "Only difference is there's twin beds 'stead of the one king."

Lesley accepted the news graciously. "I'm sure my friend much prefers it that way," she said, giving Charlie a wink, and signed the guest register for both of them.

Charlie did. His only interest was a comfortable night's sleep and a morning ride to that garage Lesley mentioned. Whatever else might be on her mind was nothing he planned to encourage.

Lesley led the way along the creaking plank walkway and into a room filled with mismatched furniture that smelled of tobacco smoke and disinfectant. A leg on one of the twin beds was propped up by a Gideon Bible. The "Modern Air-Conditioning" advertised on the motor court's roadside sign turned out to be a fan mounted on a wall shelf. Overall, it was better than spending a restless night cramped in the backseat of his car, half awake, worrying about a roadside attack.

Lesley excused herself to the bathroom toting a shabby leather suitcase whose lid identified the owner as THE AMAZING LESLEY in lettering and colors that matched the side of her car.

The moment he heard the door close, Charlie kicked off his shoes, scrambled down to his skivvies, jumped under the bedcovers, shut his eyes and lapsed into a feigned sleep. Stepping back into the room, Lesley laughed like she was on to his game. She snapped off the overhead bulb dangling from the center of the sagging tin ceiling and settled onto the other twin, the bedsprings squealing under her weight.

★ ★ ★ ★ ★

How long he'd slept Charlie wasn't certain when he felt the gentle nudging at his shoulder and warm breath on his face. A fast peek revealed sunlight pouring through the flimsy chintz window curtain. He rolled onto his side when Lesley said, "It's time for you to rise and shine, us to get a move on, sleepyhead." Opened his eyes. Discovered it wasn't Lesley hovering over him.

It was some guy, naked as a peeled grape, who looked enough like her to pass for her twin brother. Same build. Same Betty Boop eyes and pursed lips, even the same double chin; the biggest difference being his thick, curly brown hair, heavy morning stubble, and an uncircumcised pecker.

"Lesley?"

"In person."

"You're a guy?"

"The evidence is indisputable, wouldn't you say?"

"Amazing," Charlie said, sitting up, trying not to stare.

"Exactly," Lesley said, speaking now in a deeper, richer voice.

"You're a drag queen?" Charlie said, his writer's natural curiosity kicking in.

"To some. A transvestite to others. An *artiste* to anybody who has seen my solo act or my specialty numbers when I'm performing at Two Dollar Bill's Club in Liberty Belles on Parade."

"What's your preference?"

"Human being," Lesley said, dressing in clothing he pulled from his suitcase—a tobacco-brown blazer with long, broad lapels and square shoulders over a high-collar satin shirt, generous-cut Glen-plaid-check trousers, a matching beret he settled at a jaunty angle. Completed the outfit with tasseled tobacco-brown Italian loafers. Reviewed himself in the mirror and nodded approval after a tug or two. "Good morning, Leslie, my man," he said. "Welcome back."

Charlie got the rest of the story on the drive to Todd's A-1 Auto Service—how a "Leslie" blossomed into a "Lesley" after surviving childhood taunts and churchgoing blue-collar parents who banished him from their storybook middle-class home in Boise, Idaho.

"Outcasts always manage to find each other," Lesley said. "I got lucky after a few bad years I don't ever like to talk about, hearing about Two Dollar Bill's club and selling my way to San Francisco. Bill took me on and his star attraction, Screaming Mimi, took a liking to me and took me under his wing. I'm a quick study, and after a year I was one of the headliners. The rest, as they say, is history. When I'm not doing the show, I work solo gigs on an underground circuit that runs from Sonoma south into Ventura County. I was heading back from a private party when I saw you and figured to add another gold star on my ticket through the Pearly Gates."

"There's a movie in your life story, Lesley. Take my word for it."

"I welcome your word, only what pray tell do you know about movies?"

Charlie told him.

Lesley was impressed. "And they're making your picture right now?"

"Right now."

"With Sarah Darling."

"Yes."

"Really?"

"Really."

Lesley blew a whistle into the windshield.

Charlie said, "I might be able to get her interested in playing you. Jane Withers you as a kid and Sarah Darling once you're grown up."

"I don't know."

"I understand. You're thinking Sarah might be too old, but she's the kind of actress who's ageless in any part."

"Not that, Charlie. It'd make more sense to have Jackie Coogan acting me as a boy and growing up into Tyrone Power or George Raft, don't you think so? Tyrone is luscious, more than George, but George is quite the dancer, and my routines call for a good dancer."

"I don't think so, Lesley."

"You get a chance to see me at Dollar Bill's, you'll understand how important that dancing is to any story about me. . . . Don Ameche, he'd make a dandy Screaming Mimi." He correctly read the disapproval on Charlie's face. "It wouldn't have to be Don Ameche, Charlie. James Dunn, maybe?"

"No dice. Hollywood and the moviegoing public, not to mention the Breen Office, would never go for men playing women and going around in dresses and all, so it'd have to be Sarah, who's quite the dancer herself, by the way."

"Any actress playing me, that wouldn't be my story."

Charlie didn't hear Lesley's complaint. He was too busy mining his imagination and invention, deciding, "Shirley Temple would make far more sense than Jane Withers, but I doubt Fox would loan her out to another studio, although the grapevine has it Shirley may be headed over to Metro for *The Wizard of Oz.*"

When the two-door Pontiac pulled up, Charlie was relaxing on the running board, visualizing scenes for the movie he had given the working title *All About Lesley,* still undecided whether to spell it "Lesley" or "Leslie," and Leslie (or Lesley), bent under the hood installing the new fan belt, was announcing, "Another minute or two, I'll have you ready to hit the road again."

There were four of them, the driver and three passengers, one sitting alongside him, the two others in the rumble seat. Mid-thirties to early forties. All dressed like dirt farmers. Looking like trouble—or for trouble—not a smile or a fresh shave among them.

The driver stayed behind the wheel while his passengers hopped out of the car and closed in on Charlie. The six-footer of the trio, who towered over his beefier buddies, said, "Need help?"

"Fine, but thanks anyway for asking."

"You look like you need help."

"Everything's under control. My friend's been replacing a broken fan belt."

"That's not all you need to replace," Six-footer said, his words as final as a guilty verdict.

"I beg your pardon?"

"Hear him, boys? I got him begging already." The rumble seat duo laughed like this was part of some routine they'd performed dozens of times. "Save it, mister. No amount of begging's about to change the fact we're taking your car."

"You're stealing my car?"

"Isn't that what I just said? You be a smart guy and not give us any trouble, we'll be inclined to leave you and your friend behind in one piece, with your brains in their proper place. There've been some who've ignored my well-intentioned advice and—show the man what that got them, boys."

The rumble seat duo had been holding tire irons behind their backs. They put them on display, smacked their palms with the irons for emphasis.

Six-footer said, "Any more questions, or maybe best you just get your ass up and move aside?"

Charlie rose from the running board and stepped away from the car.

"You there under the hood. Hey! You about done yet with the fan belt?"

"Just now," Leslie said.

"Come out from under, lock the hood good and tight, and join your friend."

Leslie inched back from the car, lowered the hood and came around.

"Is that your buggy parked there, the Buick looks like it got painted The Amazing Lesley by some faggot fairy queer?"

"Yes."

"Not anymore. Hear that, boys? We got us a two-for-one stop this fine morning."

"None for two cars is more like it," Leslie said.

Six-footer spit out a laugh. "It sounds like you missed the part where I warned your boyfriend against making trouble. Maybe you need a taste of iron from my boys to prove I mean my words when I speak them, is that your preference, faggot?"

"Thanks, but no thanks," Leslie said, giving them their first look at the snub-nose revolver he'd been gripping out of sight, his finger on the trigger.

Six-footer and his boys froze.

Leslie said, "I'll be happy to show you I know how to use it, especially if you two morons don't drop the tire irons before I reach the count of one."

The irons hit the dirt.

"How you doing, Charlie?"

Charlie answered Leslie with a series of nods and a wave, his heart beating too fast for speech, feeling like he'd just been rescued from a gangster movie.

Leslie said, "Your buggy's in good working order, so take off back to LA, while I make certain these jerks don't chase after you."

"Maybe I should go after the cops first?"

"No. Scoot. Leave everything to me, except for one thing you can do when you get around to it," Leslie said. He confirmed he had Charlie's full attention before finishing the thought. "Tyrone Power," he said.

Charlie was planning to head for the Paramount ranch and see how the shoot was going when, physically and emotionally exhausted by the encounter with the car bandits and depressed as ever by his failure to find Robin, he narrowly avoided a head-on collision attempting to pass a Ford Woodie hogging a two-lane stretch of highway at a pace that put snails to shame.

He stopped at a roadside diner advertising "Last Good Eats Before Los Angeles," knocked back three cups of black coffee and, for ballast, two sugar doughnuts and one cream-filled doughnut, and was home by late afternoon. Ten minutes later he was soaking in the tub, where he woke thinking he might have dozed off for a half hour, max. In fact, it was six-thirty in the morning and the once-warm bathwater was iceberg cold and giving him the shakes.

He made a breakfast of Wheaties, "The Breakfast of Champions," garnished with half a brown-spotted banana, and retreated to his Royal Quiet Deluxe intent upon getting started on *All About Leslie and Lesley,* his latest title of choice.

First he called into the studio, was connected to the *Showdown at Shadow Creek* production trailer and let the girl who answered Max Moonglow's extension—a voice that was unfamiliar to him—know he was home and available if Mr. Moonglow needed him.

"Why would he need you?" she said, her voice an adventure in curiosity.

"I'm Charlie Dickens. I wrote the movie," Charlie said, holding his temper.

"And I'm Little Nell," she said, her bugle laugh beating at his eardrums before she disconnected.

An hour later, he was ripping another sheet of paper out of the portable, balling it and tossing it at the wastebasket, his aim as lousy as his writing, FADE IN the only words he considered useable, when the phone rang.

Max?

Calling to say he was needed at the ranch for, maybe, hopefully, prayerfully, some new writing on *Showdown at Shadow Creek?* Fingers crossed. Easy as pie compared to the creative void he was suffering with *All About Lesley and Leslie. Nothing About Lesley and Leslie,* more like it.

Charlie grabbed the receiver.

"Hello, Mr. Moonglow?"

"What? No. This Charlie Dickens?"

"No, this is Charlie Dickens. Who are you?"

"Red Moretti, up Sonoma way. Remember? We were talking about the family with the sickly girl I was able to help out a little?" His voice and face sank into place. "You give me your name and number, said call if I heard back from my driver? So happens I did."

"What did he say, Mr. Moretti, your driver?"

"Not nearly fifteen minutes ago, when he checked in for any add-ons. Turning into a better'n average run, pushing us close to finishing out the month in bonus money territory for the first time in a long time, ever since rotten weather come along and cut into the size and quality of our crops."

"What did he say about Mr. and Mrs. Keyes, about Robin, Mr. Moretti?"

"Exactly. You know Eden Highlands? Farming community over in the San Luis Rey Valley; more cattle and sheep than citrus; overall a pale second to what you'll find next door in Orange County."

"About my friends, please."

"Right. Well, that's where he let them off, from his description the girl worse off than I told you from when I seen her, right at the emergency entrance to Eden Highlands Memorial Hospital."

Charlie shouted his thanks, slammed down the receiver, dumped a few essentials into an overnight case and headed for Eden Highlands.

CHAPTER 37

Polly wasn't on the call sheet, but she was at the ranch house set anyway.

Two reasons.

It was a scene involving Harry Carey, one of her favorites when she was growing up, her true idea of what a western hero was all about, a man's man, much like her father, not a Gower Gulch drugstore cowboy like Earl Stanley, a boy who reminded her of all the boys back home she was able to seduce to her wishes and whims with the simple hint of more available than her tongue tickling the backs of their throats. Sometimes it was, out behind the barn, with somebody who actually stoked her fire; once, in a classroom cloakroom, with Mr. Bloomquist, her first teacher, who taught her the easy way to get an A on the report card.

More than that—

Reason two:

Earl idolized Harry Carey. This would be their first scene together, and for days he'd been—as her poppa used to put it—as nervous as a long-tailed dog in a room full of rocking chairs. He wanted her on the set for moral support. He'd been telling her that for days. Leo also wanted her there.

"Give him all the moral support he needs so he'll shine," Leo had said. "The better he looks in the rushes opposite someone like Harry Carey, the easier it'll be for me to sell the studio on the screenplay you keep nagging me about."

He meant *Forbidden City.*

"Charlie Dickens's script. You finally read it?"

"You read it, you told me how the story goes, how you wanted to play Cassandra, and that was swell enough for me, freckle face. I've already managed to set a meeting with Pan Berman, the big cheese himself."

"What if Earl flops with Harry Carey?"

"You're there to make sure he doesn't, whatever it takes."

"How was I, Polly?"

"Wonderful, every time is better than the time before," she said. "You're going to do great out there." They'd been running lines in his trailer for almost two hours, waiting for Earl's call to the set.

"You're not just saying that to make me feel good, are you?"

"I have better ways to make you feel good, but they'll have to wait until later."

"You know what I mean."

"You know what I mean."

"I'm crazy for you, honeybunch."

"And me for you." She leaned over and slathered a butter kiss on his lips.

"Let's try that one exchange one more time before we move on to the next, you don't mind. Like with flowers, it takes a lot of watering to get 'em as big and beautiful as the Lord intended for them to be."

She dropped her voice and proceeded into a lousy imitation of Harry Carey:

"Sheriff, I appreciate your wanting to be here when the McClintocks make their play, but all I want to be responsible for planting in the ground is alfalfa grass, not you."

"It's what I do for a living, not for dying, Mr. Jorgensen. I ain't gonna stand by and learn after the fact them varmints got the best of

you and ran off with your herd."

"You're a fine man, Long John Brooks, nowhere near what I expected when you rode into town and took up with the likes of Lola Jolly."

"It's not what it seems, sir. I took an oath to uphold the law when I agreed to put on this badge. She ever breaks the law, she gets treated like anyone else goes down that dusty trail."

"Take it from an old cowhand, sheriff. You're deceiving yourself when you say that, but not me. I've seen me a parcel of Lola Jollys in my time. Not one stands up to the likes of a Kate Washburn."

Instead of his next line, Earl looked at her with more emotion than he'd put behind any words from the script. "Kate Washburn, that's you, baby, in the movie and in my real life now. No one stands up to the likes of you."

"Not even Sarah Darling?"

"Sarah, she may be a star, but you're the sun, the moon, all them other planets, and whatever else is keeping this old world humming and spinning for me."

"And don't you forget it," Polly said, an answer that satisfied him, and pointed Earl back to the script.

"I grant you she's quite the woman, that Kate, but Lola ain't one to toss in her hand until she gets what she wants, Mr. Jorgensen, grant me that," he recited, like a first grader struggling to remember the Pledge of Allegiance.

Any concerns she and Leo had about Earl proved unnecessary.

He disappeared into Sheriff Long John Brooks when Max Moonglow called *Action* and the camera rolled.

His presence commanded attention.

He put strength and conviction behind every line of dialogue.

He held his own with Harry Carey, who made no attempt to upstage the younger, less experienced actor in their two-shots, no doubt confident he'd win back any losses in the reaction close-ups on his weather-beaten, world-weary face that silently told a million stories of battles won and lost.

The crew showered him with added respect, and even Max Moonglow smiled and found a few nice words to toss at him, but it was Harry Carey who drew the most emotion when he walked over, clamped Earl across the back and said, "Son, I can't remember when I last met up with somebody as talented as you. You're well on your way to big things, and I'll be proud telling people how I was there at the very beginning."

He also had enthusiastic words for Polly before he returned to the set, leaving her speechless when he said, "Goes as well for you, young lady. From what I've observed so far, you'll be nipping at Sarah Darling's heels in no time at all."

Sarah didn't see it that way.

She'd been watching the action from somewhere behind the camera, close enough to hear what Harry Carey had said. She headed in their direction, pausing long enough to say, "Don't count on it, either of you." Making no effort to hide her disdain. Every syllable laced with venom.

CHAPTER 38

Max had filmed Sarah's ranch house scene with Harry Carey first.

He knew it was unwise to have his star sitting around with nothing better to do than paint her toenails and struggle with the *Times* daily crossword puzzle before her irritation dissolved into one of her volcanic temper tantrums.

Under ordinary circumstances, she'd have demanded retakes, protection coverage, and close-ups favoring her good side—right profile or left profile, she never remembered which it was supposed to be, so she'd wind up insisting it be done both ways—because she was Sarah Darling and she could.

Not today.

Today she'd rushed through the take with near picture-perfect perfection, caught Max off-guard by declining his offer of a fresh angle she might prefer, explaining with unexpected, uncharacteristic generosity, "I'm satisfied if Mr. Carey is satisfied," and left when Carey rewarded her with a tip of his Stetson.

She could have used another take, done the scene better, and she didn't care a gnat's ass about Harry Carey. The canyon scene was shooting tomorrow and she needed daylight hours and privacy to check out the ravine substituting for off-limits Ruggles Ridge, satisfy herself that Max could die there as easily as at the ridge.

He couldn't.

There wasn't much of a drop, maybe forty or fifty feet, before the land arced onto a dense brush that would soften any fall, prevent any serious damage, unless she got lucky and Max hit a few boulders and cracked his neck on the way down. More likely, he would survive, suffering little more than a bruised bone or a sprained shoulder or a broken arm or leg, lucky son of a bitch that he was.

After that, what?

The cops?

Sarah Darling arrested and charged with attempted murder.

A scandal that brought her career crashing down around her, leaving her to rot in a jail cell while Max luxuriated in headlines that won the sympathy of millions and elevated his career using some lousy substitute of an actress like—God forbid!—Polly Wilde, who could never in a million years achieve the brilliance of a Sarah Darling.

No, damn it.

No.

No.

No.

Max would still need her more than she needed him.

He knew it.

She knew it.

She had to somehow get him back to Ruggles Ridge.

She'd figured out how by the time Max got home from watching the day's rushes, over a late supper garnished with a few bolts of Rémy Martin.

An argument for dessert.

"What's to talk about?" he said. "The canyon will be beautiful; you'll be even more beautiful. Isn't that what I've been promising you all along?"

"For Ruggles Ridge, only now we're not filming at Ruggles Ridge."

"You've seen one ridge, you've seen them all. Like Sam Goldwyn is always saying about Griffith Park, how a rock is a rock, a tree is a tree."

"I saw, Max. I went over and had myself a look. It's not the same. It's not as good. It's not for me." Every word punctuated. Irate, but not over the top. "It has to be Ruggles Ridge."

"Ruggles Ridge is condemned. What do you want me to do, go fight City Hall?"

"Ignore City Hall."

"It's dangerous at Ruggles Ridge. I went and saw for myself. I wouldn't want, God forbid, anything happening to you."

"I'll risk it. Remember the bomb explosion scene we did in *Daydreams?* You were going to use a stunt double, but realism and the Moonglow Touch demanded it be me and nobody else. It's the same thing now, Maxie."

"Ridiculous. First of all, you were younger and more adventurous when we made *Daydreams.*" He cocked an eyebrow.

"Brute!"

"We had a budget and time working for us on *Daydreams,* not like now. Now we're trapped making a shitty little B picture on a tight schedule and an impossible budget."

"And an even bigger problem."

"Meaning?"

She came around the dinner table, rubbed the tension from his shoulders and settled a kiss on the top of his head. "You want me for the scene tomorrow, you know where you can find me," she said, and strolled off.

"And you know where I'll be," he called after her, reaching for the bottle of Rémy Martin.

They spent the night in separate bedrooms, not unusual for nights they argued to no resolve, Sarah in the master bedroom, Max down the hall in the guest bedroom.

He was still sleeping when she hopped out of bed and into a quick shower, tossed on a shocking pink cardigan sweater and a muddy-brown skirt that accentuated her tiny waist and minimized her hips, and pampered her face with some rouge, lipstick and eye shadow.

She recharged her nerves with a strong cup of coffee laced with a double shot of Bombay gin; left her usual sign of ongoing battle where Max would be sure to discover it when he came looking for her; drove to the Paramount ranch.

Today was the day.

Sarah was ready for it.

She'd get him to the edge of the canyon.

Look, Maxie, you need to see from here, see why I'm so keen for Ruggles Ridge.

He would come look, of course.

Anything to oblige her, at the same time ready to plead with her to reconsider.

Not there, Maxie. Over here, my darling man. Right by me.

Over he'd come, and—

Push—

Over he'd go, plunging to his death; no way could anyone survive a fall like that.

And she'd run screaming for help.

Beside herself, crying her heart out.

Bemoaning the loss of her sainted husband.

Telling the cops she'd begged him not to check out Ruggles Ridge again. It was condemned by the county. Dangerous. Life-threatening. She'd trailed after him, pleading with him to stop, turn around, settle for the new, safe canyon location. Max wouldn't hear of it. Ruggles Ridge served his vision for a special kind of spectacular Moonglow Touch. That was that. So be it. Max had spoken and was not to be denied.

Not exactly the plan she'd worked out with that quitter Earl, but close enough.

The end would justify the means.

And all her fans would mourn the loss with her.

She reached the ranch undecided whether to ask Schiaparelli or Chanel to whip out her widow's weeds; something simple and understated; a stylish number in mourner's black that would appeal to the photographers at Max's memorial service.

It sounded more Chanel than Schiaparelli.

Max would know, but she couldn't very well ask him, now could she?

CHAPTER 39

Max sped past the gatekeeper without stopping, needing this morning to be more than his usual first man on the set. He was anxious to confront Sarah and bring her to her senses, convince her to do the canyon scene—by begging or bribing, whichever worked best, whatever it took.

She'd thrown down the gauntlet, damn her, anyway. The one-of-a-kind Tiffany's twenty-four-karat gold charm bracelet he gave her to commemorate the start of *Showdown at Shadow Creek*—left on his plate at the breakfast nook.

It was Sarah's way of telling him nothing less than having her way would satisfy her. Not the first time she'd pulled this stunt. She had done it with her charm bracelets for *Daydreams* and *An Appointment with Tomorrow,* but those were petty squabbles, easy for Max to surrender to her whims.

This Ruggles Ridge business was different.

Filming there would be breaking the law.

Somebody could get killed there.

For him to ignore the dangers inherent in moving the shoot back there, especially now, everything set to roll, would tip off the crew that something was amiss. They would have it figured out when Sarah arrived on the set like Cleopatra entering Rome. All hail the conquering movie queen, who'd be making sure in her unsubtle ways that everybody knew she'd had the best of him. Word would spread. It would make the columns. The *Hollywood Reporter. Variety.* Turn Max Moonglow into a mealtime laughing stock at all the studios, the butt de jour over Louis B. Mayer's chicken soup at Metro.

So what?

He told himself: *Your ego can take it, right Max?*

Answered himself immediately: *Hell, no!*

He parked and made a beeline for her trailer, banged on the door demanding to be let in, telling her, "I got your damn charm bracelet in my hand here. Understand? We have to talk."

No response.

He tried a second and third time.

Still no response.

Fine and dandy.

If it was a battle of wills Sarah wanted—

It was a battle of wills she'd get.

He'd outwait her.

Max covered for her absence by screaming his contempt for the transient clouds that blotted what background beauty there was in this sad substitute for Ruggles Ridge, actually grateful for them. They allowed him to buy time by moving the camera and tinkering with the lighting and sound baffles, retrack the shot, bellow other excuses invented to sustain the impression he was running the show, not his shrew of a wife, who refused to leave her trailer the several times he sent Ace Berland after her. Ace always returned with the same message, "She'll only talk to you, M.M."

After three hours of this, the buzz on the set growing louder, the crew giving him the old fish eye, he'd had enough.

Rather than humble himself to her, he intended to redeem himself in their eyes.

He marched off to Sarah's trailer working on the words that would put an end to her nonsense: *Either you get your beautiful ass in front of my camera right now or I will shoot the scene with your stand-in, her back to the camera.* No. Not a strong enough threat. *You don't want to do the scene, fine. I'm giving it to Polly Wilde.* Better. A message bound to do the trick. He should have thought of it sooner.

The door was slightly ajar.

He called her name.

No answer.

He pushed the door open and stepped inside.

No Sarah.

The trailer was empty.

A smile crept up his face and converged with his dueling scar. The little she-devil. He knew where to find her, waiting for Mohammed to come to the mountain, to Ruggles Ridge. As if illustrating her argument would win the day for her.

Hah!

Turning to leave, he tossed her Tiffany charm bracelet onto the dressing table.

The bracelet clunked against a jar of cold cream and dropped to the floor.

He retrieved it and was about to settle it on the table when something caught his eye in the Tiffany's blue jewelry box sitting open, reflecting light in a way that outshone everything else in her collection of expensive rings, earrings, bracelets, necklaces, and ornamental gold, silver and ivory doodads—

The wedding ring given his sweet Dixie by her mama, the one she had pawned in order to buy Whirlwind Wheels for her job as a skateress at the Skate Burger.

The wedding ring he rescued from the hockshop and gave his sweetheart the night he suffered his near-fatal asthma attack—

The last time he saw that darling girl, waking instead to Sarah, who said Dixie was not at the apartment when she got there.

Then how—

Then how—

Then how did she come to have Dixie's mama's ring?

Or was it?

He checked inside the band for the engraved inscription that had so moved him when he first saw it: "Forever, my love."

The inscription was there.

He could do no better now than believe the worst about Sarah.

Somehow, Sarah had a hand in Dixie's death.

You didn't have to be Einstein to figure that out.

What other explanation could there be?

Max realized he was struggling to breathe, his asthma acting up again.

He felt weak in the knees.

He braced himself with a palm on the dresser to keep from falling while he fumbled for his inhaler. Got it to his mouth and squeezed the rubber ball, once, twice, a third time, praying for the medication to begin its magic before he might lapse into unconsciousness.

He was fine after five minutes.

He pocketed the ring and headed for Ruggles Ridge.

Sarah was standing near the edge of the cliff about fifty yards away with her back to him, hands locked in contemplation, sucking up the view the way people study paintings at the museum.

When he yelled her name and cried out, "We need to talk," she turned and answered him with a smile as bright as the sunlight bouncing off the canyon wall across the divide.

"Of course, we do, my darling man," she said, in that tone she always took when she smelled victory.

"Not about here, Sarah. About this." He held up the wedding ring. "Does it look familiar?"

Sarah lost the smile. Her eyes grew wide. She hesitated before answering, "I don't understand," sounding like a line from a script, the worst reading he'd ever heard her give.

"Of course you do," Max said, rushing toward her. "What's not to understand?"

"I can explain, Maxie. It's not what you think."

"You think you know what I'm thinking, you got another think coming."

"Hear me out. You owe me that much."

"And what do I get in return, you bitch? Do I get Dixie back?"

Before she could answer, the ground began rumbling under them. Sarah quickly moved several steps away from the edge. Max jumped over a pothole and tripped on a rock. Off balance, he stumbled forward, colliding with Sarah. She bounced off him and sailed over the cliff, her scream echoing between the canyon walls until it abruptly quit.

Max melted to his knees, crawled slowly, carefully, to the edge and peered down, choking at the sight of Sarah's twisted body. He called to her, "It was an accident. I never meant for this to happen. I wanted to learn the truth in order to bring you to justice, not to your death." Was that the truth, though, he wondered, or was he lying to himself the way she had lied to him? She had a hand in Dixie's death; she got what was due her. *An eye for an eye.* If he could picture himself pushing Sarah off the cliff, what would the authorities believe? Given his own uncertainty, would he be able to convince the police, the crew or anyone it was an accident?

The answer arrived unexpectedly.

"You almost lost this," Ronald Redman said from a few yards away. He showed off Dixie's wedding ring. "You dropped it over there, right before you went on the attack after Miss Darling and threw her to her death." He moved forward, helped Max to his feet, and handed him the ring.

"Couldn't you see it was an accident, what happened—not an attack?"

The Indian hunched his shoulders and turned his palms to the sky. "Why should I?"

"Because it's the truth."

"The truth? I'll tell you what's the truth. You fire me off your picture. You have me barred from the lot. You force me to find another way in, Indian style, so I can track you down, to beg you to give me another chance. Only now, I don't think I need to beg, do I, Mr. Moonglow? The tables are turned. What my people did to Custer at Little Big Horn, I won't hesitate doing to you if it should come to that."

"You're back on the picture, will that satisfy you?"

"Not good enough, Mr. Moonglow. I'm your only eyewitness. What I saw, what I tell the police—it should be worth a lot more to you than one picture."

"Like what? What do you propose telling them?"

"Like how, when I got here, I saw you were pleading with Miss Darling not to do anything foolish, only she wouldn't listen. She was carrying on like a mad woman, about what I don't know, when all of a sudden she ran to the edge of the cliff, told you she loved you, would love you forever and a day, and leaped to her death before you could get to her and stop her."

"I'm going to make you a star," Max said, offering his hand.

Sarah was front-page news around the world.

The stories carried a heart-wrenching account by her brokenhearted husband, who explained how they had gone to investigate a possibly dangerous film location, how she had stepped too close to the edge of a canyon ridge over his warning, how the ground had shifted under her weight and fallen away, dropping the famed Academy Award–winning motion-picture star hundreds of feet to her death.

The real truth—as told the police by Max and confirmed by the only eyewitness, Ronald Redman—got no further than a confidential department report buried in the files before Sarah was laid to rest, bought and paid for at the highest government levels by Perry Lieber.

"A suicide would be lousy for business, make Sarah look bad, raise more questions than it answered," he told Max before putting his publicity boys to work. "Her accidental death is guaranteed to tug at the heartstrings and get all her adoring fans flocking to the box office for *Showdown at Shadow Creek* and a final farewell look at their divine Sarah."

"And you're certain I'm in the clear?"

"As clear as the air, Max, thanks to this Redman actor chap. Stick to the script I've laid out for you when I put you in front of the press. Make yourself a first-class hero with Pan Berman and the front office by getting the picture finished and ready to exhibit before Sarah's cold in the ground, while she's still on everybody's mind."

The Moonglow Touch became Moonglow Magic.

Max shot the safe canyon scene using Sarah's double, with her back to the camera. Plugged some holes the same way or with footage and sound strips from her earlier films. Made other scenes work by having the Indian gallop in all sweaty and breathless to report: *Miss Lola send Raging Bull to tell you what she just saw.* Or *said.* Or *did.*

And damned if it didn't work.

Preview audiences in Riverside signaled their approval with sustained applause at the final fade-out. The Santa Barbara preview produced a standing ovation after "The End" flashed on the screen.

The opinion cards left no doubt *Showdown at Shadow Creek*

represented a fitting and triumphant farewell to its star. More than that, they confirmed the rising star power of "America's New Two for You," as Polly Wilde and Earl Stanley were being billed in RKO press releases that also predicted the emergence of the Old West's first Indian hero, the new and exciting Ronald "Cheyenne" Redman.

All the while, at Max's direction, Sarah had been rescued from the coroner's office and brought to Hollywood Memorial Park Cemetery, where she was embalmed and stored under refrigeration while plans for a memorial service were worked out by the studio. He would have settled for something quick and simple, but RKO had grander ideas.

"You see the crowds that turn up there all the time for Valentino, that's what we want to create for Sarah," Perry said. "You start off with a bang and take it from there. It doesn't happen by itself. She'd love it if she could be around to watch and, of course, she gets remembered and we get free publicity by the pound year after year after year."

For starters, a crypt was purchased across the narrow corridor from Valentino's.

When the preview screenings confirmed the studio had a major hit, Perry decided Sarah deserved bigger and better than a memorial service at the mortuary chapel. "We do a double-header," he said. "Two days to accommodate the friends and fans who'll want a last look at the great star whose loss we're mourning. Maybe three days, if it looks like we can milk it for that long."

Max had a problem with the idea. "I saw her, Perry. I saw what the fall did to her beautiful face. Did you? If you did, you would know a closed casket is what makes sense, if people are to remember Sarah as she was."

"And she will be again, Max. I already have a green light from Pan Berman to put our finest hair and makeup artists on the case. The same with wardrobe. Top drawer all the way. She'll go out looking like Sleeping Beauty, like all it would take is a kiss to wake her from her eternal sleep." He thought about it. "That's awfully stylish, if I do say so myself." He pulled a note-pad and fountain pen from a jacket flap pocket, reciting while he wrote: *A kiss to wake Sarah from her eternal sleep.* "Louella's going to love it when I call and offer her those words exclusively."

The third day was added, then a fourth exclusively for journalists brought in from around the country by DC-3 and chartered trains, and for winners in "Farewell to Sarah" radio contests sponsored by Player's Cigarettes. ("I know she smoked Gitanes, but they're French, and we couldn't get those damn French to cooperate with us, you know how they are," Perry told Max.)

A deal was worked out for live radio coverage of the chapel ceremonies on both the RCA Blue and Red networks, starring Polly Wilde and Earl Stanley as the cohosts, with Ronald "Cheyenne" Redman brought out to deliver a special Indian farewell prayer in his native tongue.

Paramount, anxious to cash in on the excitement, offered Bob Hope and Shirley Ross for the program, to duet on "Thanks for the Memory," a song they were introducing in *The Big Broadcast of 1938,* currently in production. RKO approved after Paramount agreed to loan one of its players for a future production, Gary Cooper, Joel McCrea and Fredric March among the names leaked to Walter Winchell.

And Max?

"You'll be as visible as your love for Sarah," Perry told him, later sharing the words in an exclusive item planted with Hopper, and speed spoke Cagney-style what was lined up for him:

A special guest appearance on Lux Radio Theater following *An Appointment with Tomorrow* starring Polly Wilde and Earl Stanley in the roles originated for the big screen by Sarah Darling, in her Oscar-winning performance, and Herbert Marshall; introduced by Cecil B. DeMille to recite an original tone poem written by Norman Corwin, "For Sarah, With Eternal Love Forever and Ever Evermore."

"That's it? That's all?" Max said, by now caught up in the mechanics, his fingers beating out an anxious tune on Perry's desk. "I was Sarah's producer. I was her director. I was, for God's sake, her husband, not some *schlemiel* brought in off the street by Central Casting."

Perry reared back in his chair as if insulted, dissolved an expression of shock into an appeasing smile. "Come on, Max. You know how important you are to the studio. I have you down to recite the poem at each and every memorial service, right before Paul Robeson closes out the show with 'Ol' Man River,' singing a special set of lyrics by Oscar Hammerstein that's costing us a pretty penny."

"I liked that show," Max said, regaining his composure. "Even Sarah admitted to me what a swell job Irene Dunne did as Magnolia."

"She played it on the stage, you know."

"Of course, I know," Max said. "Why wouldn't I know? And Helen Morgan was Julie, both stage and screen. Sarah could have played Julie, but not without me, and the studio already had Jim Whale locked up to direct."

"I wasn't aware Sarah could sing."

"You ever hear of dubbing? It's the acting carries the day. I'd have had somebody else doing the singing, maybe even Helen Morgan." They shared a laugh. "What else you got going for me, Perry?"

"After every service, you'll lead the parade of mourners past the casket, through the gate connecting Hollywood Memorial Park to the studio, and into the giant tent we'll have up for our buffet meal catered by Chasen's Southern Pit. After that comes the screening of *Showdown at Shadow Creek,* where you'll take a bow afterward, following Polly, Earl and the other key cast members."

"And maybe say a few words?"

"Why not? Good thinking. A tear or two also might be nice for the camera boys and the newsreels."

"They should come easy," Max said. "A little raw onion rubbed on my hand, that'll do the trick. How I got it done with Sarah."

Everything was working and on schedule until three days before the first memorial service, when Perry stepped into his office unannounced, looking like he had been run over by a steamroller. "We have us a problem," he said. "The mortuary just called to say Sarah's gone."

"Gone? Of course she's gone."

"I mean gone missing. Persons unknown broke in and stole her body last night."

"Gott in himmel," Max said, reaching for his inhaler, the color draining from his face. "Who would do such a thing? Or is this another one of your publicity stunts, Perry?"

"Do you see me smiling? Not even me, Max. I already have the cops investigating."

"So we postpone everything until she's found."

"We have big money tied up, commitments we can't break, a premiere date carved in stone for here and New York—Sid Grauman's Chinese and the Radio City Music Hall no less."

"What are you saying, Perry? Spell it out."

"What you already know in your heart, Max. The show must go on."

The first memorial service easily could have been confused with a circus carnival sideshow. The noisy crowd outside the memorial grounds bookended the drive entrance, cheering celebrities in their chauffeured limousines and luxury cars, sometimes blocking access long enough to snap a Kodak or score an autograph.

The chapel had filled early and quickly to overflowing. Late arrivals were being ushered to rows of folding chairs set up outside, under a torrid sun expected to raise the temperature well into the eighties. Exceptions were made, naturally, for Louis B. Mayer, Darryl F. Zanuck and Samuel Goldwyn, who had saved places in the roped-off front row, across the center aisle from Adolph Zukor and Cecil B. DeMille. Harry Cohn, consigned to a reserved aisle seat in the second row, complained heatedly and threatened to leave; Pan Berman graciously traded places with him.

Max was closeted behind a view curtain in the private mourners' room on the left side of the stage, reciting to himself the Corwin tone poem, which he was determined to have comfortably memorized by the time he was called to the lectern, when the entrance door onto the parking lot opened and Barney Rooker was wheeled inside.

"Damn traffic," Barney said, by way of a greeting.

He settled alongside Max.

They shook hands.

Max said, "Barney, I'm glad you got my message. You were Sarah's oldest and dearest friend. She always spoke of you with love and affection. I couldn't imagine your not being present to help me bid her this loving farewell."

"Yeah. All them people. She'd have sucked up this scene like mother's milk." He appeared to choke on his words, struggling to speak above a harsh whisper. Max had to lean over, angle an ear to Barney's lips to hear him. "What bothers me, her being dead and gone like this? I can't believe it was an accident."

"It was, Barney, trust me on that. I was at Ruggles Ridge when it happened. I saw her go over the cliff. I would have saved her if I could, but it wasn't to be. For days I went around wishing it was me who died there, not her, not my Sarah."

"You want to know something?" He motioned Max closer. "It would-a been Sadie's wish, too, so better late than never," Barney said, whipping a switchblade ear-to-ear across Max's throat.

Max uttered a silent cry. His hands flew to his neck, but he couldn't stop the flow. Blood poured through his fingers. He stared at Barney with disbelieving, questioning eyes that lost focus as he pitched sideways onto the inlaid marble floor.

"Nothing personal, Mr. Moonglow, only obliging a friend past helping herself," Barney said, and ordered his attendant, "Shake a leg, Mad Dog. Get us out of here while the getting's good."

CHAPTER 40

"Mad Dog!" Charlie called when he spotted him helping Barney Rooker out of his wheelchair and into one of the limousines lined up like railroad cars in the reserved area of the cemetery's parking lot. He was drowned out by hundreds of tightly packed, noisy spectators, emotions rampant, who made it impossible for him to reach them before the limousine sped out of the lot.

He shouldered his way back to a front-row spot at the restraining ropes, no more than another face in the crowd. He'd phoned the studio after learning of Sarah's death, but was unable to connect with anyone who could get him an admission ticket to the memorial service. Rudy Bundsman, the only one he reached, was apologetic. "I had to scream bloody murder to get one for myself," he said.

Harry Carey rescued him. He was one of the stars maintaining a somber face and a steady pace on their forward march into the cemetery, pretending not to hear appeals that bordered on begging for autographs and snapshots, until he spotted Charlie. He stopped to wonder, "Dickens, right? That you? The feller what wrote *Showdown at Shadow Creek?*"

"Yes, sir, Mr. Carey."

"Our mutual friend Rudy Bundsman described you to a T. Skip under the rope and come along." Within seconds a security cop wielding a metal baton was on them, ordering Charlie back.

Carey said, "Mr. Dickens is with me, sonny boy." Sonny Boy

recognized him and withdrew. Carey said, "In we go, Mr. Dickens, as long as you don't mind it's standing room only back of the hall."

"I don't know how to thank you, Mr. Carey."

"Writing me a fine role in *Showdown* was thanks enough until Rudy let the cat out of the bag, telling me there's a dandy part due me in the script for your next movie coming up. What's it called? *Forbidden City?*"

"Yes," Charlie said, like he knew, too timid to ask any questions.

"I hear they're promoting Bobby Wise out of editing, giving him a shot at directing. Any truth to that? Good man, Bobby, destined for big things."

"I heard the same thing when I was at the studio last week collecting the last of the lady's personal belongings," Mad Dog said, more mush-mouthed than he was when Charlie phoned him after the screening and he demanded, *Get your ass over here, pal. We got us a load of catching up to do.* "That was all the talk," Mad Dog said, "about this Wise guy, him and Polly Wilde in the role you intended for the lady. Whaddaya say to that, pal?"

"Polly Wilde is no Sarah Darling," Charlie said, telling Mad Dog what he was sure Mad Dog needed to hear, choosing to forget he had once told Polly she was perfect for the role of Cassandra. Maybe she was. Maybe she would be. In this town, in this business, he'd come to understand there was no such thing as the whole truth and nothing but, or was that simply another lie? Was he past knowing the difference?

They were relaxing on the terrace garden at Sarah's Benedict Canyon home.

"So that was you and Mr. Rooker I saw taking off before the ceremony began," Charlie said, changing the subject.

"God's honest truth, yes. No sooner I got there, before I

could bring myself to put one foot inside that chapel. Same for old Barney, so I delivered him back to New Dawn and here I be. I downed a few snorts before saying a prayer for the lady. Downed a few more. Said another prayer. Got myself good and soused, in case you haven't noticed." He threw a thumb at the portable bar. "Help yourself, pal. It'll take the edge off the worst kind of sadness—feeling sorry for yourself."

Charlie shook off the invitation. "Rain check, you don't mind, Mad Dog. I need my wits about me for the long haul back home. Eden Highlands, you know the town?"

"Best little whorehouse in all of the state, Hog Heaven, I heard tell by Barney and some others. One place I never figured to go looking for you when I went looking for you. What, pray tell your uncle Mad Dog, got you down there?"

"Robin Moon."

Mad Dog arched his eyebrows, flashed a strained smile. "I shudda cudda guessed. The damsel in distress Barney and I did the rescue mission on for you. Last I heard she'd disappeared into thin air from New Dawn. Don't tell me she wound up working a mattress in Eden Highlands. You never struck me as the type to fall for a sporting lady, pal, or you been doing a snappier job than Dr. Jekyll of hiding your Mr. Hyde?"

"Nothing of the kind," Charlie said, smacking him with a look as chilly as a winter frost. "Robin got back to chasing field work up and down the state. She turned sicker than she already was, collapsed and got taken by my other friends to Eden Highlands Memorial Hospital, where I finally caught up to them. Where Robin is right now. Why I was keen to see you, Mad Dog, hoping you can help me out one more time."

"Right now I can't play Bank of America, if that's what's on your mind, pal. What spare change is around needs to go for the upkeep on this place and the monthly care and feeding of Barney over at his domicile."

"No," Charlie said. "It's just—the hospital's done all it can and I need to find a place where Robin can take it easy until she's up to full strength again. I was originally planning to come ask Sarah, but—" He blew out a sigh.

Mad Dog thought about it. "The lady wudda said yes. She liked you lots, pal, so you won't mind my speaking up for her and saying it's a done deal. Your Robin and them other friends, too, that's what you want. You, too, pal, that's what you want. The more the merrier. We'll make it work."

"You sure?"

"The lady's got no use for the joint anymore, and, besides, it's mine now, including all the trimmings. She left it to me in her will, in black and white, for friendship rendered, you got that? Not services rendered. Friendship rendered." His eyes crinkled and he freed an impish laugh. "One condition, pal. One. *Uno*, as they say south of the border."

"Name it, anything," Charlie said, unable to disguise his relief.

"You have that drink now," Mad Dog said, "so we can toast to friendship and most of all to the lady."

Charlie awoke to the chatter of birds signaling morning; stretched out on his belly on the high diving board of the pool; clothes soaking; cymbals crashing at his temples; the bitter taste of booze clawing at his throat. He remembered how one drink turned into two, three, and one more for the road, nothing after that, definitely not the road.

He took the ladder down, missing a few rungs and almost losing his grip a time or two before reaching the deck, and went looking for Mad Dog. Discovered him in the den, asleep on the billiards table, clutching an empty bottle of Ray and Nephew Jamaican rum; his buzz saw snore constant and impenetrable, no matter how hard Charlie tried shaking him awake.

He retreated to his old bedroom. He'd left behind half a rail of sports outfits when he moved back home. He threw on a casual sweater over a pair of white tennis trousers, slipped into a pair of tired sneakers, and aimed for the kitchen. Hovered anxiously over a percolating pot of coffee. Poured a cup, stirred in half a dozen sugar cubes, and settled at the kitchen table with the extension phone.

Twenty minutes to ten.

Charlie took a chance Roy Balloon would be in his office at Elegant Artists by now and dialed the direct number Roy gave out only to clients, but never answered himself. He did this time, making a sad, failed effort to disguise his voice:

"Mr. Roy Balloon's office," he said, not even close to duplicating the breathy whine of the assistant he shared with three other junior agents.

"Mr. Charlie Dickens calling," Charlie said. "Your once and future client."

Roy dropped the act at once. "Charlie, where the blue blazes you been, baby? Been trying to reach you for days going on eternity with stupendous news about—"

"Forbidden City."

"Forbidden City." Announced as if he hadn't heard Charlie. "We got us a fabulous offer from RKO for your fabulous script."

"The fabulous script you kept telling me would be right at home on a field of bull dung?"

"A sensational director the studio's high on—Rob Weismann."

"Wise. Robert Wise. He's a film editor."

"And the clincher? They want it for Polly Wilde and Earl Stanley, who couldn't be hotter right now if they were missionaries from Hell."

"How fabulous is that fabulous offer, Roy?"

"Scott Fitzgerald should be so lucky."

"Fabulous," Charlie said, and small talked his way off the call.

Left a thank-you note pinned to Mad Dog's shirt.

Hit the road for Eden Highlands, using ideas for a new screenplay to help clear his head and pass the time.

An heiress disappears on the eve of a marriage arranged by her tyrant of a father and joins a gypsy band of migrant workers toiling in the fields and vineyards of Southern California. She meets cute a handsome worker who has joined the caravan, unaware he's recognized her and plans to turn her in for a reward posted by Daddy. Cupid rears his curly head. They fall madly, desperately in love. He confesses and—

No. No. No.

He's truly a migrant worker, poor but honest, smart, a head on his shoulders, near genius, who talks in poetic terms of the future they can share and proposes they run away and get married. She can't. She's currently engaged to a decent man with good intentions and a future in faith healing. They agree to put their emotions on hold by separating for a year. If their love survives, they'll reunite Christmas Eve at the forecourt of the Grauman's Chinese Theater, by the footprints of Mary Pickford and Douglas Fairbanks. No. Up at the HOLLYWOODLAND sign. No. The upper deck of the Hollywood Bowl. No. On the rooftop of the Taft Building at the intersection of Hollywood and Vine.

No. No. No.

Nothing sounded right.

Too on the money.

The Griffith Park Observatory?

Yes, maybe there.

A reunion under the stars.

Even call the story *A Reunion Under the Stars*.

He was still undecided a mile outside the Eden Highlands city limits.

Promised himself to return to the question later, too excited now for anything but sharing with Robin the good news about Mad Dog's generosity.

He pressed down hard on the gas pedal and ignored the speed limit racing to Hog Heaven.

Hog Heaven was the first whorehouse opened in Eden Highlands more than half a century ago, whose reputation for quality, quantity and elegance quickly made it a favorite stopover for travelers journeying through the fertile San Luis Rey Valley and visitors from adjoining cities and towns anxious for a temporary respite from the realities of everyday life.

The Victorian mansion, built in the Queen Anne style, boasted perfectly balanced windows, an assortment of steeples and a spire easily confused with a church tower; housed two floors of private rooms above a stylishly furnished reception parlor overseen by matronly women of mundane appearance, in stark contrast to the smartly turned-out young ladies waiting for company in the upstairs bedrooms.

"Back so soon?" the portly woman behind the registration window asked Charlie when he reached the front of the line, trailing a pair of hunky farmhands and eight rowdy, fuzz-faced sailors on leave from the naval base in San Diego.

"I phoned ahead."

She pressed her spectacles against the bridge of her bulbous nose and ran a nail-bitten index finger down the guest register. "So you did, Mr. Dickson—"

"Dickens."

"That's right, same as the book writer you told me before," she said, like she was answering a question from the "Professor Quiz" radio show. "On time again, I see. I so adore that in a man—punctuality—and consistency, too. Once more for our Miss Robin, correct?"

"Correct," Charlie said.

"Miss Robin has become quite popular in no time at all, a real crowd-pleaser from what I hear."

She smiled.

Charlie didn't.

He pushed five dollar bills through the barred window and started for the stairway hidden behind a scarlet-red curtain that belonged in a burlesque house.

"Hold on there, Mr. Dickson," the receptionist called after him. She pointed to the row of antique chairs across the way. "Please take a seat. Miss Robin's not as punctual as you today. She's running behind with a client who at the last minute paid double-time for overtime."

Charlie spent the wait working on the new screenplay, getting nowhere, his mind too full of Robin, before a middle-aged businessman in a blue pinstripe, sporting a lousy toupee, an overgrown goatee and a gargantuan grin, stepped into view and called over to the receptionist, "Put me down for day after tomorrow, sugar. Usual time. Same honey."

The receptionist scribbled a note and after another five minutes announced, "You can head up, Mr. Dickson. Our Cinderella Suite this visit. End of the hallway on your left. Framed picture of a glass slipper hanging on the door. She's expecting you."

Charlie took the stairs two at a time.

Knuckle rapped on the door.

Tried the knob when he got no answer.

Pushed the door open and stepped inside.

The suite was decked out like a child's vision of a fairy-tale princess's bedroom, the air heavily perfumed to disguise the accumulated smell left behind by an endless parade of visiting princes. The bed was unmade. The leather armchair and a cushioned lounger were wet-stained from recent use.

Charlie parked against the wall, hands stuffed in his pockets, and called for her.

"Be right out, darling," she answered from the bathroom. After a couple moments, the toilet flushed. She stepped naked into the room and immediately struck a pose, her legs spread wide, her arms akimbo, but what trapped his eyes were her nipples, hard, erect and painted a cherry red with rouge.

At once, surprise overtook Robin's sexual leer. She clapped her palms over her breasts. "She said it was Mr. Dickson again. I forgot that's what she calls you, Charlie. Why are you back here? I told you not to come back."

"Remember what I said I wanted to try doing, arrange for you, Ernie and Millie to stay with a friend in Los Angeles while you were recovering, help get you back on your feet? It's done. I went and got it done. I wanted you to hear it first, get you packed and out of here before I share the good news with Ernie and Millie."

"Remember I told you to do what you wanted with them, but forget about me? I'm happy where I am now, Charlie. It's where I belong. I'm as recovered as I'll ever be or care to be, so I'm telling you for the last time: go away. Get out of my life. Let me be. Forget about me. That's what I need from you, Charlie. That's all I need from you."

"You don't mean that."

"I do, Charlie. Look at me. See what the cops turned me into?"

She began a series of slow quarter turns.

She looked worse than on any other day since he caught up with her and talked about rescuing her from this place. She'd lost so much weight, he would not have been surprised to see her rise from the carpet and drift away.

A sallow complexion.

Dark circles under empty eyes.

Flesh hanging loose from her bone-thin underarms.

Ribs on display.

Bruises, welts and bite marks decorating her body.

"The cops got me riding the banana boat," she said, her voice going soft. "They beat me whenever I pleaded with them and begged to get off. They turned me on to junk. They passed me around the station houses like a bowl of gravy at the dinner table. When I was all used up they sold me for beer money and a bag of pretzels to the stag-film crowd. You ever catch *Horsing Around* or *The Hole Truth* or *Lesbo Lovers on Parade,* that's me having a swell time."

"In a year, less, it'll all seem like a bad dream you once had, you'll see."

"No, you see, Charlie. Stop staring at the ceiling. Look at me when you say that. I am not the girl you first met, not anymore, never again. And you want to know something else? I like what I've become. I like who the cops turned me into. It's probably who I was all along. I'm happy to be at Hog Heaven. It's where I belong. A roof over my head, three squares a day. Making more money by the hour laying on my back than breaking my back in the fields ever paid on a good day."

"It's no way to live."

"Can't you understand, Charlie? Haven't you figured it out yet? I'm already dead."

"I hope you haven't been talking like this to Ernie and Millie. It would break their hearts."

A hoarse laugh played in her throat. "Last time they were here they read to me from the Bible, saying they wanted to bring me back to God. I told them: *I didn't leave Him. He left me, God damn it.* Hearing me take the Lord's name in vain, they said good-bye like they meant it. I haven't seen them since. So long, Ernie. So long, Millie. It's been good to know you."

Robin turned from Charlie and crossed to the dresser.

She pulled a loaded hypodermic needle from under a stack of sheets in the bottom drawer.

Moved to the bed.

Raised a foot onto the bed frame.

Prepped the needle before inserting it between two toes and depressing the plunger.

"Atta boy," Robin said. "Come work your voodoo on Mama." She tossed aside the hypodermic and rolled onto the mattress on her back, spread her legs and called to Charlie, "You're running out of time, mister, so what's it going to be? More talk or are we going to fuck?"

Charlie had staked Ernie and Millie Keyes to a room at a motor court down the hill, halfway between Hog Heaven and the highway.

They'd checked out.

No forwarding address.

He made the lonely ride back to Los Angeles with only the stars for company.

CHAPTER 41

Three months later, Charlie had settled on his usual bench by the boat-rental dock at Westlake Park and was preparing to feed peanuts to the pigeons when he spotted a copy of the afternoon *Citizen-News* someone had left behind. He reached for it and turned to the entertainment section and Sidney Skolsky's column.

He'd met Sidney a few times at Schwab's Pharmacy, chauffeured him around town once or twice, Sidney being one of those transplanted New Yorkers who'd never learned to drive. What he liked most about Sidney—Sidney greeted him by name, like an old friend.

Today's column struck him like lightning:

HOLLYWOOD IS MY BEAT
By Sidney Skolsky

The black cloud that hung over *Showdown at Shadow Creek* and took the lives of Oscar-winning screen idol Sarah Darling and her brilliant producer-director husband, Max Moonglow, has now claimed a third victim. Earl Stanley, whose star-making performance came opposite the Divine Sarah in that award-winning film from RKO.

He was pronounced dead at 3:25 P.M. today at Hollywood Receiving Hospital, after lingering for eight weeks in a coma, resulting from an accidental shooting on the set of

353

his follow-up film, *Forbidden City,* opposite RKO's newest screen sensation, Polly Wilde.

Set-side observers said Earl had been showing off for visitors when he put a prop gun loaded with blanks to his temple and pulled the trigger. He apparently was not aware that blanks use paper wadding to seal gunpowder into the shell and shoot out with enough force to bring on injury or death when fired too close to the body.

Studio spokesman Perry Lieber said the tragic accident has not delayed production on *Forbidden City.* Another newcomer, Ronald "Cheyenne" Redman, who made his own strong impression as the heroic Indian brave in *Showdown at Shadow Creek,* was available to immediately step into the role after some emergency overnight rewriting was completed by that versatile king of the keyboard, Ben Hecht.

Ronald's career is in the capable hands of self-styled "boy wonder" Leo Salmon, who also manages Polly and numbered the late, lamented Earl among his clients. Leo is rumored to be a prime candidate for a production slot at RKO under supervising producer Pandro S. Berman.

Meanwhile, Oscar talk is mounting for the luscious Miss Wilde, who won herself a Supporting Actress nod for *Showdown,* but would be a contender in the top category for *Forbidden City,* being helmed by Robert Wise, his first assignment since making his mark at the studio as a film editor.

The Gossipel Truth—Missing from all the hubbub is Charles Dickens (no, not that one), the up-and-comer who penned both *Showdown at Shadow Creek* and *Forbidden City.* Last anyone heard, he had packed his bags and taken off for parts unknown with nary a word of explanation. I can appreciate why somebody on the brink of a major career breakthrough in a business that eats its young alive would pull such a stunt, but don't get me wrong—I love Hollywood.

Charlie said, "Me, too, Sidney." He tossed the newspaper into the trash can, dug into the bag for a handful of peanuts and pitched them across the walkway onto the grass. The pigeons were at them immediately, swooping down from their perches on the phone wires, a few at first, and then a dozen more.

He thought about Robin. Pictured her in a bright summer dress and sunbonnet, the sound of her heels clacking on the pavement growing louder as she raced to join him, her smile and embrace, her lips melting on his, telling him everything he would ever need to know about love. Reminded himself, *She's no movie, Charlie.* Shut his eyes to eclipse his imagination and got back to feeding the pigeons.

ABOUT THE AUTHOR

Robert S. Levinson is the best-selling author of nine prior crime-thriller novels, *A Rhumba in Waltz Time, The Traitor in Us All, In the Key of Death, Where the Lies Begin, Ask a Dead Man, Hot Paint, The James Dean Affair, The John Lennon Affair,* and *The Elvis and Marilyn Affair.* His short stories appear frequently in the *Ellery Queen* and *Alfred Hitchcock* mystery magazines. He is a Derringer Award winner, won *Ellery Queen* Readers Award recognition three times, and is regularly included in "year's best" anthologies. His nonfiction has appeared in *Rolling Stone, Los Angeles Times* Magazine, *Written By* Magazine of the Writers Guild of America West, *Westways,* and *Los Angeles* Magazine. His plays *Transcript* and *Murder Times Two* had their world premieres at the annual International Mystery Writers Festival. Bob served four years on Mystery Writers of America's (MWA) national board of directors. He wrote and produced two MWA annual "Edgar Awards" shows and two International Thriller Writers "Thriller Awards" shows. His work has been praised by Nelson DeMille, Clive Cussler, Joseph Wambaugh, T. Jefferson Parker, David Morrell, William Link, Heather Graham, John Lescroart, Gayle Lynds, Michael Palmer, James Rollins, and others. He resides in Los Angeles with his wife, Sandra, and Rosie, a loving Besenji Mix, who thinks she rescued them. Visit him at *www.rslevinson.com.*